BOOKSALE

Distance

Distance

a novel

JACK HODGINS

⟦A DOUGLAS GIBSON BOOK⟧

M&S

National Library of Canada Cataloguing in Publication

Hodgins, Jack, 1938-
Distance / Jack Hodgins.

"A Douglas Gibson book".
ISBN 0-7710-4199-3

I. Title.

PS8565.O3D48 2003   C813'.54   C2003-902513-6
PR9199.3.H54D48 2003

We acknowledge the financial support of the Government of Canada through the Book Publishing Industry Development Program and that of the Government of Ontario through the Ontario Media Development Corporation's Ontario Book Initiative. We further acknowledge the support of the Canada Council for the Arts and the Ontario Arts Council for our publishing program.

Though some of the events and a good deal of the geography take their inspiration from real life, the events, places, and characters in this novel are fictional creations of the author's imagination.

Book design by Terri Nimmo
Typeset in Goudy by M&S, Toronto
Printed and bound in Canada
This book is printed on acid-free paper that is 100% ancient forest friendly (100% post-consumer recycled).

A Douglas Gibson Book

McClelland & Stewart Ltd.
The Canadian Publishers
481 University Avenue
Toronto, Ontario
M5G 2E9
www.mcclelland.com

1 2 3 4 5   07 06 05 04 03

for Hart Hanson

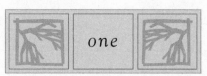

one

When he returned to his seat, the woman across the aisle was waiting for him, her knitting lowered to her lap. She was a large woman with a flushed face and bright tiny eyes, and wore a flowered summer dress that rustled from even the slightest movement. "Six hours is just that little bit too long," she said. Her bare feet, crossed at the ankles, were etched with purple scribble beneath the skin.

Sonny Aalto could not disagree. This had been his fourth or fifth journey up and down the aisles. Six hours was too long to be idle, inside a Boeing 737 or anywhere. Still, he picked up his book and found his page before responding. "True enough. Even when you're in no hurry to get there."

"Oh dear," the woman said. "A reluctant traveller!" The man beside her lowered his newspaper to see what a reluctant traveller had to say for himself.

But Aalto turned a page and made a point of frowning, to show that this book required his fierce attention. His limbs were electric with the need to get out again and move. He'd angled both legs into the space belonging to the empty window seat beside him, but shifted now in order to stretch one leg along the aisle, his sock foot tight against the seat ahead. Planes should come with exercise rooms, or a cinder track down the length of one side and back the other.

"I can't read when I'm in the air," the woman said. It might have been an accusation. Perhaps she'd noticed that pages turned were often turned back for a second look. He was having trouble with Gaston Bachelard's *Poetics of Space*. Small print, and ideas that needed concentrated thought. "When I try to read this far from the ground the words just float off the page." Apparently it had never occurred to her that people brought books onto planes in order to avoid people who had not. She yanked a length of white wool up from the bag at her feet and concentrated on her clicking needles.

The man beside her folded his newspaper in half. A teenager had murdered her stepfather with a rusty spike. Quebec *séparatistes*, who preferred to be known as *souverainistes*, were preparing for another referendum.

"At least I'm happy to be going where we're going," the woman said.

She probably wondered what Sonny Aalto was doing in Executive Class, a man with his hair stirred up like a terrified bush, wearing clothes that might have been second-hand. He supposed he did look a little too casual. He hated wearing new clothes, he got attached to certain items and wore them out with washing. The knees of these jeans were nearly transparent.

He turned his watch back, one hour, two hours, three. Time zones were being crossed without acknowledgement from the people running this plane. Time would not be mentioned until they'd arrived in Vancouver, where the captain would tell them whether it was or wasn't raining outside and then remind them that after a six-hour flight they had lost only three hours out of their lives. Sonny was aware that thirty years of *his* adult life were being rapidly reversed below them – a garden shop in Thunder Bay, a landscaping firm in Winnipeg, another in Regina – landmarks in his slow progress eastward to join his growing children. He was being dragged backwards across the surface of his own life even as this plane was taking him forward into a future he wasn't prepared to face.

He knew, or thought he knew, what he was going home to: the farm in ruins, his father in hospital, neighbours wondering what had taken him so long to get there. It was August, the days already growing shorter. Blackberries would sag with dusty fruit; ocean-spray flowers would be dry as swatches of brown old lace. Like anywhere else, nature's marvels happened without much fuss. That Sonny Aalto was heading west, on the other hand, was a marvel brought about by a good deal of fuss, including months of phone calls, faxes, and letters. And finally the message: "You'd better get home fast. Your father has taken a turn for the worse."

No one would have been surprised if he hadn't come, he knew this. His father's friends might not know precisely why he'd left home but they knew that in thirty years he had not returned often to visit. He usually came without warning, at his own convenience, and never because his father might have needed him. That he never stayed long was noticed as well. "By the time we know you're here you're already gone. All we ever see is your coat-tails snapping around a corner." They were disappointed because even after all this time they still wanted to *like* him. Even after all this time they still thought of Sonny as the energetic, good-natured, hard-working boy that Timo Aalto had raised by himself on that back-road farm, where father and son had been an insep-arable pair, like rustic figures in a fairy tale.

He was remembered as a figure perpetually on the run, the boy they'd called the Flying Finn, "Our own Paavo Nurmi." Like the great Olympic athlete, he'd been a long-distance runner in his youth – one-mile champion of the district, the Island, and even-tually the province as well. The mystery, even to him, was that he hadn't needed to practise. He'd just showed up at meets and won. Observers swore his legs moved too fast to be seen, like a sand-piper whirring along the beach. They'd not been entirely sur-prised when those legs took him out of the settlement and into the greater world.

What he'd left behind was there to drive by still, next to his old man's farm – his first nursery garden, now thirty years overgrown.

Once, people had driven out to buy shrubs for their houses in town. Some had treated his property like a public park, wandering through to admire the exotic plants draped over his trellises and coiled beside his ponds, poking around inside his glass houses filled with brilliant tropical blooms. None of this was any longer accessible or even visible from the road. Everything was hidden behind a barbed wall of Himalaya blackberries, a tangle of thick rust-coloured coils piled year after year upon itself to twice the height of a man and ten or twenty feet deep. By now, fragile imports may have been overwhelmed and choked to death by alder, willow, and Douglas fir. Perhaps a jungle of monstrous hybrids lived in there now, or a colony of reclusive pygmies with their own civilization, no one knew for sure.

A youth in a red T-shirt appeared from behind the curtain separating them from Economy Class, and made his unsteady way up the aisle, grabbing with one hand at the seat-backs to keep from toppling into someone's lap. "Excuse me, excuse me." He seemed confused. When he turned back, Sonny pulled in his leg to prevent an accident, but the young man took this as an invitation to stop. His eyes looked out from a narrow face that seemed to have been given a twist, throwing the nose and chin off-centre. He grabbed at the back of Sonny's seat for support and raised his voice to address the man with the newspaper. "You, sir. How old do you think I am?" He spoke slowly and carefully, forming each word as though it were a burden to his tongue.

Heads attached to headsets did not turn. The knitting woman smiled and kept her eyes on her needles, giving her white wool a sudden jerk to bring more of it up from her bag. When her companion did not respond, the youth turned to Sonny Aalto. "Know how to tell how old I am? Cut off my head and count the rings!" This struck him as so funny that he stomped his foot.

His tongue passed across his bottom lip. "I think," he said, "that it was really this that offended the people back there." He pointed at the back of his skull where a patch had been shaved from his hair. At the very centre was a dark puckered hole, like the rear end of a dog. The hole was shown off to the knitting woman as well. "I nearly died on the operating table. The drill went into my brain!"

The woman narrowed her eyes. "What's it for?"

For a moment the boy seemed unsure. Then he remembered. "It's a drain-off valve for geniuses! When you know so much there isn't room in your skull!" He laughed, *aha, aha, aha*. A child in an eighteen-year-old's body.

He was still laughing as he tried to push himself in past Sonny Aalto's legs.

"Where do you think you're going?" the woman said.

"Returning to my seat," the boy said, though he quickly stepped back into the aisle to say it. Frightened. Probably confused.

"You're lost," the woman said. "You're not even in the right cabin."

"I'm sorry, sir," he said to Sonny Aalto. "You won't have them throw me off the plane?"

"For heaven's sake!" the woman said.

"I won't," Sonny Aalto said. He stood up and put a hand on the boy's bony shoulder. "I don't even care if you sit there, so long as you're quiet." He leaned close so he could lower his voice. "But sooner or later there'll be someone in a uniform chasing you back to your seat."

The boy's eyes widened but he did not lower his voice. "They'd better not open the exit, though. We'd all be falling out of the sky like dying stars." He looked about the cabin, as if trying to remember why he was here. Then he started jerkily away. "Excuse me, sir. I'll just duck into the can so I won't get anyone else upset." Pushing past the grey curtain, he left them with only the muted roar of engines and rushing air, the faint chemical scent of upholstery.

"A moron," the man said, and shook out the folds in his paper. "We all have scars we could be showing strangers – but we don't."

The woman held her knitting still, as though an idea had occurred that needed some thought. Then she put her needles

down on her lap and addressed Sonny. "The flight attendants must
all be asleep." When Sonny smiled without taking his eyes from
his book, she added, "We have children of our own, of course.
Perhaps you have as well?"

The aggressive quality in this woman's voice was not visible in
her bright little eyes. "I have," he said, though it seemed strange
to say so. What did it mean to "have" children? He had *caused*
them, but had not had the opportunity to raise them. They had
been raised mostly out of his sight. "One girl, one boy, both of
them grown up."

"We had four girls and a boy. They leave us behind, as they
should, but we go on feeling as though we'd lost them in a super-
market somewhere and ought to go looking for them one more
time." She seemed cheerful enough about this.

The man beside her was not so cheerful. "Even from as far
away as Peru they have a way of making you feel you've disappointed them."

Sensing that he'd allowed a door to open that would not be
easily closed, Aalto attempted a return to his book. He would not
exchange horror stories about the younger generation. There
would be photographs crossing the aisle before he could put a stop
to them.

"I recognized you while we were boarding," she said. She waited
until he'd looked her way again. "You owned that landscaping
firm. The Garden King. You advertised yourself on TV."

"Not lately I haven't," he said. "I sold the business a couple of
years ago. The whole chain, from coast to coast. I have nothing
to do with it now."

"I know that," she said, as if he were a fool not to have guessed
this. "But not before you'd done the roof garden for that new
hotel. We almost bought one of your ready-mades – Japanese –
but changed our minds when we decided to sell up and move."

She was referring to a marketing approach that changed his life.
Meant for the modest budget as well as the undecided, this was the

opposite of customized landscaping, a cousin to the off-the-rack suit and prefabricated house. At Garden King you could choose from an array of styles, including Subtropical, Japanese, Spanish Desert, and Easy Care. For a Japanese garden, this couple would have got a tiny concrete pond, three bags of crushed gravel, ten stepping stones, one square yard of small river stones, three black pines, two mugo pines, one Japanese maple, three evergreen azaleas, one Japanese holly, a flowering cherry tree, and drawings that pictured four different ways in which these elements could be combined. There were no further decisions to make, no substitutes allowed. Sonny Aalto's success had been secured by people who wanted to take home an instant landscape much as they would a matching set of bathroom towels and mat.

Now, of course, someone else was making a nice profit from the ready-mades, while he had become the new owner of a fleet of chip wagons. M'sieur Patates. His face all over town, painted on the sides of his vans – wild pale hair and bony jaw, an ear-to-ear grin. *M'sieur Patates, lui-même.* Youthful employees passed steaming food in cartons out through an opened window. Chips, hot dogs, a variation on the Beaver Tail. You came upon them leaking steam in parking lots, against a curb in Centretown, amongst the vegetables in the ByWard Market. Bright red rhyming letters invited, "Have a treat – *patates frites.*"

Those who saw no practical reason for buying a chip-wagon business shortly after selling a firm he'd spent three decades building accused him of trying to belong. They were probably right. He wasn't interested in the actual day-to-day business, he left everything to his young managers. But after selling up his life's work, he'd discovered he didn't like the sense of disappearing from the public face of the city. After living in Ottawa for only eight years, he wanted to belong.

He supposed he belonged there now. Strangers greeted him on the street, "Harya, lad!" Half-familiar faces smiled, *"Bonjour, M'sieur Patates!"* People regularly seen in newscasts stopped to speculate about plans for his property in the Glebe, to ask about his trip to Spain or New Mexico, or to inquire about his son's new business venture out in the Valley. So far from his original place, he had almost put down roots. Sometimes he could close his eyes and swear he knew everything that went on in the city. Even now, for instance, high in the Prairie sky and heading west, he saw the manager of that new Centretown hotel step out from behind his desk to shout at his wife. "Stupid cow, am I to have no life of my own?" In the Museum of Civilization, an archivist paused to accuse her young assistant of sloppy work. "I don't know how much longer I can tolerate this." And in the parliamentary restaurant, a senior Cabinet minister lowered his voice: "You fellows think you have only to cross the river and give me this list of complaints?" Similarly, all over town, people of influence made the noises that would guarantee control for the rest of the day.

"Your children," said the woman across the aisle. "They live in Ottawa too?"

He decided not to hear this. There was too much of his father's voice in it. *And where are your children now, or do you know?* It would be one of the first things the old man would ask, an edge of sarcasm in his voice. Whether Sonny knew where they were was not the point – of course he knew where they were. His father would simply be making sure he knew what they had in common.

That they had *anything* in common was a notion he resisted. Sonny Aalto's children had not been raised by a lazy wife-abandoned drunk, as he had himself. When he and Elaine had separated, he stayed on in their Vancouver house while she took the children east to her parents' mansion beside the Rideau Canal. Even after Elaine's death, the grandparents continued to raise them. Judith Buckle, who'd been Sonny's Grade 2 teacher long before she'd become his mother-in-law, was as devoted to the children as she'd been to her students. By the time he'd worked his way across the country to join them, opening up small branches of his business in a number of towns, his "children" had pretty well grown up.

For a while, at first, he'd hoped that Warren would give him a chance to make up for what they'd missed. "But it's too late now," the boy said. At seventeen, he wasn't inclined to explain. "Maybe you should start a new family from scratch."

They hadn't seen much of one another after that. Recently, Warren and his Lori had bought an abandoned flour mill up the Valley in a stand of birches, and converted it into a shop for local arts and crafts. Stone-block walls. Cement floors. A stream below. When Sonny first saw it, icicles as thick as his arm hung from the eaves right down to the frozen stream. He had handed over the down payment when it was asked for.

"Well, for heaven's sake," said the woman across the aisle. "If we were going the other way we could watch that movie they shot up the Valley." She held up the opened in-flight magazine so that Sonny could see the miniature reproduction of the famous poster. "You remember when they filmed it."

This poster could be seen in the windows of video stores. A railway trestle spanned the foreground, with a lone male figure standing near the centre. A distant village was buried under snow. A single spire, a single thread of smoke rising to sky. New Hampshire, it was meant to be. This photo had come to represent the stark frightening beauty of backwoods New Hampshire. Possibly it had even come to represent New Hampshire to the Ontario villagers who lived beneath those roofs. Sonny had read somewhere that the state of New Hampshire was thinking of using this Ottawa Valley photo in its tourist brochures.

"A violent story," said the woman across the aisle, shuddering melodramatically. "I wouldn't watch it again but I think it's clever of them to show it for people going to Ottawa. If nothing else, it will remind them how cold it can be in the winter." She shuddered in an exaggerated manner, hugging her knitting to her chest with both hands. "Now tell me," she said. "Would you have guessed we're heading home ourselves after enduring thirty Ottawa winters? As soon as George retired we bought a little house on the beach, not far from where we grew up!"

"Pacific salmon," said the man beside her, his long face flushing up with apparent pleasure, "returning to the river where we were spawned."

You would think he had never heard that salmon returned in order to lay their eggs and promptly die. Sonny considered this a trait that humans were fortunate not to share.

No movie poster was needed to remind him of the Ottawa cold. As a man raised on the Coast, a man who could not sit still, who had to get out in all weathers just to be in motion, he was only too aware of how the air in winter could be dangerous. Human flesh, they said, would freeze in a matter of minutes.

Of course this didn't stop him. Visitors said that although he'd run away from home he certainly hadn't settled. Even with a briefcase in his hand he looked, to them, as if he were out to win a marathon. Down along the side of the canal he sailed on his bike, to visit his office and give a few orders to his employees. Out along the Queensway he sped in his BMW, to check up on work sites. Up and down the streets he strode, hair and jacket-tail flying, just to run a few errands. Even in temperatures that would have people back home expecting to perish, he was out and on the run. If the canal was frozen over he was on it. If you could just move fast enough you might not freeze to death.

On the coldest evening in his recent memory one hundred thousand people on skates went flying down the canal, their movement all that kept them from turning to ice. For seven kilometres they streamed through the frozen city, laughing, linking arms, and brushing snowflakes from their lashes while they called out greetings to one another. Old people in furs, heavy as bears; young people in zippered ski-suits of yellow and blue; mothers in quilted jackets that made them look like oven mitts, with babies trailing behind on sleds – all stroked past to the Viennese music that swirled from black bouquets of speakers strapped to the railings above. Occasionally, from somewhere beyond the apartment towers, fireworks shot up and flowered like coloured ink stains on the snowy sky.

It was mid-February. The occasion, according to the lamppost banners, was "Winterlude," or – if you looked from the other side – "*Bal de Neige.*" A terrier in a red felt vest came streaking out of a throng, pulling a boy on a leash. A group of youngsters, skating backwards, parted to avoid the dog but nearly ran over a gentleman pulling a rocking chair on a rope. "Atti*shon!* Atti*shon!*" cried the backward-skating youths, to the dog, to the man, and to Sonny Aalto, who whirled past with Bathsheba in his arms.

"*Bonsoir, M'sieur Patates!*"

He laughed, and pulled her closer to him as he stroked, glided, swept past others. Bathsheba turned up her teeth to the sky and roared out a laugh. All of the city could see.

All of the city could see she'd made little concession to climate. The brilliant red-and-yellow dress was meant for Nigeria or Chad, though it was impossible to tell how many pairs of long johns were underneath.

The two of them swooped into the crowd, and moved swiftly down the ice beneath one bridge and then another, past the glowing windows of canal-side houses, including the house that Aalto shared with Judith Buckle. Past the faces of diners in the Canal Ritz. Past apartment buildings with rooftop gardens he'd designed, some of them under glass, most of them under snow. A man who couldn't stand still, he rejoiced in the sleek mobility of skates. To drive himself through resistant air was to experience life. He bared his teeth in order to taste it, though it tasted fiercely glacial. Ice crystals formed in his nostrils; wind bit at his ears. His lungs were an aching chandelier of fragile ice.

They stopped at a Kurbmaster van with Sonny Aalto's face on its side. He paid for two coffees and handed one to her. Both of them were shivering. So were others who'd stopped – beating their gloves together, flailing their arms, dancing on their skates. Exposed ears were a dangerous red.

"You're a champ. You'll skate the length of the Congo the minute it freezes over."

She had never seen the Congo in her life. The Mississippi was her river, New Orleans her town. Though she dressed like a Nigerian market woman, she sometimes spoke like Scarlett O'Hara's mammy. North for a jazz club gig, she'd looked up Sonny Aalto, who sometimes looked her up in her flat near Jackson Square. She was known only as Bathsheba. If she had another name, he was never told it.

To sip their coffees, they shared a bench where an abandoned newspaper served up the day's events. Two frozen bodies had been found in the trunk of a car. Elsewhere, someone had taken a road-salting truck for a spin and got a surprise – the front page showed it being hauled up through a hole in the river ice. A farmer had found a pig that had been missing since fall, buried behind his barn. You never knew what waited beneath the snow.

Stout Darryl Maclean, dressed head to foot in green-and-blue horizontal stripes, screeched to a halt in a spray of ice and removed the frozen scarf from the lower half of his face. "G'day, g'day." He shook Bathsheba's hand. "I recognized ya there from TV." His breath escaped in broken trails of steam.

Sonny introduced them. "Darryl has a woodlot up the Valley. Delivers firewood to keep us city folk warm."

"Might take a leaf from this lad's book," said Darryl Maclean, tilting his head towards the van. "Paint my handsome mug on the side of my truck." He laughed. His face belonged on a Hollywood thug. "M'sieur Le Bûcheron, lui-même. 'On the road to keep you chaud!' Whaddaya think?"

Bathsheba laughed. So did Sonny Aalto, though he'd heard it before. Darryl Maclean told you all his business every time you saw him. The first time he'd delivered firewood to the house, he said he'd been dispossessed by the St. Lawrence Seaway project. Sonny's late father-in-law, a Cabinet minister at the time, had voted for it. "My childhood home's in one of the Lost Villages. Drowned when they raised the water."

It was his claim to fame. If he'd wanted to go home, he'd have to wear diving gear. "I visit in my dreams," he told Bathsheba. "Swim from room to room. Last week I baked a two-headed cod in my mother's oven." He claimed he could read what time and the river had written on the walls.

Darryl Maclean was a family man – thirty years married, the father of four, the cousin or uncle or nephew of just about everyone in the Ottawa Valley. Sonny Aalto, on the other hand, was about as free as a man could get – a father half a continent away, a mother lost since childhood, no wives within a thousand kilometres, and adult children who didn't need him. Not a single guy-line, as he put it himself, to hold him pinned to one spot. Maclean disapproved. He especially disapproved of women, like Bathsheba, who inspired a man to bare his teeth in this cold and fly like a boy down the ice.

Once Maclean had moved on to join his family, Sonny steered her into the traffic again, and skated down through crowds towards the concrete towers and greenish spires of *centre-ville*. They cut left around a group of skaters, swerved right past another. His every molecule participated in this motion, every muscle of his legs, every nerve and bone, every hair of his head and wrinkle in his restless soul was engaged in this headlong joyful progression up the squeaking ice through this city.

It seemed to him that the cheerful greetings from half-familiar faces were for the sight of him swooping past with this grand bright woman in his arms. They'd known him once as a devoted husband to the beautiful Janis Truscott, the two of them an inseparable couple seen everywhere on one another's arm, and they'd shared his grief when she left to take up another life in Halifax. They believed the sight of him laughing in the company of another remarkable woman meant that he was happy once again.

They didn't know, nor did Sonny Aalto yet know himself, that while they were removing their skates a few minutes later, Bathsheba would tell him about the clarinet player from Chicago. Another of her many "admirers," this gentleman had shown up

today with a diamond necklace and photographs of his newly purchased house.

He was startled out of a shallow sleep by the voice of the woman
across the aisle: "Oh dear, I don't think you should be here.
Where is that stewardess?" The boy with the hole in his head
pushed his way past Sonny Aalto's legs to claim the empty seat
beside him. He laid his narrow head against the seat-back, then
turned his pale crooked face towards Sonny. "Sir?" he said.
"When I came up behind you? I noticed, there are marks. Scars
on the back of your neck."

"What?" Sonny put a hand on the back of his neck, then ran
it up through his hair where the unseen dents were deeper. "It's
nothing. Jesus. They're nothing. What are you doing here?"

Perhaps he'd sounded too fierce, too cranky. The boy slid closer
to the window and pulled his thin legs up under himself. "I'm
sorry. The people back there are not very nice."

Well, he *felt* cranky. "There's nobody back there wondering
where you've got to?"

"I tried to stop him," said the woman across the aisle, "but he
wouldn't listen."

The boy closed his eyes. "You shouldn't say it's nothing, sir.
They looked like teeth marks to me." His tongue passed back and
forth across his bottom lip.

Sonny stared hard at the blur of words in his open book. Darryl
Maclean was always harping about the importance of combatting
what he called the "Age of the Grouch," something a man had to
watch for once he'd passed fifty. Acquaintances had already suc-
cumbed, with disastrous results. Sonny made some effort to resist,
but the temptation was sometimes too much – to rail at the
foolish opinions of youth, complain about dishonestly advertised
items, protest the politicians' obvious lies. He'd accused police,
firefighters, and even librarians of assuming authority while still

in their baby-faced adolescence. If he got away with it, it was only because of his robust infectious laugh. But there was something about this kid that provoked the Grouch without inspiring the laughter.

"They look like teeth marks because that's what they are," Sonny said, almost savagely. "Something that happened a long time ago. They don't matter now. They especially don't matter to you."

"I've pushed the stewardess button," said the woman across the aisle. "But of course they show up only when they aren't needed."

The boy's eyes opened wide. "A vicious dog?"

"Do you have any idea how wide a cougar can open her jaw? A mountain lion? I was a toddler playing out in the backyard and this cougar came out of the bush and started dragging me off with its mouth around my skull."

A shadow of doubt crossed the boy's face. This adult could be pulling his leg. "Why would he want to drag you away?"

"She," Sonny said. "To take me home for dinner, I guess. I was only three years old. I only know what my father told me. He was the one who fought 'er off."

"And saved your life!" The boy was happy to believe. "Can you feel them? After all these years?"

"I can't feel a thing," Sonny said. "I can't even remember when I *did* feel them. I don't see them, I don't feel them, I don't even remember they're there until someone without any manners mentions them."

"I'd have nightmares if it was me."

"I've had fifty years to come across scarier things."

"You ever dream your father still needs to save you from something bad?"

"My father tries to worm his way into my dreams but I fight him off. If you have a father yourself you'll discover they eventually give up saving your life and start trying to wreck it instead."

"No one seems to care," said the woman across the aisle. "We're on our own, in a plane without any staff."

The boy gasped, and leapt to his feet. Something on the far side of the cabin had caught his attention. Something he could see through the windows on the far side clearly frightened him. "I can see God out there."

Heads turned. Where? What did this lunatic see? Headsets were removed. Sonny tugged on the leg of the boy's jeans to encourage him to sit. There was nothing out there, not even clouds.

"He follows me everywhere," the boy explained. "Since my oper-A-tion, He's been watching me."

"Sit down," Sonny said, tugging still at denim.

The boy did not sit. "Maybe He thinks He made a *mistake*, letting me pull through." He turned to Sonny. "Are you afraid to die?"

"Sir! Sir!" A flight attendant had appeared from somewhere, a frowning middle-aged woman with pinned-up greying hair, who, Sonny imagined, resented being pulled out of a happy retirement to fill in for someone who hadn't returned from Hawaii. "Young man, please return to your own seat. You are not supposed to be in this cabin."

"So you say," the boy said, quickly sitting again and moving close to the window. "This gentleman gave me this seat so I could take my last ride in comfort."

"You really must go back where you belong," the flight attendant said. "I will have to call the chief steward." When the boy remained where he was, both thin arms crossed on his chest, she turned away as though to go for help. But after two steps she turned back, her lips pressed tightly together. No doubt she was someone's mother. She reached across Sonny, took hold of one skinny arm, and hauled him out. The boy did not resist, but it was necessary for Sonny to stand up and get out of the way if he wasn't to make things worse.

The attendant gave Sonny Aalto a look that suggested he was as much to blame as this youth for disrupting her otherwise uneventful shift. She pushed the boy into the curtain that was meant to discourage this sort of invasion, and then went through behind him.

"Did you notice his complexion?" said the woman across the aisle. "He's been in an institution. You pay a fortune for your seat but that don't mean you're safe."

Sonny ignored this obvious invitation to report the boy's conversation. He returned Gaston Bachelard to the leather bag at his feet and withdrew a book he knew would be less demanding. *John Graham, Convict* contained engravings, and larger print. This was something he'd bought months ago, next door at Mr. Percy's permanent yard sale in his glassed-in porch, but hadn't got around to reading. To encourage the old man, Sonny sometimes bought a book he would never read. This one seemed to be a kind of illustrated diary, events following a shipwreck in Australia. Naked black people danced around a captive white woman, who hung her head in shame. A black man stood with spear raised level with his eyes. "*Marriage was by abduction.*" He supposed he'd forked over the seventy-five cents in honour of the poor freezing Aussie who'd shown up out of nowhere one minus-twenty night down on the canal.

The figure had stepped out from beneath the Mackenzie King Bridge to hail him, moving stiffly on unlaced boots, gloved hand upraised like a traffic cop. This was a stranger in a fur coat and bright scarves, holding a long slim pole in his hand. A shepherd's staff? A spear? He meant to block Sonny's way with it.

A boyish face on a man in his late thirties. When Sonny had scraped to a stop that sent ice spraying for several feet, the stranger removed a glove and offered his hand. "Jerrod Hawkins. Looking for Dennis Aalto. Your mother-in-law told me you'd be here. One of the blokes in the stag line pointed you out."

"Hawkins?"

"Javelin-throwing champion of Queensland, mate – once was, that is. Too bloody far from home." He slipped his hand back into the glove and shuddered.

"It isn't the track meet season here," Sonny said. "In case you haven't noticed."

"I've been to Montreal – law conference. But brought you this." He jabbed the javelin into the ice with such force that it vibrated in the air between them. "Found it in a pawn shop and thought I'd be clever. I would've heaved it onto the ice and surprised you but I might've done some other poor bugger damage." A piece of paper was folded behind an elastic band at the chord grip. "I'm here to deliver a message."

Of course Sonny assumed the message was from his father. "I know what it says, they're all the same. Though it seems he used some imagination this time."

The stranger shuddered. "Bloody hell, it's cold." He looked desperately around, perhaps hoping Sonny would suggest meeting somewhere warmer. "Doesn't it worry you to think your country's governed from a block of ice? Thirty-eight degrees is what I left behind."

"Then you were a fool to come," Sonny said, pushing back to leave.

"I am that." The stranger opened wide his pale blue eyes and grinned. "One more thing I am is this – I'm also yer brother, brother, believe it or not."

Sonny laughed. "There you're definitely mistaken, pal."

"Just because yer mum shot through don't mean she quit on ya. Viira's been busy as a bushfire for fifty years."

The name set up such an electric clamour in Sonny Aalto's head that he couldn't think what it meant. "Viira?"

"The white-haired crone of Kalevan Station. Old gal that spawned us both – whaddaya reckon? After all this time she wants t'see ya. Yer own neglectful mum."

Aalto studied the face for signs of a practical joke. He *had* no "mum." He hadn't had a mother since he was two years old.

The Australian could read his doubts. "Believe me, mate, I would not risk frozen gonads for the sake of a prank."

As a boy, Sonny Aalto had believed she'd run off to be a movie star like Ingrid Bergman. Sometimes he'd hated her, for leaving him with his boozy father on the back-road farm. More often he envied her escape. For a while he'd imagined that she'd signed up with Hitler's army, destroying Russian lives on the Karelian front, her ancestral home, and had been captured, tortured, and then herself destroyed by the enemy. A few years back he'd made an effort to discover if someone knew where she'd gone, but had failed. Lately, he hadn't thought of her at all.

At the top of the paper, "Kalevan Station" was embossed in black. Three short uneven lines of blue-ink scribble followed, and an illegible signature. The scribble, once he'd squinted to decipher it, said, "October 31. Annual shooting party. You're invited."

"Shooting what?" he said. "Each other?" He skated over to lean against the concrete wall while he read the scribble again.

"Grunters," said Jerrod Hawkins, once he'd stiff-legged his way across the ice, holding his javelin with both hands. He'd probably hoped that Sonny would grab the javelin and turn their meeting into a rowdy competition. It would be something to tell about in the Queensland bars. "Feral pigs," he said, and sat on a bench where people perched to put on their skates. A row of boots was beneath it. "They come up the dry channels and eat the lambs. Once a year she throws a party, we go out and shoot what we find."

"You serious?"

"Yer ol' mum is always serious, cobber. Her parties are bloody sought-after. People of influence beg to be invited."

"Kalevan Station?" Aalto sat on the bench and read the letterhead again.

"Her property. Three thousand acres, an hour from Mistake Creek – the nearest town. Trevor stayed to manage the station now the old man's dead. Reckons he does. She gives the orders still. I work for a law firm in Brisbane."

"Are there others?"

"Errol's a dentist to toffs and CEOs in Sydney. Never see him, except once a year at the shoot."

"A family affair," Aalto said.

"Mostly rellies, yeh." The Australian watched a chain of backward-skating adolescents swoop by, all screaming. "Sometimes there's a mob of strangers for the novelty. She sends the invitations, she doesn't tell us who. I've seen them come from Adelaide, Cunnamulla, and Broome. They camp in the shearers' quarters. Drink enough grog to flood a good-sized town. So far, hardly anyone's been killed."

Aalto folded the note and pushed it into a pocket. "I haven't held a gun since I was twenty. I'd be a hazard with a rifle in my hand."

"There might not be any rifles, mate. Sometimes she wants us to act like a mob of Abos. Or the ancient bloody Greeks."

"I seem to remember that Greeks hunted buck-naked," Sonny said.

"And carried spears," said Hawkins. Beside him, a fat man lowered himself to the bench and, breathing heavily, bent to remove his skates.

"You carry spears?" Sonny said.

"She reads. Too much, if you ask me. You can use my javelin to practise. I wouldn't practise naked, though, in *this*."

Aalto tilted back his head and addressed the sky. "Who's running this universe, anyway?" The woman had shown no sign of having thought of him since the day she'd left him behind, but now expected him to traipse halfway around the world to shoot her pigs. If he weren't sure his father had no idea where she'd got to, he'd believe this was a scheme cooked up between them. The old man was capable of it – imagining that the prospect of meeting his mother in Queensland would increase the appeal of travelling the mere five thousand Ks to pay attention to *him*.

"Why would I want to see her? Tell her she left it too late, she's wasted your time."

He set off down the canal again, weaving through the crowd in the direction of the Château Laurier, the broad stone sentry beside the locks that dropped this canal in steps to the frozen river.

The Australian hadn't given up so easily. A few days later he appeared on the Buckle doorstep, stomping snow from his boots and breathing steam into his hands. Clearly he'd used the time to do some research, and knew of Sonny Aalto's restless passion for chasing after the world's sacred sites. Santiago de Compostela, the Great Serpent Mound, and the Island of Iona were all dismissed as mere appetizers. "If the chance to shoot a tusker won't bring you to Oz, I'm told that Uluru might. Ayers Rock to you, I reckon. The crossroads of several Dreamings. Or, if you fancy the Devil's Marbles we could drive a few days out to sticky-beak around." Those giant stones, he'd explained, were eggs laid by the Rainbow Serpent when he created humans. "If we cracked one open we might find humans as we were meant to be – if some poor bugger hadn't forgotten to hatch."

Sonny Aalto held firm. He could visit those places one day without having to meet his mother. "I'd rather stay as far from her as she has stayed from me." He searched the Australian's face for hints of a family resemblance, but found none. His accent seemed less pronounced here. Maybe he played up the Australian only in public.

"Like Uluru, there's only the one Viira in the world. Nobody worships her, but she makes them nervous. If we survive the shooting party I could drive you out to my favourite spot. Jump-ups, cave paintings, site of a dinosaur stampede. You can see the tracks in the stone. Hundreds running to escape an attack. Not far from the old woman's property. You can stand in all that silence and almost hear them."

In the John Graham book there were no drawings of dinosaurs. There were no drawings of wild pigs uprooting the landscape either. Maybe there were no wild pigs in Australia. Wild boars belonged in the European woods. Boar hunts belonged to the corrupt nobility, who afterwards dined on roasted pork while planning to devour one another. If you had a mother who behaved as though she belonged to that crowd – perhaps importing pigs for the pleasure of behaving like a Prussian countess – you might want to go down for a look, see what the life of outback royalty had to offer that would keep her from staying home to raise her first-born son.

It didn't matter. It didn't matter now because his father had captured him first. The boar hunt was still a couple of months in the future while his father's letters and phone calls had become urgent. No polite invitations arrived on embossed paper. Neither letters nor phone calls had promised anything as exotic as a hunting party or dinosaurs.

He'd ignored the letters, he'd evaded phone calls, invented excuses, and cancelled flights, even those booked for him from his father's end of the country. He promised: soon, soon. There was always something – a crisis amongst the staff of his chip-wagon fleet, plans for a possible trip to the fairy chimneys in Turkey. He held out until they convinced him that waiting any longer could be a mistake that he would regret, as they put it, for the rest of his life. As Dora Mitchell wrote in an exasperated note at the beginning of August, matters had gone and got urgent. In the end he had little choice.

He knew what to expect, he knew what he would find. He'd left it too late to go directly to the farm. The old man had been taken down-island to the Royal Jubilee Hospital. A report of "complications" had been vague, though it sounded like pneumonia. After six hours in the air and two in the Vancouver airport, Sonny would then have to fly to Victoria International, where he would rent a car, drive to town, and check in at the Ocean Pointe Resort on the harbour, then follow Fort Street until he came to the sprawling pile of pale orange bricks called the Jubilee. He wouldn't need to ask the way to his father's room. He would hear the old man's neighbours shouting across his bed. In public they bellowed at one another as though they were obliged to entertain the whole vicinity, including the deaf. Nurses would roll their eyes and look at the clock. With that long drive ahead, up-island visitors couldn't stay forever. Surely these old buzzards would want to get home before dark.

He would be met with accusations, he was sure of that. "Did you hope you'd be too late?" They would blame everything on the East. Something happened to people who moved there. "I'd a mind to go back and drag you home myself."

Dora Mitchell would see him coming and shout his name. With eyes closed and arms thrown wide she would wait while he completed the long walk down to her hug, then lay her puff of white hair against his chest. "We thought you'd hightailed it off to China or somewhere." Stepping back, she would give him a swat to show the welcome was not deserved.

If his father heard him coming he would make an effort to look as sick as possible. He could muster up a pretty good death rattle when he wanted to, so that he could rally later and look for disappointment in Sonny's traitorous eyes.

What he couldn't predict was whether this would be a farewell deathbed scene, or some sort of con to trick him into staying, or even an elaborate hoax for the pleasure of causing Sonny as much inconvenience as possible. The old man wasn't likely to jump out of bed and shout "Gotcha!" but the thought would be visible in his eyes. You needn't think you could escape this man forever. With luck, it would mean hanging around Victoria just until he was strong enough to go home, then driving him up-island and doing a few chores around the place before returning to his life in the East.

He supposed he would make an attempt to see Charlotte while he was there. Contrary to what the woman across the aisle assumed, his daughter did not live in Ottawa. Soon after Sonny had arrived she'd run off to the States with a trumpet player named Ryan DeWitt. Since then she'd returned to this country, alone, though not to this country's capital.

"Excuse me, sir. Excuse me."

The youth was back, standing with his narrow denim legs against Sonny's thigh. Sonny's whole body reacted, jerking his leg away from the touch, half-rising from his seat. "What? What do you want now?"

"Oh, for heaven's sake," said the woman across the aisle. "You've made me drop a stitch."

This time the flight attendant had arrived with the boy, and was holding a boarding pass. Her pinned-up hair was beginning to fall loose around her ears. Clearly this flight had tested her patience. "There are only four empty seats on the plane," she said, through gritted teeth, "and this young man has managed to occupy them all. Caused trouble in every one. Somehow he's convinced the chief steward that this is where he should be for the rest of the trip."

"Like a cat," said the woman across the aisle. "The people who hate them are the very ones the cats can't leave alone."

The boy had climbed over Sonny's legs before Sonny had a chance to stand out of his way. He sat, and closed his eyes, and tilted back his head. Maybe he would sleep.

"He seems to be relatively calm up here," the attendant said. "The chief steward will come by later with a better explanation. Apparently we've had word that he's to be sent home on the next flight and it will be easier for us to keep an eye on him here."

Sonny Aalto closed his eyes. Inside the Château Laurier, the premiers of several provinces had gathered with selected federal ministers for a reception. Tomorrow they would try once again to prevent the country from tearing itself apart. "The same old blackmail," said the premier of a Western province. "'Give us everything we want or we won't play.'" His companion nodded: "While desperate refugees line up around the block to get in. We should arrange a trade." A senior Cabinet minister rattled his Scotch and joined in. "We have to show them they'd be crazy to go their own way, when they're already living in the best damn country in the world."

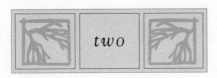

two

I f he had been in a hurry he'd have taken the stairs. This elevator could be counted on to groan and moan and give him a little more time. At the second floor, it stopped to take on a slump-shouldered young orderly pushing an empty gurney. Both men nodded a greeting. "You could wheel me straight to the morgue," Sonny Aalto said. "My life's about to take a downward turn."

"Morgue is below," the orderly said, though not without a smile. "We're heading up. If things are as bad as that, you can jump from the roof."

Nurses at their station paused in their work to watch him approach. This man in his fifties looked like a boy faced with some awful punishment, his hair stirred up as if he'd been trying to pull it out. The air vents hummed. The departing elevator loudly grieved as it sank in its shaft. A yellow sandwich board warned of wet lino that would break your neck.

No shouting came from his father's room, no laughter. Yet he had only to stand in the doorway to see there were three visitors sitting quietly around the bed. Rob Mitchell half-dozed with his head against the wall. Dora Mitchell, seeing Sonny, sprang to her feet for a hug. Tom Reimer did not raise his immense body from the chair near the head of the bed. He tilted forward to regard Sonny out of dark, expressionless eyes, his hands wrapped around both ends of the walking stick that spanned his wide-apart knees.

Elastic braces curved out to bracket a stomach that spilled over the unbuttoned top of his pants. "Too damn busy making money to think of the poor old fellow that raised him." He was not about to waste precious energy struggling to his feet for Sonny Aalto.

"Don't start," Dora said, dropping into the one vacant chair. "His father needs him. Here he is. Be glad!" She straightened the thick square glasses on her Pekingese nose and crossed her ankles, her runners swinging inches from the floor. Dora's husband Rob raised a hand in weak salute from his chair against the wall.

Aalto had hoped to find the room empty and a sign that said it was all a mistake. But here was his father laid out on the high white bed, his head thrown back, his long ropy throat and Adam's apple offered up to anyone's knife. Beneath his sharp yellow nose his mouth was a fluttering hole, his dentures riding the waves on the chest of his hospital gown. The old man was asleep, probably drugged, or wanting you to think he was breathing his last.

Sonny lightly placed a hand on his father's shoulder. One pale eye opened in its pocket of wrinkled flesh and then abruptly closed. The old bugger was awake but refused to speak a welcome. Sonny leaned close to draw a long deep breath but did not smell any booze.

"We almost lost him," Dora said. "But now he's nearly ready to go home."

"Looks about as healthy as he ever did," Sonny said. "The only time he looked better was when he was chasing that mail-lady woman who wouldn't have him." He searched for her name, knowing his father could hear. "Rose Somebody. Wouldn't *marry* him, anyway."

Dora slapped at Sonny's thigh. "Lower your voice. She's right behind you here in the can."

"Her thirtieth cigarette of the day," Tom Reimer said, one hand dispersing imagined smoke. "We're waiting for the sprinklers to go off and get us all kicked out."

Rob Mitchell struggled harder than any patient for each breath. "She insisted . . . on coming," he said. "Wasn't . . . our idea."

A half-dozen "Get Well" cards stood beside a single rose on the bedside table. They were joke cards, tall and narrow and garishly coloured, with cartoon figures on the front. He imagined his father glancing at each and grunting, then allowing someone else to set them out on display.

The toilet door swung open and Rose Ferguson shuffled out, jamming a wad of Kleenex into one eye and then the other. She checked the buttons of her pink cardigan and tucked the wad beneath the rolled-back cuff. Since he'd seen her last her narrow shoulders had begun to curl forward, as though her body would roll itself right down to rest on her shoes.

Dora jumped to her feet and closed the toilet door. "They get a whiff of that, we'll all be slapped in chains. I swear she knows how to turn off alarms."

Discovering Sonny amongst them, Rose Ferguson threw up both hands and flung herself against him. "Dear God, you finally came!" Her voice sounded as though it had had to fight its way through pockets of loose pea gravel to get to open air.

She smelled like last night's ashtray. This was the memory that came to Sonny now: cleaning up the morning after one of their drunks, emptying ashtrays, collecting the bottles, mopping up the mess that never quite reached the toilet. And, often as not, guiding Rose to the sink, where she could wash her poor ruined face.

Dora slapped both hands on her knees and jumped to her feet. "Well, now that you're here and Rose has a fresh coat of tar in her lungs we can hit the road!"

But Rose dropped into Dora's vacated chair in order to gaze at Timo Aalto's closed-off face. The ball of Kleenex reappeared. Ceiling light reflected off pale scalp beneath the thinned-out dyed-black hair. She'd been a wreck at forty – at least he'd thought so then – and time had not been any kinder since.

"She's got more than cigarettes in that handbag," Dora said, as though Rose were deaf. Perhaps she was. "Nothing fills the heart with devotion like a few quick snorts and the sight of a helpless man in bed."

Rob Mitchell raised a walking stick from the floor and waggled it. "Lookit this!" A chuckle rumbled through his wheeze. "Yer dad . . . made it himself . . . out of somebody's . . . ol' umbrella!"

Even stripped of its spokes and tipped with a rubber cap off the leg of a table or stool, it looked like what it was, a long-handled umbrella rescued from the dump by someone too cheap to buy a walking stick.

"Because buying one would mean admitting something," Dora explained.

In the second bed, someone bald lay motionless and barely breathing. Hoping, Sonny imagined, to remain unnoticed.

Reimer pressed his lips together in a shallow smile. He gave the impression that his large inanimate body had been propped up by his arms so that his head could do its minimal business without troubling any muscles or organs below the neck. He couldn't believe, he said, that Swampy Aalto had let himself be driven directly from his doorstep to this hospital without a single side trip into the bush. "I was sure he'd make the ambulance take him." He bulged his eyes to imitate Sonny's father: "*Up here's a road I never been down, let's see where it goes.*"

"Showing his age," Sonny said. "Once he would've bullied them down some back road trying to find where Edgar Peterson got lost."

It had been their only recreation once. Sunday afternoons were set aside for a drive, the only way Timo Aalto knew how to entertain his son. Sometimes they drove south, to Union Bay, and sometimes north to Campbell River. In either case they stopped for ice cream at the farthest point and started home. Going, they stuck to the highway, but coming back was a different story. "I wonder what's down this road," his father would say. "Snowsells built a cabin somewheres here, we'll see if we can find it." Narrow roads led towards mountains or sea, one or the other. They had come upon forgotten garbage dumps. They'd found a deserted wartime practice range, where the ground was littered with shell casings. They'd found themselves in the private yards of unpainted, unfinished houses. Unnamed lakes were discovered, a sudden expanse of beach, wildlife throwing up its head to sniff the air. "I don't remember no bridge across that creek. Let's see where it goes." Roads divided, where decisions had to be made, and eventually divided again until they were shuddering along the edge of a gravel pit or stopped at the top of a cliff above the sea.

"I was always scared he'd disappear down one of them roads and never find his way back," Dora said. She gestured for Sonny to notice Rose, whose chin rested on her buttons. Asleep but not yet snoring.

"The question is how far down *this* one has he gone," Sonny said. "What does the doctor say?"

No one told him anything more than what Dora Mitchell had already said. Maybe that was all they knew. Dora slapped both hands all over her hips in search of a pocket, and pulled out a set of keys. "Wake up, Rose, let's go!" To Sonny she said, "Once we're out of your hair you two can have a good talk." She danced a few steps in her Reeboks, to show she could hardly wait to get this journey started.

They had a four-hour drive ahead of them. Reimer no longer drove; Rose had never learned; and Rob Mitchell's eyesight had begun to fail. Also, Dora explained, his legs could not be trusted to respond to emergencies, though he still owned a licence that gave him legal permission to drive half-blind and crippled in anyone's car.

Reimer rose slowly from his chair, his bent arms expanding like an accordion car jack in order to lift that belly and wide expressionless head without disturbing anything inside. "Well then, make sure you stay with him," he said to Sonny Aalto. "Make sure you bring him home." His tarnished-penny eyes were deep in folds of dark sad flesh. He raised his walking stick and jabbed Sonny hard in the ribs. "Damn you, anyways."

"Hey now," Sonny said.

Dora Mitchell grabbed Reimer's sleeve and stepped between them. Then she pulled Sonny down by his ears and kissed him on the mouth. "Be nice," she said. "You knew they did tests on your dad? Well, now he's got something to tell you."

But Tom Reimer raised his stick again and, before Sonny could tell himself to step out of the way, brought it down hard on his shoulder. "Where have you been, you sonofabitch?" he said. "That there father of yours has been waitin' for you since back in the middle of winter. Where the blazes have you been?"

He was not surprised that this sterile box of a room made his legs itch to escape. Blank white walls, high white ceilings, square panels of fluorescent lights. Someone ought to bring a truckload of boulders and potted shrubs into this lifeless sharp-edged monotony. Of course he would not be allowed to bring soil, nor introduce boulders where nurses might bark their shins. But was there a law against shrubs? He detested topiary – a frivolous brand of cruelty promoted by Wm. Cutbush and Son – but he could imagine a row of waist-high yew along one wall, each shaped like a surgical instrument. He had never shrunk from a difficult challenge, even if, more often than not, this meant having to do some landscape reconstruction to the customers' thinking first.

Rubbing his throbbing shoulder, he watched his father's neighbours cross the parking lot. Dora Mitchell strode ahead of the others, a tiny stick-lady tossing keys in her cupped palm. Visitors came and went around them. Some approached the building carrying flowers, others went out towards their cars with noses buried in white handkerchiefs.

"Thank Christ they're finally gone," his father said. "A person's a sitting duck in this goddam place. They'd talk your bloody ears off."

Here it came – the crowing. "Not asleep the whole time after all?" Sonny didn't turn from the window.

"Gave you hell, didn't they." The voice was weak and phlegmy but there was no mistaking the man's pleasure. "They're watching you. What are you gonna do now – run?"

"I might. Don't want to take advantage of a sitting duck."

"It's the damnedest thing," his father said. "Parachutes. Dozens of them outside that window."

"What?" There were only a few white moving clouds in the August sky.

"Not now!" The growl was addressed to an idiot. "Last night! Parachutists landing on horses. I never told them others about it."

Sonny turned. His father had pushed himself up into something close to a sitting position against his pillow. "Horses in the parking lot?"

His father's grin was sheepish. "Mostly pintos. I seen the soldiers landing on them. They started stabbing the poor beasts while they were galloping back and forth. Blood everywhere."

Laughing seemed the safest thing. "A nightmare. Must be the drugs."

But his father's eyes were filled with alarm. "What's out there, then?"

Of course from his bed he could see nothing but sky.

"Parking lot. Street traffic. A row of chestnuts past their bloom. Dora trying to get her car started. You know you're in Victoria, don't you?"

His father hated this city, though he'd been in it only three or four times in his life. Government bureaucrats, tourists, university professors, retired Prairie farmers, and doctors. That was the sort of people Timo Aalto believed were housed in those buildings out there, all of them confident that the rest of the island was their private playground. In order to ensure this, they camped on logging roads, lay down before logging trucks, burned logging company bridges, demanded that the government convert all timberland to park. They believed the towns and villages to be populated by stupid and brutal subhumans whose main purpose in life was to lay waste to every living tree. His father believed he was amongst the enemy here.

He'd been amongst the enemy here three years before as well, when a specialist in this hospital had opened up his back. The idea was to free trapped nerves that were cutting off the feeling in his legs. But he'd sent the old man home without doing a thing except sewing him up again. Nothing could be done. His local physician had waited too long to send him down. Timo Aalto wasn't surprised. There was little point in wasting your time with an eighty-two-year-old hick from the up-island bush.

He would sometimes lose his balance, and didn't have enough control to stop himself from falling. According to his letters, and Dora's, it could happen anywhere, in his own kitchen, out in the yard, on a concrete sidewalk in town. Sometimes he bounced off a wall and righted himself. If no wall was close, he went down. Others would have to help him to his feet. Usually he made a joke of it. "You just witnessed the fall of man," he might say. Or, "I can do it again to music if you want." Once, he'd grabbed the peaked cap off his head and held it out as though expecting money. During one of his doctor appointments he'd fallen against the nurse, taking both the nurse and the doctor with him to the floor.

None of this had anything to do with the short wooden stump attached to the remainder of his right leg. He'd worked in the woods, a faller like most of the Finns, but only for a short while in his youth. One day a tall hemlock, instead of falling where it was supposed to fall, bounced off a second tree, swivelled, and crashed down to smash the bones in his shin. The lower part of his right leg had had to be removed. He was so furious that he went back out into the woods with a chainsaw and cut the offending tree into lengths, harvesting a lifetime supply of wooden legs. He borrowed the use of a lathe and turned a few of them himself. A friend had made the leather harness. No fancy artificial leg for him; his every step would be a blow to the sonofabitching tree that had turned him into a cripple.

"I didn't know that Rose was back in your life."

His father snorted contemptuously. "Neither did I. She was shacked up with Rudy Vanderhorst till some damn fool told her I was sick. She likes the idea of being a widow."

Once the Mitchells' Honda had bullied itself out into the Fort

Street traffic, Sonny turned again from the window to find his father struggling to get out of bed – grunting, kicking his foot out from under the blanket. "What're you doing?" He crossed the room to restrain him before he pulled himself free of the tubes.

The old man fell back against his pillow. "Get me the bottle there, willya?"

"What bottle?"

"In the locker there. You don't think I'd let Tommy leave me here without a Johnny Walker?"

"They'll smell it," Sonny said.

A loud disgusted heave of breath. "I don't know why you bothered to come."

That sharp old nose was a network of blood vessels laid against pale yellow cartilage – had always been. A drop of moisture hanging from the tip was also a common sight. The shiny snail trail on his sleeve showed that at least he still made an effort to wipe it before it dropped. The rest of the flesh on that accusing face now looked as though it were made of stretched-thin paper, bloodless, except for the blue satchels slung beneath the eyes. Only a few white hairs grew on his scalp, ghosts of the thick blond mop that had disappeared while Sonny wasn't looking. What he saw now was the top of a stranger's head.

This old wreck had been his partner once, his closest friend. His father had believed that the partnership would last forever. They'd both believed that nothing would ever change. But he had to remind himself of certain things. That this parent, for instance, had once left his seven-year-old down one of those back roads he liked to explore, for complaining about the potholes that had him bouncing off the window glass. He hadn't come back for six hours, after dark, reeking of gin. Once, he'd left Sonny to tighten the Maguires' fences while he went to borrow Sid Bested's come-along, but hadn't returned. He might have gone to the Riverside to drink with his pals, he might have gone home and got lost in a book. By dusk, Sonny had used the iron bar, the hammer, and a bag of staples to tighten a half-mile of barbed wire the best he could. Maguire drove him home and paid him, instructing him not to tell his old man about the money. But such secrecy between them was unthinkable. When Sonny confessed, his father agreed to an even split.

However unlikely it seemed now, none of this had caused him to doubt the partnership. Each new betrayal was a surprise within the unquestioned facts of their life. Even now, it was necessary to remind himself that none of this was what other children – or other partners, for that matter – were expected to consider normal.

Inside the metal locker, the bottle of Scotch was hidden behind clothing and a stack of paperbacks. The old man had brought some of his Russian novels with him. Turgenev. Dostoyevsky. Already second-hand when he'd bought them, they'd been read so many times that some were held together with elastic bands. A man who avoided work had plenty of time to read.

"You didn't bring your Plutarch?"

His father took hold of the bottle, turned it up, glugged down a few gulps, then wiped his sleeve across his mouth, "Why would I?" and turned up the bottle again. Then he handed it back to Sonny, a smile of guilty pleasure transforming his face.

"So you could rub my nose in it, the way you used to. *Coriolanus was raised by only one parent and still became a great man.*"

"That still rankles, don't it. Most people would've forgot it years ago."

"I read it for myself. You never told me the parent who raised him was later the cause of his death."

"Then you didn't read it very close." The old man was trying not to look too happy. "It was his own resentment that did him in. And filling himself with rage."

Sonny had read enough of Plutarch to find reason not to read more. When Brutus sent his own son off to be executed, Sonny slammed that volume shut and vowed not to open the others. He'd begun to suspect that every story would hold some unsettling message. He hadn't seen the irony, then, of the world's laziest man promoting men of accomplishment, a drunk promoting virtue. "*Virtue is a self-sufficient plant and can flower anywhere,*" the old man liked to quote. In case Sonny had missed his point he'd added, "Even in nowhere places like here."

Sonny picked up a crumpled newspaper from Rob Mitchell's abandoned chair and sat to glance through headlines. He might know all that went on in Ottawa but he no longer had any idea what went on out here. Immigrants from Vietnam were shooting one another in what was believed to be a drug war. A provincial Cabinet minister was being investigated for a conflict of interest. A father whose son had been stabbed by a classmate claimed to have forgiven the killer. "I refuse to blame someone who's only error's thrall."

"You find us in there?" his father said. Though he could lose himself in one of his Russian novels for hours at a time, he couldn't stand to have you read in his presence. "*Timo Aalto and son in town. Government House alerted, in case they drop in for tea.*" His fingers dug at the blankets, scratching where his right leg ended, just below the knee. "You haven't gone and got your mug in the papers again, have you?"

From the gloating edge to his voice, Sonny supposed the old man was referring to the Memorial Garden incident. A bitter memory he'd rather not talk about. He'd been delighted when his firm got the commission, an Ottawa memorial garden for wartime nurses, women dedicated to healing in the midst of horrors. Using mostly water and local stone, he'd modelled it after a pool he'd visited in the Canyon de Chelly in Arizona – a place of pilgrimage with a reputation, amongst the ancient Navajo, for its healing powers. The garden was meant to inspire awe: a towering stone wall, an oasis of living plants and deep reflecting water. The figure of a uniformed woman was barely suggested in relief amongst the curves and striations of the stone wall, as though by some innocent act of nature. This had made headlines in the local weekly: VALLEY SON WINS NATIONAL RECOGNITION.

But the Valley Son hit the national papers when hundreds of indigenous people marched to protest his design, frightening parliamentarians and their deputy ministers into ordering the thing dismantled. Fortunately, the "cultural expropriation" had been seen as accidental, and the National Capital Region permitted a "revised" version, so long as it didn't give so much as a nod in the direction of Arizona Navajos or the sacred sites of any other people. Sonny had thrown up his hands but Michel, his partner, had taken over and given them a place of bland grass and curving walkways, with a statue of two nurses (presumably one of them English-speaking, the other French) silhouetted against the distant Gatineau Hills, a fallen soldier and his rifle laid out at their feet. It hadn't made it onto the tourist maps. Perhaps some locals used it as a shortcut to and from work.

When Sonny did not respond to his father's question, the old man raised his head to look at his sleeping roommate, then dropped back with a sigh. "If you'd been around, you could've talked me out of coming down here."

This tone of voice had once sent Sonny out of the house to throw tools around, or to punch sacks of chicken feed until his fists were raw. "Don't be stupid," he said now. "It was an emergency. Anyway, it all happened before I even knew."

"You'd say the same if I'd arranged to cut off my head."

His father hadn't asked how Sonny was doing. Hadn't asked about the chip-wagon business, which he'd referred to as a hobby for a man who needed an excuse to avoid returning home. He hadn't asked about Warren or Warren's business either.

A heavy-set woman clutching a pot of yellow chrysanthemums stepped in through the open doorway, her face arranged in a rigid expression of cheer. Sonny hoped it was someone to relieve him. But "Oh!" she said, startled to find herself in the wrong room, and hurried away.

Sonny stood up and went to the window again. Outside was a world of movement – cars roaring past, leaves shivering, people free to walk the length of sidewalks. Waves, unseen but only blocks away, would be crashing against the shoreline. There were bicycle lanes and sea-wall promenades and, not far away, horses that could be rented if you needed to feel your skin pushing itself through the air.

He had lived out there for a while, in this city, he and Elaine and the two children when they were small. A tall old whaling captain's house in James Bay, a view of the blue Olympics. But it hadn't been far enough. There'd been too many phone calls from the old man, too many demands, too many emergencies he was close enough to deal with. Foreseeing a lifetime of racing up the Island Highway, he'd moved his family to Vancouver and opened a new branch of the business. Gardening had expanded to landscaping by then, though not yet to landscape design. In Vancouver, even the psychological distance provided by the Strait of Georgia wasn't enough, but he'd stuck it out through the marriage breakup and several years of absorption in work, and hadn't got around to following his orphaned children east until (he was alarmed to discover) they were all but grown.

"Before you jump out the window, get the checkerboard outta the locker, willya? We mizewell play a game or two, since you're here."

They had never been able to stop after one. On certain occasions they'd played right through the night. Anything was an excuse – a run-over pet, a bad report card, a letter from the small-debts court. "You can skip school tomorrow," the old man would say. "We'll sleep until we feel like getting up."

Sonny and Darryl Maclean had talked about how easy it was for their fathers to make them feel like boys again. It was because they'd never been put to any great adult-making tests. They could have gone off to Africa with CUSO in the sixties. They could have switched places with draft dodgers who'd fled north from the Vietnam war. The problem was that nothing *inescapable* had been put in their paths. Maclean, a churchgoer, looked to Moses as his model – a tongue-tied nobody until God showed up and told him to do what he was sure he couldn't do. Gideon, too, was a humble

farmer who turned out to be a great military leader – no choice!
God didn't need your ability, said Maclean. He only needed your
availability. "Look what you can do with a little shove." Maclean
was available and waiting. For Sonny, that "little shove" should
have happened years ago; he didn't want it now.

He cranked the old man's bed so that he was more or less
sitting up. His father opened the box and unfolded the checkerboard out onto the cantilevered table that Sonny slid into place
across his lap. As always, he took the reds to himself.

"Charlotte agreed to meet with me tomorrow," Sonny said.

"You looked *her* up before you even seen if your old man's still
alive?"

"I'm *her* old man – remember? I phoned as soon as I'd checked
in. It didn't hold me back ten minutes from rushing to your
ungrateful side."

His father always made the first move – a privilege of age, he'd
called it.

Charlotte hadn't been especially pleased to hear from him.
"Ah, yes," she'd said. He imagined a small ironic twist to her
mouth. She hadn't called him "Dad" since she was six or seven
years old.

"Do you think we could meet while I'm in town?" He'd felt like
a sixteen-year-old, asking the school's cruellest beauty for a date.

"We could, but I don't see much point in it." She'd been blessed
with a rough-edged sexy voice though she claimed never to have
smoked, except for the occasional joint. "I was going out the door
when the phone rang." He could imagine her tucking strands of
blond hair behind her ear, making a face to show the waiting door
she hadn't asked for this delay, perhaps tilting down her head to
smile at herself in a mirror.

"Somewhere tomorrow then?"

"Tomorrow I work."

"So where you meeting her?" his father said. He played without raising his eyes from the board. Sonny played inattentively,

knowing he would eventually lose. If he were to take the lead the old man would find a way to cheat.

"You braced for this? She's taking pictures at Butchart Gardens." His father laughed.

Sonny had been careful not to laugh. "Have you fallen on hard times, or were you commissioned by people from Mars?"

She'd let a moment of silence go by, for him to reconsider his tone. "Believe it or not, there's one or two magazines on *this* planet haven't done it yet."

"At least people who like pictures of flowers don't often issue death threats."

There was another moment's silence before she'd responded. "You've been talking to your father."

"His neighbours send me clippings," he said. "Out of the purest motives, of course."

"I hope you talk some sense into her stubborn head," his father said. "She's got the place in an uproar up there. Last month the tires on her Blazer were slashed. I heard she come down here to lay low. If she's got any sense she'll stay."

For a while the old man had had a grudging respect for this granddaughter. Thanks to Charlotte, he'd even enjoyed a brief celebrity when his photograph had been chosen for a Toronto exhibition of photographs by young women. This was what had brought her home from the States. But at the last minute a sub-committee insisted the old man's photo be removed. A male was not acceptable as a subject. Newspapers wondered if the title had something to do with it. "Man of the Woods" suggested the evil logger. In the end, she'd pulled out altogether as a form of protest. Once again his father's face was in the papers, this time beside a photo of Charlotte. "Beauty and the Beast," his father had scribbled on the copy he mailed to Sonny.

The title had been a fiction. The lines on the old man's face had not been etched by a life in the woods. Though he referred to himself as one of those "dirty-rotten overpaid bush monkeys," quoting, as loggers did, from some never-forgiven letter to the papers during a long-ago strike, he had been a logger for only a very few years. Once that rogue tree had ended his career as a faller, he'd expected to live off workman's compensation for the rest of his life. But the company talked him into returning for less-demanding work, though his general incompetence and his hang-overs made him a safety threat to others. Rather than fire him – a wife-deserted man with a child to raise – the bosses moved him through a sequence of ever-easier jobs until they finally shifted him to the road crew. A swamper filling potholes behind a gravel truck. When he was found too often napping behind a stump, they'd had to let him go.

Because of the women-only incident, magazines began to seek Charlotte out. It so happened that some of her photos were of Vancouver Island mountain slopes, their ancient timber slated to be logged by the international companies. Some slopes were already denuded by clear-cut logging. Magazines began to attach these photos to articles supporting efforts to save old-growth forests. Fundraising groups sold posters made from her photos, printed over with sentimental references to Mother Earth. One of these hung in storefront windows. Torn-up earth, a blackened stump as broad as a garage, devastation that seemed to go on forever. WANTED, the sponsoring organization had printed below, PUBLIC ENEMY NUMBER ONE. *Help Us Stop These Butchers.*

Sonny Aalto had always loved areas of recent logging. Summer afternoons were sometimes spent filling milk pails with trailing blackberries. He'd stalked deer where fir seedlings had grown just high enough to poke through the charred slash. He knew the thrill of disappearing into a stand of second-growth timber barely taller than himself. He thought the poster's foreground stump was beautiful in the manner of certain abstract sculptures. This was clearly not how he was meant to feel. It was taken for granted that you found this landscape ugly, like all right-thinking people of the world. Ugly and, of course, iniquitous.

"She might not even show," Sonny said. "Or I could not show up myself – fly off to Hawaii tomorrow with some woman I meet at breakfast."

"And leave me here to rot."

Sonny studied the board, unsure what he'd had in mind before that last move to the left. "Well, I could call Rose, I guess. Tell her to get down here and grab you fast if she wants you. Take you home and tuck you into her big guest bed."

"It ain't her guest bed worries me. Pay attention here, for chrissake – you forgotten how to play?" The gnarled old hand moved Sonny's checker back to where it had come from. "Old age done something to that woman – she don't think of nothing *else!*"

Sonny laughed. "She probably used to say the same about you."

A red king hopped, a hand scooped up the captured black. "If it's not Hawaii it'll be somewhere else. You'll walk out that door tonight and that's the last I'll see of you."

The white plaster surface of the wall behind the bed was not as perfectly flat as you'd expect. If they'd hung pictures and living vines you might not notice that unsteady human hands had finished it. One of Charlotte's posters, maybe – though "*Help Us Stop These Butchers*" might not please the surgeons who worked in this place.

His mind was beginning to wander. The old man had crossed the board and earned two kings already, though Sonny hadn't noticed it happening. Now one of them started back – hopped once. His father's free hand scooped up Sonny's man, and pushed Sonny's hand aside. "Wait your turn."

"Dora said you had something to tell me."

His hand dismissed the question as it had dismissed his hand. "Later." The black king hopped a second time, and then a third. The captured checkers were deposited in the box lid without glee or even apparent satisfaction.

"Never mind *later*. I'm here now. I only have to go out there and ask those nurses. Or call the doctor."

"You're not paying attention," his father said. "I mizewell play by myself." He swept the checkers aside, scattering them over the bed, and folded up the board. A few checkers clattered to the floor. "If we're gonna be stuck with each other you'll want to put a little more effort into it than that."

H is promise not to look at their world-famous flowers meant nothing to the woman in the ticket booth. She made him fork over the admission fee like any tourist. There was a time he would have entered this place eager to discover new hybrids, eyes open for innovative layouts. Not any more. His first glimpse of blazing red tuberous begonias sent him ducking for cover. You could hardly avoid the flowers at Butchart Gardens but in the Blue Poppy Café, where they had agreed to meet, you could keep your eyes on your coffee.

He'd brought Gaston Bachelard's *The Poetics of Space*, which promised insights he should have explored long ago. "Outside and inside form a dialectic of division," he read, "the obvious geometry of which blinds us as soon as we bring it into play in metaphorical domains." Faced with so much small print, he replaced the bookmark and went next door to the gift shop for a package of poppy seeds and a matching card for Judith Buckle. Then, draped across the table with his legs sprawled to one side, he wrote: *You see how far she will go to humiliate me – risking my life amongst 20,000,000 Japanese tourists oggling* Cynara cardunculus! One spelling error was required in every correspondence between them, to remind them both that she'd been his Grade 2 teacher. Slamming the pointer down across his knuckles: "Keep your mind

on your work, Master Aalto!" *Aalto Senior survived the pneumonia,*
let's hope the rest of us survive him.

More immediate was the need to survive this meeting with
Charlotte. He wasn't sure why he was here – only that it seemed
necessary, since he was in the city. He supposed he should encourage her to be careful for her professional reputation. Express
concern for her safety. He knew better than to hope for her
support in this situation with his father. Since their accidental
reunion in Helsinki nearly five years ago, he'd known better than
to hope for anything much at all.

At least it wasn't raining today.

It had rained off and on throughout his week in the Baltics.
It had rained in Oslo, where he'd visited Gustav Vigeland's garden
of tortured stone figures, seeking inspiration for a sculpture
garden he'd been commissioned to create outside Toronto. In
Finland it had rained through most of his Karelian travels, while he
looked up his grandparents' village, and then on a whim searched
for the location of the "wanton Lemminkäinen's" encounter with
the Swan of Tounela immortalized in both the *Kalevala* and Jean
Sibelius's music. He'd found neither swans nor river, nor anyone
who would admit they existed. "The Russians ate the swans,"
amused villagers had told him. "And probably drank the river."

In Helsinki the third downpour of the day had begun as he
hurried down the Esplanade towards his hotel. His shoes sloshed
in a gravel soup; tree limbs slapped heart-shaped leaves at his face.
Presumably the people who looked out through the glass walls of
the Kappeli were dry. Coffee drinkers held pastry between their
fingers. Lovers leaned towards one another across small tables.
One young woman sat alone inside a glass corner turret, perched
on a wooden stool at a high round table. Her gaze was somewhere
off in the direction of the harbour market, her chin resting on an
index finger. He stopped running, struck by the way the weak
interior lighting seemed to isolate her in a floating cage – herself
floating within it, since her long legs were tucked back, her feet
behind the rungs of the stool.

Her hand moved, jotted something in a small book. Then she rested her chin again, this time on a cupped palm, and looked off across the cobblestones towards the Presidential Palace. A poet waiting for inspiration? In that glass tube she looked about as Finnish as you could hope for, with her white-gold hair. He decided to greet her with something from Lönnrot's epic:

> . . . *shall I open the word-chest*
> *and unlock the box of tales*
> *unwind the top of the ball*
> *untie the knot of the coil?*
> *I will sing quite a good tale*
> *quite a fair one I'll beat out*
> *after some rye bread*
> *and some barley beer.*

He scanned memory for something more appropriate but by the time he'd carried his coffee across the room, his socks squishing like sponges in his shoes, he was no longer thinking of poetry. "*Anteeksi*," he said, instead. "*Hyvää päivää. Puhutteko englantia?*"

"I suppose you could call it English," she said, "though I've been told there's a hint of the South around the edges." Because of the high stool, her eyes were level with his.

He was so shocked at his mistake that he was barely aware of her words. She was out of context here, of course. And she had done something with her hair – perhaps dyed it even paler than it naturally was. She had, of course, grown a little older since he'd seen her last, after tracking her (with Bathsheba's grumbling help) to a flat above a courtyard off Canal Street. His face burned, to think he'd planned to impress her with poetry.

"You're dripping on my notes." She pulled her notebook closer to her breast. Her eyes were the pale translucent green of gooseberries.

He perched on the stool across her table, and pushed his wet hair back so the water would run down his neck instead of his

face. She sighed and tapped her fingernail while he expressed surprise at their unlikely meeting. The trumpeter was in town,
touring with a jazz group, she said, and she was taking advantage
of the opportunity to use her camera. She had been published
recently in a few magazines in the States. A gallery in Baton
Rouge had featured some of her photos.

And what was he doing here? She asked this with the feigned
interest of a distant cousin enduring an unwelcome meeting. She
showed little interest in his Karelian family quest, and even less
in his horticultural tours, but seemed a little curious about his
half-hearted search (since he happened to be in the country) for
some news of his mother.

"And no one in that village knew where she'd got to?"

"No one spoke enough *englantia* to help." All he'd got from his
excursion was the view from the train window, little Nordic farm-
houses and hay fields that looked exactly like the houses and
fields of the Finns who'd settled amongst the meagre branches of
Portuguese Creek. "Yesterday I went to see a cousin – a second
cousin of my father's, across the bridge in Lauttasaari. She had
nothing to tell, but gave me a huge lunch, with a view as far as
Estonia, and afterwards a walk through a cemetery."

"Filled with Nazi soldiers," she said.

His father's family left Karelia in the 1800s, he reminded her,
his mother's family in 1903. This may have had something to do
with Czar Nicholas's plan for the Russification of Finland. "It isn't
easy living next door to a Selfish Giant, as we know."

She had perfect ears. In this light, her hair shone with hints of
pink, like the tips of nearly ripe hay. The sharp cheekbones were
real, not merely suggested by makeup. Because the bottom two
buttons of her dress were undone, he was conscious of the long
splendid calf of the crossed-over leg. Her mother had been a
subtler beauty. Not so tall. Not so assured. Not so self-contained.

While she was here, she said, she would photograph buildings
designed by the famous architects. Carl Engel, Eliel Saarinen, and
others. Perhaps he'd heard of them? Obviously she was sure he

hadn't. But he had, he'd read of them in the books his mother's relatives had sent. Gesellius. Alvar Aalto. He may even have been some distant cousin to Alvar Aalto, as she would be herself. "He designed the concert hall."

She was almost impressed. Even so, there'd be little point in mentioning his visit to the Paavo Nurmi statue outside the Olympic Stadium this morning, since she would only feel obliged to look bored.

She put her notebook into a leather bag and stood up, allowing him to help her into a light raincoat. "Rain's letting up. I've work to do."

She was off to a church burrowed into the bald stone crown of a hill. "The Suomalainen brothers," she said, "quarrying after God." Though this may have been meant to discourage, he accompanied her. He would suggest dinner later. The Kosmos was the restaurant the cousin had taken him to after the cemetery. Above their table there'd been a pair of lady's high-heeled boots behind glass.

Before he went home, he said, he was hoping for a tour of the recently discovered Lost Gardens of Heligan in Cornwall, a family estate that disappeared beneath a jungle of brambles and ivy, all of its gardeners having been killed in the First World War. His feet sloshed inside his shoes, as they walked up one and then another side-street until they came to the glass doors that provided an entrance to the hill.

His father's root cellar had also been dug into a slope, and was sealed with a rough plank door. Inside was the smell of apples and potatoes, the darkness unbroken except by a single pencil line of light through a crack in the door. It was where his father, as a boy, had hidden while the forest fire went through. It was where Sonny had gone to keep out of the old man's way. That it might have something in common with a church had not occurred to him.

"Amazing what can be done with a hole in the ground," he said.

But she turned him away at the wide glass doors. If he followed her inside, he would interfere with her way of seeing. He could come another time, if he wished, on his own.

He'd gone back the following day, to discover for himself what had been made of the hole in the ground. Daylight spilled through ceiling glass that rested on spokes from a central copper disc, and washed down the pink and grey streaked surfaces of the rough stone walls. This was a church a gardener might have designed, given an abandoned quarry to work with. He too would not have set anything before that unevenly chiselled front wall but a long granite slab, a small cross, and a bowl of white orchids. And would have planted those few leafy maidenhair ferns beside the steps to the communion rail. Charlotte must have known he would want to explore every bend in the walls, examine every plant, figure out how the water leaking down the side walls was carried away at the base. Or she might simply not have wanted him to see the place at all.

He wasn't made for sitting long. He especially wasn't made for sitting long in crowded coffee shops, waiting for someone he wasn't entirely sure he wanted to see. He searched for the time amongst the excessive information his watch was determined to give. This was his latest purchase from the Franklin Mint, who'd been sending him catalogues weekly since he'd ordered a jack-knife advertised in a flyer. He'd had no need for the jack-knife but hadn't been able to resist one with a picture of a 1940 Ford pickup on its flank – his first vehicle, rotting now in one of his father's sheds.

Judith Buckle had warned him. First a jack-knife, then a watch. Would porcelain dolls be next? Marilyn Monroe with her skirt inside out, or Scarlett O'Hara twirling her parasol? She had never mentioned his ring, whose lions were from King Richard's heraldic symbol. According to the Franklin Mint, the ring had been especially designed by Her Majesty's jeweller, "a symbol of power for today's man of destiny."

When he went out from the Blue Poppy onto the pathways, today's man of destiny tried not to look at the thousands of pots and hanging baskets of begonias. He kept his eyes on the toes of his Rockports and followed the painted footsteps, twisting his ring and calling up King Richard's courage for the encounter ahead.

If she had been following the footsteps herself she hadn't got far. She stood on the high rim above the old limestone quarry. Stairs went steeply down to the gardens fifteen metres below, where cement walkways curved out past beds of scarlet *Salvia splendens*, variously coloured pelargoniums, and petunias meant to take your breath away. Tall evergreens stood up like pillars and conical sentries. The rough stone wall on either side was draped with gleaming ivy. Someone had planted a Garden of Eden in what might have been Dante's pit.

She liked to wear loose skirts that emphasized her height and graceful long-legged walk. He'd come upon her just as she'd made an abrupt stop, the skirt still in motion about her calves. His blood tried to rush in all directions at once, but seemed to collide with itself somewhere behind his lower ribs and go boiling around in a flurry. He was *shy*, before his own child! "Amazing what you can do with a hole in the ground," he said, hoping she might remember the Suomalainens' church.

She crouched to search through her camera bag. When she looked up at him from close to the ground, she tilted down her head so that her blond hair fell to one side. This was a calculated pose, a chosen angle. The smile was also calculated. You noticed the perfect mouth, the small white teeth. Someone had photographed her like this and she'd used the picture ever since with her promotion material. People seeing her in magazines wondered why they couldn't put a name to the movie star she resembled. They didn't wonder if the pleasure shining in her lovely half-closed eyes was sincere.

"Guess how hard it is to find an original shot," she said, standing again to put a hand on either side of his face and kiss his cheek, one side and then the other. Then she turned aside, as if that had been a farewell kiss, and frowned, lowering her eyelids to reduce the field of her vision. Something down in that quarry had possibilities. One hand reached for the camera at her hip, the gesture of a gunfighter, the graceful gazelle had become an Annie Oakley ready to drill a rattler. "I should have known better than to take this damn assignment." The camera was left after all at her hip.

"You've forgotten how to say No?"

"Every magazine on the continent is begging for more clear-cuts," she said. "Each has to be more horrifying than the last, to show that things are even worse than we thought. I'm tired of trying to outdo myself."

"Which is why you refuse to cash their cheques." He moved up to stand beside her.

She looked away. "Careful, if you don't want to be pushed off this cliff."

"You've thrown *yourself* off a cliff, I understand. Professionally speaking, I mean. By getting yourself adopted by a Cause."

Her gaze was busy calculating possibilities in this view. "While you still refuse to see there are sides to be taken, I suppose, on the grounds that you wish to be open-minded." But she quickly dropped the high moral tone. Perhaps she had little energy for it. "I'm trying to get a little distance but you can see where it's brought me. Azaleas!"

"If you're looking at what I think you're looking at, that is a bed of dahlias."

"Whatever." She started down the switchback stairs. "You're as restless as ever, I can see it in your eyes. You've probably started three more careers since I saw you last. Added sixteen countries to your travels. How's your father?"

"You haven't paid him a visit since he's been down here?"

"You know what he thinks of me. He'd start telling me where I should and shouldn't take my camera, keep my nose out of local conflicts blah blah blah. Pretty soon we'd be shouting. Anyway, you're a fine one to talk! How long has it taken them to drag you out here just to say hello?"

"I think I'd prefer the bare original rock to all this friendly growth," Sonny said. "If I were a photographer."

She stopped at the bottom of the steps to lower her lashes at him. *As if*, she meant. As if he could ever stand still long enough to take pictures. "In fact I'm trying to find a patch of bared stone somewhere myself, to suggest what's covered up." Her fingers barely touched his arm. "Find something you haven't seen a thousand times, my eyes are crossed from looking."

"Uncross them now. Here's something that doesn't get into magazines." He meant three women silently dead-heading a rhododendron the size of a shed. They stood inside the branches in their green shirts, moving only their hands, slowly dropping withered blossoms like gathered fruit into green buckets at their feet. Late in the season, but perhaps this giant was a hybrid he didn't recognize. A relative of the *ponticum*. "Invisible employees. You can break the news to an astonished world: it doesn't happen by itself, there are armies of unseen workers spilling sweat."

"They'd never print it," she said, glancing to either side as though someone in authority might leap out from the bushes and confiscate her camera.

If the workers noticed that someone was photographing them, they didn't let on. So confident of their camouflage, they believed they would not show up in a photo. Once she'd taken three or four shots, she lowered her camera and frowned at his shirt. "You were wearing that a year ago. Don't you ever change?" She ran her gaze down the length of his jeans.

"I take them off to wash them," he said in his own defence. "Since I saw you last I've probably worn out a couple of shirts and two or three pairs of jeans."

She moved on down the pathway. "And how many of the world's 'sacred sites' have you worn out since those jeans were new?"

She'd never missed a chance to mock his habit of chasing after ruined cathedrals and the sites of pilgrimages. Wasting money, wasting time, wasting hope. Even the most restless of men got over that sort of thing by their thirtieth birthday. Or should have. She had a father, she'd suggested, who was less mature than she was.

He looked down at his faded knees for help. Glastonbury? Moose Mountain Medicine Wheel? He'd stumbled against one of the rocks at Moose Mountain and was yelled at.

Janis, too, had complained about his restlessness throughout their short marriage. It had nearly driven her crazy. At least that was what she'd told him. Even now he found himself explaining his reasons to her, in his head. Occasionally he lay awake at night imagining her, recalling her dark hair on the pillow, her grey eyes watching him in the dawn light of that last day, her mind already on the life she would resume away from him.

Others before her had complained as well, and others since, including Bathsheba – who had chosen stability. At a certain age it seemed that people wanted to feel settled; they wanted you settled too. Apparently he gave the impression he was still looking for something that would lead him into adulthood – a true vision, a special place, a career to dedicate his life to. It put people off, his habitual dashing off, throwing too much energy into too many directions at once. As Darryl Maclean put it, "Your life will be over and you'll still be waiting for it to start."

The crowd ahead had come to a halt on the pathway, treading on one another's heels. Some stepped onto the grass. Two youths were the obstacle, standing nearly nose to nose and shouting. "That's the stupidest idea I ever heard, you gotta be nuts!"

A red gash on the youthful cheek was a bullet scar. This boy was familiar. Sonny had seen him on his way out of the hospital yesterday, outside the front door in a wheelchair, smoking.

This morning his photo had been in the local newspaper. UP-ISLAND BOY SHOT BY FATHER RECOVERING. After the boy had been charged with a gas station theft, a shouting match with his father had escalated until the man lost his temper and went for his gun. The boy had then been airlifted down here in one of those ambulance helicopters.

Apparently he'd been released, and was seeing the sights before going home to face an investigation. Perhaps there were police behind the bushes, letting him enjoy a bit of freedom before they locked him in their back seat and drove him home.

There was something stagey about the way he spoke – a little too loud, a self-conscious belligerence. He wished to be the focus of attention. In this old cement plant dressed up as a series of gardens he could be pretty sure of having the largest audience available in this part of the world. He was waiting for someone to say, "Aren't you the boy in this morning's paper?"

"Okay, numb-nuts!" he shouted. "You think I'm crazy, why don't you just take off!"

"Sounds like a good idea for the both of you," fearless Charlotte said, as she led the way around the pair. The youth sneered at her, at them. Sonny raised a hand, as a caution against a too-hasty reply, and then walked on, expecting a body tackle from behind.

"I would think you'd jump at the chance," Sonny said. "You could stand him against the wall, rough stone and baby face with scar – first blow from life's hard chisel."

She crouched to consider crimson petals floating on the pond. "I'm trying to do a job here. Flowers, remember? A *spectacular carpet of colour*?" She stood again, dismissing the floating petals. "You show up out of nowhere and give *advice*? Can't you even see that what you had in mind was a big mistake?"

"I'm not sure what I had in mind."

"You had in mind what you always have in mind," she said. "Though this time you've put hardly any effort into it." She started away, her long strides setting that skirt in motion. "At least I used to be able to laugh at your efforts." She turned back to him, unsmiling. "Hired planes dragging signs across the sky. Flowers replanted to spell out your paternal affection. You must be getting tired. Or old."

"I was in the neighbourhood," he said.

"You just wanted to witness my humiliation," she said. "Charlotte Aalto photographing dahlias for *Western Homes*. You should be able to work it up into a story for your father. He'll love it."

"Well," he said. He couldn't deny that the old man would find it amusing.

She disappeared behind the heavy boughs of a western red cedar. The interview was over. She was a woman of ambition – of accomplishments, success – with little time for him.

Sonny started for the exit by way of the Italian Garden, which was usually less crowded than the others. Few of the visiting hordes had resources of wonder left for this subtle formality after following the arrows through the sunken garden, the roses, and the mono-chromatic peace of the Japanese garden. Legs ached. Feet hurt. Eyes could take in only so much in one day. Most passed through the Italian Garden in a hurry, removing film from cameras, collecting their children, discussing where to go for dinner.

He understood that his efforts had been wasted here. He might as well have spent the afternoon with *The Poetics of Space*. Passing down the concrete flags, he paused for a moment to admire the cross-shaped pool's twelve sentries – a rose tree at every corner. In Vancouver, he'd designed gardens much like this one. Low box hedges, symmetrical flower beds, concrete pools, and fountains. At first it had been for troublesome corners of a few large estates on Southwest Marine Drive. But once his work was better known, he'd become the favourite gardener for members of the Italian community. Signor Aaltoni, they called him. Soon he was installing small-scale replicas of Florentine gardens in the tiny backyards of East Van – miniature pools, a bit of cement, a row of conical shrubs, a couple of plaster statues. Leaping fish and sim-pering Venuses. Families greeted him loudly on the street, intro-duced their children, insisted that he attend their backyard wedding receptions.

On the open plaza inside the exit and entrance gates, weary tourists sat on varnished benches or stood to have their photos taken in front of a large copper boar beside a pool. The beast's heavy front-quarters and great tusked head were raised, its forward legs apart, as though ready either to bolt or to charge. But he was anchored by his hindquarters to a metallic green earth populated by metal snakes, frogs, snails, salamanders, and crabs.

This was a copy of the *Il Porcellino* he'd seen in the Uffizi, itself a copy of an earlier version in Greece. He'd been told there were versions everywhere you went, offspring watching over far-flung corners of the world. It was tempting to think the javelin-throwing half-brother had arranged to have it erected here especially for him, in case his sales pitch had planted seeds that needed encouragement.

Like the brochures he'd mailed a few weeks after his visit. Photographs showed gold and ochre sandstone, a three-toed footprint the size of the hat beside it, and dozens of tiny three-toed prints going the opposite direction. *Lark Quarry Day Tours.* According to the explanation, a carnosaur had left eleven three-toed tracks in the mud – now hard stone. The thousands of smaller footprints were made by dinosaurs racing to escape. The attached note had said, "In case the Devil's Marbles aren't enough. Gerard." Gerard must have been what the Australian thought he was saying when he was actually saying Jerrod.

Charlotte appeared from the direction of the sunken garden. "I can't do this," she said. "I hate flowers! I've always hated flowers. I hate the very idea of gardens. What are you doing?"

He stepped up onto the boar's metallic garden amongst the snakes and crabs, and draped an arm over the animal's neck. "I may liberate this fellow. What do you think?" He rubbed a palm down the long metallic jowl, and imagined the boar coming down off his pedestal after dark, to root up daffodil and tulip bulbs, to wallow in the Italian pool, and run grunting up and down the deserted pathways, Italian arias ringing in his expatriate head, until the early morning arrival of the first employee. He gave the long metal snout a ringing slap that widened children's eyes.

As they walked together towards the exit, he told her about the Australian's invitation. "Of course I don't have much interest in going. *Didn't* have. But the thought of dealing with the old man has given the idea some appeal."

"At least you're consistent," she said. "Keep yourself on the run so no one can nail your feet to one spot and make you responsible for something." She started away towards the parking lot, then stopped and turned back. "On the other hand, if your up-island rednecks make good their threats, or gardens are the only assignments I get, I may be looking for a new continent myself."

While he watched her leave, quiet laughter rose up his throat, threatening to become more vigorous. He had dreaded this meeting. He hadn't known what it might lead to and it had led to nothing. He would not have guessed how good this nothing could feel.

He withdrew the postcards from his pocket. On the way to the hospital he would stop for stamps and drop them in the first red box he came to. Judith Buckle would be stepping down from the bus about now, to buy cut flowers on Bank Street before walking home along the canal. Darryl Maclean was just about to end his day's work, splitting birch or oak in his woodlot, cataloguing in his mind the infinitude of injustices that kept him amused and furious with the world. The manager of the Centretown hotel, having sent his wife to Montreal on a shopping spree, locked the door of his office and instructed his receptionist to remove her clothing. "If we understand one another correctly." She understood, she said. In fact, she'd had much the same thing in mind. The archivist left the Museum of Civilization, stopped at a M'sieur Patates wagon for ice cream, then set out to cross the bridge to the National Gallery, hoping to burn off the anger she felt for her young assistant. Speeding along the road to the airport, the senior Cabinet minister leaned back against the seat with his eyes closed and spoke to his driver. "Man, I am going to give those people a piece of my mind, I'm telling you. They have to make sure the choice is clear: Yes or No to independence from the most civilized country in the world."

He thought of the highway as a river of pavement that started modestly near the island's northern tip, five hundred kilometres to the north. After meandering for a while, it gradually widened and straightened a little as it worked its way through mountains and timber and the towns and farms of the eastern coastline, becoming finally a four- and six-lane freeway emptying its traffic into the capital city here at the southern tip. They were working their way upstream.

Or trying to. The drive north became a series of side trips onto backcountry roads, sometimes winding so deeply into farmland and forest and mountain canyons that finding their way back out to the highway became a series of experiments. The road to Cobble Hill had to be explored because, his father said, "Hollywood come up and shot *Little Women* back there." A few miles farther on he instructed Sonny to turn onto a road newly cut into the woods because "I heard they'd started a place for old folks somewheres back in here." The rented Buick LeSabre was filled with his father's smell. The old familiar nose-tickling odour of his Copenhagen snoose was overlaid by the faint hospital scent he'd brought with him. Soap, maybe.

"You want to reserve a room?"

"Ha," his father said. "I'd rather you dumped me in the chuck." He rolled down his window to spit a stream of brown juice into the wind. He'd promised the doctor he would try to resist the booze but warned that this would require a wad of Copenhagen behind his lip every waking minute. Occasionally he scratched through his dark wool pants where the wooden stump was attached to his leg. A sign of agitation. It was enough to start an itch along the back of Sonny's neck.

Instead of an "old folks' home" they found only a farm, whose fields had been cleared but not yet cultivated. Buildings still waited for paint. "Must've heard wrong," his father said. "Unless they're penning the old folks up in the barn." He hauled out a handkerchief and swiped it across his nose, where a small drop of moisture had been glistening since Victoria.

At a fork in the road his father said, "Take the left." A narrow gravel road followed a winding creek. Low limbs scraped the car. Tires dropped into sudden holes. Soon they were passing through muddy swampland. Ducks flew up.

"Water parsnip," his father said. "Deadly."

Sometimes during their Sunday afternoon drives they would stop and get out for a hike. His father carried a book for identifying plants but seldom needed to consult it. They would follow a creek or a canyon while his father pointed out what Sonny ought to notice. A clear-cut ablaze with orange tiger lilies. Mossy ravines with patches of mountain lady's slipper and coral root and rattlesnake plantain. Swamp areas of white bog orchid. Sonny recalled a marsh marigold blooming in a tiny recess under the melting snow, high up a mountain in July.

What gave his father the greatest pleasure was to point out a beautiful flower – foxglove, say – and inform Sonny that it was dangerous. "That's Indian hellebore over there. 'Skookum root,' they used to call it. Frothing at the mouth, blurred vision, lockjaw, vomiting, diarrhea, unconsciousness, death!" Sonny had checked with the books. The old man was always right. "Cow parsnip," he would say, and shudder. "Fatal!"

"This could be the road George Williams moved down," he said now. "Remember the Williamses? Eight or nine kids."

The road was mostly uphill through unfenced pine. Probably Crown land. "Out here's where drug dealers pick up their shipments," Sonny said. "We'll get ourselves shot."

The only house they came upon was a small shack, its rough boards weathered dark, its metal chimney flue stuck out through a window. "You think George Williams raised nine kids in that?" A woman's head appeared at the window, then disappeared.

"I heard old Williams died," his father said, while they travelled downhill through the pines. "I see people more at funerals now than I ever seen them before. I have to tell them every time where you got to. Stick to the right."

The road led at a slant past grazing cattle, fenced off from fields of hay stubble. A large barn with twin silos stood on the hill. "Lily," his father said. "Death camas, that one. Poisonous roots." He could recognize every type of lily from just the leaves. False Solomon's seal, clasping twisted-stalk, Hooker's fairbells, false lily-of-the valley, queen's cup, white fawn lily, yellow glacier lily, Hooker's onion, camas, death camas, tiger lilies, mountain bells. "Consider the lily of the field," he would sometimes say. For most of his life, Timo Aalto had lived like the lilies, avoiding toil wherever he could. Counting on God and Sonny to keep him fed and clothed and out of jail.

When Sonny had decided that Plutarch was not for him, he'd made a point of reading Theophrastus instead. This student of Plato and Aristotle had classified all the plants in the known world. Reading him was a way of keeping up with the old man. Occasionally it could be a weapon, when his father pushed too hard. "Theophrastus freed *his* slaves – what about you?" Unfortunately the old man went to the trouble of reading up on Theophrastus himself. "Only at his death, my son! And only on the condition that they work in his gardens for another year afterwards."

"I remember when I seen that shack before! Me 'n' Tommy Reimer come down this road looking for a hay wagon advertised in the paper. It was grouse season so we had our shotguns. The fellow selling the wagon lived there, crazy as a loon. When he seen our guns in Tommy's truck he must've figured we come to rob him so he grabbed his twelve gauge and drove us off his place. Shot over our heads. We never even got to see the wagon."

Eventually they found a road back to the highway, and remained on the pavement long enough to pass through the town of Ladysmith. "They shot *Big Bully* here," his father said, raising his walking stick to point across in front of Sonny's nose. Ladysmith had played the part of some small town in Minnesota. If they had the time for a side trip to Port Alberni they could see where *Dante's Peak* was shot. "They made it look like a town at the base of a volcano – some other part of the world." To his habit of rereading Russian novels he'd added a passion for videos.

Sonny would have been grateful to avoid the gaudy signs and commercial outlets along this stretch of highway approaching Nanaimo. Where once you'd driven past timber and cattle, you now passed body shops with their write-offs up on pillars, chain-saw statues, and fenced-in stockpiles of septic tanks. "Makes you wonder why the protesters go after the loggers when you see what developers can do," his father said. "Years from now the logged-off woods'll be forests again but their damn 'improvements' will still be buggering up the place."

Where a stretch of new freeway had been pushed through wilderness, his father chose to follow the older highway curving along the coastline, where monster houses were the blight. "Indians got millions for this here stretch of land," he said. "Smart buggers, they stopped the developers in their tracks till they got what they wanted. Claimed there was a graveyard. Can you imagine anyone stopping a subdivision because *your* grave was in their way? Who decides what's sacred and what's not?"

Soon they were burrowing into timber again, and eventually came to a lake whose shoreline was crowded with so many summer cabins that they could see only narrow slices of the water through the spaces between. Above the roofs, the steep timbered hill across the lake was clearly visible, and beyond that, the snowy peaks of the mountain range. They passed along the base of a sheer vertical rock face and came to a government parking lot in the soft green light beneath cedars. A sign pointed out a pathway that led to caves.

"Looks like a bit of a walk," Sonny said.

His father opened his door and began to struggle out. "Let's try. It's been years since I seen them caves."

He wiped the dampness off his nose again and started towards the trail with one hand jabbing his walking stick into the gravel. He stayed close to the bumper log, his free hand poised as though he'd decided this was the direction to fall if he lost his balance. According to Dora Mitchell's reports he refused to consider a metal walker. Instead, he'd learned to roll onto his shoulder when he fell, and only occasionally gashed his forehead. The shoe at the end of his good leg was a cheap black runner, Sonny noticed, worn down at the heel and turned over along the outer side. They would have to shop for new ones.

Not that you saw much of his shoe. He wore his trousers so wide and long they collapsed in folds around one foot and dragged on the ground where the other foot ought to be.

It took them several minutes to work their way across the narrow creek on the suspension bridge, Sonny holding onto his father's arm while his father held on to the railing. Ahead, a wide pathway curved uphill through giant cedars. Where it was steep, wooden steps were there to help. Breathing heavily, his father lowered himself to sit on the first of the steps. "I always wanted to go in for another look."

They stared in silence for a few moments at the sword ferns down along the creek. Sunlight flickered and shifted with the moving boughs of the cedars.

"I don't weigh nothin' no more," the old man said. "You could piggy-back me up these steps."

Behind them, the parking lot was almost empty. Sunlight poured down onto the gravel from directly above, through a gap in the cedar canopy. A red Ford Fairlane sat at the far end.

Abandoned, maybe. No vehicles could be heard coming up the road. Sonny crouched before his father and directed him to put his arms around his neck, and to clamp his knees to his sides. Once he was standing again, bent forward with his hands under his father's bony thighs, he began to climb the steps, the old man's walking stick clamped beneath his arm.

The opening to the first cave was an inverted V, like a tent door in the rock face of the mountain. But there was too little light to see in. They followed the trail along the base of the rock face to a second cave. Moss grew here and there on narrow ledges. Cracks and pockets of soil sprouted ferns. This might have been a wall in the Suomalainen brothers' quarried church.

From the second cave, a narrow stream gushed noisily, and gurgled downhill through the trees. Sonny crouched, to set his father on the path, then handed him his cane. "Where Moses struck the rock!" his father said. He jabbed the end of the converted umbrella at the rough stone cliff. Then he looked up, mouth open, as though expecting his own miracle to drop from amongst the heavy boughs of the cedars.

The pale green light entered the opening just far enough to illuminate curves and shadows and gleaming wet stone. Sonny bent and stepped in, and breathed the chilled, metallic air. There was clearly a tunnel beyond the light, behind a large curved lump of stone. The surface of the cave walls did not seem like stone at all, but was coated with a pattern of lumps you might expect to find on the hide of an ancient lizard, like blisters of rust on old machine parts.

If there were a tour guide he might have asked if these caves had once had special meaning to local Indian bands. Places they feared, perhaps, where evil creatures emerged from the bowels of the earth. Maybe they'd left their dying elders deep inside for the journey to the next world. Of course these caves may have had no more meaning for them than, say, the caves of northern Spain had had for Sonny Aalto, who'd hoped for revelations of a life-changing nature but only developed a headache from the underground air.

He stepped across the spilling water and discovered, behind the boulder that half-blocked the entrance, an antechamber dimly lit by a slice of sunlight slanting down from a fissure in the rock. The temperature dropped abruptly. Water trickled through worn channels beneath his feet.

"Me 'n' Tommy Reimer went down there once," his father said, from close behind. "I never seen nothin' like it. Like going down a giant's throat and finding an art gallery in his gut – coloured sculptures by a crazy artist in hell. We went from one room to the next. Some places we had to crawl on our bellies." He moved forward a step, wobbled a bit, and put a hand for balance on Sonny's arm. "Once we had to strip and swim underwater to get through to the next room. I went first. Tommy got stuck, he was fat even then. I had to go back under and help him, the whole time thinking he was going to drown where he was and plug up my only way out. Damn, but I was scared! We weren't hardly more than boys." The old man was silent a moment, then added, "If I could trust these legs I'd go down there now. Listen!"

Muttering came from deep in the tunnel. A flickering light appeared, then disappeared for a moment, before flashing against the wall. Eventually the glaring suns of two flashlights floated in the dark. Sonny crouched for his father to climb on, and then carried him out through the narrow entrance to get out of the way. His thighs in Sonny's hands were frail sticks wrapped in loose rough wool.

A bearded man stepped out of the cave mouth, speaking over his shoulder to someone behind him. "Well," he said when Sonny stepped back to let him pass. He smiled a mocking "caught you" sort of smile, to let you see how foolish you looked with a man hanging off your back. The second man – a redhead – wore heavy boots and work denims hacked off at the ankles. Both were probably in their late twenties. The second recognized

Timo Aalto. "Jesus, Swampy, I never knew you had servants to pack you around."

Sonny made a warning sound in his throat, but his father said, "It took a while but I finally got him trained."

Both men laughed. So did Timo Aalto, who'd always enjoyed attention.

"What else you train him to do?" the bearded one said. "Does he mop up yer puke?" They shook their heads, grinning at their cleverness, and started off.

Sonny had spent twenty years mopping up his father's mess. "Just a minute," he said.

"The redhead's a Maguire," his father said. "I forget the other fellow's name."

By the time Sonny had left his father and reached the parking lot the two young men were getting into the Fairlane. "Just a minute," he said again. "I think you owe my father an apology."

The redhead turned inside the opened door. "You think so, eh?" He seemed to believe this was funny.

"Come on," said his friend behind the wheel. He started the engine.

"Fuck off, asshole," the redhead said. He got quickly inside and shut his door.

Gravel sprayed out from behind the back tires, the Ford leapt ahead. Sonny slammed a fist on the roof as it passed. The car cut a wide curve around the parking lot and came back, straight at Sonny. He stepped up onto the bumper log. The car skidded to a stop. The driver leapt out and came at him, fists ready for a fight.

Sonny leapt down off the log and blocked the fist with his own raised arm, struck out himself and knocked the driver's shoulder hard enough to spin him away. The driver came back and slammed one fist into Sonny's chest, then with the other drove an uppercut into Sonny's chin, hard enough to drop him, sitting, onto the bumper log. Pain shot up either side of his skull.

A door slammed. Gravel sprayed again. The car roared off.

He put his head in his hands. Shit. Already he was back where he'd started, fighting the old man's battles, even though he had better reason than those two thugs to mock the sonofabitch.

Local men had always taken that slightly amused and contemptuous tone when they talked to his father. Even those who liked him sometimes did it. He was a home-grown joke, a boozer whose evasion of regular employment had become a comic legend. If he'd noticed this himself he'd mistaken it for affection. He'd even played to it. "Yer jealous," he'd laugh. "Bustin' your asses for men that get rich off your sweat."

Sonny had seen how they grinned at one another behind the old man's back. They were experts at the smirk that suggested they knew something repulsive about you that you couldn't know yourself. As Timo's boy, Sonny had sometimes felt it directed towards himself.

Of course he'd hated his father for the confusing mixture of shame and indignation. He was furious to see his father mocked but embarrassed to be his son. What made it even worse – and maybe this was what rankled the most – was that the old man seemed to identify with the others against him. *Took me long enough but I finally got him trained.*

The redhead had called his father Swampy, a nickname attached to him after he'd been fired as swamper with the road crew. "Timo" did not come easily, except to the neighbouring Finns, though someone who knew of his love for most things Russian once made a kind of singsong out of it: Timo-Timo-Timoshenko. For a while the Timoshenko stuck. He hadn't discouraged this, maybe because it made him feel like someone in his Russian paperbacks. But then someone drinking in the Riverside had slipped from Timoshenko to Timbershanks. Silence followed, in case this had been going too far. Even the man who'd said it was shocked. Eyes glanced at the tip of wooden leg that showed below the pants. But Timo Aalto laughed, and danced a few steps, tapping his stump on the floor. Timbershanks he was, to some, from then on.

Sonny had hated the nicknames. He'd especially hated the Timbershanks. He would have thrown himself at anyone who used it if his father hadn't stopped him. While the old man seemed to be flattered, Sonny heard only the mockery. When they weren't mocking they were patronizing. He'd never, even once, heard his father addressed as Mr. Aalto.

The taste of the Fairlane's dust was still in the air when they pulled out of the parking lot. At the first stop sign, Sonny waited to be told which way to go. They sat in silence, both of them staring ahead. Sonny refused to ask.

His father spat his wad out the window, drank from the water bottle in the glove compartment, then fetched the small, round Copenhagen container from his shirt pocket, opened it, and stuffed a pinch down behind his bottom lip. He held the open container out towards Sonny, who pushed it away with the back of his hand as he had done all his life. One taste, long ago, had been enough.

"I figured you wouldn't show up this morning," his father said. "You done your duty – I figured you'd took a good look at me and then flew off again."

"You can thank Judith Buckle. Her teacher-nagging wore me down."

His father grunted. He'd never had much good to say about Judith Buckle. He'd known she had little good to say about him. "Turn left," he said. "There ought to be a shortcut up this way."

"Shortcut to where?"

"Supper."

He had phoned from the hospital for a reservation, he explained. Some place he'd read about in a magazine. "Movie stars fly up from L.A. Before I go home I want a decent meal and a night of luxury."

There was little point in resisting. Not only was this fancy lodge likely to be filled with movie stars, but, even more impor- tant, it was up one of the few back roads the old man hadn't yet explored.

The pink "luxury lodge" appeared to be a cross between a Spanish castle and a wedding cake. All archways, turrets, and fancy trimming, it stood high on a rocky knoll amongst a towering stand of pines. Sonny had never heard of this place. His father knew only what he'd read in a magazine: it was popular with actors seen on his videos.

At the door, they were welcomed by a dark-haired woman in a long dress the colour of the building. She looked a bit confused, but stood smilingly by while Sonny signed in. The photographs of wedding parties on every wall may have had something to do with her bewilderment. "The wedding chapel is outside to our left," she said, when she saw Sonny frowning at the pictures. "The pool and sauna are just beyond it. I'm afraid your unit does not have its own hot tub."

The units with hot tubs, Sonny saw in a brochure opened out on the counter, were three times the price of their own unit. The price of their own unit may have reflected the fact that it was downstairs, a long narrow room with window and glass door on the end wall, looking out across a tiny low-walled patio to a view of the mountains. A dog run, his father dubbed it, and claimed the double bed for himself. "You can have the couch."

He made a show of grumbling about everything, as though someone else had made the decision to stay here. Gold taps in the bathroom were showing off. The paintings of pink flowers, pink birds, pink lace made him want to puke. In the dining room he said he couldn't believe the maitre d' was paid for putting on a penguin suit and smiling while he pulled out your chair. With the menu gripped in both hands, he wondered why anyone would pay $56 a plate for venison when they could go out and shoot it themselves. If he didn't want Sonny to think he was impressed with these things, it could only be that he was.

Except for themselves, every male in the dining room had put on a suit and tie. Sonny had changed into a fresh shirt and cotton pants with a crease up the leg, the dressiest clothes he'd brought from Ottawa. He hadn't known he'd be dining with Hollywood stars. His father had no clothes but those he was already wearing.

The owners had spent a fortune on the gardens below the windows. Flagstone walkways and lush amoeba-shaped lawns were wrapped round with crowded beds of flowering shrubs and the more dramatic perennials – Japanese anemone, golden *Ligulara stenocephala*, and pampas grass amongst them. A waste of money, since the dining room looked out above that expensive land-scaping and down the length of a narrow valley. Ribbons of mist shredded out across the pale-blue timbered hills. "If they got out and did a bit of exploring," his father said, "they'd see views as good as this any day for free."

Few would care about the view, Sonny imagined. He and his father were probably the only diners not on a honeymoon.

Peering at the wine list, the old man groaned. "What kind of people pay $40 for a bottle of wine?" He ordered a beer for himself. "Just one," he added quickly, before Sonny could invoke the doctor's orders.

When the beer arrived, along with Sonny's Scotch-and-water, the old man discovered he needed to get rid of his wad of snoose. "What am I supposed to do with it here?" He looked on either side of the table, as if expecting to find spittoons or coffee cans on the carpet. He swept a hand across the pale pink linen tablecloth – "No ashtray." He eyed the maitre d', who stood smiling at atten-tion near the entrance. "You think that fellow would mind if I called him over and spat it into his hand?"

"He wouldn't show it," Sonny said. "He'd just call the giant bouncer they've got chained in the basement and quietly have us removed. I guess you'll have to swallow."

His father made a face. "If I slip it under the cloth you think they'll find it?"

Sonny imagined the two of them using glasses and plates to iron out the lump. "You'll have to eat your dinner with it in your mouth."

But his father hauled a polka-dotted handkerchief from his pocket and carefully opened it out on the tablecloth. Then he lifted it to his mouth, cupped in his hand, and brought it away, grinning straight at Sonny while he folded it up again and put it back in his pocket. Then he quickly swiped his sleeve across the drop of moisture at the end of his nose.

Maybe they would be able to get along after all. For long enough, at least, to get the old man home. Though his father's flesh was the unhealthy colour of putty, small splashes of pink had risen in his cheeks. His eyes were bright. He was enjoying himself. Possibly he was even happy, having dragged his son to this place. "I don't know why them others bother with supper," he said. "They can't think of nothing but the one thing. Look at that pair. Probably race back to bed between courses."

The man and woman at the nearest table were holding hands while they ate, gazing into one another's eyes. The woman wore a corsage on her blue lace dress. She offered a spoonful of her soup for her balding bridegroom to take into his mouth.

His father squinted to study every face in the room, clearly hoping to find people he'd seen in his movies. None yet, to judge by his disappointment. But there was still the possibility that one of the diners facing away from them would turn out to be Kirk Douglas. Or Jean Simmons. The shaved head could be Yul Brynner, who'd played one of the Karamazov brothers in the movie. That is, if Yul Brynner were still alive.

There was a peculiar hush in the dining room. No clatter of dishes could be heard. People whispered, if they spoke at all. White walls, white pillars, white archways, pink and pale-blue watercolours. This might have been a funeral home if it weren't for the plaster cupids high in each corner, aiming their arrows down on the diners. People starting new lives. When the crop-haired young woman with the guitar began to sing "The Way We Were" she was careful not to intrude much on the quiet.

Discovering that his hips had slid ahead to the front edge of his chair, his legs sprawled out like someone in his own home, Sonny yanked himself up to sit like a gentleman. He became aware of his feet in their shoes, of his knees locked into right angles, his hips pressed to the shape of the chair.

Janis would have liked it here. It would have been an excuse
to dress up, to be elegant amongst elegant people. She'd have
responded to the romance she would claim was in the air.
Bathsheba, on the other hand, would not get through the meal
without a disaster. She wouldn't be able to restrain her laughter,
or see any reason to try. Her sarcastic comments about the dewy-
eyed couples, her mockery of the decor, her critiques of the timid
singer, and her laughter at Sonny's discomfort would have forced
that maitre d' to escort them out of the room, and perhaps from
the hotel itself. He smiled, hearing the uproar of Bathsheba's
boisterous laughter echoing off the pristine walls as she shook off
the maitre d' and marched like the Queen of the Mississippi Delta
out the door.

"I don't imagine you stayed in a place like this for your honeymoon," he said.

"With your mother?" His father made a scoffing noise with his
mouth. "We took off down to Nanaimo and tied the knot there.
Stayed in a cheap hotel for a couple of days before we dared go
home. She was visiting relatives, don't forget. They went up the
wall when they found out."

"You never told me this."

They ate the mushroom soup in silence. The couple at the
next table had abandoned their soup and sat holding both hands
while the singer moved up to sing, just for them, Dean Martin's
silly list of the symptoms of *amore*. They would have to be Sonny's
age to remember that one.

"We didn't eat nothin' like this," his father said. "We probably
had liver and onions. Stayed in a room with a view of the alley."
He finished his beer and signalled the passing waiter for another.
"You notice mirrors everywhere you look? They think this is
bloody Versailles."

Sonny had noticed mirrors of the kind you found in some
clothing stores, somehow constructed to make you look tall and
slim. Everyone here was meant to look beautiful. Mirrors at home
would deliver shocking news.

His father gazed at the view for a moment, his spoon dripping soup on the tablecloth. "I just remembered, I been up here before. Whistle-punked for a week just up behind us a ways. Probably sat on this knoll to eat my lunch. Behind us is where the haul-back cable snapped and killed Martin Green, dug that scar right up my arm going past. Nearly took off my head."

Sonny knew the scar. He knew about the nearly severed head.

When the soup bowls had been taken away, Sonny stared at the tablecloth in front of him, trying to imagine what it was that had his stomach in knots. Some of it must be the shame he felt at losing his temper with those yahoos at the caves. Some, too, his embarrassment at being hijacked into this place.

Since his mother had been mentioned between them while they were surrounded by these honeymooners, it was almost impossible not to wonder about his parents' marriage. "Maybe if you'd taken your bride to places like this she might not have been in such a hurry to leave."

Timo Aalto hissed while he searched for words. "You think I chased her off?"

"I think she saw what things would be like if she stayed. What I want to know is why you didn't let her take me. I was always scared to ask."

"She didn't want you." They'd kept their voices low until now, but this was loud enough to bring other conversations to a pause. His father glared around at those who frowned at him, then lowered his voice again. Menacingly, Sonny thought. "What do you think of that? She didn't even talk about it, she didn't ask, she just left. We never talked about what would happen to you. I did what I could."

"You kept the kid to raise as your bloody slave."

"Gentlemen." The maitre d' bent low at Sonny's elbow to whisper. "Our guests expect a harmonious atmosphere while they dine."

Plates of warm duck salad were placed before them. They looked in silence at the colourful heap of mixed greens. His father stabbed a forkful and raised it almost to his mouth, then lowered it. Sonny drove his own fork into the heap, pushed greens apart in search for slices of duck. Again he pulled in his legs, which had strayed out onto the floor, his feet cutting arcs from the need to move. His father raised his fork again and this time put the greens in his mouth. "She didn't even run off with nobody," he said through his chewing. "Old Man Karamazov's wife run off with some other man. Afterwards, when he heard she'd starved to death, he ran into the street hollering and dancing with joy."

Timo Aalto had always been pleased to find common ground with someone in a Russian novel. There was no point in reminding him of Karamazov's own eventual fate. It made more sense to shift the tone of the conversation. "Maybe she didn't run off with another man but she did run off, as you told me a thousand times, with your lunch bucket!"

It was the one thing the old man had been willing to talk about. Had harped on. His lunch bucket had disappeared about the same time as his wife. It had been dented and beaten up from his time in the bush. Sonny did not know why it was important. Nor did his father know why she'd taken it. "Spite," seemed to satisfy him. To Sonny it looked like a way for her to draw attention to what, or rather who, she *hadn't* taken. To his father it eventually became a convenient sign that he wasn't meant to waste his life holding down a job.

"Look," his father said. "You better brace yourself for something here." He stabbed a second forkful of salad and ate it while Sonny waited. He was already braced. Being braced and stiff was the only way he could keep his body from sliding into a natural sprawl. "I didn't say nothing before. I wanted to get away from that hospital first. About the Tests." He chewed and swallowed, his sharp Adam's apple shooting up and down.

The chill that had been growing all afternoon in Sonny's bones took on an identity now. "You sure you want to talk about this?"

"Keep eating. You don't want the cook to yell at us. The doc, he didn't want me to leave – whatever he said to you. There's a whole rigamarole of things they want to do. I threatened to raise hell if he told you himself, so he said he'd wait a day or so before he phones."

"Jesus," Sonny said.

"He'll want to twist your arm to take me back. The sonofabitch gives me half a year at the most."

Sonny's brain was hearing now what his body must have known already. He pushed back his chair. "What are you talking about? What's the problem?"

Not wanting to know – or rather, not wanting to hear. But here it was, it had arrived, the mountain falling on their heads.

"It don't matter what the problem is. At my age it's nobody's business what I die of."

The old man could be lying. "Okay, it's nobody's business, but if you want me to believe you you'd better give it a name."

"Eat! Eat! Let's put it this way. If I stood up right now and pointed to where the goddam problem is that fellow in the penguin suit would throw me out." He turned his face away, as though from something distasteful. "Old Man Trouble. Gone too far to stop."

There was another reason for a son to express indignation while he held his inner reactions at bay. "And you're just going to let it happen?"

"Keep eating or they'll be over here hounding us about what's wrong with their food. This is why I never said nothin' before. If you try to take me back I'll throw myself under a truck."

"Jesus," Sonny said again. "He didn't tell me any of this."

His father kept his gaze on something in the valley mist below them. "I'm eighty-five years old. Did you think I was gonna outlive you?"

Sonny picked up his fork and poked at the greens. "Why would a doctor put a date on it?"

Why sound incensed about a date? Did he believe that if he faulted the doctor's prognosis this would throw doubt on his

diagnosis as well? Of course there was no purpose to the question
except to shift a little off a topic about which there was nothing
really you could ask.

"The bastard didn't want to tell me how long I had." Apparently this was worth a chuckle. "He quoted statistics – you know
what they're like. But I nagged until I wore him down. I took him
through a guessing game until he finally threw up his hands and
said, *Okay then, six months.*" The old man was clearly pleased with
himself. "He was so fed up with me by this time, he made it sound
like a curse."

For a few moments there was silence while they both stirred
their forks in the salad. Other diners murmured predictions of
more palatable futures. Sonny Aalto had the feeling that if he permitted silence while he adjusted to this shock he'd be in danger of
discovering something about himself he didn't want to know.

"So what are we going to do about it?" There was still the possibility the old man could add: *But if I rest and take my medication
I could last another decade.* "You can't just do nothing."

Timo Aalto drew lines in the tablecloth with the tines of his
fork. "I have a few things figured out."

"Such as?"

"We don't have to talk about this now."

"We do have to talk about it now. We have to make some
decisions."

"The decisions are mine to make," his father said. "When we
get home we'll rest up for a day or so and then get back in your car
and keep going."

"To where?"

"To the end." When he saw that Sonny didn't understand, he
added, "Cape Scott."

Cape Scott was the northern tip of the island, three hundred
kilometres of highway north of home. *There's no hospital at Cape
Scott*, he almost said. Did his father mean that he wanted to
explore all the side roads to the north? Sonny didn't want to
think how many there would be.

"I mean to the cape itself. Where you can see the waves coming in from both sides at once."

The waiter brought their entree, a circle of overlapping slices of roast venison with a juniper-berry-and-mushroom sauce. Sonny looked at his plate but did not pick up his fork. Nor did he make any comment about the few tiny vegetables at the edge of the plate – slivers of red pepper, carrots the size of sinus-congestion capsules. He felt as though he were still down one of those unfamiliar roads discovering no way out.

"I was born not far from there, don't forget," his father said.

The old man's folks had lived for a while in the Utopian socialist colony of Sointula, but had moved when Timo was still an infant. Timo Juhani Aalto, too, had been a child.

"The road doesn't go the whole way," Sonny said, barely able to believe he was talking about this. "Just to the park. There's a long walk through the bush on a muddy trail! Even hikers in top-notch shape take most of a day to walk in."

The old man regarded the venison on his plate as though he weren't sure how it had got there. "That's the one place left I want to see." He raised one slice of meat to his mouth and looked out at the valley while he chewed it. "Hasn't got that wild taste," he said. "Raised in captivity. Might as well be beef."

Now the singer was serenading an elderly couple at a corner table. "The Anniversary Waltz." Sixtieth anniversary, Sonny guessed. The old fellow looked as though he wasn't too sure he wanted to be where he was. He kept attempting to stand but his wife put a hand on his arm and held him in place through the song.

"You can't take vehicles past the parking lot at the trailhead," Sonny said. "I'd have to carry you in."

His father stabbed a miniature carrot and chewed on that, not raising his eyes to Sonny. "A person could stick these up his nose."

"You think I should carry you on my back like this afternoon?"

The old man spoke to his plate. "You could tell yourself, 'At least I'm not having to give the old bastard injections, I'm not having to wipe his arse.'" He looked up and grinned.

"And you'd let me? Carry you up a muddy trail for six or eight hours or however long it takes? When you should be in hospital." Sonny picked up his fork and then put it down again. "And then the whole way back."

But the hostess stopped to ask if they were happy with their meal. Sonny nodded. Did anyone ever say No? His father said, "This three-spike could've done with some foraging for himself in the bush." The woman smiled insincerely and moved on quickly to another table.

"Just pretend you're an Eskimo putting your old man onto an ice floe," his father lowered his voice to say. Then he added, "You wouldn't need to carry me back." He laughed and sat back to look around the room.

"Sure," Sonny said. "Why don't you tell me the names of all the movie stars you've recognized so far. For all I know I could be rubbing shoulders with Meryl Streep."

His father ignored this. "Well, I'm sorry, but I meant it about the Eskimos." He corrected himself. "Inuit, I guess I'm supposed to say."

This time Sonny's brain veered off so abruptly from the implications that for a moment his body believed the floor had been removed. "Don't be ridiculous," he said.

"I spent my life on this island," his father said. "I'd like to get to the one part I never seen and then step off its end." The idea of stepping off the end seemed to amuse him.

Of course this should not have been a surprise. His father had told him long ago that he didn't want any goddam undertaker handling his carcass when his time came, he'd rather be the old dog that just wanders off into the bush and disappears.

"If you'd come home to stay a few years ago it might've been different, but it's too late now. You don't need to think I'll let you nurse me. I won't have Rose move in and do it neither, which I know she would. I figure me and you we mizewell make an adventure out of it." He chewed another piece of venison and swallowed. "Hell, I'd rather be like that fellow in the Old Testament.

'Translated,' they called it then. Never mind leaving a corpse. What I figure is, just letting the waves take me away is the next best thing."

Sonny rearranged his knife and fork on either side of his plate. Maybe the old man really was getting senile. *Senile dementia* they called it now, in case the one word wasn't enough to send chills down your back. He talked as though none of this were difficult for him, as though he were almost enjoying himself. "You think some killer whale will take you off to live in an undersea heaven? What kind of movies do you watch?"

His father did not look up from his plate.

"I should've guessed," Sonny said. "You mentioned that 'translation' business once before. What you didn't say is that the reason Enoch got to skip over the dying part was because he'd pleased God. Maybe you'd better tell me how this is true about you."

The singer, having performed for every table but theirs, regarded them from across the room. Feeling numb and helpless, Sonny watched her make the decision. She took a deep breath and forced herself to approach them. "Is there anything you gentlemen –?"

His father did not let her finish. "Ah shoot, honey," he said, giving her a wink. "We're just commiserating. We come here for our honeymoons but both our brides ran off and left us."

The singer laughed a small, surprised laugh and moved on, but her suddenly flushed face betrayed anger or hurt. Sonny would have to apologize. She would not be used to people like Timo Aalto in a place like this. Or himself, for that matter. Men whose lives had stalled. This was a place for beginnings.

"So what's the big rush to do this," Sonny said, "if you've got a few months before things get really bad?"

"Because I know you. Always in a hurry, always on the move." His father stood up and reached for his cane. "If you go back to Ottawa now that'll be the last I see of you." He put a hand on the table to establish his balance. "You can finish the meal if you want, I've had enough. I know what all these others are going to do when they've finished here but I don't know what you've got in mind for yourself. I'm heading back to the dog run. If I don't break my neck on the stairs I'll just crawl into bed and sleep."

"Wait a minute."

Without turning back, the old man waved his free hand as though to dismiss Sonny altogether, and headed towards the stairs. But he hadn't taken three steps across the dining room floor before he began a sideways stagger that his walking stick could not stop. It was necessary for Sonny to leap to his feet and take hold of the old man before he landed in the lap of the alarmed bride at a nearby table. Even so, they both thudded against the wall in a tangle of limbs. For a moment, as they collapsed towards the floor, Sonny's face was mashed against his father's sandpaper jaw.

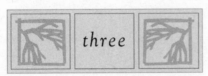

three

Anyone making infrequent visits home would naturally expect to be surprised every time by change. But here, the surprise was that this place never changed much at all, at least on the surface of things. The General Store and Post Office had undergone renovations over the years, but most of these were inside, where they couldn't be seen from the road. If Connors's machine shop appeared to have shrunk, this was because the surrounding firs had continued to grow. Sam Cochrane grew pumpkins in the field where Richardsons had grown them long ago. And Will Thomas lounged on the same front porch where Old Man Hueffner once entertained boys like Sonny and Will with tales of his misadventures while digging the Panama Canal.

Constitution Hill could still be seen from the road leading inland towards the river. Once a whiskered silhouette of fire-blackened snags, it was covered now with a lush green coat of second-growth timber – but was still a solid reference point between the settlement and the mountain range behind it. In the scrub near the first bend you could still see the rotted pile of timbers from the original community hall, mysteriously burnt after the Halloween dance where Caro Macken knocked out Arnie Prince's front teeth. No changes had been made to the house that Ivan Telsky created out of four old bunkhouses arranged around the well that everyone knew was really a secret tunnel, a radio transmitter down inside for reporting local events to Joseph Stalin. A little farther on, where you turned onto gravel, was the perfect little Finnish house, surrounded by a grove of birches, where Timo Aalto met the Koskelas' visiting cousin and supposedly fell in love.

You didn't even have to get as far as Timo Aalto's gate to see that the only change to the farm was its continued deterioration. Coils of Himalaya blackberry had overwhelmed the roadside fence. Once a sturdy gabled box of white weatherboard and coloured trim, the house was clearly in a state of collapse. The paint had peeled away to raw grey wood; one wall had buckled inward; shakes had fallen from the sagging roof.

Over the years the old man had restricted himself to fewer and fewer rooms until he'd confined himself to the kitchen – the sole remaining corner he considered safe. But eventually he'd moved out of the house altogether, and taken up residence beneath the orchard trees behind it, living in a trailer stained with rust and sharply dented in the midsection. It had been on its way to some-where down the road when it turned over outside the gate. The disgusted owner had sold it where it was. Colin Macken sent his son and one of his trucks to haul it into Timo Aalto's yard, then came over himself with lumber to slap up a porch. Still unpainted – good-quality fir exposed to weather.

Half the orchard trees were dead. Caterpillars had bound whole limbs in their gauze. One heavy snowfall could bring the swaybacked barn roof down. Alders had invaded the fields behind the barn. And moss and slimy lichen coated the slabwood walls of the chicken shed Sonny had built one summer. Nothing that remembered his touch was any longer part of the visible world. Yet his hands did not forget picking rocks in this field, or cutting and stooking and hauling the hay. Doing much of it alone, while his father BSed in town. A boy's life of work added up to little – a pale scar on his left wrist from a boulder that had resisted him for most of an afternoon.

"I thought my old man was crazy trying to make a farm outta

this," Timo Aalto had once explained. "All I ever did was keep it up, so long as you were here to help. After you left, I figured nature didn't want no tidy Scandihoovian farm along this road." Obviously, this was how he justified not spending any of Sonny's regular cheques on repairs.

Parked in the yard, with the Buick's engine turned off and the windows down, they could hear the chickens humming, unaware that a roof could fall on their heads any minute. Not far away, his father's '74 Dodge Dart, its licence long expired, was parked beside the little shed that housed the sauna – the "steam bath," friends had called it, when they'd sometimes asked to use it on Saturday nights.

Dora Mitchell burst out through the trailer door and onto the porch, her hands upraised like an apprehended thief. "Caught before we even had all the silverware into our shirts!" A tea towel hung from the strap of her plastic apron.

White Reeboks danced down the steps. Through Sonny's open window she said, "Lunch is on the table. I Saran-wrapped the sandwiches. Tea won't take a minute." Up on the porch again, she used the towel to swat at cobwebs around the door. "I couldn't hold Rob back. He's eaten." She slapped the towel against her leg. "Now I've gone and got this filthy."

Sonny braced himself for what lay ahead. Nothing had been resolved in his head, though his thoughts had churned like laundry through a sleepless night and the morning's silent drive. He was ashamed of half his thoughts and horrified by the rest.

Inside, the trailer did not smell of sour dishcloth and unscrubbed toilets as the house had done. There was a hint of pleasant chemicals in the air. The neighbours had obviously given the place a scrubbing in his father's absence. Over lunch, they made it clear they'd spent much of yesterday at it while they watched for father and son to return. They didn't blame Timo for the delay, Dora Mitchell said. A man who'd been in the hospital had no obligation to phone and tell his friends his plans. "Tommy waited for you well into night. Rose was inconsolable." Dora removed her glasses and wiped them on a sleeve. "She forgets you haven't gone near her in years. Wants to be at your side in your hour of need."

"I'm not on my deathbed yet." His father's face was a danger-ous shade. "I can look after myself."

"Can you mend a broken hip if you fall in the night?" Dora cried. She poured tea all around, into mismatched cups, then put the pot in the centre of the little table. "Don't make Dennis think he isn't needed here. He is!"

It was a shock every time he heard his given name used – his *English* given name. Dora was nearly the only one here who used it. Some of the local Finns still thought of him as Risto, his second name, though most people had long ago got into the habit of calling him Sonny.

Rob Mitchell sat back while they ate, running one hand along the countertop and down the face of a cupboard door beside him. Everything was thin metal – warped and dented, with rusted gouges chipped out of the paint. Maps were taped to the cupboard doors, each a different segment of the island, with most of the roads traced over with purple lines. A television set was mounted on the wall, a row of videos on a shelf beneath it. Down at the end of the narrow hallway, stacks of books spilled out through the door of the second bedroom.

A welcome-home party had been discussed, Dora said, using the community hall, with an open invitation published in the newspaper, a volunteer orchestra, and food donated by everyone who came. But when it came to doing it, they hadn't the energy.

He could see what was going on. They wanted to shame him, to show that his father was cared for by people as old and crippled as he was himself. A father was not a garden you could neglect without causing human damage. "We know Finns are famous for being hard-working and trustworthy," Dora had told him once, "but there's always the chance an exception to the first could spawn an exception to the second."

Rob leaned forward and slurped his tea. He had always drunk

like a horse, baring his top teeth while he noisily sucked, but unlike a horse he said "Ahhhhhh" and replaced his cup to his saucer. He explained what they had decided if Sonny hadn't shown up. Tommy would sleep here at night and go home after breakfast. He put a hand on his heaving chest, to help himself breathe. "Me and Dora . . . would come . . . in time to make lunch."

His father scrunched up his paper serviette and stuffed it into his almost-empty teacup. "Everyone out. I'm ready for a nap."

Dora leapt to her feet. "I'll just throw a chicken in the oven first."

"No you won't," his father said. "Sonny can put a chicken in the oven. I don't even feel like chicken. I feel like steak. You wouldn't believe the tasteless venison we paid a fortune for last night."

"Your Ford," Rob Mitchell said, "is still . . . in the lean-to." Even Sonny's old pickup would be used for their cause. He knew where it was – amongst shadows and spiders in the shed off the end of the barn. He could see the gap-shingled, sway-backed building from where he sat, its walls stained with the shapes of ancient manure piles long ago spread across the fields. A rusted wringer-washer stood aslant in the grass. An icebox lay flat on its back, its insides probably green with stagnant rainwater.

"Your dad has 'er all tuned up," Dora said.

His father looked away. "Colin's boy come over and worked on the brakes."

"You'll have to . . . get your . . . own insurance," Rob Mitchell said.

The local newspaper seemed to think he'd returned for good. A copy had been left on the countertop, folded back to display the two-inch column. FATHER AND SON REUNITED. Circles had been drawn around it in red ink. Sonny Aalto was still the "Flying Finn," though there was no mention this time of Paavo Nurmi.

The front page, when Sonny turned it over, was devoted to a showdown in the woods planned for today. Protesters had camped across the approach to Lost Man's Bridge up Saunders Canyon, intending to prevent loggers from going to work this morning.

Some were high in the trees, others had pitched their tents on the road. Cans of gasoline were set in a row down the length of the old plank bridge, in case nothing but fire could stop the loggers from going to work. Two men had chained themselves to the railings, prepared for martyrdom.

When the old man got up from his nap, Sonny was sitting with his feet on the porch railing, peeling carrots for their supper, the strips dropping into a chipped enamel basin on the floor. He could tell from the kathumping of his father's progress through the trailer that he was steadying himself at every step with a hand against the wall. "We've got to get you a walker. One day you'll fall and break your neck."

"This stick'll last as long as I need it," his father said, pushing the screen door open. "If I wanted one of them things I'd've rescued some old grocery cart from a ditch."

"A helmet, then," Sonny said. "To protect what's left of your brain."

The old man held a folded paper in the hand he used to steady himself against walls. When he got out onto the porch he let the paper drop onto the paint-chipped table, then shuffled himself into position to drop onto a chair, "Ungh!" as though someone had punched him. Once he'd got himself straightened around, he unfolded the paper once and then again so that it covered half the table. A map. "Come have a look," he said, tapping a finger.

Sonny groaned.

The park was a sizeable chunk of the island's northern tip. San Josef Bay. Sea Otter Cove. Hansen Bay became Hansen Lagoon and nearly severed the claw-shaped end from the rest. With his finger Sonny followed a hikers' trail from the end of the road, at the park's southern border, up past a lake, along a creek, and through a campsite. Then, at the remains of a failed Danish settlement, it turned left to cross an isthmus and pass through remains of dikes and fences and buildings, another even narrower isthmus, until it came to Cape Scott itself. On either side of the cape was the drawing of a ship going down. You could almost hear the wind.

"Just a minute," Sonny said. "How long is that trail?"

The map-makers had anticipated this. Twenty-three-point-six kilometres, from the parking lot to the cape. The hiking time in good weather was estimated to be eight hours. "But not if you're walking with a cane," Sonny said. "Or even with a walker and a helmet on your head." By reading just a little of the small print he saw that the notion of cane or walker was ludicrous. In the best of weather much of the trail was mud. "You'd better think of some other place to make your exit," he said. "You'd be dead from exhaustion long before you got there." He was surprised to hear himself using this tone. He'd heard wives tease in this way about things that frightened them, when husbands were being unreasonable. "I'd be left with nothing but a corpse to heave in the chuck."

His father removed the little round Copenhagen box from his shirt and opened it, and offered it to Sonny, who pushed it away with the back of his hand. Then he scooped out a wad to tuck behind his bottom lip and closed the lid and slipped it back in his pocket. "We'll think of something," he said. "Just about every other road on this island leads to somewhere I been – except for that trail to Cape Scott." He smoothed out a fold in the map and pointed with a swollen-jointed index finger to a spot alongside the trail. The nail was thick, stained yellow-brown from years of snoose and divided long ago by a kindling axe. "I figure we could camp out here on this last little point. Before I go in for my swim." He chuckled softly, as though he saw this as some sly joke he was planning.

"What do you think you are, an old-time Indian?" Sonny said. "Waiting for the Great Spirit to swoop down in the shape of an eagle and take you away?"

"I'd just as soon be taken by the waves."

Sonny picked up a potato and dug out a bruise with the tip of the peeler. "And eating *what* while we wait? Am I carrying a month's worth of groceries up that trail as well?"

"They say you can see a line in the water where the two seas meet from either side," his father said. "Sea lions play along it. Up there –" His finger indicated some indefinite place off the northern border of the map. "Up there somewhere, there's a big cliff above the sea I read about, with the imprint of a man in the stone at the top. The Indians say he fell from the sky."

"What we've got to do is take you to your regular doctor. Make sure someone's keeping a proper eye on you. You know you're asking your son to risk a manslaughter charge?"

"Bah! All you have to do is get me to them rocks. One good wave should do the rest."

He was enjoying this! "Listen," Sonny said, "This sort of thing isn't *discussable* until someone's in terrible pain. On life-support systems. Right now you can still sit up and fork venison into your mouth! And complain about it afterwards."

Because his father's face had pulled in tight and resentful, Sonny made an effort to change his tone. "You told me once about one of your Russians who went out with a bang – stood up on his roof and started tearing down his own house? If I had to go, I think I'd rather go like that. Noisy!"

His father laughed. "Ol' Martin Kharlov!"

Turgenev's Lear. He stood up on the roof of the house he'd built with his own hands and started tearing it down in a rage. Tossed planks and rafters and chimney bricks down on his horrified guilty daughters in the yard, and all his gawking peasants, until he came crashing down himself with a pair of rafters and crushed his skull.

His father's eyes shone with merriment. "My God, that was something! Old Kharlov throwing timbers in every direction!"

"Furious that he had to die."

"He didn't have to die." The contradiction came quick and fierce. "He chose this, to show what he thought of the people who'd let him down." All signs of pleasure had gone from his face. "You want me to make a spectacle of myself? Toss timbers down on your head?"

Sonny held up his guiltless hands. "Your roof would collapse the minute you set foot on it, it sags from the weight of *air*!"

His father looked away, his chin aimed at the distant firs. The sky was populated with moving clouds, all travelling separately but at similar speeds, as though a meeting had been called somewhere to the east. "Would you rather I slit my throat?"

"Can you really see me doing what you want?"

"Unless you'd rather clean your old man's brains off the ceiling." A nasty note of triumph had once again entered the voice.

"Maybe we ought to get you to some kind of counsellor." Sonny's teeth ached. Lines of pain ran from his eye teeth up through his sinuses. "If you're supposed to have six months you can wait another five before you start talking like that."

"Take me seriously, will you? I have to do it while I'm good enough to get there. Pretty soon some nasty things'll happen and I don't want to be around for them."

Maybe it was the "don't want to be around" that caused Sonny to remember that he didn't want to be around here himself. And that he had somewhere else he could go. "I didn't tell you I heard from my mother," he said. "She has another family in Australia. Owns a sheep ranch there."

"She was born in Australia," his father said, looking down again at his map. On the top of his head a dozen white hairs, weak as threads, stood up and twisted this way and that in the moving air.

"You never told me that. You never told me anything."

"She left a two-year-old kid with a drunk who couldn't keep a job. There's nothing more to know about a woman like that."

"I kept thinking she'd come back. She left some things behind. Her books."

"They were sent by relatives who didn't know she'd gone. How much did you learn from them?"

He'd memorized long passages from the *Kalevala*. He'd read *The Unknown Soldier* twice, sent by an uncle who was convinced that Lieutenant Lammio was based on a brother who'd died in the long "Continuation Wars" along the border with the Soviet Union.

"She's invited me down to a big boar-hunting party on her spread."

The head shot up this time. His father was used to getting postcards from foreign places but sneered at this one. "Australia! Snakes and spiders and God-knows-what-all waiting to kill you. It's a wonder any of them live to be adults." He looked off towards the barn. "That's one hell of a distance just to chase a pig. We could rustle up a few tame ones and save you the time and expense."

"I didn't say I was going."

"You seen *Queen Margot*? Fellow got invited to a boar hunt so they'd have a chance to kill him. In the end, a mother kills her son with poison. I'd think twice if I was you." Grinning now. "She'll be surprised to hear I raised you myself. She probably thought I'd dump you in some orphanage. What would you tell her?"

Sonny bent and gathered up the basin of peelings off the floor. "That at least you didn't dump me in an orphanage. Were there orphanages?"

"I guess I could've found you a family in town."

"So I should tell her – what? That you stopped drinking the minute she left, got a good job, married again, bought me real toys, paid for me to go to university."

The reference to university was unfair. He could have paid his own way if he'd wanted to. It was only lately that he wished he'd got a proper education, instead of having to get it all out of books and picking the brains of others and examining the results of his own guesswork. Amongst his educated colleagues he felt – had always felt – an impostor.

His father dismissed the sarcasm with a sneer. "You could tell her it's a wonder you weren't burned to death while I was in the Riverside some Saturday night. Tell her I showed you where to turn in the beer bottles you collected from the ditches for your spending money." He pushed back his chair and set off towards the door. But he should have waited until blood had got to his legs or sluggish messages reached his muscles. He staggered and slammed a shoulder against the thin metal wall. By the time Sonny had stood up, he'd righted himself and yanked the screen door open.

After their supper, the old man went directly to bed. Sonny went back out to the porch table and unfolded the map. There was a native midden near Experimental Bight. A sailing vessel sunk for a breakwater had broken up and washed ashore. At the turn of the century a group of Danish settlers had tried to estab-lish a farming colony – but had failed because the government reneged on its promise to provide the road they needed to get their products to market. He wondered if anyone had ever dragged a travois up that trail.

A safety warning mentioned abandoned wells, black bears, wolves, and cougars. They would have to sleep under the sky in places that bears and wolves and cougars considered home. Too often you heard about wounded or hungry cougars attacking humans. As one had attacked him long ago, out there behind the sauna.

At least that was his memory of it, or his memory of being told about it. Not yet three years old, Sonny had been playing with his toy trucks on the roads he'd gouged into the grass. His father was inside the sauna, screwing a coat hook into the wall of the change room. When he came out to Sonny's cries, the cougar was already dragging him off towards the woods. "Ordinarily she would've killed you outright," his father said. "I don't know what she had in mind." He'd assumed the cat would drop the boy once she saw an adult waving his arms and yelling. But she hadn't let go, even when Timo Aalto jabbed his screwdriver into her skull, her ribs, the back of her neck. Then he'd driven fingers up her nostrils and used both hands to pry her jaws free of the boy's skull, more or less inviting her, as he'd explained to Sonny later, to turn on him instead. Fortunately, she'd decided to run for the woods. Waiting to catch him again, Sonny had thought for years. He had the sharp punctures to remind him of how close he'd come to death.

As a boy he had imagined a thousand deaths for himself. Most had been inspired by the Saturday coloured funnies. He'd been tied to a piling while the tide came in, the water rising towards his mouth and nose. Roped together with other prisoners against a concrete wall while soldiers aimed their rifles at the white circle over his heart. Sewn into a gunny sack and dropped to the bottom of a river. Strapped into an electric chair; positioned over a trap door with a noose around his neck; walking the gangplank with gunshot in his pocket. He had imagined these dyings in delicious detail but had not imagined being dead. If being dead was something you could imagine being conscious of, then being dead wasn't being dead at all.

He'd often wished to see his father changed, even vanished, but he'd never wished him dead. Nor had he imagined the afterwards. To think that someone you knew this intimately might no longer exist was some kind of metaphysical contradiction in terms. He could not imagine his father not *being*. He could not even imagine his father not being here, in this place, even if it was only for Sonny to curse and resent and blame.

It seemed that he would be forced to imagine the impossible, whether he wanted to or not. And yet, so long as it was still *now*, the prospect of afterwards was only hypothetical. The fatal slash of that dividing line was still an illusory thing you might brace yourself for even as you refused to believe in it. Six months gave you that. What he had to face was how to handle the time between now and then.

"Another twenty years and this place'll look pretty much like it started."

Startled, Sonny tilted back in his chair. Big Tom Reimer stood in orchard grass a few feet off the end of the porch. "How long have you been there?"

"My mother's people thought the settlers were *mesachie peltoon*, trying to make something out of this timber land that it wasn't meant to be. They'd laugh to see what's happened to your place!" He took a few slow steps towards the porch and leaned on the rail, breathing hard, and looked down to follow his own hand smoothing out the shirt on his monstrous belly.

"My shoulder still hurts," Sonny said. "You think being old gives you the right to knock people around?"

"You're thirty years younger than your ol' man. Thirty years goes by pretty fast." His tarnished-penny eyes studied Sonny's face, not even glancing at the open map on the table.

Sonny held his gaze as long as he could, then broke to look for something that did not look back. The roof of the chicken shed. "You wanted something?"

The eyes were still on him when he looked again. "Something's up with you. I can smell it. Don't forget there's more than you have got a stake in this."

"Just don't poke me again with your stick, or I'll break it over your head."

Tom Reimer's laugh resided somewhere deep in his belly and did not reach his eyes. "These days they put you behind bars for hitting old folks, didn't you know? That was just a little tap I gave you there, in case you thought I'd got tame and toothless in my old age."

Sonny's elbows were on the opened map. He stared down between his forearms at the drawings of sunken ships until the swishing sound of Tom Reimer's steps through the grass had faded away. Had he really imagined dragging a travois up that trail? He went cold to the bone to think he might be bullied into this.

After his father had gone to bed, Sonny went out to the sagging lean-to beside the barn to admire his 1940 pickup, still convinced that nothing could compare for simple beauty. Someone had recently polished it up. Shovels, rakes, mattock, clippers, and hoe stood up in their places behind the cab. With this eighty-five-horsepower V8 engine and three-speed manual transmission, he'd first gone into business for himself – cutting lawns, planting vegetables, pruning trees, clearing brush, and designing flower beds for people in town. The licence plate was dated 1963.

"I gotta tell ya something. I used to turn green every time I seen you go by in that."

Sonny turned. Colin Macken stood in the doorway, broad and ruddy and grinning. His hair had gone white, though he was younger than Sonny by a year or so. He was wider, too, than he used to be – a huge stomach strained the buttons of his dress shirt. Broad-faced Colin's beard opened up to a big red grin as he held out his calloused hand. "Sorry I scared you." He tilted his head towards the pickup. "She's a beauty even now."

"I hear one of your boys did some work on her."

"Nearly killed him, he wanted that truck so bad. He'd sell his kids to buy her if he could." He studied a toe of his elaborate cowboy boot. "Your dad's inside, I take it."

He'd brought along a daughter who'd agreed to stay with the old man – she was reading a magazine up on the porch – if Sonny would come on over to say hello to Colin's in-laws. "No one refuses me on my birthday." He scratched at his beard as though he were truly uncertain how to go about saying this. "T'rese's folks've been nagging ever since they heard you might be coming home. Korhonens always thought the sun shone out your butt."

He'd driven over in a motorhome he'd left parked by the house, its rounded corners and shiny cream-coloured surface giving it the appearance of a peculiar kitchen appliance for giants. "Your bedroom," Colin said. "I'm leaving 'er there. I figure you two might kill each other cooped up together in that trailer. If you wash the sheets once a month you could last the winter in it."

"I don't think so," Sonny said.

Colin was not to be argued with. It was easier just to cross the sagging fence with him and go on into the woods, following a grassy ditch that in times of rain became one of the nameless tributaries to Portuguese Creek. Already Sonny suspected that Colin Macken would have more to do with his future than anyone ought to have. Eventually they came to Colin's fence – in perfect repair, of course, wires tight as cello strings – cutting through a stand of Lombardy poplars beside the little house he'd built when he was barely out of school. Plain and square, plastered over with stucco and broken glass. His father had given him these few acres off the back of his property, a wedding present for a seventeen-year-old kid. Now Colin owned the entire farm and rented out his parents' house to a family of dope fiends, as Timo put it, "growing pot to pay the rent."

The driveway went up the slope to a newer house built of cedar posts and glass, where, like his Finnish in-laws, Colin had planted a stand of birches. Inside, a crowd sat around a dining-room table, the adults drinking coffee while the children spooned ice cream into their mouths. Colin pointed out his children, their spouses, and his children's children. The two sons came forward to shake

Sonny's hand, both of them wearing beards exactly the shape of their father's, though not yet grown as thick.

Of course Sonny remembered Colin's wife Theresa, and was not surprised that she'd grown as wide as her mother. Short, shy, chubby Mrs. Korhonen stood up and held both arms out wide. "Risto!" she cried, and gathered Sonny down for a hug. She'd always insisted on his Finnish name. Embarrassed about her poor English, she'd tried hard to teach him Finnish.

Tuomo Korhonen was a little cloudy in the eyes but still had his own snoose-stained teeth, and showed his pleasure by sucking laughter through them. *"Khee-hee, khee-hee."* He half-stood, reaching for Sonny's hand, but fell back into his chair. He'd been a highball faller once, his chest and shoulders broad and powerful even now. "You look like you could still win a few axe-throwing contests," Sonny said. The old man couldn't speak for grinning. He would have been a father to Sonny once, if Sonny had let him.

The lush fields and the straight fences were what you'd expect of a Macken, but the inside of the house bore the mark of the Korhonens. Stark red cedar walls and fir plank floors. Of course you never saw Mrs. Korhonen's floors, since she kept them covered with newspaper pages except when special company arrived. No doubt she'd woven these colourful *ryijy* rugs. Glass Iittala candlesticks stood on the sideboard under the tinted photo of an old-country farmhouse – a picture that had once hung in the Korhonens' own front room.

Sonny refused a piece of birthday cake, but one of the sons placed a cup of steaming coffee before him – as dark and strong as the old woman's *kahvi* had been. He also set down a plate of cookies. This was proof they'd expected him. No doubt they remembered when he would invent excuses to drop by the Korhonens', in order to gobble these S-shaped sugar-and-cinnamon cookies while drinking the cups of coffee he wasn't yet old enough for at home. He was almost afraid to taste one now, knowing he would then go on to eat the entire plate.

Mrs. Korhonen watched, grinning, knowing very well how his salivary glands were reacting.

Without asking if Sonny cared, Colin – who had taken up his in-laws' habit of drinking through sugar cubes clenched in his teeth – brought him up-to-date on old acquaintances. The Winton boys had kept their old man's turkey farm going. Neil Maguire had retired early in California and come back to take over the family homestead. Sandy Stewart had quit teaching in the Peace River country and come home to live in his parents' house on the beach. Sonny thought of the couple on the plane, with their salmon instincts. Had these people spent their working lives waiting for this?

Colin's parents had recently died, Theresa said, and most of the uncles as well, but Aunt Nora – oldest of them all – was still alive. "She lived with us for a while but got too much to handle. Now we've got her down in Extended Care."

Family members glanced at one another but didn't speak. "I bought her farm," Colin said. "My grandparents' old home place. Part of the deal was we would look after her for life, but we didn't know what a handful she could be. And she didn't warn us she'd outlive us all." He winced at Theresa's thump to his arm. "I don't suppose you've kept in touch with Rusty. Still with the Forests ministry in Victoria."

"He's up to visit his folks," Theresa said. "You knew that Eddie and Frieda sold out and moved to town?"

In Macken eyes, Sonny had been the perfect son. "Better than a wife," they used to tease him. Timo Aalto didn't deserve him, is what they meant. While the Mackens had admired him, the Korhonens and the other Finns had worried about him. Because the old man's drinking and laziness reflected on them all, they'd tried to give Sonny their support without offending his father – invitations to family picnics, weekend jobs, the loan of books, casual invitations to the movies. *Suklaa* cakes and pies and loaves of sweet braided bread were left on the doorstep. He had not resented their kindness but if he'd fallen in with them altogether he would have had to see his father as they did themselves. That he refused to do this did not diminish their affection for him. They had probably foreseen how it would end.

"Mama still thinks you should have married Lilja," Theresa said, "so the two of them could keep you stuffed with *kalakukko*."

The old woman had watched Sonny's face while Theresa said this, then tilted her head in a small bow of acknowledgement, smiling shyly. One of his earliest memories was of her hauling cardboard cartons out of her attic in 1944 the day the Finns finally turned against the Germans. Now that Finland was no longer an enemy, she could send relatives the socks and sweaters she'd been knitting throughout the war.

"Your daddy?" she asked.

"Home," Colin answered for him. He leaned forward with his elbows on the table and cleared his throat. "He won't be able to stay at home much longer." He said this in a voice that suggested he was sorry to find it necessary. "It's been tough on the women. Even the government workers call me over to help get him up off the floor."

"Colin," Theresa warned.

"Well, it's the truth. Sometimes they're in tears. Harry's niece goes over twice a week in her spare time. Theresa goes. Our Linda goes." He lowered his voice to add, "You'll have your hands full, I'll tell ya. Sooner or later you'll have to get him into a home."

"He'll never go," Sonny said.

"Auntie Eila's in the Finnish Rest Home in Vancouver," Theresa said, "but your dad'll never leave the island. Take him to visit Nora. Tell him you'd come down to see him every day."

"He'd have Davy Chalmers for company," said one of the sons.

"Not that it's easy to get in," Theresa warned.

"I'll take you down myself tomorrow," Colin said.

"Careful," Theresa said, reaching for the coffee pot to offer refills. "Sonny'll think you want to get your hands on his father's land."

Colin laughed and thrust back in his chair. "I've got more land *now* than I can handle." Both sons laughed as well.

That Colin had survived while all around him loggers had been put out of work was something he attributed to going into business for himself. He was logging his own property now, he said. He'd bought Svetich's forty acres when Andy Svetich died, then added his in-laws' 160 beyond that, as well as Aunt Nora's. He'd been making a half-decent living for twenty years with selective logging. "Started with a team of horses. Now I've got that little Timberjack out there – tractor, cat, yarder all in one. It's like thinning the carrots in your garden – give 'em the room to grow. I've got more standing timber now than when I started. Chris here could log it all his life if he wants, and his little monsters too if they don't run off to be rock stars."

He saw this as a kind of joke. "The settlers broke their necks clearing the land only to find out it wasn't meant for farming. Had to take work in the logging camps. My ol' man let his hundred acres grow back and started a Christmas-tree farm. Now it's thicker than it was before they settled here, and I'm logging at my own darn pace." He drained his coffee cup and pushed back his chair. "Let's you and me head up to the Blueback for a beer. T'rese'll call up Rusty and tell him to join us." To his mother-in-law's protests he said, "Don't worry, Ma. He isn't going nowhere. We won't let him."

They rode in Colin's blue Dodge truck with the extended cab. The glass from the passenger door had been replaced by a sheet of rippling plastic. Being on the move did nothing to change Sonny's sense of having been immobilized. Colin drove with his arm on the sill and his hand on the roof, but Sonny could not roll down the duct-taped plastic to stick his head outside or even hold out a hand to shred the air with his fingers.

"You won't catch me retiring," Colin said. Maybe he thought this was what Sonny had done. "It's a dangerous time of life, ours." He was quite important, his stomach pushing against the wheel. "I see guys all the time start acting old at fifty. No more mountains

to climb. Me, I've only gotten started." He had the look of someone who could hardly wait to get into the woods again with his
Timberjack. He might have been still in his thirties.

Sonny had made a practice of hiring people in their thirties,
still burning with dreams – ambitious and energetic. People at
Sonny's age – especially men – had either achieved what they'd
hoped for or had been so disappointed they'd given up their
dreams in order to criticize others'. He sometimes felt in his thirties himself. The trouble was, he experienced the hunger but
could not identify the dream.

"You see Hollywood moving all their equipment onto your old
man's place? They're making a movie – I guess he told you that."

"Never mentioned it."

"This outfit come snooping around for locations. Some story
set in the American Civil War. They want to turn his place into
a Kentucky farm. Some hillbilly's property left in ruins by the
Yanks."

"Maybe he hopes to meet Clint Eastwood," Sonny said. He felt
oddly bereft by this news, as if something had been stolen. "Of
course, he'd rather the civil war was Russian."

For a while the road followed the river. Oregon grape grew
along the ditch, amongst the salal, sword ferns, willows, and
salmonberry. Yellow yarrow was in bloom. *Achilla.* The river was
slow and shallow and dark. It had always marked the edge of civilization, or settlement, at least. Everything beyond was Crown
land, timber-licence territory, logging roads, a land of bear and
elk and cougar, of alpine meadows and snowy peaks all the way
to the Pacific.

The road shifted away to pass between his father's farm and
Tom Reimer's, then tunnelled through overhanging alders along
the bottom of Sonny's overgrown nursery garden. Blackberry
bushes were higher than this truck. "Them walls in there should
bring back memories," Colin said.

Through gaps in the brambles there were glimpses of concrete
gable ends standing high in the trees. The shell of the old sawmill.

By the time of Sonny's childhood there'd been nothing left but the walls, like some bombed-out old-country prison, the gables thrusting into the upper branches of the willows crowding in around it. As a boy, he'd imagined this a great medieval dungeon, the site of famous adventures worthy of Sir Walter Scott. He dreamed himself an imprisoned knight who used his time behind bars to plan his crusades for justice, waiting for the day he'd be freed to do something good for the world, worthy of Plutarch's praise.

In childhood, Macken cousins had often joined him there. They'd built campfires inside and imagined they were soldiers during a lull in the fighting. Once he and Rusty had set up a dinosaur museum. At first they'd had nothing to put in it but books and pictures. They'd gathered up some deer legs out in the woods, the ribs from Will Pearson's horse that he hadn't buried too deep, and a few roast bones from their own garbage, then wired together a skeleton of what they called a *Tyrannosaurus rex*. They'd charged admission, but the deception was quickly seen through and classmates demanded their money back.

"T'rese's sister says she used to meet you there," Colin said.

Lilja Korhonen had allowed him to bring her to the mill after a movie. He'd brought Ursula Winton there, too. He'd brought Elaine Buckle there nearly every evening in the months before they'd married. A blanket was all they'd needed, and a case of beer, and some newspaper for a fire. They'd often found they were sharing the place with figures whispering in corners. They would not get near the sawmill now without machetes or a D8 Cat.

"You got no objections, I might send the boys to clear out a trail," Colin said. "Them movie people told your father they may want to use it."

"They want to pretend it's Kentucky?"

"It's the movies, they can pretend any darn thing they want," Colin said. "I don't suppose it'll put money in the pockets of the out-of-work loggers but their wives might earn a few bucks making sandwiches. If some folks are gonna survive, it looks like we got to sell the scenery to do it."

The Blueback Restaurant and Pub was a structure of raw posts and vaulted ceilings, sitting out near the high-tide line. Fake pilings smelling of creosote had been planted along the borders of the gravel parking lot. Eelgrass and blooming calendulas grew inside a disintegrating rowboat that sat at a tilt amongst a tangle of vetch and bleached driftwood. In the fading light, seagulls wheeled and cried above the dredged marina filled with yachts flying the U.S. flag. Beyond the breakwater, the pale surface of a full tide was so swollen that waves were only wrinkles smoothed from a satin sheet.

Colin's relatives had owned this stretch of coastline once. Now there were RV campsites and cabins on either side, and motels and private homes beneath the giant firs. The pub had been built near the spot where a little family hotel had stood in horse-and-buggy days, burned to the ground and rebuilt and then sold not long ago to pay off Toby Macken's debts.

In a roped-off portion of the parking lot, people were setting up telescopes. When a slight, bearded man offered them a look, Colin waved the idea away. "Naw."

Sonny seldom looked at sky. He'd kept a watch on what was offered by the earth – streams, roads, houses, gardens to be redesigned – and had no idea what went on above, or what it meant. Sky was just sky. Stars were stars. It could be just a painted dome.

A group of children listened to a young man's enthusiastic speech. A youthful astrophysicist, or a teacher. "Okay now, look over there and you'll see the shadow of the earth. A dark curve across the sky. See it? In the next hour or so it'll climb to become our night – or all we get of night this time of year, mostly twilight through till dawn."

Rusty Macken stepped out of a long, sleek two-door Jag. Dark green. Dusty. Not a recent model. He hadn't put on weight as Colin had. A blue cotton shirt hung loose; tan cotton pants were too wide for the bony legs. His red hair had faded to the colour of weak tea. "Theresa let Colin out of the house without her?" He adjusted his little round spectacles and led the way up the steps. Inside, he pulled back a chair at the nearest table. "She denies him nothing, she thinks she's got the world's number-one provider."

"And so she has," Colin said, twisting in his chair in search of a waiter. "So she has." In his enthusiasm he showed all his teeth. Probably most people couldn't help but feel good in the presence of such satisfaction, Sonny thought, but you might not want to be around it for too long. In contrast, freckled Rusty was pale and gaunt, less satisfied, perhaps, but apparently more amused.

Raw cedar had been used in the posts and exposed ceiling beams. Along a railing separating the pub from the restaurant a few steps lower, upended wooden "Explosives" boxes displayed pieces of old logging equipment – a pulley, a coiled bit of cable, an axe with a broken handle. When a young woman had taken their orders – two Heinekens, a Molson for Sonny – Colin asked for a bowl of nachos as well. He raised a hand in greeting to someone at a distant table, his eyes already travelling through the crowd for other faces. Someone bending over the pool table. Boaters came in and went down the steps to the dining room. "Anything free on the patio, hon? I want to smell that *sea!*"

"Annual invasion," Colin said, nodding towards the couple dressed in tennis shoes and yellow flowered shorts. "You notice they don't complain like they used to – how things are not like home?"

"That's because things are more like home than they used to be," Sonny said.

Colin sucked at a tooth. "That's right. We sat on our hands while Ottawa gave it away. They call it the Global Village but they mean the 'Merican Corral." He added the words *Free Trade* like a curse. "You could've raised some hell about it, living back there."

"Colin was never patient with democracy," Rusty said.

Sonny hadn't seen Rusty for nearly twenty years. He'd seen Colin occasionally but never for more than a quick exchange of pleasantries. They were trying to find out how much of a stranger he'd become.

"I still can't see you living in Ottawa," Colin said. "I keep expecting to hear of some prank you've pulled, pissing everyone off."

"A greased pig let loose in Parliament," Rusty said. "Or a model
of a horse's ass delivered to the PM. The Sonny we remember
would have everyone holding their breaths."

A woman passing with a stack of dirty plates veered over to
pause by Colin, who introduced her. "Holly Fitzgerald. Harry
Sylvester's niece."

Sonny stood to take her hand. No introduction was needed. He
and Holly Fitzgerald had spent some time together on earlier
visits. She tilted her head a little to one side and smiled, her
manner suggesting that she was delighted to present herself for
his admiration, *Aren't I something?* suggested with such pleasure
that he was inclined to agree.

She was nearly as tall as he was. Her ginger hair was cut close
to her head, making her ears stick out a little and her rust-
coloured eyes seem almost too large. Half a dozen freckles were
sprinkled across her nose. She was not wearing the tight black
jeans and white blouses worn by the other women who worked
here. Instead, she wore a long grey skirt and a red velvet top that
hung loose from breasts you were meant to notice. She was
pleased to present *all* of herself, it seemed, for your admiration. A
hostess, temporarily pressed into busboy service.

Before she could move on with her dishes, a small boy ran in
from outside and tugged at her skirt. "Hey there!" Colin wrapped
a headlock around the boy's neck and ruffled his hair. "This here
is Rohan. Say hello to Sonny – just home from the wars!"

The trapped boy peered through lowered lashes at Sonny
Aalto. They had met before, when the boy was an infant, before
that pale worm of scar had been scribbled across his forehead.

"He nagged to come because of the telescopes," his mother
said. Then she narrowed her eyes for the boy's benefit. "But promised not to bother me at work – right?" She turned sharply away
and headed for the kitchen. Majestically, he thought. A queen
who carried dirty plates with the same delighted *hauteur* as she

employed in carrying those strong shoulders, that long straight back, those splendid breasts.

Colin hauled candies up from his pocket and dropped them into the boy's hand, then sent him running outside through the front door. Just as the door slammed shut behind him, a heavyset white-haired woman in a floral-print dress came up the steps from the dining room, laughing at something the man behind her had said. Then her foot slipped and she went down on one knee, "Shit," and flung out a high arc of musical laughter.

"Good grief, George," Colin said. "Can't you take that woman anywhere without her making a spectacle of herself?" Once she was on her feet again his arm went out around her cinched-in waist.

"I only had one glass of wine, so help me." She placed a hand against her bosom and released another peal of laughter.

"That's what they all say," Colin said. "You recognize anyone at this table you hoped you'd never see again? Come all the way across the country for my birthday?"

The woman pulled in her chin and considered Rusty, then frowned and dismissed him with a swipe of her hand. She studied Sonny Aalto. She fumbled in her purse and brought out a pair of glasses. "I hate these goddam things." She peered again at Sonny through the lenses. "Oh, for Christ's sake!" She sang a few more notes of laughter as she removed the glasses; then she came around the table. He stood up to receive a kiss on the cheek.

"Ursula Winton herself," Colin said, possibly to jog Sonny's memory. "Mrs. Kerrigan and her poor old husband George – henpecked and still homesick for 'Prins-Aird Island,' as he calls it."

For a confused moment Sonny thought he was looking at Ursula Winton's mother. But this wasn't her mother, this was his steady date through much of Grade 10. A white-haired heavy woman in a flowery dress.

Sending her husband off to chat with friends across the room, she pulled up a chair between Rusty and Colin and sat with both hands on the purse she'd plopped on her lap. She shook her head at Colin's offer of a drink. "Good lord, no. If I can't keep my

footing after one glass you can imagine what I'd be like after two."
A sigh was filled with nostalgia and regret. "I used to be able to
drink." She looked at Sonny and pulled a long sorrowful mouth,
suggesting perhaps that no one knew better than he how she'd
loved her booze.

"You used to be able to drink the rest of us under the table,"
Rusty said.

She laughed again and put a hand on Rusty's arm. "Because I
knew that once I had a guy under the table I could do anything I
wanted with him." She looked hard at Sonny, then tore her eyes
away to show indifference. "That was how I met George." The
face she made suggested this was something she hadn't yet come
to terms with.

It was clear she'd installed herself amongst them. She wanted
to know why the three of them were here, then answered herself.
"Oh. I know. Your birthday – right?" She pecked at Colin's cheek.
"Didn't bring your wives?" she said. "Or are our womenfolk all
gathered somewhere for a Tupperware party?" She made as
though to stick her finger down her throat.

"Sonny had a woman with him last time," Colin said. He
turned to Sonny. "Janis somebody. You were talking marriage
then."

"Didn't last," Sonny said.

Ursula Winton's gaze had rested on the table's nearly empty
beer glasses. "Maybe I'll have that glass of wine after all. No I
won't." She slammed a hand down on Colin's wrist to prevent
him from doing anything drastic. "Don't let me."

Sonny supposed it was polite to ask a classmate what she had
done with her life. "You're not still typing up contracts for Central
Motors?"

This was a woman who pulled faces. She rolled her eyes to
heaven for this. "Worked a few years after you took off. Raised
kids." The eyes aimed straight at Sonny. "Now I've got eight grandchildren! What do you think of that? My daughters married men as
horny as George." Her jaw dropped to release a cascade of laughter.

Rusty pushed his chair back and stretched out his legs so that his body was a long thin curve. His loose clothes might have been draped over a construction of stiff ropes. "Eight grandchildren and a horny husband from the Maritimes," he said. "That wasn't in the yearbook. What did the yearbook say would become of Sonny Aalto?"

"Ha!" said the former Ursula Winton. "Said we'd find him still driving his old man's wartime Jeep in sixty years, still chasing girls, and not a grandchild in sight." Her fingers snapped open the purse on her lap, then snapped it closed again. "Just released from jail for the fifteenth time for brawling at a dance."

"I avoid dances," Sonny said. "What did they say about Colin? Did they see Timberjacks in his future? Half the district eating at his table?"

Again Colin showed those teeth. "I wasn't in no yearbook. I dropped out to work in the woods – you forget? Teachers told me I was wasting their time." His laugh suggested the teachers hadn't known the half of it. When he leaned forward with his elbows on the table, his broad back and shoulders told the world this was a man of substance. His right hand travelled back and forth between the bowl of nachos and his mouth. He gobbled up the world with relish.

Rusty had probably never gobbled a thing. With his hands behind his neck and his ankles crossed, he looked as though he'd never needed food.

"Rusty's one of the brains behind the new Forest Practices Code they're workin' on," Ursula said, swinging her purse to whack against Rusty's shoulder. "Going to put a stop to some of the clear-cutting, bring peace to the war in the woods."

"Don't hold your breath," Rusty said.

"I told him one sure way to do it," Colin said. "Give half the timbered land to the logging companies and tell them they can log all they want for the next twenty years so long as they end up with more standing board feet than they started with. Give the other half to those eco folks and tell them they can preserve as much of it as they want, so long as they've produced x number of board feet in twenty years."

Sonny laughed. "You'd turn it into a contest?"

"They'd both win, don't worry. Neither would take the chance of missing out on the second twenty years."

"It has to be somebody's fault, is the trouble," Rusty said. "Who can we pin this on? We've been infected like everyone else these days with a passion for assigning blame." He leaned forward long enough to take one cheesy nacho from the bowl. "One day both sides'll stop blaming the other and put all the blame on the government. That's the way we do things in this country. Loggers and eco-freaks will get together and march on Ottawa, demand apologies and financial reparation. After some years of squawking they'll get it."

Ursula laughed her musical cackle. "If this was the United States of Lower North America we'd have bullets and bombs and flame-throwers roasting children. If we believe their TV. Everything ending up in a courtroom trial to fill up the nightly news."

They were quiet for a moment. Sonny watched Holly Fitzgerald pass by with steaming dinner plates. She moved with the elastic grace of a dancer, making him conscious of the body within that long grey skirt, the velvet top. When she saw him watching she veered off course just long enough to pass one of the plates beneath his nose. "Salmon," she said. "No charge for the smell. How often do you dream of eating sockeye back East?" Then she was gone, weaving past the other tables, avoiding suddenly thrown-out hands and pushed-back chairs, the plates held high. She knew, of course, that he watched.

"Well," said Ursula Winton, who'd been watching Holly herself. "I better drag George home, he'll be jabbering over there all night." She put both hands on the table and pushed herself upright. For a moment she stood looking at Sonny. "You need a haircut, Aalto. Christ!" She started away, then turned back. "You've got a haunted look about your eyes, like you just woke up and can't believe you aren't nineteen any more, with all the world waiting to see what you'd do." She started away again, dropping her hand in that dismissive gesture again, "Ah hell, what do I know?" Her voice trailed away. There was an uneasy, tentative edge to her manner, as though she were self-conscious about leave-taking. Maybe she was accustomed to thinking of better exit lines. To make the break she hollered "George!" and set off through the crowd.

"One glass," Colin said. "That wine must've been in one of them bottomless glasses I heard about." He drank from his own glass of beer. "I think you shook her up a little there, Sonny-boy. There was a day she thought them grandchildren would be yours."

"Writing forest codes isn't what Rusty set out to do, either," Sonny said. Rusty had wanted to make movies. Since they'd dragged him here and turned this into a reunion, he might as well ask the sort of questions you asked at such events. "You satisfied?"

Rusty shrugged and placed a single nacho on his tongue. The top of his thinning hair was reflected in the window. "I'll be up for early retirement soon. If Ruth still likes her job I'll get out and dabble a little in my son's business."

"Rusty's boy went to film school in New York," Colin said. "Works for this company in Vancouver."

"Says they might hire me for some lowly job if I'm humble enough to let him teach me the ropes."

Sonny didn't doubt that Rusty would be a good father, as Rusty's own father had been. Once they had joked that if they'd traded fathers all four of them would die of shock.

"My oldest boy has worked beside me since he quit school," Colin said. "If I croaked tomorrow he'd run things like nothing changed." He reached for more nachos. "You got kids." He tapped his wrist against Sonny's forearm before raising the handful to his mouth. "What they got in store for you?"

A chilly shaft of alarm shot up through Sonny. "The question is, What's my old man got in store for me."

Holly Fitzgerald moved about the room lighting candles in the centre of the tables. When she leaned forward he saw the curve of a hip, the faint arc of elastic across it.

No doubt Colin had moved his parents into his house when they needed help, as he'd done with his aunt Nora. Sonny leaned forward to address Rusty. "You managed to put a little distance between yourself and the family. Would your folks expect you to drop everything and come home to look after them?"

"Ha!" Colin said. "Rusty shows up for every wedding or funeral or dog-christening comes along." This was boastfully said, holding Rusty up as a model Sonny might emulate. In case Sonny thought he was the world's only inconvenienced son.

Rusty said, "Well," to cast a little doubt. "I'm far enough away to feel helpless and guilty, but close enough to call on every time there's a need. My car has done the trip so often it can find the way by itself. Sometimes I haven't been home a day before I get a call asking when I'll be back."

"Sheepishly, of course," Colin said. "You can't imagine Uncle Eddie coming right out and asking for help. Or Frieda."

There was a time Rusty might have said, "If I had your dad for a father I'd stay as far away as I could until it didn't matter." But it was a long time since he could guess what Rusty Macken might say.

Rusty may not have got what he'd wanted at seventeen but at least he knew what he hadn't got. Sonny had only wanted, without knowing what. He hadn't known about any landscaping schools in this country, there probably weren't any then. Landscape designers were immigrants imitating gardens of another place. He'd taught himself what he could, while doing a gardener's work – reading the few books he could find on the subject, studying photos. In the end he'd become a pretty good imitator, but in the end had discovered more talent for business than for art or botany.

Two men in work clothes stood up from a corner table and started towards the door. One of them saluted Colin. "Old lady's

gonna spit tacks," he said. He grinned as though he were reporting a joke on someone. "Shift ended at four." He wore a week-old
beard on a leathery face. Eric Pearson. Dropped out in Grade 9.
He looked hard at Sonny. "The Flying Bloody Finn."

"We were talking about what happened to people," Colin said.
"Eric's a foreman at the pulp mill. His brother was head of some
corporation down in Seattle but he quit and moved home."

The second man had moved up to stand beside Pearson.
"Look who we got here," he said. "Mr. Independent Logger and
Mr. Government Lackey, cousins in cahoots." A friendly sort of
mockery.

"You remember Sonny," Colin said. Not so friendly, Sonny
thought. Maybe those who stayed behind got to know each other
too well.

"Garden King," the man said. He looked like a Horton. He'd
said "Garden King" as he might have said "Bozo the Clown." The
sleeves of his green plaid shirt were rolled to his elbows, revealing
thick-veined hairy forearms. "Yer not with yer famous daughter,"
he said.

"You Mackens still tryin' to figure out which side you're on?"
Pearson said.

Rusty leaned back and concentrated on the ceiling, as though
waiting for this to be over. Colin dropped a handful of nachos into
his mouth. Then he said, "Rusty here is on the inside – where he
can do something more useful than pointing fingers. Me, I'm on
the offside, waiting for someone to notice I might just have the
solution you rest are looking for."

"And Sonny sends his daughter out to stir up trouble," said
Giddy Horton.

"You remember Ward, don't you?" said Eric Pearson. Ward
Marsden, he probably meant. "Had his own show – gyppo outfit
over in Stamper Inlet. Them protesters kept him at home for a
month last year. You heard what happened to his wife."

Rusty had the good sense to ignore them in favour of the
ceiling. Colin was patient enough to wait them out with a small

amused smile in his beard, as though they were mildly entertaining but of little consequence. But Sonny imagined driving a fist into someone's gut, his whole body tight with a need to kick these cretins out the door.

"Ward's wife spent three days in hospital. She stood up to the cocksuckers that closed him down and got a boot in the head for her trouble."

"Your girl shoulda got a picture a that," the Horton fellow said. "Hilda Marsden getting her head kicked in."

"We should ship her and all them goddam tree huggers off to Quebec," Pearson said. "Let the lot of them separate and leave the rest of us alone."

"Why're you shouting at *us*?" Sonny pushed back his chair and stood up. "Nobody at this table kicked Hilda Marsden's head."

"Well, fuck me," the green shirt said, stepping back. Both men laughed. "Whoopdeedoo!" And turned away to leave, their boots heavy on the wooden floor.

Once Sonny was again in his chair, Rusty spoke to the ceiling, imitating someone else's voice. "If I only had my lunch kit back." Both he and Colin laughed.

"What?" Sonny said.

"A local joke," Rusty said. "People got so used to hearing your ol' man harp about his missing lunch kit, they got so they say it whenever they want to complain – about anything. *If I only had my lunch bucket back everything would be fine.*"

"Well, it's a little more than that," Colin said, getting serious. "Somebody noticed he'd been bitching about his bucket since around the time the big international company bought up Valley Logging. At the time it seemed like the beginning of prosperity around here. Well, it *was*. But what nobody guessed was that it was also the beginning of this mess we're in now. Big profits for men in San Francisco, ruined fish streams, violent protests, closures. If they'd kept on logging in the old way we'd be poorer, sure, but there'd still be timber out there and fewer grandmothers lying across the roads."

"You haven't seen the big poster inside the store?" Rusty said. "Your father's lunch bucket –"

"A cartoon," Colin said. "Imitates your daughter's poster with the stump. *Save Our Community*, it says. *Bring Timbershanks's Lunch Kit Home!*"

Both men laughed. Sonny supposed he was smiling.

When Colin had gone in search of the men's room, Rusty waited until he was out of earshot and said, "Those two jerks forget that Colin helps more people around here than just about anyone else."

"How's that?"

"Hires some that were laid off. Helps some get started logging their own land like him, some with horses. He sponsors a softball team for kids that are, you know, handicapped. Buys their equipment, their shirts. Sometimes even shows up at their games."

They fell silent for a moment. Maybe Rusty, too, was wondering why it had never occurred to him to sponsor a team of handicapped children. When their eyes met, they held for a moment. Wondering – at least Sonny was – how two best pals could become strangers without deciding to. They'd built a treehouse once together, and when it was no longer of interest to them they'd studied Eddie Macken's stump-blasting handbook and blown the thing to bits. They'd made that dinosaur museum together in the abandoned sawmill. They'd travelled up and down the island on the same track-and-field team, they'd hiked in Strathcona Park, they'd double-dated, they'd worked on one another's car. Best friends for life, they'd both believed. Sonny, at least, had believed. Neither had made an effort after the first few years apart. You wondered if there'd been all that much between them in the first place.

The door flew open and Theresa came in, with a laughing crowd behind her – faces from the dining-room table. Children had been left behind, apparently, along with Theresa's parents. "Why should we miss his birthday while he's drinking with the boys?" She was already dragging a neighbouring table over to ram it up against theirs. One of the sons went after another. "Besides, we wanted to welcome Sonny home!"

Later, he and Rusty waited on the steps for the others to join them. Moonlight had drowned everything in a pale yellow flood. Crowds were taking turns at the gleaming telescopes behind the ropes. Holly Fitzgerald's boy danced up and down, waiting for a chance to peer at the stars. "Be patient," his mother said. "The sky's not going anywhere." To Sonny she said, "I wish his teacher had never told him the universe is expanding." This set off a rumble of laughter in her chest. "She might as well have said it was falling apart. He won't admit it, but I'm sure he thinks it's up to him to hold it together."

"Big Dipper's about the only thing I recognize up there," Sonny admitted. He went down the steps to join her. Rusty followed.

"Ursa Major," the boy corrected him. He pointed out Polaris to Sonny Aalto and then to Rusty, and showed them how to go about finding Ursa Minor. But when a young man stood back from the nearest telescope, the boy ran off for his turn.

"He thinks he's got the stars and star clusters figured out," said Holly Fitzgerald. "What's got him stumped is all that black space they haven't been able to penetrate."

"Penetrate?" Sonny said. Moonlight seemed to have found the gold flecks in her eyes. She stood with arms crossed beneath her breasts, perhaps chilled by the outdoor air.

"It drives him nuts that they don't know what it is. Light just won't go into it. Could be a big wall painted black." She laughed. "Or the side of an old black dog." It was her laugh that had attracted him first, five years ago, six. It was more than her laugh that had caused him to stay on, that time, for a summer.

"I'm off," Rusty said. He shook Sonny's hand. He'd always known when to leave Sonny to his own pursuits. "Will we see you again, do you think?"

Sonny hesitated. "You up for long?"

"Not sure."

Sonny laughed and said he wasn't sure himself. Then Rusty set off for his two-door Jag and drove away, waving one long arm out the window.

"Your boy's so eager, he must be good at school," Sonny said to Holly Fitzgerald, who'd gone inside and come out again with a white shawl draped over her shoulders.

"He hasn't even learned to read!" she cried. Dismay was mixed with amusement. "The only one in his class. His teacher tries but he says he can already read – the sky."

They watched in silence as the boy alternated between looking through the telescope and questioning the man who owned it.

A man in a captain's cap straightened up from his telescope. "Want to see Venus?" he said. Maybe astronomy buffs had much in common with pornographers. Sonny did not particularly care to see Venus. He was aware of Colin and Theresa coming down the steps. But the boy seemed to think this was impor- tant. He looked into the eyepiece himself, and then stood back to find Venus without help. "There it is." He pointed, for Sonny's sake. He came closer, so that Sonny could see the angle of his pointing arm.

Sonny could see nothing above the dark folds of the forested hills to the southwest. Pale blue silk stretched tight. Stars and planets shone elsewhere in the sky, but he could see nothing in the direction the boy was pointing.

Colin's noisy crowd had come out onto the parking lot. Doors slammed. One and then another truck pulled away. Sonny waved a single goodbye to them all. Colin and Theresa walked across the gravel to the blue Dodge but didn't get inside.

Holly Fitzgerald bent to the telescope, and then stood back to discover she too could see with her naked eye what she hadn't before. "Your turn," she said, and took Sonny by the arm, guiding him over to the telescope. She was prepared, it was clear, to find him amusing.

He put his eye to the small black ring, and saw something small and white and blurry-edged at the centre of a pale blue disc. That was supposed to be Venus. Then he stood back, looked at the same spot, and saw nothing.

"See it?" Holly said.

"No."

"Awwwww?" the boy protested. He looked again through the telescope himself, and then stood back. "Above that tree," he said, "just a bit to the left."

Sonny saw nothing above the tree and a bit to the left. Was this whole thing set up to make him feel stupid?

"Hold your hand sideways above the tree," the owner of the telescope said. "It's just to the left of your thumb."

Sonny did as he was told. He squinted, tried to detect some flicker of light. Still, there was nothing. He shook his head. Holly, the boy, the owners of the telescopes, all pointed out something that did not materialize. He considered lying. He could see it would make them happy.

"You wear glasses?" the man with the captain's cap asked.

"No."

"Maybe you should," said Holly Fitzgerald. There was a muttering of laughter all around. The boy didn't laugh. He narrowed his eyes suspiciously at Sonny.

"I'm sorry," Sonny said, backing away. He raised his hand in a manner he hoped the boy and his mother would see as a friendly farewell, then turned and started towards Colin's truck, trying not to seem as though he were fleeing.

At the sound of tires on the gravel he went outside thinking Colin had come to take them to Extended Care before he'd got around to warning his father. But the car turning in at the gate was a green Honda hatchback. When it had pulled to a stop on the grass, Holly Fitzgerald stepped out dressed in military camouflage pants. Was there a Uzi in the car? Over a T-shirt she wore a work-shirt hanging open, its sleeves rolled back to her elbows.

Rain had stirred up the rich scents of earth and grass and washed gravel. It had paused for now, but a heavy dark cloud threatened more.

"I got up early," she said, hauling a cardboard carton out of the hatchback and passing it into Sonny's arms with the same apparent self-delight as she'd had in presenting herself last night. He looked in upon the golden crust of a pie leaking red juice, a Zip-Loc bag of cookies pressed with fork tines, a lidded bowl. "What you don't eat you can put in your father's freezer."

She went over to the old man, who had come out to sit on the step, and kissed his cheek. "We missed you. Scared you'd take to city life and decide to stay." She laughed at his growled response and lightly passed a finger along his jaw. "All those nurses and you couldn't charm one of them into giving a decent shave?"

"Saved it for you," Sonny's father said, sticking out his chin. He tried to hide his pleased half-grin with gruffness. "I told 'em I was saving myself for someone who can cook as good as shave."

"Look." Her boy had got out of the car holding a magazine open to a full-page map of the sky, a blue disc populated with small white dots. His finger jabbed at what Sonny was to look at, a dot slightly larger than the others. The word *Venus* was printed beside it, as unfortunately it had not been printed on the actual sky last night.

"Venus," Sonny read aloud, thinking this was expected.

It wasn't. "I don't need you to read it. Here's the ecliptic." He pointed to a yellow line that curved across the sky. "There's just two planets on it this month and this one here is Jupiter." He jabbed at a yellow dot to the left. "So this one's Venus. I could've told you anyways because it's next to Libra. But lookit this." He turned to the magazine's centre, where a *Tyrannosaurus rex* walked across a barren landscape. "What's he doing in an astronomy magazine?"

"Don't tell him," Holly said. "If he takes it back to school next month his teacher can show him how to read it for himself."

"Forget it." The boy slapped the magazine closed and turned back to the car. Sonny had liked him better when he was an infant, too young to show contempt for adults.

Holly turned a rueful smile on Sonny. "We're not getting along too well today. He nagged me into reading the list of sky parties coming up, and now he's mad I won't take him to Arizona." She briefly threw up her hands to show what she thought of this. "I'd better get to work."

He assumed she meant at the restaurant, a lunch shift. Dressed like a hostage-taking terrorist? "You been at the Blueback long?"

She paused behind the opened door of her car. "I mean at my uncle's. I've started – Timo didn't tell you? Since I saw you last I've started a business back along the river. Selling native plants." She laughed, as though this information were a surprise even to her.

Selling native plants. "People pay you money for what they could dig up themselves?"

She was not intimidated. She looked him square in the eye. "Bigleaf maples. Sword ferns. Chocolate lilies. Ocean spray. That sort of thing. Devil's club." Her ears were big – it wasn't just the haircut.

"No one's going to pay you for devil's club."

"One man already did. It makes a great fence if you're plagued with trespassers – those big, poisonous spines." Smiling, she conceded that this man had had to buy a lot of them to do the job. She looked across the old orchard, then at his father on the step, and then at him again. "I even have a few western wahoos over there."

She waited, grinning, forcing him to ask. When he did, she said, "Grows along this river but nowhere else. Nowhere else that I know of. *Euonymus occidentalis.* I'm surprised you don't know it." She ducked in behind the wheel of her car. "I'll be there till late afternoon if you want to meet one."

While they were backing out onto the road, her son's eyes made it clear that the man who had failed to see Venus last night had let him down again.

There was barely room for his limbs inside the pickup Ford. But the simple dashboard shone, recently polished. The interior did not smell damp or musty – someone had kept it aired. He jiggled the long-stemmed stick shift to test the forgotten feel of it. He put his foot on the narrow clutch, turned the key, and pushed the starter button. The engine groaned, and turned over, and caught. "Yes!" The idle was rough by modern standards but he let it run for a minute or so until the engine settled into a steadier hum. Then he released the hand brake under the dash, eased up the clutch, and felt the wheels begin to turn beneath him.

In the driveway he left the motor running while he got out to admire it from every side.

"Don't get it into your head that we can take this up to Cape Scott," his father said. He'd come up for a closer look, jabbing his walking stick into the dirt for something to lean on. "We don't know if it can take the distance. I'd rather ride in the Buick, myself, since I won't get to ride in a fancy hearse."

Sonny used his handkerchief to rub at a smudge, and flick away specks of dust. "I'm just taking it out to the store for some groceries."

"Without a licence? Without insurance? You better hope some cop don't stop for gas while you're there."

Fortunately there was little traffic on this road. Neighbours would have to shoot one another before police would bother venturing down this way. And if that ever happened, they'd be in too much of a hurry to notice his licence plate dated from when you turned them in for a new one every year.

A red and black truck was parked where they'd caught glimpses of the sawmill last night, a narrow canyon already sliced through the Himalayas. Somewhere out of sight a chainsaw growled, as chainsaws did when they'd got their teeth into something – as though some measure of fury was important to their work. Colin's boys, he imagined, clearing a trail. He hadn't given permission, but Colin must have guessed that he didn't care.

There was a public phone booth outside the store. Before going to sleep last night he'd taken the Yellow Pages out to Colin's motorhome, copying down numbers of intermediate-care facilities in the district. Of course, his cellphone didn't work here. He hadn't thought to make arrangements. He hadn't thought he would need to.

Within half an hour he had received more or less the same response from six different institutions. "Of course there is quite a hefty waiting list. The person currently at the top of our list has been waiting for three months." Or two months, or in one case a year. Worse, they had only to ask a few questions about his father

– "Can he dress himself? Can he get to the bathroom on his own?"
– before they were surprised at how much he didn't know. "Your
father's case should be evaluated by the people in Provincial
Health Services. Do you have their number?"

The General Store and Post Office had changed hands fairly
often. In recent years someone had installed a coffee counter and
a few booths in the front corner where an ice cream freezer had
been. A later owner had pushed a portion of the back wall into
the living quarters and devoted the space to video rentals. A
lottery ticket dispenser sat beside a Coke machine. Over the door
– he remembered to look for it – the homemade poster was
thumb-tacked to the wall. BRING TIMBERSHANKS'S LUNCH KIT
HOME. The thick paper was discoloured, its corners curled. The
cartoon lunch bucket was as sway-backed and battered as Timo
Aalto's old barn.

The young man behind the counter did not look up from his
newspaper until it was necessary to clear space for Sonny's groceries. Long-lashes blinked behind a pair of tinted glasses. "Good
to have you home," he said, as he ran the items across his scanner.
"I expect we'll be seeing quite a bit of you in the months ahead."

His father kicked up a fuss when Sonny warned him about the
plan for the day, but eventually agreed to a very brief visit with
Davy Chalmers. But Colin, when he arrived, took Sonny aside to
express second thoughts. "Look, I laid awake all night wondering
if I shoulda kept my mouth shut. Maybe this little excursion's not
such a good idea." For a moment Sonny thought he'd somehow
learned of his father's obsession with Cape Scott. How many
"little excursions" were in the works? "I've got so used to visiting
Nora, I didn't think how the place might look to your dad."

"I can't leave things as they are," Sonny said.

Colin held his opened hand a few inches above the hood of the
pickup, still wet from a short cloudburst, and watched the bent

reflection of his fingers. "Nora's happy as a clam there now, but she kicked up one heck of a stink at first. I'd kick up a stink myself if someone was tryin' to stick me in there." He looked up at the dark sky and chuckled. "Everybody with someone in there knows you couldn't ask for better care for your folks when they've got so you can't look after them yourself – but nearly all of them will tell you that when it comes their turn they'd rather you took them out and shot them."

"We're just looking," Sonny said. "Shooting may come later."

As the blue Dodge led them south towards town, Colin drew their attention to the number of old pioneer farms whose gate posts had recently acquired hand-lettered signs. *Hay for Sale. Woodworking. Handcrafted Furniture. Dog Training. 4 × 4 Backhoe for Rent. Bunnies for Sale. Firewood. Income Tax Help.* Right where the Returned Soldiers had slaved to clear and cultivate the land, their inheritors had apparently decided to try something new. "So many out of work, they'll dream up anything might bring in a buck."

"Some of our generation are coming back," Colin later said. "But they're coming back to what they see as a pretty place to take their leisure in. You go down any of these new roads into the bush and you'll find old soldiers' farms chopped up into five-acre mini-estates. Little 'farmettes,' I call them, with shiny new houses that would look just fine in town. Painted fences, paved drive-ways, manicured grass, grape arbours, horses. They've put our grandparents' old farm machines on display in their front yards, like statues. I guess that's what they like to call folk art." He spat out the window and rolled up the glass as though erecting a barrier between himself and these unsavoury facts of life.

Between them, his silent father looked braced for something indescribably terrible, like those French aristocrats in movies who were being hauled in carts to the guillotine.

They entered the long single-storeyed wing of the hospital by a rear exit door, which opened when Colin waved a hand in front of a black sensor machine as it would open to any thief or murderer who knew how to lift his hand. Inside, he led them down a hallway past a row of open doors, the names and photographs of the patients posted on the wall beside them. "They'll have finished lunch by now," he said. He gave the impression of leading a parade – his large stomach out ahead, his wide, white smile revealing teeth as eager to devour this experience as any other. *If I wanted to be any kind of a decent son,* Sonny thought, *if I wanted to be any kind of admirable human being at all, I suppose I'd stick close to Colin Macken and learn how to navigate successfully through a useful life.*

The fact that everyone was in a wheelchair, moving more or less in all directions throughout the large dining hall, gave the impression of a collection of life-size windup toys. Some didn't move, but stared into the space between their feet. Some faces glared at other faces as though trying to recall where they'd seen them before. No one seemed aware that an entire wall of windows looked out on a view of the bay and the snow-peaked Beaufort Range. Music fell from the ceiling, a dance tune from the forties. Like a parent shopping for a kindergarten, Sonny hoped to find just one old codger here who might befriend his father.

"Dave Chalmers? Oh dear." The woman behind the counter looked uncomfortable. "His daughter's down in his room gathering up his things."

"He's gone?" Sonny said.

The woman nodded, widening her eyes as though to suggest *in a manner of speaking.* "Early this morning. I'm sorry. He'd been failing. We'd had him over in Intensive for a few days."

"Somebody must've told him I was coming," Timo Aalto said. His eyes had gone a little wild. "We mizewell get ourselves outta here."

"We'll just say hello to Nora first," Colin said.

Nora Macken's wheelchair was pulled up to a long table, where several women sat on either side of her. Burgundy plastic mugs were lifted and sipped at and put down. Her hair was dyed as dark as it had always been but hacked off short and pulled severely back, giving her long bony face an exposed and slightly startled

look. Like the other women, she wore a flowery dress-front that
didn't entirely hide the flannel nightgown behind it.

She remembered Timo Aalto, or pretended to. She gave Sonny
a shallow nod – royalty with more important things to do. "Some
of us enjoy an extra cup after lunch," she said. "When these
lunatics let us enjoy it in peace." Scornful eyes flashed about the
room to make it clear that "lunatics" included almost everyone.

"Open up, Margery, it's lunchtime!" A woman beside the
piano was apparently talking to herself. "Open up, Margery, it's
lunchtime!"

"Oh, for Pete's sake," Nora said. "That one don't even know
we've eaten." She stretched her neck and raised her voice. "Be
quiet, Marge, there's company!" Then she lowered her voice
again for guests and admirers. "She better watch it or they'll
throw her in the old folks' home!" To Colin she added, "You
won't get any tea, you know. They pick and choose who they wait
on around here." Resentful eyes shot accusations in the general
direction of the nurses' station. "They wouldn't know a Macken
from a piece of driftwood."

Family was everything to Nora. Sonny remembered this about
her. Everyone else had only bit parts to play in the family story.
Even relatives were judged according to how well they measured
up to the family norm – some amalgam of her workaholic father
and her madcap brother Toby, whose death in a car crash while
he was drunk was everyone's fault but his own.

On the side of the room away from the view, windows looked
inward to a paved central service area where a milk truck sat
parked by a delivery door to the main hospital. Sonny's peripheral
vision alerted him to a white hearse pulling in beside the truck.
A stocky man in a jacket and tie got out with a handful of papers
and walked past the milk truck to disappear inside. No one else
seemed to notice.

One of the women having tea at Nora's table was suddenly agi-
tated about something. "I wonder where my family got to?" she
said, putting a hand on Sonny's arm. "I need to get home, I've got

to put supper in the oven." A tiny freckled lady with huge glasses.

"T'rese said to tell you she'd bring flowers Friday," Colin said.

Theresa's promise warranted only a nod. Though Theresa had taken Nora into her home, she was a Macken only by marriage, and no doubt deficient in some additional way that Sonny didn't want to imagine. Nora had sacrificed her life to raise her brothers after her mother died in the big fire of '22. Having done what was right so early in life, she'd expected nothing less of everyone since. She was quick to condemn those who failed – though blood relatives, if not exactly forgiven, were provided with excuses.

"I wonder where my family got to." The tiny lady touched Sonny's arm again. "I've got to put supper in the oven."

While Colin took Nora through his whole family, relating the latest accomplishment of every child and grandchild in a voice that suggested to Sonny he'd gone through it all many times, the diminutive woman who believed she needed to put her supper in the oven gazed first at one and then the other, whoever was speaking, back and forth, an expression of little-girl awe on her face. When Nora noticed this, she set her plastic cup down with a thud. "Go away," she snapped. "Why are you sitting there? What are you looking at?"

The lady's expression didn't change. She looked at Colin, as though she believed Nora was still speaking to him.

"Go on, shoo! You're always poking your nose in where it isn't wanted." To Colin and the others Nora said, "Never had a pot to pee in, that one. I used to give her all my nice things when I was through with them, never got so much as a thank-you. Dirt poor, without a speck of manners, no better than the rest of that Cumberland tribe she comes from."

"I don't think you knew this lady before," Colin said.

"Dirt floors!" Nora spat this at the woman, who had still not moved away. "Wouldn't say 'Thank you' if their lives depended on it."

But the woman did not understand. She looked at Nora and blinked. To save them all from any more of this, Sonny pushed her chair towards the windows. The card on the back of her chair said *Rosalyn*.

"Open up, Margery, it's lunchtime!" It was the woman at the piano again. "Open up, Margery, it's lunchtime!"

"Shut up!" someone screamed from the far end of the room.

The woman in the pink sundress who came in from down a hallway did not appear shocked to be walking in on this. She looked familiar to Sonny. Big-boned, a dyed blonde, with slightly crooked front teeth. Edna Chalmers. In one hand she carried a battered square-cornered suitcase. Her other arm was clamped against a rolled-up quilt. She smiled weakly at Colin, who gave her a brief hug. She greeted Sonny with a nod.

"He was a physical wreck when we signed him in," she said. "We had no choice, we couldn't do it all ourselves. But he was still as sharp as a tack."

"I seen him reading off in the corner there," Colin said. "Sometimes playing cards."

"Not for long," Edna Chalmers said. "He couldn't take the humiliation." She looked this way and that, as though collecting her words from the walls. "Strangers giving him his shower. Wearing other people's clothes half the time. His watch stolen. He started going downhill within the month." She glanced around the room again, and laughed. "I must be crazy, I've just signed up to volunteer!" Her mouth remained open for a moment, as though the words had escaped on their own and might be withdrawn. But she shuddered, and apparently decided to believe what she'd heard herself say. "I want to feel what these *heroes* must feel at the end of a day's hard work."

Little Rosalyn had taken hold of Sonny's hand and pressed it to her cheek. Despite the toothless gums, her adoring smile could not be seen as anything but beautiful. "If you'll just take me home now, dear, you can stay for a bite of supper."

"Christamighty," Timo Aalto said. He'd taken his Copenhagen out of his pocket and opened it, and hooked a wad of snoose in the curve of his finger. But he hadn't yet tucked it behind his lip.

Across the service yard the man in the jacket and tie was wheeling a gurney out towards the hearse. There was not a coffin on it. The shape, bigger at one end than the other, was wrapped in a burgundy blanket. In full view of all these patients. Someone who'd failed to show up for lunch at this table, perhaps. Davy Chalmers.

The others seemed not to notice. Timo Aalto started away, then stumbled and grabbed hold of a wheelchair for balance. But the wheelchair and the woman in it moved under his weight, and he tilted, staggered, and, as Sonny rushed across the room towards him, finally went down on the floor. The Copenhagen container rolled across the tiles, spilling its dark brown powder as it went.

Now you've done it, Sonny thought.

His father must have been thinking the same. "Quick," he said, as soon as he'd rolled onto his back. "Get me up!"

But down or up, there was no escaping the damage. He'd scraped the left side of his face against the wheelchair. The flesh was coming to life already with tiny beads of blood.

"Excuse me, let me –" Sonny was gently pushed aside by a young man in a blue smock. His father would not get away until he'd been given first aid. Sonny would be given a lecture, no doubt, as the one who allowed this man to go about the world unaided.

His father was silent the whole way home, paying attention to nothing outside his own head. Sonny could imagine what he was thinking. What he was thinking himself wasn't fit to be spoken aloud. In fact, there weren't any words, only a tumbling mixture of disappointment and anger and frustration turning behind his eyes, a monologue of curses and protests and fears. He could imagine banging his head against the windshield, driving a fist right through this stupid plastic sheet rippling and snapping at his shoulder where there ought to be glass.

Behind the wheel, Colin was also silent. His first words were "Doggone it, anyway!" when they turned into the yard. Dora and

Rob Mitchell were waiting on the trailer's porch. Rose Ferguson stood frozen in the middle of the driveway, her hands to her face while she waited for Colin to run her down.

"Where is he?" Rose said. "What have you done with him?" Her sparse hair stood up like a crown of muddied feathers. Her lips were thickly painted a brilliant red. An irradiant green swept out like parrots' wings from above her eyes. When she saw the old man climb down out of the truck, she screamed, and spread her arms. "Dear God, he's alive!"

"I'm sorry," Colin said. "I blame myself for this."

"Get them outta here!" his father shouted. He was yelling even as he crossed the yard to the steps, his wooden leg sending bits of grass sod flying. Rose Ferguson's open arms embraced nothing but air. "Someone get these people off my property." Sonny thought he meant Dora and company but the old man flung out an arm in the direction of the truck. Dora Mitchell was to rescue him from *them*.

"What's happened?" Dora shouted. "My god, where have you been?"

"He's had a stroke!" Rose cried.

When Dora learned where they'd been she looked as though she might explode. "Are you crazy? You might as well have taken him down to the cemetery and showed him a fresh-dug grave! I can't believe you'd do a thing like that."

Colin Macken knew better than to hang around. He was already backing out of the yard.

"He did everything but sign me in," the old man said.

"We won't let him," Rose cried. She'd got herself as far as the bottom step but stalled, unable to talk her foot into attempting the second.

"You mizewell kill me now!" The old man turned this way and that as if looking for a gun. "Take one of them sticks of wood and knock my brains in, get it over with."

Sonny might have walked away if the Mitchells hadn't been here, and Rose. He might have taken his father inside and then gone for a run. He should not have snatched his father's walking stick out of his hand, but discovered that this was what he had done. Discovered, too, that while his old man staggered back to catch himself against the wall of the trailer he slashed with the stick this way and that as if he would destroy the world around him. Slammed it against the cheap metal wall. Slapped it down on the railing. Stirred up the newspapers and maps left on the table and tossed them over the railing and onto the wet grass. Jabbed at the potted plant to his father's left, jabbed at the wall to his right. Shouting, "The same old thing! The same old thing! Nothing changes! This time I thought I might help but of course you make it impossible, you make impossible demands and then sit back so you can watch me fail!"

Of course Rob Mitchell said, "Here now!" while Dora was trying to grab the walking stick from his hand, screeching, "Stop it, stop it, you'll hurt him, he *will* have a stroke!" still screeching even after he'd dropped into a chair and put his face in his hands.

Rob's voice said, "You okay, Timo?"

"You'd better go," Sonny said.

"We will not," Dora said.

When he looked up he saw that she'd set her feet apart, as though to resist great forces gathered against her. "We can't leave you two alone. I'm afraid you'll do something stupid."

"We've both done plenty of stupid things already," Sonny said. "We'll probably go on doing them, but not for your entertainment."

"I'll make us a cup of tea," she said. "Then we'll all calm down."

"No," Sonny said, standing up. "I'll go."

"Then don't come back till you've cooled down!" Dora said. "You forget, we know what damage you left behind the first time."

He drove with the pickup's window open, the wind whistling at his ear, his hand and arm down the outside of the door in order to feel his movement through the cool resisting air. "The damage he'd left behind," Dora had called it. A disappointed father, he supposed she'd meant. A man cheated of the respect, companionship, and servitude he considered his due. She didn't know how much worse it could have been.

He could not recall, now, what had triggered that break – only flashes of a remembered argument. Chopping firewood in the yard. His father hungover, somehow giving the impression that the boy ought to be not only chopping wood but inside making supper as well. Implying that this business he'd started, this making fancy gardens for people in town, this nonsense of the display nursery, was not only keeping him from doing what was needed here, but was also some sort of betrayal. A few months past his twenty-first birthday, the perfect son and partner had awakened as if from a prolonged state of hypnosis. Had discovered, in the act of raising a double-bitted axe above the old man's head, that what he'd believed and felt almost since birth had vanished, revealing the resentment and blame he had kept secret even from himself.

If the neighbours were so hell-bent on keeping a watch on the old man, they could have him. Let him find out how he liked having Dora Mitchell or Rose Ferguson moving in to cook his meals. Let him try to talk Rob Mitchell into a hike to Cape Scott. Sonny would return for his bags and move to a hotel in town until he'd arranged to fly home, or found something temporary here. Clearly he wasn't meant to stay on the farm.

A yellow half-ton Chev came barrelling down the road towards him. Flashing headlights made him aware that he'd been driving down the centre. He swerved to the right just in time – the Chev didn't slow. A voice wailed past – "Asshole!" – in a flash of yellow. The pickup shuddered from the slap of wind. The other driver, who'd dropped his right wheels into the ditch, sprayed gravel as he fishtailed up to regain the road.

He slowed, aware of the world he was passing through. Familiar crowds of sword ferns, mossy boulders, rotting man-high stumps with whole gardens of baby cedars and huckleberry bushes growing from their tops. The wall of Himalaya blackberries along the face of his old nursery was sharply interrupted by the gash of Colin's new trail. No trucks were parked here now. No chainsaws growled or whined in the bush. He pulled over to the side and stopped.

The new trail was narrow enough for fir boughs to meet overhead. It felt, when he started to walk it, more tunnel than trail. The dry stalks of chopped-back blackberries smelled of dust despite the morning's rain. Hacked-off alder bled from naked wounds, its pale flesh already darkening to orange. Leaves on tossed-aside branches had not yet lost their shine, nor started to curl. The strongest smell was the sap from young white pine. Once, he'd liked to puncture their blisters of pitch with his thumbnail, just to have that scent on his hands the rest of the day.

On the raised threshold of the doorway to the old sawmill, the red and white of a beer carton was a sharp contrast to all this shadowed greenery and the pebbled grey of old cement. He put a hand to the wall and heaved himself up to the floor. Old concrete had, amidst all this growth, a foreign smell. Patches of moss had spread partway down the nearest wall. He placed a hand against it – soft, damp, and cold.

Moss was not all that had spread across the walls. Tall letters had been spray-painted high above his head. *Silence Violence. Youth Revolt.* Up near the windows: *Judy Doesn't Do It Any More.* Nearby, THIS BUILDING IS POSSESSED was printed in big black dripping letters. Then a row of Oriental symbols that meant nothing to him. Clearly someone had been getting in without the convenience of a trail. Black heaps of recent campfire ashes were here and there amongst the broken bottles. Colin's boys had ruined someone's meeting place.

A teenage sex club, maybe. A heap of limp, feathery greens had been left in a corner, enough marijuana to fill the bed of his truck. No doubt someone had got wind of a raid and pulled up their hidden plantation. Hadn't thought of rain.

It had not been a prolonged battle, the day he left. It had been the emotional equivalent of repeated jabs in the ribs. "Not finished yet?" "You think firewood can cut itself?" "I suppose you think you're too good for this sort of chore?" Self-pity masquerading as bewilderment. The world as Timo Aalto had constructed it was falling apart.

Of course he had been afraid. The look on the old man's face in Extended Care had been pretty much the face he'd worn thirty-five years ago. Desertion panic.

A car door slammed. Someone hallooed from down the trail. Colin's voice. Colin's footsteps crashed through the brittle violated bush. "They told me they finished," he said from the doorway. "I figured I'd come down and check it out."

"People have been getting in without your trail. A tunnel, maybe, like rabbits."

Colin heaved himself up onto the raised floor and stood, with feet apart and fists to hips, to look around. He shivered. "Behaving like rabbits when they get here too, I bet." He put a hand against a wall as though to test the quality of 1912 cement. "This'll give Hollywood a chance to get in and see if they want to use it while they're in the neighbourhood. Maybe they'll film a manhunt through a Southern jungle – dogs baying at runaway slaves. What can we see?"

What they could see from the tall narrow window space, in the faint light that penetrated the canopy of firs and alder, included things Sonny hadn't seen for years. He stood up on the pedestal of some vanished machinery for a better look. Statues fallen and half-buried in English ivy. Sickly Norfolk Island pines. A monkey puzzle tree. One poor stunted hibiscus with pale flowers. If they were to walk farther into the woods – pushing through the waist-deep sea of underbrush, risking poked-in eyes and twisted ankles – they would probably come upon ponds gone to muck and choked with bulrushes, bridges collapsed under fallen trees, and shattered greenhouses wrapped in runaway vines. Himalayas would snag your clothes and rip gashes up your arms.

"My old man thought you were crazy," Colin said. "But he changed his mind when he saw what you made of it. A shame you didn't leave anyone to keep it up."

"Someone could have if they'd wanted to," Sonny said.

"It doesn't end, you know," Colin said, his gaze still some-where in the dim stripes of forest. "Three years and I still can't get it through my head he's gone. My dad, I mean. Someone who's been moving ahead of you all your life just disappears, the footsteps you've been following just *stop!*" He gently hammered a fist against the rough concrete. "I think about him ten times every day. The thing of it is, I remember him telling me the same. He must've been nearly eighty before he admitted it: he never got used to losing his folks." He stood back on his heels and sucked air, a reverse sort of sigh. "When his mind started to go towards the end he'd ask to see them. Every day I had to remind him they were gone. After a while I just told him they were resting."

"Your old man wasn't Swampy Aalto."

"No he wasn't, but he was one of those men who could always do everything better than you." Colin spoke as though to the heap of marijuana. "It was almost the end before he admitted he needed me to do some of the things he couldn't do himself."

Did he need to run into Colin Macken's expansive generosity of spirit every time he turned around? "I'll have to look into private care. There must be outfits that send trained workers out to the house."

"Twenty-four hours a day? Seven days a week?" Colin glanced sidelong at Sonny Aalto. "You any idea what that'll cost? I looked into it once. Let's put it this way – if you sold the farm you'd go through the money in less than a year." He jumped down off the threshold and started towards the road.

Then he stopped and turned back. "They'll wait until he's completely dependent and phone you back there in Ottawa to tell you one helper at a time isn't enough. Are you so determined to let him die without you that you'll fork over twenty-thirty thousand bucks a month for three shifts of teamed-up strangers just because you can?"

Above the whitewashed rocks at the entrance to Harry Sylvester's driveway a small hand-painted sign was nailed to the trunk of a fir: *Native Plants*. Holly's invitation to come see her "western wahoo" had sounded something like a dare.

He followed the pea-gravel tracks that wound gently down through a stand of cedars towards the river. It was a long driveway, overarched by heavy boughs. Graceful sword ferns grew like green explosive fountains on either side, and rows of cedar seedlings along the backbones of rotted windfall trees. He passed dense thickets of salmonberry and patches of different tribes of grasses, from blue wild rye to reed canary. All familiar childhood brands against which everything elsewhere had seemed exotic, hinting at beauty, pleasure, and adventure.

Maybe the weak sunlight winking in the beads of moisture drew new attention to things. Maybe it was his anticipation – he was about to visit a woman he'd been close to one whole summer years ago, who believed she could make a living selling native plants. Maybe driving his 1940 pickup Ford had caused the years to roll back, allowing his eyes to see it all as he had seen it when the world was new.

Harry Sylvester's unpainted cedar-shake house sat in a clearing on the bank of the river, the moss thick as a good green mattress on his roof. Sylvester himself came into view in the grassy yard, stooped over a border collie. Though an admired high school teacher and coach, he was about as ordinary as the trees that surrounded him. Old now, like Timo Aalto and Tuomo Korhonen, bent and broad-hipped and a little off-centre when he walked.

Harry Sylvester's face could look as if it had got out of the practice of smiling until you got close enough to be recognized. A hand came out, its grip firm. There was probably no one he wasn't pleased to see, at least for a while. "Come in, I'll make us some tea."

"Can't stay, Harry. I stopped for a look at your niece's new business here."

"Oh that." He laughed. One long hand gestured down along the bank of the river. "She's around somewhere." Her truck, if it was hers, was a flat-deck GMC of some sort, its green cab mottled with patches of rust.

Sylvester led him to a wooden bench beneath a gnarled hawthorn. "I'd show you around but she'll want to do it herself." He took up a book from the bench. "I was reacquainting myself with Euclid here. Keeps my mind from wandering. Now tell me, what was all that racket up at the road this morning?"

"Colin's boys cut a trail to the old sawmill."

Harry Sylvester placed his book beside him on the bench, where his hand explored its surface as if memorizing its shape. "I thought of trying to go in a few times but decided it would be risking serious death. I'm curious to see what it is you keep running away from."

"You wouldn't find it," Sonny said. "Not in there."

"I didn't really think so." He bent to scratch the ears of the dog at his feet. "Tell me how your father's taking things."

When Sonny told him about his phone calls and the visit to Extended Care, Sylvester narrowed his eyes in a manner that suggested he was listening to more than you were saying. It could have been birds singing a mile away or your unspoken thoughts. "I was thinking more of *his* bad news than yours."

"I could go home if he were some place safe, and come back later. Closer to the – to when it starts to get bad. Naturally, that's not what he was hoping for."

Harry Sylvester said, "I don't imagine it was," and turned to the sound of footsteps from around the side of the house. When Holly had come out from behind the building, brushing dirt from the knees of her combat pants, he said, "They're opening up a trail to the sawmill."

She raised a hand to her brow to study Sonny Aalto – the sun had broken through cloud just in time to blind her. "This mean I can go in to see what's hidden in that mess?"

"Not if your son still needs his mother," Sonny said. "Even if you don't break your neck you might never find your way out again. There's no castle in there, if that's what you're hoping. No Sleeping Beauty waiting for the Big Kiss."

"There could be a whole civilization in there," she said, "lost to the world." She leaned against the nearer side-rail of his pickup and looked him up and down. "Well, I didn't think you'd have grown horns and a tail since I saw you last, but something – I guess I expected a citified kind of snooty indifference."

"C'mon, Dog," Harry Sylvester said. "Let's skedaddle." The black-and-white collie got to its feet and panted at his master's heels all the way to the door of the house.

"It pisses you off that I came home at all." He'd meant to sound amused.

She hauled her work gloves out of her back pocket and pulled one of them on. "What made me mad was how long it took you to get here." She slapped the free glove repeatedly against the side-rail, and didn't seem to notice the flakes of dried mud flying into his truck bed. She seemed unaware that what she was leaning against was no ordinary vehicle, probably didn't know one truck from another. "Come, I'll show you around."

She led him down a chip trail past a small blue spruce, a dogwood in second flower. A spindly western trumpet honeysuckle curled around a cedar stake. Small bushes of ocean spray drooped against a strange construction of bicycle wheels that spiralled upward around a rusted centre pole. A red-flowering currant, long past blooming, leaned against a chainsaw statue of an upright life-sized grizzly. She hadn't spent much on commercial start-ups but must be pretty handy with a shovel. He imagined her digging up these plants at night, on Crown land or some farmer's property, her boy holding a flashlight and babbling on about stars.

"Do you have an answer for people who want to know how they'll tell their paid-for plants from the weeds?"

She smiled, but otherwise ignored the question. "I've started a few junipers up ahead, to see if they make good ground cover."

The junipers spread themselves around the base of several upright lengths of rusted railway tracks, welded together in a variety of sharp angles. "This some kind of newfangled trellis?"

"Sculptures," she said, a quick reproach. "A few local artists have lent me their work." She pointed out a series of long, glittering blades turning beneath the high branches of an old fir. "My dream is to create a sculpture garden, to attract people to the place."

The boy stood up from weeding to watch them approach. There were frayed holes in the toes of his unlaced running shoes.

"Fireweed's in a clearing down that trail," she said. "Beekeepers can plant their own fields. Housewives can plant them against the house instead of snapdragons. That's what I'm hoping, anyway."

Sonny laughed. To the boy he said, "And where's this fabled wahoo your mother was bragging about?"

The boy pressed his lips together and led them down the trail. The river here was dark in the shade of overhanging bigleaf maples, and studded with boulders large enough to cause eddies and a quiet backwash.

He supposed he'd seen the western wahoo without knowing what it was. Tromped on it, even ploughed it under. It wasn't something that drew attention to itself. He crouched and turned up a leathery leaf. Seeds the shape of cashews. "Looks a little like mountain boxwood," he said to the boy, who'd sat on his heels beside him. "Kinnikinnick, too."

"Florists like it," the boy said. Rohan.

"Does your mother send you out with a shovel, trespassing where you might get shot?" The boy grinned, but shook his head.

"Anyway, I'll have to pull all this up and go somewhere else when Uncle Harry sells. Developers come by every week, he won't resist forever. You can imagine how much respect they'll give our wahoo when they bring their bulldozers in."

She had a way of brushing the back of her hand across her forehead, as though she were used to pushing hair aside and hadn't adjusted yet to this radical cut. It was a version of what they used to call a pixie cut but there was nothing coy or cute about her, nothing of the pert young thing. It was just that someone had found a way of cutting her hair so that it made you notice the line of her cheekbones, her large eyes, the full curve of her bottom lip. There was something brave and sexy about showing off those ears. A tall, strong-boned, proud-breasted woman, as pleased to be in her forties as she seemed to be with everything else, she had a way of smiling that suggested she was confident you were as pleased with her as she was herself.

"Where did you study?" he said. Since he'd seen her last she'd probably got a degree in botany, environmental studies, landscape design, all the things he hadn't gone to school for himself but wished he had. She'd have picked up foolish notions about landscaping with native plants from some professor. But she'd have had other instructors, too, who'd researched and digested and passed on all the books and articles he'd had to find and read for himself – usually in a panic when the need had suddenly cropped up.

"Never spent an hour at a desk. Not for plants!" She dipped a quick mock-curtsey. "My school was across the road. Most of what I've learned I learned from your dad!"

He could imagine. Had the old bugger talked her into taking him on his explorations down back roads, his field-guide book between them? Did she think that knowing the names of things was the same as knowing how to make use of them? When she'd walked him back to his truck, he said, "You flirt with the old man so he'll leave you his place in his will? For when Harry caves in to developers?"

He thought he'd made it clear he was teasing, but she narrowed her eyes. Colour rose up her throat. "Maybe you think I'm poisoning him too, with my baking?"

"Sorry!" He held up both innocent hands. "All I know is the look on his face when you were fussing over him."

"If you're jealous I can flirt with you as well. There was a time you didn't need me to, but I guess you've forgotten." She waited through his embarrassed silence. "All I do is go over twice a week and clean up a little – wash dishes, that sort of thing. Run his clothes through the wash. Sometimes I bully him into a bath. I started nurse's training once, long years ago. I couldn't properly nurse anything higher up the chain than a *Pinus monticola* but I can listen while he talks."

"Stories meant to make you despise the son off living amongst the swine." He waved goodbye at the boy, then put a hand on the roof of his cab while he opened the door.

"It isn't your father's farm I want," she said. "What I want that isn't mine is that jungle of yours. I see these sculptures in there, and my plants, once it's been opened up a bit. What's so important in the East that you have to go back?"

She'd switched too fast. He looked at her, breathing with her fine mouth open just a little, a front tooth gleaming. Behind her, the boy had gone back to yanking weeds from the sawdust. A raindrop hissed on the hood. "Your business will fall apart without you?" she said "Some woman might find a man with more money?

There must be something more important than that trip to
Turkey." Naturally, everyone would know his excuses. "Those
fairy chimneys will be there a year from now. What are you in
such a hurry to go back to?"

There was something in her eyes that dared him to tell the
truth. "The habit of being not here, I suppose. Being glad I'm far
away from him."

More raindrops fell. There would be a cloudburst yet. He got in
behind the wheel and shut the door. She put both elbows on the
sill and rested her chin on both gloved fists. He imagined running
fingers along her jaw, or down her freckled nose, he imagined
touching the blue veins in her wrist and slipping fingers inside the
loose wristband of a dirty glove.

If she knew what he was thinking she didn't let on. "It isn't just
that you're mad because he's old and there's not a thing you can
do about it? Maybe it never hit you before that he would die one
day. Well, here it comes! Maybe you're scared to admit you don't
want him to." She slapped both gloves on the sill, scattering bits
of dirt inside the truck and down the front of his shirt, then
backed away as though to give him room to leave. "*Now* – before
you disappear again. If you aren't scared of getting a little dirt
under your nails and some rain in your hair, you could help me
move a mock orange I'm supposed to have ready this afternoon.
My occasional helper's recovering from bullet wounds inflicted by
a father *he* can't get along with. Also dealing with police. There's
a coffee waiting for you afterwards, if you do a good enough job."

After the coffee and lemon meringue pie and an hour of arguing
about the wisdom of selling native plants in a place like this, he
turned towards home. He would have to face his father – possibly,
to make amends. It irritated him that he was sure the old man was
expecting exactly that. At this moment, if the neighbours had
gone home, he was probably sitting before the television set and

watching one of his videos. Or maybe rereading one of his tat-tered Russian novels, where the son would have not only threat-ened his father with a walking stick but beaten him to death with it too, and afterwards suffered a life of self-torture, knowing he would be in torment for all eternity.

In that imaginary novel written by a Russian version of his father, how much of what the old man had become – a drunk, a local joke for his laziness, a man who'd raised his son like a prisoner-slave while thinking he was creating a lifelong partner-ship he was terrified to let go of – how much of that would be laid at the feet of the woman who'd deserted him? Deserted *them*, in order to live amongst the kangaroos and wild pigs of another con-tinent. Had she been a beauty who hadn't loved him in the first place and knew that if she'd stayed she would have betrayed him with other men? Had he loved her so much that losing her had turned him into something he mightn't have otherwise become, or was he just an inadequate man forced to raise a son on his own without knowing how to go about it? In this Russian melodrama rapidly approaching its final pages, as his son was beating him with his own walking stick, what did the old man believe had brought him to this moment where he was forced to confront his own death?

Faced with it, he supposed he was able to imagine his father's dying. But he could not, even now, conceive of the world without him. He supposed that in his place Colin Macken would take all of this in his stride. One more person to include in his extended tent of generosity. It seemed that the school dropout and stay-at-home had become a Good Man, a living example of what naive and simple-minded Sonny Aalto had once hoped to become. What he had become instead was a wandering fool, a seeker who didn't know what he was searching for, a successful businessman who hated what his business had become and didn't know what to do with the money it had brought him. How much of that could he blame on being born to Timo Aalto instead of to one of the Mackens?

If he'd been born to one of the Mackens he might never have left. This was something else to resent. It wasn't this place he'd run from, it wasn't anything about this place that kept him away. Darryl Maclean had recognized that but Sonny had mocked him for it. Disbelieving, or fearing to believe. Maclean had flown out with him on one of his quick visits and had fallen in love with the place himself. Afterwards he'd said, "If it weren't for your father you'd have gone home long ago. I watched your face as we walked along the river, when you put your hand against the old rough boards of the barn."

It was absurd to be driving through this overabundance of nature while having to deal with – what? A chill somewhere in his bones. *The sinister presence of death* – the phrase had leapt from somewhere in the distant past, something his father had quoted from his old pal Leo Tolstoy, who'd been stopped in his tracks by some spiritual crisis. Interesting enough for a conversation in the sauna, but something else altogether when it descended not upon Leo Tolstoy but upon you.

In case life hadn't already become impossible, the dark broad bulk in the middle of the road in front of Tom Reimer's place turned out to be Big Tom Reimer himself. He sat on and completely engulfed something that was probably a chair, with his knees wide apart, his hands resting on the walking stick he'd planted in the gravel between his running shoes. A stained fedora was tilted down to put his eyes in shadow. To swerve around him on either side would be to risk the narrow shoulder and the ditch, ploughing scratches into the paint. To run straight into him (it occurred, fleetingly) would do more damage to the pickup than it was worth.

Solid and immovable as any mountain, Tom Reimer glared out from under his hat at the chrome hood ornament until it was less than a metre from his nose – as close as Sonny dared. He didn't even appear to blink when Sonny honked the horn. In his sloppy brown shirt and the huge draping folds of his khaki pants he might have been a statue of himself formed from scooped-up earth.

Sonny put his head out the window. "You collecting a toll or just waiting for another chance to break my ribs?"

Reimer made no answer to that. The gaze from his dark half-curtained-off eyes shifted from the hood of the car to Sonny's face but took on no new expression. He said something Sonny couldn't hear, so he got out and stood inside his opened door, arms resting on the roof of the cab. "If you wanted to join the protesters with their roadblocks you picked the wrong road."

"Never mind your smart talk. I mean to have a word with you."

"I don't think there's any point. None of this is your business."

"Whose business is it, then, if it isn't ours? Me and Dora and Rob and a few others around here." There was no trouble hearing him now. "Who's gonna care how you treat your old man if us old-timers don't? You can run over me if you want and no one'll be surprised. It's no more than we'd expect from you now. There's more than one way to run an old man down."

"There's more than one way to deserve it, too, and heaping shit on someone already ankle-deep in manure is one of them."

The muddy tip of the walking stick rose from the gravel and aimed for Sonny's heart. "A fellow's got to *earn* a claim on someone else's dying, and you haven't done it yet. The way I see it, you got two choices. You can stay and look after your father for as long as he needs you, and do it cheerfully like a decent son, or you can go back where you come from and let the people who care about him do it the best we can." The rubber tip barely wavered. "Anything else, you'll have me to contend with. You ain't even begun to imagine how mean old age has made me. I'd knock you senseless as soon as look at you." He rose from a wooden kitchen chair as though a hydraulic jack were propped beneath his butt, all his weight concentrated on the top of his walking stick. He exhaled a brief sharp grunt from the effort. "Now go home to your dad. That woman's with him now."

"What woman?"

Tom Reimer dragged his chair away, two of its spindle legs cutting furrows in the gravel. "That's all right. I'd try to forget her too if I was her father, but she never looked to me like someone who'd let you. If she was in one of your old man's books you'd have to kill her pretty soon. Strangling's what I recommend. She's got the neck for it."

Charlotte sat out on the trailer's porch, a finger in one of his father's paperbacks. She'd set a bottle of Scotch in the middle of the table. Beside it, her glass was less than half-full. "He locked me out," she said. She did not tilt her head and smile her movie-star smile. She was indignant. "I banged on the door but he told me to go away."

"And you haven't gone." He sat on the railing at a distance from her, one foot braced on the rough planked floor. "Maybe he's afraid there might be trouble right behind you. You're a danger-ous woman. People who slash tires one week may decide to slit throats the next. He doesn't want to find himself in their way."

"I drove up because of a woman in a tree," she said. She laughed, or almost laughed, though not in a way that suggested she would share the humour with him. "You knew the protesters left last night? Called it off? Some agreement for more negotiations."

Sonny nodded, though he hadn't known. The radio had not been turned on this morning. This meant that when Rusty was at the Blueback last night he'd just come from something of a success but hadn't bragged about it. Hadn't thrown it up in Horton's face.

"When the protesters left, this woman refused to go with them. A college instructor of some kind."

"She'd rather live in a tree than face her classes." He'd heard of teachers going to extraordinary lengths to avoid the terrors of Monday morning.

She did not acknowledge his interpretation. "She got herself into the upper branches and wouldn't come down. Even when the protest was called off. She said she would stay there until the logging company changed its practices. One of the magazines asked me to get her photo but I changed my mind when I got there."

"Not a crusty old granny after all, nor an open-faced young beauty."

"You don't have to be a shit, you know." Her shoulders shook his shittiness off. "I just didn't want to do it, okay? It could have made a great picture – woman blending into tree, giving the forest a human face, blah blah blah. A good story, too – she's a logger's wife gone over to the other side." This was stated from her favourite sidelong tilted stance, pale hair held back with a single finger so that she could see past the edge of the curtain. You were addressed but not exactly confronted. "They sent a local reporter out to write it up, but I couldn't go through with my part. If the picture turned out to be as good as I imagined, I could already see what they'd do with it. 'Metamorphosis of Woman Martyr' or some stupidity. I don't have the courage for it. Not any more." She lowered the finger and allowed the curtain to fall across her profile for a moment. Then she tossed it back and looked up at the clouded sky. "I thought I'd drop in to say hello, but he acts like he despises me."

"He despises both of us right now. Don't take it personally."

"You don't take it personally?"

Was there any other way of taking it if you were the old man's son? "I do, but I know how it was earned."

She wasn't curious about the reasons. "Anyway, he can't despise me as much as he pretends, I noticed he has the poster hanging in his house. The old house, I mean."

"Maybe he plans to use it for a game of darts."

"Maybe," she said. She raised her glass and looked in at the golden liquid. Then she touched the top of her little finger to the surface and brought out a tiny dark spot – a fly of some kind, or mosquito – and scraped it off against the edge of the table. She put the glass down but did not remove her hand, as though she was uncertain whether to drink from it now.

"He'd probably like to drag you out in the bush to take new pictures of that stump. That is, if you could find it amongst the new trees grown up around it."

The trouble with that poster was that it missed the point. He would not remind her that he'd praised the photo, had even confessed to a love for that stump, if not for the message beneath it. It was taken for granted that people were too stupid to understand good reasons for saving forests and had to be encouraged to hate the people responsible for the damage. This scene was ugly, we were meant to think, and so we were meant to think it was evil as well. Confusing aesthetics with morality.

She appeared to be watching something in the lower sky. When he turned to straddle the railing he saw a hawk circling above the trees behind the barn. Eyeing the old man's chickens. "A baby would do," his father used to say. "They'd as soon snatch a baby from its buggy." Someone local, Sonny could not remember who, had lost a child this way. He remembered wondering if a hawk could be big enough to take an adult, had taken his mother, perhaps. Maybe she'd offered herself in order to save young Risto. Giving up her life that he might live. This was an explanation no one had ever suggested.

"I thought you might take me out to dinner while I'm here."

Here was something new. With Warren he had wanted the comfortable companionship that sometimes happened between father and adult son, but it seemed he hadn't earned it. With Charlotte the problem was the built-in certainty of failure. She was too complex, too hostile, too changeable. He had learned long ago that trying to be her father required an exhausting amount of effort even as you braced yourself for the next rejection. His trip to New Orleans where he'd tried to talk her into coming home had made that clear enough, as had Helsinki and every encounter since. It seemed she knew how he hoped for the smallest sign of success and provided it only for the pleasure of seeing him stumble once again. Now she wanted to be taken out to dinner.

"Did your grandfather sound like someone who would be willing to eat in public with us? I'm not sure you should be out in public yourself in these parts. There are people who'd like to teach you not to meddle in local affairs." He held up his hands against her protest. "I know, this is more than local. But you have to remember that all affairs are local to the people caught in the middle."

She made a show of refusing to look at him. The old sag-roofed barn was more interesting, the chickens more sympathetic to her cause.

He could hardly blame her. He too would prefer hen cackle to a sermon. "I'll ask him." He got down off the railing and crossed to the trailer door. But the door swung in on silence when he knocked. "You said he'd locked you out."

"I didn't say he was still in there. He came out after a few minutes and went around and down the back. I found this bottle in a cupboard and decided to read something till he came back." She looked at the front cover of the paperback and wrinkled her nose. *A House of Gentlefolk.*

By walking to the open end of the porch Sonny could see smoke from the sauna chimney, shredding into the neighbouring trees. "How long has he been in there?"

She shrugged. "Long enough. One minute is too long for me in that place."

"Think of the great pair of photos you're passing up. *Woman Hiding in Tree. Man Hiding in Sauna.* Give me the camera and we can make it a triptych: *Woman Sulking on Grandfather's Porch.*"

"I'm not leaving until he apologizes. Just because he's old doesn't give him the right to be rude."

The two-room shed was as weather-beaten and tilted as the rest of the buildings, propped up by two-by-sixes at an angle to the ground. Inside, the change room had been kept clean and tidy enough, smelling of soap. Soap and sweat. Tendrils of steam leaked in from the sauna itself through knotholes in the door. "It's me," he said, and began to strip off his clothes.

In movies, men sat with towels across their laps, but in the Aalto sauna you left your towel in the change room. You sat on the risers if there were anyone there besides yourself, but if Sonny was alone he lay out on the highest row of planks with his hands behind his head and waited for the heat to relax his muscles. Above him, the rafters were softened and bleached from seventy years of steam. He knew their patterns of ceiling knotholes as well as Holly's boy knew the stars. He would lie on his back while a slick of hot sweat formed on his chest, and would run a hand down through it and over his belly and groin. This was a chance for a seventeen-year-old to examine the body he expected to have through the rest of his life, the body that women he had yet to meet would come to know. He did not sit up until he could bear the heat no longer, time to use the soap and loofa to scrub away the grime.

This was where they had come every Friday night. To talk, facing one another from opposite benches. Other families talked at the supper table, he'd understood. At their table his father had shovelled in the food as though he feared it would be snatched from under his nose. Things that got talked about at other families' tables got talked about in here. Sonny's week at school. Work done around the place. Work that needed doing. Some woman his father had hopes for, who might or might not be someone Sonny had met.

Of course that man, his inseparable partner, his one-time "best friend" – even the little of him that remained – would soon disappear altogether, no matter what they did between now and then. The hard taskmaster, his constant companion, the lazy bastard who had presumably loved him the best he knew how, who had brought him up the only way he could, was about to step off the earth, whether he did it at Cape Scott or somewhere else.

He had no idea what his father thought he was facing once he'd allowed that wave to sweep him away. He had no idea what he was facing himself, or how he would handle it. His more immediate need was to find a substitute for the picture he had of his father and himself heading north, the trunk of the rented Buick stuffed with camping equipment, Tom Reimer and the police not far behind.

Once he'd draped his clothes over the back of a bench and stuffed his watch and King Richard ring inside one of his shoes, he tapped on the door and opened it. "Coming in!"

The heat and thick steam caught his breath, as it had always done. This time the steam was denser than he'd remembered being used to. His father must have been pouring regular dashes of cold water onto the stones – stones that his own father had picked from the fields. Also jamming sticks of wood into the forty-five-gallon drum they'd made into a stove. It was nearly impossible to see any depth into the room.

He felt his way along the right-hand wall and climbed to the top riser. His father, he eventually saw, was sitting on the bottom level facing him from across the room, his accustomed place. Dressed in his long johns.

"I was going to ask if the doctors would approve of you being in here, but I can see you're just trying to rot the clothes off your back. To save taking them off yourself."

"That place today," his father said. "I don't mind tellin' you it scared the crap out of me."

"Me too," Sonny said. He should phone in a complaint about that hearse.

He imagined them being pulled over by police somewhere north of Campbell River, his father taken away in a government car, himself arguing with men in uniform who wanted to put him in handcuffs. Tom Reimer scowling from the back seat of the Health and Welfare car as it pulled away.

"I'm sorry I behaved like a bastard when we got home."

His father grunted. He was an indistinct figure in the steam. The top of his tilted-down head was pale, except for the scabs from recent falls. Today's bandages were still on his face. His hands in his lap looked as though they were reassuring themselves about one another. Of course the old man's fear was not only for the threat of Extended Care. Here was a man who had run out of back roads to explore, left with nothing but a one-way exit route he wished to travel down as fast as possible.

"I been trying to think how we're gonna get through this business," his father said. "I know I'm a stubborn sonofabitch but I'm not stupid. Maybe we'll just have to come up with some kind of deal."

"You going to make me an offer?"

"I figure I already done that. It's your turn."

"It's been my turn since I got here. Nora Macken's little kingdom was not a roaring success. I think we've backed ourselves into a corner. You going to sit in your underwear till it falls off on its own?"

His father's thick fingers started fumbling at the top buttons. "Damn things get harder to take off every week. Nurses helped put them on." His sheepish smile suggested pride or guilt, or maybe both. "I thought I'd just stand under the shower afterwards."

"And catch pneumonia again while they're drying?"

"Hell, no. They stretch when they're wet, easier to get out of." This was delivered like a scientific discovery Sonny ought to have known about.

"Undo those buttons. We'll throw them in the wash and look for clean ones."

If he was expected to propose some sort of "deal," and was doomed to play nursemaid anyway, he might as well be playing nursemaid while seeing something of the world besides this back road farm. "Cape Scott can wait – okay? No matter how much you nag. But I don't intend to sit here while your neighbours plot ways to nail my feet to your floor. Since you seem to think you're up for the trip to the Cape, you must be strong enough to go somewhere else instead. I know *I've* got to get out of here. This place is already starting to look pretty good and I've only just arrived. I could end up like all those others Colin told me about, coming back to retire where they were born."

His father's snort was unbelieving. "It's that Holly."

"And the bloody sword ferns and the Douglas firs! It's the

feeling I got when I looked in towards the dark centre of my old nursery garden. There were no sirens singing but if I don't get out of here fast I may start hearing them."

"You'll never get me to Ottawa, if that's what you're thinking."

"If I took you to Ottawa, Judith Buckle would kill us both. I've had my eye on Cappadocia. What do you think? That's in Turkey. Mushroom-shaped rock chimneys hollowed out for homes. Some of them eighteen storeys deep into earth, a whole secret village where twenty thousand Christians lived in persecution times."

"I'm not going any place I might get shot."

Sonny laughed, but bit his tongue against temptation. His father was entitled to his contradictions, he supposed. If you'd made a decision to walk into the sea you might resent the bullet that stopped you.

Now that he had his long johns unbuttoned all the way down to his waist, his father stood up and struggled to step out of them. But once they were around his knees they were too tight to shake off while standing up. When he sat down again, he couldn't reach far enough to force them off.

Sonny crossed the room and pulled the long johns down his father's legs and off. It had been a long time since he'd seen the old man's hide. There wasn't much flesh but what there was was pale. What there was was loose, too, as though it would fall from his bones. Decorated with bruises from his falls – some purple, some yellow, some faded into grey. Long white hairs grew on the top of his big toe. It had been even longer since he'd seen the leather harness and the joint below the knee. It ought to be taken off as well, but Sonny decided to consider his job complete. He tossed the long johns against the door and went back to his side of the room.

"I should go off to the old woman's boar hunt," he said, "and hire a pair of babysitters to keep an eye on you while I'm gone."

"You'll dump me in that place, that's what you'll do! Why not take me up to Cape Scott before you go? Then you won't have to think about me again."

"I could advertise for a pair of buxom nurses trained in Russia, lady wrestlers. Unless you wanted to come with me."

His father abruptly straightened, as though pulling back from a blow. "You crazy? I never heard nothing about Australia I wouldn't hate. Red dirt and bloody heat. You think you're Virgil, planning to drag me through a practice run for hell?"

Sonny knew who Virgil was but hadn't read him. "A chance to look up your runaway wife?" He felt curiously exultant at the imagined risk in this. He and his father arriving at the hunting party, his mother's other family armed with spears or guns, looking for something to kill. "Though that could be a lot more dangerous than Turkey."

"Christ!" His father snorted. "The shock might kill her."

"A showdown in central Queensland."

Judith Buckle would be horrified. *You can't take that sick old man so far from home*, he could hear her say. *What's got into your head?*

"You'd have to have a checkup with your doctor first," Sonny said. If it was a foolish idea it ought to be stopped before they took it seriously. "There'd be medication to take with us. There'd be the name of someone there to contact – another doctor, if you needed one. A few days in Vancouver would make more sense. Your friends would never let us go to Australia. You've never even been across to Vancouver."

His father's hand dismissed Vancouver. "We'll have to come up with good reasons or they'll have the authorities down our necks." He seemed pleased to see himself a fugitive.

This had begun to feel like some kind of dangerous game they were testing. "We could tell them my mother's been a prisoner all these years and we're going to bring her back." A father-son adventure was how he would present it to Judith Buckle.

She was certain to say that at his age just living through another day was adventure enough. *Spiders and snakes are only the beginning. Kangaroos can rip you open with their back feet. Do I need to fly out there and knock some sense into your head?*

"It might be an idea to take Holly along. Keep you clean-shaven for when you come face-to-face with the woman who stole your heart."

"Jesus! You mean her and you are already back where you –?"

"Not yet. But we've got more than a month before packing our bags."

He felt a little giddy now. Maybe it was the steam. Maybe it was the thought of taking Holly so far away from this place. "With a little luck we could return with your lunch kit. Put it in a glass case up at the store, for people to gawk at."

His father hadn't listened. "I can see the look on her face. You think she'll feel bad enough if I manage to expire at her dinner table?"

Sonny assumed a "let's get serious" look. "You realize this would mean an eighteen-, twenty-hour flight crammed into a plane."

"So long as she don't crash I won't mind. Crashing wouldn't please me much. I need to get home in one piece to finish our little excursion." He was quiet for a few moments, running a hand along the plank he sat on. "Sooner or later you're takin' me up to Cape Scott!"

He would have to send another postcard to Judith Buckle. *It looks as though we may be travelling farther than anyone inttended.* Since he hadn't told her about his father's camping trip to the end of the world he could hardly tell her it was being postponed in favour of something more ambitious. In fact, a postcard could not contain a proper explanation. He would have to telephone.

Telephone calls could wait until tomorrow. Hearing his news this time of day would have Judith Buckle up all night. Darryl Maclean as well – who at this moment was probably nodding off in front of his after-supper television program, swimming through the open window of his family home in order to snooze amongst the underwater weeds on his childhood bed. While standing at his office window to observe the queue beside the M'sieur Patates chip wagon, the manager of the Centretown hotel made it clear

to his receptionist that, since she'd tempted him in the first place
with her provocative clothes, her future employment depended
upon her continued co-operation behind his office door. Closer to
home, Colin Macken and his two sons ran up the steps to the
back door of the glass-and-cedar house, one of the sons standing
aside while the other put a hand on his father's back to let him go
in first. Farther down the road, Dora and Rob Mitchell watched
the early news while eating their macaroni and cheese, the senior
Cabinet minister explaining to a reporter that tomorrow he
would fly out to Vancouver, "to knock some sense into a few thick
heads out there. Some people just don't see that we need the
provinces to help us keep this country from tearing itself apart!"

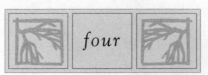

four

J errod Hawkins had suggested they approach Mistake Creek gradually, to lessen the shock. "This is a small town, far from everything. Expect heat. Expect sunlight so harsh you can feel the colour drain from your eyes." He warned of a flat dusty landscape that might have been made from broken crockery, with bits of scrub and dry old tufts of grass. Flies would nip at your ears and get trapped in your hair. "Expect a world as different as you can imagine from the glass towers and white frozen air of your Ottawa."

Jerrod would have had them come to Brisbane first, and stay with him and his wife. He would have driven them out to Kalevan Station himself. But Sonny's plan was to spend a week in Sydney, giving them time to adjust to the continent on their own, and then fly with a regional airline up to central Queensland. He knew better than to take his father directly from the plane to a stranger's home, where they would no doubt be bullied with hospitality.

And he'd been told that Sydney would be as familiar as it was exotic, a natural place to start. Here were the salt smell and gleaming towers of Vancouver, the lacy balconies and louvred windows of New Orleans, the ocean views and outdoor cafés of San Francisco. Yet all of it was flooded by sunlight so harsh that it was transformed into something new. In Sydney there were palm trees, hibiscus in bloom, laughing adults dressed like children in shorts and undershirts, licking ice cream cones. The city was a lush sort of garden for grownup children to play in.

His father's neighbours had raised every objection they could think of. Tom Reimer had even called Social Services and tried to get Timo Aalto made a ward of the province. Only the old man's claim that it had been his own idea silenced them, though not for long, since they believed it was a son's responsibility to override his foolish whims. A journey into the scorching plains of Queensland was more than just another of Timo Aalto's backroad explorations. "We should've . . . left you . . . in Ottawa," Rob Mitchell said, fighting hard for every breath.

That Charlotte had insisted on coming along reassured no one. She didn't really care about her grandfather, they said. She was going because things had got too hot for her at home. That Holly Fitzgerald planned to join them later did not impress anyone either, since she'd agreed to meet them at Kalevan Station, and only if they really thought she was needed. His phone call from Sydney did little to calm their indignation. When he reported to Dora Mitchell that the city was so beautiful they we're thinking of staying for good, she shouted at him. "Don't you try to make a fool of me! I'm mad. I'll still be mad when you get home, so you better just watch out!"

Harry Sylvester's voice replaced Dora Mitchell's. "Dora's got a long and terrible memory, son, as some of us know to our sorrow. Tommy's is even worse. Most of the rest of us are too busy to stay pissed off for long. We're planning a party for Colin and Theresa's anniversary!"

There was no point in mentioning that for the first few days his father hadn't left the little Victoria Street hotel that Kalevan Station had booked for them. The hotel manager's doctor had checked him over and recommended rest. When Sonny went out into the city himself, he came back to the hotel two or three times a day to make sure his father was recovering his strength.

On these explorations his brisk pace slowed to a stroll whenever he came to anything green and growing. He examined weeds in the concrete (lantana? pigface?), ran his palm up the trunks of unfamiliar trees, identified flowers he had seen little of at home: banksia, bottlebrush, frangipani. He pinched leafy twigs in order to examine them in the privacy of his room. In the Botanical Gardens there were rows of various palms, and Moreton Bay figs with their curtains of aerial roots and voluptuous trunks like the hides of polished elephants.

Charlotte seldom joined him, having found a whole new world to photograph. Once she'd satisfied herself that the famous harbour, the famous opera house, and the famous coat-hanger bridge looked precisely as she'd known they would look, she'd determined to seek out her own version of the city. She went down alleys and under bridges where no sane person would go alone. She strayed onto nude beaches, into the patio parties of the wealthy in Double Bay, and through some of the sleazier bars in Kings Cross. Sonny soon discovered how little she intended to listen to him here, which was more or less what he'd learned to expect at home.

She joined him once, amongst the crowds of tourists looking for local handicrafts in The Rocks, but only, it seemed, to mock his interest with a light-hearted cheer that strangers might have mistaken for affection. While he tried on wide-brimmed hats she stood indifferently by, but afterwards told him the one he'd chosen made him look a fool. "For God's sake, tilt it down in front or they'll think I'm a nursemaid to a retarded Boy Scout." What could he do but re-arrange it at several ridiculous angles, mocking himself in a storefront window? She rolled her eyes so that no one would think her amused.

She warned him to stay clear of Macquarie Street downtown where she'd come upon another of those metal statues of *Il Porcellino* outside a hospital wing, a brass plate inviting you to throw coins into the pool to help the sick. "He's followed you here to remind you why you've come."

"Looks like my mother, you think?" He had never seen a photo of his mother.

On the shaded sidewalk outside their terrace-house hotel, it was wise to watch where you stepped. The roots of trees had pushed up heaves and zigzag cracks in the pavement. There was also the chance you might put your foot on a syringe. Half-eaten fruit lay about, tossed aside by the young people who sat under the plane trees and flowering bushes in front of the backpacker hostels, talking or writing letters. The doors of cars and vans were opened all along the curb. Inside, youths brushed their teeth, or lay snoozing on a slab of foam. "For Sale – $1,200" was taped to a window. "Make Me An Offer." Fords, Holdens, Volkswagen vans – hand-painted with flowers or the flags of various countries – all were for sale, presumably so those who'd driven them around this continent could afford to fly home.

"*Morgen*," a few muttered without smiling, though it was afternoon.

In front of their little hotel, a shirtless youth leaned against a battered LandCruiser painted over with zebra stripes, a hooked thumb pushing the waistband of his corduroy pants as low as he dared. His short hair had been bleached or dyed white, his eyebrows as well, giving the appearance of a wild creature in a photographic negative. Charlotte and Sonny seemed of equal interest, though blue eyes quickly shifted to someone more deserving across the street.

Inside, the hotel manager went into an impassioned swirl of welcome. He had fallen in love with Charlotte. With both of them, maybe. When they entered the glassed-in patio at the rear of the building, he leapt down off a chair from watering the hanging plants. He poured coffee with a flourish, offered bowls of fresh mangoes and passion fruit, and insisted they sit at one of the little breakfast tables. He asked questions about their day in the city, and gave advice for tomorrow. He sailed into his kitchen to turn down the volume of his little radio, which seemed to play nothing but opera, and smiled at them from the pass-through before rushing out again with a plate of cakes.

Stanley, he'd asked them to call him. He wore crisp white shirts and black slacks and hard leather shoes that clicked on the tiles. His dark hair, slicked back in a ponytail, shone with oil. He'd insisted upon hearing about the photos Charlotte had taken, having quizzed her enough to discover she was known to magazine editors at home. "Watson's Bay is a must for tomorrow. And of course South Head." He shuddered, a man standing in wind above the sea. He disappeared inside his little kitchen and reappeared as head-and-shoulders in the pass-through, adding, "And Darling Harbour." Irony this time. "One hopes to have a camera when that glass monstrosity collapses, though I suppose the shoppers could be a mess." He wiggled fingers sticky with imagined blood. Behind him, Leontyne Price sang something from *Aida*.

"Your father has had a lovely afternoon," he said, coming out again with another bowl of fruit. "Our lady New Zealander in the lower front was not up to being a tourist either, so I threw the two of them together and they hit it off quite famously. She took on the challenge of putting a smile on his face, while he heroically resisted. Horror stories were exchanged. It seems the two of them have had equally difficult lives, working their fingers to the bone, as it were. Ungrateful children were also mentioned, but I made myself scarce when I saw things going so well." He gasped, suddenly remembering something. "And there is a telephone message." He consulted a piece of paper. "From a Dr. Hawkins. His receptionist, rather." Stanley raised the paper a short distance from his nose. "Dr. Errol Hawkins, the woman said. An invitation to dinner tonight at his home. I've written his address for you – rather posh, I must say. Your father has already refused, but has no objection to your going without him."

"That's good of him," Charlotte said. "Where is he now?"

Stanley looked pleased to be asked. "Upstairs, snoring away on his back. I peeked. His dentures are parked on his chest. Perhaps he fears he'll swallow them in his sleep?"

Sonny went upstairs to check on his father, but stepped into the narrow telephone room on the second landing and closed

the door. Eighteen hours behind would be nine o'clock yesterday evening. He dialled the long sequence of numbers necessary
to ring up the Blueback while charging it to his Ottawa telephone card.

She was on her way to the kitchen, she said, with a stack of
dirty plates. "A few grains of risotto. Strips of green pepper. Crusts
of focaccia bread. You want me to save it for you? I'm thinking of
mailing it to Eritrea."

"You thought of an answer yet?" he said. He hadn't known
what he would say, only that he'd wanted to hear her voice.

Her voice, at the moment, was impatient. "Answer to what?"

"How to tell indigenous plants from weeds."

"I have people waiting, for heaven's sake!" The upswing of her
exasperated voice reminded him of the way her eyes would flash,
amused and impatient, when she thought he was being unreasonable. She would be wearing a long skirt and a loose top, he
imagined. Not necessarily the grey skirt and the red velvet top.
He and his father had eaten at the Blueback every night of the
week before they left, and after taking his father home to bed he'd
driven back to meet her at the end of her shift. She had three or
four of those skirt-and-blouse combinations, different colours but
all long and slimming, all drawing attention to the pride with
which she presented herself to the world.

He lowered his voice in order to sound mysterious. "I phoned
to remind you of your promise."

"You've been gone just two short days!"

"It seems longer. How do you know you can trust me not to lie
to get you here? Tell you he's sinking fast and needs you."

"You'd be ashamed. At least I hope you would. Also, you're the
one who'll pay for my flight. Australia must have warehouses full
of half-trained nurses that married losers and ended up escorting
customers to their tables."

"I meant what I said. If anything goes wrong I want you here."
This, of course, was the truth. Before leaving, he had seen for
himself how the old man responded to her flirting. By the time

he'd returned from a week in Ottawa she'd made herself an essen-
tial part of his father's life. She'd looked in on him twice a day,
she'd taken a turn at sleeping overnight in his trailer. But it was
Sonny who, upon his return, had discovered reasons to spend as
much time as he possibly could with Holly Fitzgerald.

He didn't know how serious she was about their agreement.
He'd told his father she wanted to be called if his health deterio-
rated. His father was flattered. To Holly he'd said, "Frankly, I
think he's got the hots for you, he wants to know you'll come if
he needs you there."

"Look," he said into Stanley's phone. "I want you with me
now."

"The boss is making threatening gestures with his payroll
book. I still don't know why you called."

"I keep thinking of how you're missing this. What if you joined
us right away?"

"I've got a job, a business to run, and a kid to raise, I don't have
time to go gallivanting around the world like the idle rich."

"You see, I was right to wonder if you could be trusted."

She ignored this. "I got in as far as the first pond today. I crawled
as far as I dared. There's wisteria gone wild. There's a giant
dogwood that I haven't got to yet, into its autumn bloom, covered
with bright white flowers that show up like lights in the shadows.
Vines have got so huge they've burst through every pane of your
glass houses and lifted them off the ground. I'm dressed like a nun
to hide the scratches. I'm not sure I'd be willing to restore the
gardens if you hired me to."

"I don't want the gardens restored. Concentrate on your
western wahoo. I'll phone again."

Errol Hawkins's home, a forty-eight-dollar taxi ride across the
coat-hanger bridge and into the northern suburbs, was a sprawling
mansion with a porte cochère, surrounded by hedges and towering

cabbage palms. Though they arrived after dark, he could see that
the house sat high enough to have a wide view of borrowed
scenery – city lights and distant hills and possibly even ocean.
Obviously this half-brother did a good business. An oral surgeon,
maybe, or orthodontist, rather than just a dentist.

The house was already noisy with guests. When conversations
involved the names of bridge-playing friends, or fellow volunteers, Errol Hawkins or his wife Carmel would explain. "We're
talking about the ex-minister of Mines," or "This is Dorea
Carstairs we're slagging – you must have seen her films?"

Paintings on the walls were of red dirt, dusty shacks, and figures
of the elongated rural poor – definitely not their neighbours.
Tapestries might have come from old Persia. Hand-carved chests
were made from ebony. You had the feeling that a private home
was hiding somewhere just beyond these rooms, which were
meant for the public in the manner of foreign embassies.

"Not Yanks, are you?" One worried old fellow seemed to be
seeking reassurance. He brightened a little when Sonny told him
they weren't. Even his moustache perked up. He asked if they
planned to stay.

Their host said, "Sir Roger can't imagine anyone not wanting
to live here."

Others felt much the same. Though they spoke of their recent
"hols" in Fiji and six-month visits to Europe, they insisted on the
pleasure they took in coming home. "Missed me footy, for one
thing," the host admitted. He was a broad, ruddy-faced, good-
natured man, with sandy hair and a short rust-coloured beard.
Nothing about him suggested a blood relative, so far as Sonny
could see. And he showed little curiosity about Sonny Aalto –
just one more foreigner amongst them. "Couldn't find better
tucker than New Australian cuisine, even in Paris."

Sonny shouldn't have looked at Charlotte. Mischief was
clearly on her mind. As soon as they were seated at the dining-
room table, she began to sing the praises of Sydney. Already she
wanted to live here, she said. "My – uh – father may look for

investment opportunities." The pause was meant to raise doubts about the relationship. "I'll visit your glossy magazines."

The others assumed her enthusiasm was for the climate.

"Oh, but it isn't just your sun," growled Charlotte, who could make herself sound fierce. "It's your country we want." She sounded as though she would wrench it from them in a minute. "We've given up on our own."

It was true that she had given up. To Sonny she had spoken of plans to move south again to what she called a "real country," to help her photos earn a reputation in New York. The reason she gave these strangers was that their own country had decided to throw in the sponge. "It's all but turned itself over to the neighbours. Meanwhile, it stands around with its finger up its bum while its own citizens try to break it apart." She was in fine style, having found a way to mock him with his own opinions even while mocking the others for his benefit. "You're so lucky to have a continent all to yourself." She smiled, and placed a shrimp between her teeth with deliberate ceremony. Her eyes, in this light, were a startling green.

Their host said, "Oz looks pretty good to folks whose countries have gone crook. We get plenty wanting in."

"So do we," Sonny began, in case they were taking Charlotte too seriously.

"Ironically!" Charlotte quickly added, with a small laugh. She pushed aside a fall of her shining pale hair and spoke as though from behind it. "Safe haven for all the world's unhappy victims while they wait for things Back Home to change. The country's become a holding tank where they carry on battles they should have left behind."

"The Air-India explosion?" the hostess offered as an example. Carmel Hawkins wore a long lacy gown, with glittering sapphires against the freckled tops of her breasts.

"The only country in the world that's pledged to redefine itself every time a new immigrant steps onto the soil," Charlotte said. "All values are up for grabs, local traditions irrelevant. You have to read the morning paper to see what sort of country you'll be living in today."

Errol Hawkins grinned. "Mounties can wear coolie hats now if they want." He instructed the others, his ruddy face shining with pleasure. "The English language illegal in the shops of one whole province. Government money would be available – am I right? – to help me fight to replace the Bible with 'Waltzing Matilda' when I take a courtroom oath."

Since others clearly doubted this last assertion, Charlotte declared it less far-fetched than it seemed. "No values are better than others," she said. "You are a racist if you demand an end to gang wars amongst people from Asia. A choir in Victoria was instructed to delete Christ from their Christmas carols on the Legislative lawn. The national anthem is revised every few years so newly discovered offences may be replaced with even safer blandness."

Sir Roger took this as encouragement to confess his own opinion. "When the Olympics were in Calgary? I couldn't watch!" He cleared his throat. "Everything in two languages! Drove me nearly bonkers. I don't know how anyone can live in a place like that."

Their hostess mentioned a recent editorial in a Sydney newspaper. "Apparently, we look to you as a model for what we're supposed to be trying here? Multiculturalism and all that? The editor's opinion is that we don't want to see you fail."

"Nonsense," snorted Sir Roger.

Thus was Sonny Aalto's homeland written off before the second course. Charlotte directed a triumphant smile his way. What had she wanted to accomplish? When conversation broke up into smaller exchanges he felt compelled to explain to the professor of health sciences on his left that he did not entirely agree with his daughter. He believed in the strength of this mix of new immigrants, a country with a unique flavour, respecting differences. Judging by the number of people who wanted to come there, the world seemed to need such a place. "The problem, for me, is a government so eager to please the neighbour-to-the-south, to be whatever they want us to be, that we'll soon no longer be *us*. We were the North American Alternative, once, but that country is disappearing fast."

"I see," said the health sciences professor, though it was clear she had little interest in his opinion. She ran the tip of her index finger over the face of his watch. "You haven't adjusted the time?" He had, of course, but allowed her to lift his wrist so that she could see this for herself. "Nice," she said, and asked him to explain the confusing amount of information it was determined to give.

Charlotte was no longer interested in getting under her father's skin. She was nose-to-nose with Errol Hawkins, who was getting the full benefit of her tilted movie-star smile. It seemed he'd seen some of her magazine photos somewhere, or pretended he had. "We have to keep an eye open, to know what's going on." Sonny was too far away to hear who "we" might be. Dental surgeons in search of posters for the waiting-room wall? The professor of health sciences, through with his watch, seemed to think he wanted to hear about the financial difficulties her "uni" would face in the coming fiscal year.

When they'd finished the honeyed figs and withdrawn with their coffees to the "lounge room," their host explained that the travellers were on their way to his mother's annual pig shoot. Several in the company gasped, as it seemed he'd known they would. He added, "Unless they've changed their minds."

"We've got this far," Sonny said. "There's no reason to back out now." He'd chosen a black leather armchair, with bouquets of giant feathers at his elbow.

The hostess said, "Oh, there are reasons," but didn't voice them.

Her husband passed out brandies. "Could be wild, if you haven't been on a shoot before. And dangerous."

Sonny drew in his legs. "My father taught me how to use a gun. We were poor. It was up to me to bring home something to eat – ducks, venison, bear." In fact, he had never shot a bear, and wouldn't have eaten it if he had. But saying less might disappoint.

"Grizzly?" the professor said. She seemed to hope it was. She had perched on the arm of his chair, one leg crossed daintily over the other. A slender calf brushed lightly against his knee.

He looked up into her plain round face, which hovered a little too close. "There's only little black bears on the island," he said. It would be prudent to stick to some facts.

However, because the professor repeated the word *bears* as though it were magic, he could not resist explaining that the one truly dangerous animal on the island was the cougar. And then only when wounded or starving. "This is a big cat, about as long as that dining table if you include the tail. They sometimes drag your children off for food."

The satisfying gasps suggested they understood his country had more to offer than grizzlies, *séparatistes*, and Mounted Police in turbans. "How terrible!" said the health sciences professor, shifting her hips so that they put a little more pressure against his shoulder. In case she was looking for teeth-marks, he obliged by tilting down his head. She saw this as an invitation to rest her hand on the back of his neck.

A red-faced fellow with a large moustache stood over Sonny in order to explain the nature of the country they would be visiting. "Some of it's as hostile as Mars. Don't get separated. You'll be well beyond where explorers disappeared."

"Snakes worry you?" The hostess brought her own cup of coffee and sat on a black leather couch. "There's a dozen kinds of venomous snakes in the area, including some that can finish you off in a minute."

"Speaking of venom," said their host, "they haven't met Viira yet." He chuckled. So did others. Sir Roger shook his head, sad and amused, as though recalling some experience of his own. "I hope I'm there when you do," said Errol Hawkins. "I hear she's feeling a bit crook this year so she could be even more dangerous than usual."

"Has it occurred to you," said the professor of health sciences. "Well of course it hasn't – that she's capable of bringing you all this way for no other reason than to humiliate you?"

She looked to their host for confirmation. He nodded, and confessed that sometimes he believed that was the only reason she invited him, her eldest son. "Her eldest *Aussie* son, that is."

His wife agreed. "I was invited once? I wouldn't go again if she begged me."

"Viira Hawkins begging!" The very idea sent them into gales of laughter.

The professor's hip had become oppressive, her calf now heavy against his leg, which had begun to sweat. He excused himself, and wrestled his way up out of the chair, to seek out the coffee for a refill he didn't want. He remained standing after he'd stirred in the cream. Charlotte, catching his eye, made a face depicting amused surprise.

The professor, perhaps giving up on him, slid down into his leather chair and closed her eyes. Her chest swelled as she took in a long deep breath.

"You say you've shot bear?" said one of the other dentists, who must have been brooding on this since before the subject had changed. "You ought to come with us on one of our weekends. Though I reckon you'd find it pretty tame, shooting bunnies down the Murrumbidgee, Pisstank Bluey begging us to give him back his moleskins."

The men laughed. Women smiled politely, either because they had heard this before or had hoped not to hear it at all.

Errol Hawkins explained that he and Blue and Murray over there, and a Jacko who couldn't be here tonight, sometimes went off for a weekend of shooting in the bush. "To get out of the city. Forget cavities and impacted wisdom teeth." Sometimes they shot kangaroos up behind Bourke, sometimes wallabies down near Goulburn, or went spotlighting for roos again just west of Broken Hill.

"In Texas once," Charlotte said, "friends took me out at night in their truck. I sat on the roof of the cab with a spotlight while the men shot rabbits from the windows. I remember their screams."

"Screams?" the professor said, her eyes springing open.

Women could be seen reassessing Charlotte. If the men were true to their reputations they were probably wondering why they hadn't abandoned the ladies and gone to the kitchen.

"We play poker till midnight," Errol Hawkins said, "we drink till dawn, sleep a little, and then get up and find something else to shoot."

"Not unlike your mother's parties," their hostess said. She turned to Sonny, "Don't let her get you into a poker game, she'll own your house and car before you know what hit you, and your grandchildren, too, if you're careless."

"I told the old woman you'd fly up with us," Errol said, "but as usual she had her own idea. She'd already hired a driver."

"Driver?" Their hostess was shocked. "That will take days!"

"It would be a way of seeing the country," Charlotte said.

"Some of that country's better seen from the air," Sir Roger said. "You'd be going where you need to carry water. Extra food. Petrol stations are far apart."

"An adventure, then," Charlotte said, in a tone that suggested Sir Roger's objections were frivolous.

"Not sure I'd trust her," the red-faced gentleman said. "She probably thinks you'll never make it."

Errol Hawkins sighed. "There's no use arguing, mate. I've known that all my life. She said the driver will contact you at your Potts Point hotel. Some Abo she's befriended, no doubt, or a crim she's sprung from jail."

Later, in the taxi, Charlotte said, "Your father will be glad. He's had enough of flying." She looked out the window at the passing mansions and their floodlit banks of blooming oleander. "Besides, you wouldn't want to travel with those awful people. Far better to die in the desert."

When they'd plunged down into the tunnel that would take them beneath the harbour and the downtown office towers, she added, "I'm almost sorry I won't be going with you."

"Of course you're going with us," Sonny said. "That's why you're here."

She shook her head impatiently. "No, no, I'll meet you up at your mother's place for the party. I've got other things to do first."

"An assignment in Sydney?" Photos of the city for some travel magazine, he imagined, though she hadn't mentioned this till now. He realized that his annoyance was mixed with a certain amount of relief. So long as she was with him – here or anywhere – he sensed there was always something he ought to be doing that he hadn't thought of yet.

"It isn't here. Not in this city, I mean. I'll be leaving early tomorrow."

"Looking for what?"

He was supposed to know better than to ask. She'd warned him long ago that she owed him no explanations.

"Not for meaning," she said. "I'll leave that sort of fruitless search to you. I'm happy with textures, composition, light. And colour. I don't expect a pile of rocks to tell me the meaning of my life."

"So much for your promise, then. To help with your grandfather."

"You heard Errol," she said. "A driver's been hired. A chauffeur will know his way around, he'll be better help than I could ever be." She dropped her voice to a growl. "And besides, if you get into trouble you can always call up the moon-faced lady professor, who'll come panting to the rescue in a flash."

When he came down in the morning, it was clear from Stanley's blush that he had talked with Charlotte on her way out. Sonny Aalto was to be pitied, an estranged incompetent father. Perhaps because he could think of nothing else to say, Stanley expressed the hope that his guest had slept well. "The Cross was quiet last night."

He probably meant only that no one had been murdered. Kings Cross was never quiet. From his room, Sonny had heard laughter, shouting, police sirens well into morning. Unable to sleep, he'd gone out for a short run and seen its night activities for himself: young men urging you into the strip joints, hookers slouched against the walls in leopard-skin shifts or little-girl pinafores, old men sleeping on benches.

"Last week a backpacker's hostel burned to the ground, killing ten sleepers," Stanley regretted to say. "Parents in Germany will be mourning." He scooped up his coffee pot and led the way to the glassed-in breakfast patio. His radio opera was playing softly – *Eugene Onegin* he thought it might be.

"You've been out there where we're going?" Sonny said. "Central Queensland?"

"Good heavens, no!" Stanley's lashes fluttered. A hand dismissed the very notion. "Mobs of roos and filthy sheep." He swept a previous breakfaster's crumbs off a tablecloth and into a cupped hand. "When I'm not here I am down at Bondi, greased and splayed on the sand." He raised both eyebrows high as though to say, *You probably wouldn't have guessed.*

The old man was up and dressed, sitting behind a little wrought-iron table and looking morosely into a bowl of cold cereal. He considered these continental breakfasts hardly worth getting out of bed for. Cold cereal, cold toast, croissants. "Chook food," another hotel guest had described it the day before.

"You've heard," Sonny said to his father, sitting across the table and leaning a little to one side while Stanley poured his coffee. He stopped himself from massaging the fingers of his right hand, something he'd often found himself doing since his ring had disappeared while he was pruning his father's orchard trees.

The eyes his father raised to Sonny gleamed with amusement. "A hell of a thing when you can't count on your own children!" He added, clearly for Stanley's benefit, "I've had some experience with this sort of thing myself." To Sonny he said, "I can't say I'm sorry. She was never my idea of the perfect travelling companion."

"My father's disgusted with me," Sonny explained.

"My father," Stanley said, setting sail for his kitchen, "hasn't spoken to me for fifteen years." From inside the kitchen he raised his voice at the pass-through. "Hasn't spoken *about* me either, I understand. I might never have entered this world."

"You should thank him for it. Makes your life less complicated."

But there were beads of moisture in Stanley's lower lashes when he came out with a basket of croissants. "I will go home when he has reached unconsciousness – not before. My mother will call. Otherwise he would throw a heart attack and blame me for his death. I'm fortunate to have no children I can burden with my presence."

Timo Aalto cleared his throat and unfolded the copy of the *Sydney Morning Herald* beside his bowl. "On the other hand," he said from behind pages that were awkwardly larger than either of them was used to, "you're missing out on the fun of watching your offspring deal with the burden."

Breakfast was interrupted by a short phone call from a cheerful Jerrod Hawkins. "Just checking. You find the hotel comfy, I hope?" He hoped, too, that Sydney was treating them well. "Errol and his mates didn't scare you off?"

After breakfast he set off for a run. He had thought of looking in on a few sessions at a landscape designer's exhibition mentioned in a brochure, but decided that he would not be able to sit still, even through a talk on local trends. From what he'd seen, it seemed they went in for mostly jungle here, in any small corner not filled with buildings. A chaos of fragrant trees and exotic flowering plants fell over each other in tiny spaces set off with wrought-iron fences. Front yards of terrace houses, like cemetery plots, were caged rectangles of figs, tree ferns, windmill palms, and flowering hibiscus. Clusters of tilted palms looked like faded barber poles that had somehow exploded into green bouquets at the top. Today this bright sunny playground for adults was not the paradise it had been. With Charlotte's defection he felt the oppressive weight of failure without knowing what he might have done to stop her.

Research done at home had brought no Sydney gardens to his attention, though he might have visited Kennerton Green if it weren't a two-hour drive out of town. That it was on a road called Bong Bong in a town called Mittagong was almost reason enough to rent a car, but he was not eager to see an entirely blue-and-white garden of silver birches and Louisiana iris.

At the foot of Victoria Street he counted aloud the 113 steps down the escarpment to Harry's Café de Wheels, where tourists were placing their orders at the closest thing to a chip wagon he'd seen in this city. Pies 'n' Peas instead of poutine. He ran along the curve of Wooloomoolloo Bay past the docked warships and up the narrow concrete stairs to the park. The Botanic Gardens. Already he knew why he hadn't seen others running here, why he should restrict his runs to the relative cool of the evenings. Down a curving walkway through the palms, and past the flowering shrubs and the little restaurant , to cross through a host of ibises poking their crooked beaks into the grass. A little cooler here, along the seawall towards the clamshell roofs of the Opera House. At Circular Quay he stopped to have flowers wired to Holly Fitzgerald.

He returned by way of a long street that sloped up to a gigantic Coca-Cola sign high on the side of a building, then started down towards their little hotel, past the row of cars and vans with their signs. MUST SELL TODAY. The $1,200 in one window had been crossed out and replaced by $1,100; then that crossed out as well and $900 scribbled beneath it. Two pairs of bare feet protruded through the rear window of a mud-covered, dented station wagon. You imagined plane after plane taking off without these children while they pleaded for funds. Were their fathers somewhere going mad with worry?

According to Stanley, this street, now a marketplace for abused cars, had been the scene of violence twenty years ago when a citizens' uprising stopped developers from erecting office towers where these terraced houses stood. One of their supporters, a wealthy socialite, had been murdered, presumably for betraying her class.

To his left, a youth darted inside the pawnshop. GRACE'S MONEY LENT. Steel bars protected the window display. Musical instruments, cameras, sound systems. He came out again, almost immediately, to stand against the wall. Lost his nerve about something. There were beads of sweat on his forehead.

"You all right?" The boy may have been in his early twenties. Like many of the others on this street, he was barefoot, barechested as well – his shirt sleeves knotted around his neck. The bleached-white hair was familiar.

He looked at Sonny Aalto a moment, his nervous eyes an unusual shock of blue. Sonny tried to think what gem they suggested. But the boy turned away, trying to keep from sight whatever he had in his hand. Something black. A camera with a telephoto lens attached.

"That camera." Even as one part of Sonny's brain was trying to come to grips with the camera – a Minolta Maxxum 5000i and a Magnicon lens – another part was recognizing the zebra-striped Toyota LandCruiser parked at the curb.

He should not have shown alarm.

"I didn't –" the youth began, then leapt for his truck, fumbling and dropping the camera to the pavement as he did so. He yanked open the door, ducked inside, and, even as Sonny tried to open the door himself, drove off.

To yell "Stop him!" meant nothing here. Youths turned to look but didn't otherwise move. He thought of running up to the Cross for a police cruiser but instead picked up Charlotte's camera and carried it in his arms down the street like a run-over pet. Scratched, but nothing broken that he could see. Down past the row of battered vehicles he walked, and through the little clusters of languid backpackers. He passed by the steamy laundry and the restored houses a socialite had been murdered for protecting until he came to the familiar pink hibiscus outside the little hotel that was, for the time being, his home.

Stanley refused to believe the camera thief had dragged Charlotte into an alley and murdered her. "You frightened him," he said, when Sonny had described the boy. "He's a familiar sight around here. If he hasn't shot through to the bush, he'll be in Manly. I'm told that's where he goes when he isn't up at the Cross."

"Is he dangerous?"

Stanley made a doubting face. "Harmless, I would say. He's a sullen kind of loner, slinks around. My guess is, if he's silly enough to pawn the camera on this street he probably hasn't the sense to leave town."

Poor Stanley then discovered the excitement had felled him. "All my fault," he said, lowering himself to the nearest chair.

"What do you mean, your fault? You know him?"

Stanley closed his eyes and sighed. When he opened them again they were large and damp, hoping for mercy. "A little, yes. I called your daughter a cab, as she requested, but it didn't show up. She was afraid she would miss her plane. I saw the boy loung-ing across the street and called him over."

He took the camera with him on the harbour ferry to Manly, where he plunged into the crowd heading down the Corso towards the beach. Why had Stanley thought the boy could be found in this horde? Most of these people were young, more than half of them male. He ought to have phoned the police instead of coming here. Never mind the boy, the urgency was to find out what had happened to Charlotte.

Along the esplanade he found a space on a slatted bench where he could look out upon a multitude of bodies. Some were prostrate on the sand. A few rode the modest surf. A loudspeaker warned against a strong current, swimmers must stay between the red and yellow flags. One of these swimmers laboured from one side of the designated area to the other, and turned to start back again.

He couldn't imagine why he had brought her camera with him. Had he thought it would recognize the thief and start buzzing? Possibly he had the instincts of a spy. The telephoto lens could act like binoculars while he appeared to be one more camera-happy tourist amongst the many. With his eye pressed to the viewfinder, he twisted the lens to bring the houses on the southern headland a little closer. At the command of a finger's lightest pressure, a humming engine would bring that white house and that rocky outcropping into clearer focus, a green light would tell Charlotte to go ahead and do what she had to do. If what she saw was not quite what she wanted the world to look like, an invisible com-puter card would compensate.

The shortcomings would not be her own. She'd claimed to see things with frightening clarity. He, on the other hand, had never had any such dominion over the external world. He had thrown away his Brownie box at the age of ten, disappointed by its habit of reducing mountains to mere hills and pushing houses to the far side of vast empty fields.

He believed he might have dreamed of this bay at some time, and of Warren and Charlotte in it. Not the adult Charlotte, and not the Warren who had opened the craft shop, but the young children he'd lost when they'd gone off to Ottawa with their mother. In the dream it was the sea and not the East that swallowed them. Sonny Aalto saw them swimming amongst the seaweed, sporting with dolphins, riding the backs of killer whales. When they appeared above the waves they called out, begging him to join them. But his limbs refused to move. They smiled sadly then, as though with pity for his cowardice, and sank beneath the surface to swim away.

As though to mock him, a man and small boy chased one another on the sand. Both were sunken-chested, with little protruding bellies and long, sloppy bathing trunks. The boy was faster – ran circles around the short-legged father, who trotted like a dainty show pony with his head thrown back. The boy circled around, snuck up behind, and leapt on his father's back. They fell, laughing, and rolled over, and were up on their feet again to go plunging into the surf. The boy came back again and again; the father would pause, breathing hard with both hands on his knees, then set off, laughing, in a kind of endless arabesque race with his son. There was no point to any of it that Sonny could see, beyond the obvious animal pleasure both took in the exercise.

The swimmer who'd been crossing and recrossing the bay had started in towards shore. He walked up out of the water wearing a pair of grey corduroy trousers cut off high on his thighs and passed unseeing between the father and son, who'd paused to catch their breath. When he stood up on the sea wall and started along it, Sonny felt a jolt of recognition. With the zoom, he brought him closer, saw the pointed face, the ribs in his narrow chest, the cords in his throat. Dark hairs descended from his navel. He stepped down off the sea wall and walked across the pavement, moving slowly, gracefully, as though pulling his limbs through water. Then he passed along the row of palms, gathered up a red cotton shirt off a bench, and wrapped its sleeves around his neck. When Sonny lowered the camera and stood to go after him he had disappeared into the crush of bodies pouring into the Corso.

He hadn't thought to snap a picture for the police.

The police, he learned when he returned to the hotel, had given Stanley sympathy but little encouragement. No promise, yet, of help. If the young woman hadn't turned up by tomorrow he was to call again. Had he checked with the bus depot, the trains, the planes?

"I have only just begun," Stanley reported. "I had no idea there were so many airlines."

Sonny's father came out of the lounge room with a magazine in his hand. "You'll probably find her where there's trouble brewing," he said. "If I thought there was any timber in this country I'd look for an anti-logging protest."

"Well, there is!" indignant Stanley said. "You wouldn't see timber in Sydney, would you." He closed his eyes and thought hard. Then he jerked with sudden insight. "There is a priest in the papers who insists that logging is a sin. 'Destroying the beautiful images of God.'" He fluttered his lashes at the notion, then gasped at a second inspiration. "Protesters this week in Melbourne! The cast of *Neighbours* has been protesting the export of wood chips. A rugby union star has been hired by the other side."

"A four-by-four with zebra stripes must be well-enough known around here," Sonny said. "I'll go up and ask at the Cross."

"Not until you've had coffee," Stanley said, placing cups and saucers on the table. "I was about to pause for smoko myself. I've all these fresh croissants."

The Cross in daylight was not too different from the Cross at night. Prostitutes stood against the walls, men in white shirts invited you inside, men and women slept or lounged on benches, drunks staggered across the street oblivious to the traffic, which, fortunately, moved at a crawl. Occasionally a police car crept by. Crowds of tourists were out to witness depravity in daylight safety.

At one end of the little concrete park, the walls of the Fountain Café were open, its waitresses rushing out to serve customers in their little corral of umbrella tables.

The waitress with the Spanish accent did not know the youth Sonny described. Nor did the blonde waitress with the Swedish accent know anyone with a zebra-striped truck. In the magazine shop the clerk just shook his head – "too busy, mate." The heavy young woman behind an ice cream counter made an effort to look as though she were thinking. But, "No," she said. "Don't know him. You see how many blokes go by here every minute."

"But this is someone who spends a lot of time around here."

"Maybe he's a stripper," she said, and laughed. "I wouldn't know him in his clothes."

Defeated, he sat on a bench near the fountain to watch for a while as people passed by. He couldn't imagine what he thought he was doing here. He couldn't imagine what else he might have been doing. An elderly woman at the next bench smiled when he looked her way, and tilted her head to acknowledge him. She held a shopping bag on her lap. "Lovely, innit?" she said. He nodded agreement, though he had no idea what she thought was lovely. Surely not this concrete square with its pigeons and down-and-outs, most of whom looked as though they'd spent their food money on drugs.

A youth in T-shirt and jeans caught his eye and veered off course to stand at the end of his bench, though gazing nonchalantly away. "You looking for a boy?" he said. A conspirator's tone.

"I am," Sonny said. Maybe one of the waitresses had pointed him out. "You know the driver of a striped Toyota truck?"

The youth scowled. "Forget *him*," he said. "I've got a room down the block."

Sonny felt his face heat up. "I'm sorry. I misunderstood. I had something else in mind."

"Fuck you, then," the boy said, already moving off.

On the neighbouring bench the elderly woman smiled at Sonny Aalto and shook her head. "Diseased!" she cried. "All of them! Riddled with plague!" A flock of pigeons lifted from the concrete across the square and flew over to alight at her feet. She had scattered crumbs and seeds, he saw, or someone had before her.

He would have to go back and see if Stanley had made progress with the airlines. Forget the camera thief. He didn't need to find the camera thief if some airline could confirm that Charlotte had been delivered safely somewhere.

He would never know if the boy prostitute had sent him over or if one of the waitresses or clerks had alerted him. The owner of the battered LandCruiser materialized suddenly at his elbow, sitting on the bench just as Sonny was about to vacate it. The boy threw himself back and propped one bare foot on a knee, then removed it and leaned forward with his hands between his knees. "Look," he said, "I know I didn't have no business pawning that camera – orright? But I only thought about it, I didn't do it."

Sonny resisted an urge to grab hold. There was nothing he could grab but naked flesh, which didn't seem a good idea in a place like this. "The camera is not the point. What happened to your passenger is. How do I know you didn't leave her in a ditch?"

His dark beard was perhaps a day or two old, or purposely shaved in a manner that made him appear unshaved. A small gold stud glittered in his earlobe. A tiny hole had been punched through the side of his nose – another stud or a ring had been removed. Sonny's insides cringed from the piercing tool. The white hair, this close, had a yellow tinge to it.

"I took her to the friggin' airport! You can ask whoever checked her in – orright? Would I park my arse on this bench if I'd strangled her? The only thing I got to apologize for is the camera."

"I can't imagine her giving it to you willingly."

The boy looked at the filthy concrete between his feet. "She left it behind in me truck." He hadn't yet looked Sonny in the eye. A miniature tattoo on the back of his shoulder might have been a flower, or some symbolic knot.

"She's a photographer," Sonny said. "She wouldn't leave a camera in a stranger's truck."

"There's a better one in her bag, you'd know that." He spoke as though addressing the fountain, where water sprayed from an elevated sphere. "She took the Minolta out for some buildings she fancied and didn't put it back. At the airport she ran off in a hurry and forgot it – orright? I reckoned there wasn't no harm in turning it in for some cash."

"Look," Sonny said. "Tell me where she was going. I can call and make sure. What airline, at least."

The boy was silent, watching two large gulls bully their way to the front of the crowd of pigeons, wanting all the crumbs and seeds for themselves.

"It might be easier than explaining to the police."

When the boy sighed, his skinny rib cage briefly swelled. "I don't know what friggin' airline," he said. "I just dropped her off and left, didn't I." He leaned forward and pressed both hands to his knees, presumably to help him think. The fingers of the nearer hand were long, though the nails were not clean. There were no nails at all on the other hand. The fingers had been cut off at a straight-line angle that left the index finger close to whole and the little finger almost non-existent. You couldn't imagine this fellow at a table saw. You might imagine someone with a cleaver.

Then he slapped both hands decisively on his naked thighs. "Orright, I lied – orright? I'm a bloody boofhead, aren't I." He slapped his thighs again. "I shoulda taken the friggin' camera to yiz like she told me to, but I reckoned I could get some cash for me tea instead. You wouldn't know until y' join her up there in the bloody bush."

"Hold it. She told you to bring the camera to me?"

"You could use it, she said. When I told her why I've been loitering outside your hotel she said yiz could use it on the drive. I'm a friggin' nong, I shoulda done what she said!" This time he drummed a fist on his thigh.

Sonny drew in a deep impatient breath. "You weren't hanging around just to sell your truck?"

"Just tryin' to decide if I'd do what me old lady asked me – orright?"

"Which was?"

"Go up to the friggin' door? Tell yiz I'm yer driver? Hired to take yiz all the way to Mistake Creek."

Sonny's laugh was involuntary. "I don't think so!"

Of course he'd begun to suspect something like this. The quick involuntary denial was for the whole confusing route it had taken to get here.

"Why would anyone hire you to drive?"

"Old lady from Kalevan Station sometimes helps me mum. I reckon she thinks it's time I went home for a visit. I get paid when I get yiz there. You turn me away you're dooming me to a life of crime, you seen that for yourself – orright?" He looked directly at Sonny Aalto for the first time now, innocent as any small child: My fate is in your hands.

"Also," he added, as if this were an inconsequential postscript, "the LandCruiser int exactly mine. It belongs to the old woman."

"At Kalevan Station?"

The boy nodded.

"You stole it."

"Naow!" The boy reared back, offended. "She lent it to me mum for a week or two. It was there when I went home for Christmas so I borrowed it to bring m'self back here."

"Christmas was ten months ago." The boy had stolen the Toyota from both Sonny's mother and his own.

"I meant the Christmas before that. She didn't send the cops so I reckoned she didn't mind. Now she wants it back – orright? You and me are supposed to take it to her." He leaned forward and shook his head as though this were a terrible burden. "I hate it out there. But if I don't do what she says she'll have the friggin' cops down me friggin' bloody neck."

Before Sonny could think what he could do about this, a sudden explosion occurred amongst the squabbling pigeons and gulls, a convulsion of wings and indignant shrieks as feathered bodies flew up in all directions. The elderly woman on the neighbouring bench leapt to her feet, spilling her shopping bag to the pavement. "Oh dear!" Watery grey globs slid down her forehead and over her face. She fumbled blindly in her purse and brought out a small lace handkerchief to mop up the mess, starting with her lips, getting it away from her mouth.

Anyone could see that one dainty hanky would not be enough. Sonny stood up and pushed a hand into his own pocket. But the boy was faster. He leapt to his feet, hauling a blue polka-dotted handkerchief from his cut-off corduroys, and crossed the space of concrete to offer it. Too slow to be of any help, Sonny sat again on his bench, certain the gull had meant the mess for him.

"Oh, but you must go with him!" Stanley clasped his hands together high on his chest, delighted by the latest turn of events. He'd been waiting near the door, led Sonny into the little front lounge where leather chairs and piles of magazines reminded you of a dentist's waiting room. "You would be giving him a chance, don't you see. To redeem himself. I am confident he will be grateful."

The old man appeared in the doorway. His colour had improved, his eyes were clear. He looked much healthier now than when they'd arrived. "Toyota LandCruiser. Nineteen ninety-one or two." To show that he'd heard.

"He's probably a drug addict," Sonny said.

"I don't think so," Stanley said. "At least not any more. He wouldn't be walking around with his shirt off if his arms were riddled with needle tracks."

The old man said, "I wouldn't mind seeing some of this country from the road. Better than one of them little planes."

He believed that small planes went down every day of the week. He'd also refused the bus. Too cramped. He might have gone along if they'd rented a car, but he was sure that Sonny would get them lost. "It'll be better with someone who knows the country. Stanley here's our witness – if anything happens it's Viira Whatsername's fault."

"This kid is a thief," Sonny said. "He admitted as much. We'd be riding in a stolen vehicle."

Timo Aalto's disgust was for Stanley's benefit. "My son has got so used to travelling first-class he's forgotten the pleasure in being poor. Rent a wheelchair. Shove me in the back, you'll hardly know I'm there." Since coming into the room, he'd been stirring a small oval rug with the end of his wooden leg.

"So you say," Sonny said. "You've never been that easy to ignore before."

"There'll be air conditioning," Stanley said. "I'm fairly certain there'll be air conditioning. A comfortable ride."

"You think all those dents were there before he stole it?" Sonny said. "He's probably rolled it over any number of times. We'll end up at the bottom of some gully." He was beginning to feel a bit disgusted with himself. Stanley would think him a *whinger*.

"Put it this way," his father said. "You dragged me across the Pacific to put off carrying me on your lazy back to somewhere. Why would you complain about riding in a Toyota LandCruiser instead?" He laughed. "You wouldn't want to report to Dora Mitchell that me and the boy went off without you."

Sonny knew his smile was the grim smile of the defeated. "If we go anywhere in that Toyota, I can tell you this – it'll be me behind the wheel."

By late afternoon the landscape had begun to level out – a gentle rise and fall, an expanse of rust-coloured dirt, and a scattering of tortured-looking eucalyptus trees. "Scrub," the boy called this, disdain in his voice. Occasionally, where you'd expect a bridge, the road merely dipped to cross a riverbed. White stakes, marked off in metres, were there to show how much water flowed over the road. So far, they had not seen a trickle.

The Blue Mountains had provided constant change through a couple of mid-morning hours – moments of possible danger, spectacular views of sudden bluffs dropping away at their side. Since then, the world had ironed itself out, the horizon now receding at precisely the speed of the LandCruiser. The boy assured them they were making progress, but with the sun travelling in the wrong direction across the wrong half of the sky you could easily be confused.

You also could not be sure he would tell you the truth. A thief, why not a liar as well? Mingary Booligal was what he'd said his name was. He'd invited them to call him Gary, like his mates at the Cross. But Sonny had noticed a Booligal on the map and suspected a Mingary as well if he looked long enough. Though Booligal sounded vaguely native, it was unlikely the boy had Aboriginal blood. He was pale. His face was narrow, his features pointed. His slightly slanted eyes gave him an air of permanent suspicion.

Though he'd permitted Aalto to drive, he wasn't pleased about it. He sat over against the door, a plastic water bottle leaning into his crotch, and occasionally a twisted joint smouldering in the cup of his hand. With his angled finger stubs he adjusted the radio so he could listen to Australians singing American country songs.

He resented the air conditioner. Rather than put on a shirt, he would tolerate the cold air for a while, then turn it off. "Friggin' Eskimos." They opened the windows, but the air, seasoned with the medicinal smell of eucalyptus, was blast-furnace hot. They couldn't rest their elbows on the door without getting a burn off the metal. Eventually Sonny turned the air conditioning on again. "That heat's not good for my father."

His father seemed interested mainly in cataloguing everything. "Magpies in that tree," he said. He sat behind the boy, with an open field guide on his lap. On the floor was a plastic oil container, its top sawed off, so he wouldn't have to spit into wind. A few paperbacks, bought in a second-hand shop near the Cross, were stacked beside him on the seat. The rear space was filled with their luggage, the folded wheelchair, and cartons of beer cans stacked within easy reach. XXXX stubbies. Beer was not on the doctor's list but his father had promised there would be nothing stronger. "Hopbush there, I think."

If someone were to ask what Sonny Aalto hoped to gain from this journey he was no longer sure of an answer. *Blame Viira!* had become his father's war cry, but had they come to the far side of the globe just to confront an old woman? When the men of *Kalevala* sailed north to "the dark Northland / the man-eating, the / fellow-drowning place," they intended to liberate the Sampo when they got there. But did they know what the Sampo was? He'd tried to get his father's opinion once, but the old man, who read the Russians, his Plutarch, and some of Shakespeare, cared nothing for Finnish legends.

Scholars had not decided what the Sampo was. An idol, a treasure chest, a stolen Byzantine mint, a list of tasks for a suitor to undertake? It was something created

From a swan's quill tip
a barren cow's milk
a small barley grain
a summer ewe's down . . .

and yet capable of sending roots nine fathoms into the earth
when Lemminkäinen tried to lift it in his arms. Sonny had always
assumed that the men themselves knew what it was they were
after, but now he was not so sure. It could be anything stolen, he
supposed, so long as it was important enough to retrieve, though
it was unlikely that Elias Lönnrot had a logger's battered lunch
bucket in mind, or someone's mother.

Because she owned a sheep station, he imagined her riding
horses, fixing fences, shearing sheep between her knees. He also
saw her welcoming high society to her door. Weren't the wealthy
outback families called "squattocracy" for grabbing up the best
and largest portions of the landscape and making their fortunes
early? She was probably rich, an outdoor type of healthy woman,
but no doubt a poor excuse for a mother to her second family –
though at least she hadn't abandoned them. Vague images from
The Thorn Birds occurred, but he could not recall who had played
the matriarch on that giant ranch. What else did he have to go
on? Australian movies were about schoolgirls disappearing from
picnics, or aunts fighting over an orphaned boy until one of them
drowned in Sydney Harbour. He doubted that these would tell
him anything about his mother's life.

It certainly wasn't to shoot a pig that he was going. The
weekend excursions of Errol's friends had amused but not excited
him – except, possibly, in some dim adolescent corner of his brain.
The thought of killing a wild pig, however dangerous and dramatic this might be, had little appeal. Yet he imagined it waiting
for him, as *Il Porcellino* had been waiting for him at Butchart
Gardens, and again outside the Sydney hospital. This dark,
bristly, foul-smelling beast had come snorting and grunting out
from some dark cave of his dreams to trot across his inner field of

vision, turning a tiny malevolent eye his way and daring him to try something. He didn't know what "something" was but sensed it was inevitable.

Maybe the only reason for this journey was the simplest: curiosity about his mother and a need to avoid Cape Scott. To avoid Cape Scott and at the same time hope that an adventure might kindle in his father some interest in staying alive as long as he had that option.

A battered and dusty black LandCruiser, much older than theirs, caught up and passed them. The round faces belonged to Aborigines – matte-black skin and woollen toques. A sign on the rear bumper said, "BOUND FOR GLORY." Probably there was a town named Glory somewhere. Or a reserve, if reserves were what they had in this country. Or maybe they were missionaries to their own people

"Just dumped their dots and squiggles at the city galleries," the boy said. "Goin' home with pockets full of money for the grog."

"Artists?" Sonny said.

"Scribble on a piece of bark, smear the walls of caves – Neanderthal graffiti! People overseas can't tell."

"Wild melons," Sonny's father said. Alongside the road dozens of small green balls were connected to one another by wandering leafy vines.

"They claim all this?" Sonny said.

"Yeh," the boy said. "Every speck of dust and wombat shit is friggin' sacred, i'n'it? Step out and get a spear through your throat."

Sonny doubted this would happen but did not protest.

"They c'n have it," the boy said.

"Yea, though we drive through the Valley of the Shadow!" his father said. "That's a wedge-tailed eagle back there. Feeding on something dead."

They were nearing the Queensland border when a tire blew. The rear end dropped. Shocked metal grunted, and then squealed along the pavement. Sonny pumped the brake and hung onto the wheel while they went off the road, scraped through low grey bushes, and came to a shuddering stop in the cinnamon-coloured dirt of the shoulder.

"Christ," his father said. "I thought we'd been shot!" His eyes were wide. Mostly, Sonny thought, with pleasure.

Sonny and the boy got out to view the damage. Shredded rubber and a shiny wheel rim rested on the crumbling edge of pavement. The boy cursed, and looked one way and then the other down the road. Nothing in either direction. Then he started walking back in the direction of Sydney. Maybe he was heading all the long way home on foot. But after twenty-five or thirty metres he stopped, bent over, and reached to pick something off the tarmac. "Nails," he said when he returned. He held one in his open hand. A short nail with a wide flat head, the kind you used for drywall. "Dozens of them," he said. "Maybe they didn't bring their spears."

A short way off in the rusty dirt the body of a gutted sedan sat with its nose up a scrawny tree. It was the third or fourth abandoned vehicle today. Had they all begun with a blowout? Sonny wondered if the picked-clean bones of passengers were inside. Dingoes were probably watching them now, anticipating lunch. Sun broiled the silent world from a huge enamelled sky.

The map had warned them. Places had not been given names like Mount Despair and Mount Misery without reason. You started to believe that people really had disappeared out here. It was a habit of Australian historical figures to set off into the interior and never return. This was what Errol had told him. This was how you became famous in this country.

Together, they helped the old man down out of the truck. Sonny led him over to the striped shadows of a scraggly bush – the closest you could come to anything called shade. Then he went back and got his father's baseball cap off the seat and put it on the old man's head. "Doctor's orders." Timo Aalto's skin was to be kept from the sun.

"Myall," the old man said, about the shrub at his back. He read this from his book: "The shape of a half-opened umbrella."

"I hate the bloody bush," the boy said.

"It seems the bush feels the same about you," Sonny said. "You have a jack?" It looked as though he would have to be the adult.

"Somewhere." Judging by the vague look on the boy's face, "somewhere" could be in another state.

"And a spare?"

A jack was eventually located, but not until the boy had removed some of their luggage and placed it in the shade-stripes of a second scraggly bush. A spare tire was found as well, tucked under the rear bumper. The boy released it and stood to watch it bounce and wobble down the pavement and into the soft dirt. Sonny went after it and rolled it back. This was an old tire, almost denuded of tread. Worn along the inner edge as well. He couldn't even be sure it was the same size as the others.

The boy had set the jack behind the wheel rim and stood back. Since it was clear he had no idea what to do next, Sonny got down on his knees and started cranking.

"What happened to the spare that belongs to the truck?"

"One of me mates needed it, for a drive around Australia."

"And he hasn't come back?"

"Not coming – orright? He met a bloke in Perth."

Sonny went on to change the tire, skinning his knuckles and mixing his sticky blood with the dirt and grease on his fingers. The boy stood by with his hands in his armpits and waited.

"How long would you be here if you didn't have someone to change it for you?"

"I wouldn't *be* here, would I? I'd be in Sydney living me life without you two old nongs from the friggin' Arctic."

Sonny tried to laugh this off – *nongs?* – but the skinned knuckles and the irritating sweat in his eyes didn't make it easy. Before tossing the jack inside he swung it against the back corner of the truck, adding one more dent to the others.

"Whoa!" The boy yelped, as though he'd felt the blow himself.

Sweat ran down from Sonny's hair and into his eyes. Once they'd helped his father up into the back seat, he stripped off the pale blue dress shirt he'd worn open and loose, filthy now with grease and dust and the blood from his hands. In this heat, clothing was one more source of irritation. He balled it up in his fist and prepared to toss it into the back of the truck with the jack. But, seeing the boy's amusement, and struck by a wave of exasperation for this whole stupid business, he threw the shirt into the scrub instead. It snagged on a naked bush for a moment, then dropped to the ground.

The boy laughed. He wore nothing himself but a pair of shorts. "Next time you see that shirt some blackfella will be wearin' it to a dance." He reached into the truck and removed his tin of hand-rolled joints from the glove compartment. After selecting a thin, crooked tube of twisted paper, he closed the lid and returned the tin. Then he held a match to the hairy end.

Sonny turned up the bottom of his damp T-shirt to mop his face. Then he walked back down the pavement and picked up all the scattered nails he could find, and tossed them into the scrub. Their "Gary" would have left them on the road. This was beginning to feel like a punishment for something. Or a test. Did Viira Hawkins know what sort of travelling companion she'd saddled him with? Just to get her battered Toyota back.

"Your friend in Perth take anything else we should know about?" he said.

They were back on the road and moving again, a hot breeze blowing in the opened windows.

"I'm asleep," the boy said, though he wasn't. He hadn't even closed his eyes. "I can't hear you. Wake me when we get to some place where there's better company."

They said very little after that. All three pairs of eyes watched the pavement for a fresh scattering of nails. The door to the glove compartment had begun to rattle. Sonny's rolled-down window clattered inside the bottom half of the door. You didn't want to think what kind of treatment this truck had endured since it came to the city. Would his mother recognize her vehicle when she got it back? No doubt the boy had painted the stripes himself, and was responsible for the dents.

For a while it seemed they were travelling through a slaughter-house of sorts. The windshield had been thickly peppered with the bodies of flying insects for some time, but now they passed the swollen carcasses of kangaroos and wallabies and cattle alongside the road, their stiff legs pointing at sky like a spilled truckload of peculiar tables. Sonny noticed a discomfiting amount of exploded rubber scattered over the pavement. Abandoned vehicles sat half-hidden amongst the bushes growing in dry riverbeds, behind signs that said ROADS SUBJECT TO FLOODING. INDICATORS SHOW DEPTH.

The dusty black LandCruiser passed them again, dark round faces observing them without interest. Sonny's greased and bloodied shirt flapped from the aerial. Was it a justified reprimand for his abuse of their ancestral land, or merely flaunted booty?

"How'd they get behind us?" the boy said. No one mentioned the shirt. "There's no way they could get behind us again out here."

"I wonder what's down that side road there," his father said.

Two rutted car tracks curved across the sandy earth and disappeared into scrub. A piece of cardboard leaned against a mailbox post, awkward letters spelling out *LORETTA ANNE 8 lb 5 oz!*

"You bring pictures of your kids?" his father said. "To show your ma?"

"Friggin' fuck!" the boy said. "Did yiz put the luggage back in?"

Sonny braked, and pulled to the side of the road. "You didn't?" He'd assumed the boy had fetched them while he was picking up the nails.

The boy said nothing. The old man said nothing. Sonny got out and opened a back door. The jack was where he had tossed it, lying across the boy's rolled-up sleeping bag. His father's bag was where it had been from the beginning. His own and the boy's weren't there.

It would take too long to go back, on this bald tire. By the time they had come to a town and replaced the tire, the luggage would be even farther behind. He supposed that where there was a service station there'd be police who could be asked to look out

for it, and send it on. Of course the dusty LandCruiser flying his
shirt could have their bags stored in the back. If someone wore
his shirt to a dance, as the boy had predicted, they would have
new underwear and socks to wear as well, and aftershave.

The important thing now was to get rid of this fellow before he
brought them more bad luck.

"I brought mine," his father said, once they were moving again.

"What use is your luggage to me?"

"Pictures!" his father shouted back.

"Of what?" Sonny said. "Your collapsing house?"

"Warren. Charlotte. Who else?"

Sonny turned to study the old man's face. His father glared
back. Judith Buckle must have sent them. Grandparents looking
out for one another.

Eventually, they began to see fences, a few scattered buildings,
some evidence of irrigation. The sign "PED AHEAD" was presumably meant to warn of a zebra crosswalk at an intersection.

The young woman attendant who filled their tank regretted that
the repair shop was closed. The same would be true of the Ampol,
she said, and gave them the home address of a mechanic who
might be willing to sell them a tire. But the mechanic answered
the boy's knock with his plate in his hand, and didn't stop eating
while they talked.

Sonny raised Charlotte's camera to bring the man's face closer
with the zoom. What did a person look like who lived in a town
like this? Bald, he saw. In need of a shave. Grey hair exploded
from above his greasy undershirt. Tank top. Singlet, they called it
here. His shorts were smeared with black grease, as were his bare
knees and the fronts of his thighs.

A woman appeared in the window, barely more than a shadow
at the back of the room. Listening. There was a small electric
shock when he saw that it was Charlotte. But the woman moved
out of sight and reappeared in the doorway at the mechanic's
shoulder. Not Charlotte. You couldn't imagine Charlotte listening

with her mouth open, scratching at her arm. He put the camera on the floor at his feet. His anger and the heat between them must have triggered some kind of hallucination.

"Judith Buckle sent you pictures?" He turned to look at his father. All windows were open but the heat inside was intense. Both of their faces were wet.

The old man looked up from his guidebook. "Warren sends them. Charlotte used to. In their letters. What did you think – they shouldn't?"

"I'm not sure I believe you," Sonny said. He turned back to face the world outside the filthy windshield. The boy was returning from the house.

The mechanic had refused to sell them anything until morning. There was some television program he had to watch. "No point in looking up another mechanic neither, he said, because the bastards are all addicted to the same friggin' series. *Come in Spinner* or something. We might as well go somewhere for our tea and find a place for the night – orright?"

Inside the small café, the soap in the washroom wasn't strong enough to remove the grease from Sonny's hands. If there'd been a shower, he would have used it. His hair was stiff with sweat and dust, his T-shirt as filthy as the shirt he'd thrown away.

An orange poster above their table advertised something called "Waratah." It didn't appear on the menu. They ordered chicken and chips and studied their hands while they waited. When their meals arrived the old man buried his in ketchup and forked it up, swallowing almost without chewing. At least the beer was cold. The boy ate one long chip at a time, slowly, as though he intended to make the meal last all night. If he'd had a choice, his every gesture implied, he would have dined with better company.

"I haven't seen a place to rent cars," Sonny said.

"Wait till we see about that tire," Timo Aalto said. "Of course we might not live that long if these chips are as lethal as they taste." He pushed his plate away. "Fried in sheep dip."

The boy held up a golden chip. "Safe from all diseases sheep are prone to. Whatever happens tomorrow we won't wake up with foot rot."

This was supposed to be funny, Sonny assumed.

Three enormous trucks were parked outside the window. At the counter, one of the drivers read a newspaper, tabloid-size. "Floods're getting bad up north," he said to his mate. "Says here a bloke in Emerald lost two hundred cattle."

"Let 'em keep it there," the waiter said. "Me arms still ache from humping sandbags last time she come through."

When the truck driver opened out the paper to read the inside pages, Sonny could see the front was devoted to a coloured photo of a farmer in an oilskin coat and wide-brimmed hat crouched over a drowned sheep. Beside it, a lamb lay half-submerged in the milky water. The plundered look on the farmer's face told you sheep were not the floodwater's only victims.

Timo Aalto got up to fetch an abandoned newspaper. *The Australian*. "Yeltsin Rushed to Hospital Over Heart." He read the headline aloud. "Let's hope he didn't damage it too much." He raised the paper high and opened it wide. "Aha. That damn referendum again. Listen to this. 'The tragedy may well be the erosion of one of the world's few truly civilized societies . . .' Whaddaya think of that?" He looked so pleased he might have conceived the civilized society himself.

"You must be getting homesick," Sonny said.

"You see what we have to do to hit the news in this neck of the woods – threaten to fall apart." The old man folded the wide pages back. "Listen to this! 'Canada's Indians vote to retain federal ties.'" He laughed. "'Quebec natives threatening to separate from the separatists!' I guess they figure what's sauce for the goose is sauce for the gander too."

The referendum shared space with other news that Sonny could see for himself. According to *The Australian*, a tribe of lost Indians had been discovered in the Amazon rainforest. Had they

known they were lost? They may have begun as a small group of
travellers – father and son and sullen street kid – heading into
hostile territory in order to find a runaway mum.

Each of the three parked trucks was hauling two trailers, as
long and high as this café. Three tiers of crammed-together sheep
peered out at the world through horizontal slats. The "ROAD
TRAIN" signs on the grilles made it clear that these were not to
be thought of as mere transport trucks. "If we didn't want to wait
for a tire," Timo Aalto said, folding up the newspaper the best
he could and twisting back to put it on the table behind them,
"we could hijack one of them rigs. We wouldn't have to stop to
eat, we could just yank off a leg of mutton to chew on."

It was probably the relief – that they had actually got to somewhere more or less intact. Or it might have been that he was tired
of Sonny's cranky face.

When he opened the door to help his father through, the air
was warm even now in the dark. Two youths were leaning against
the LandCruiser, in a pool of light from a weak street lamp. A
third sat on the hood. They were fourteen or fifteen years old.

"Seen yer truck before," said one of the teens, a tall lad, thin as
a rail, whose hair had been shaved from his bony skull. He looked
at his companions with a smile that was mostly sneer. "When I
was down to the city with me da'." He narrowed his eyes and
pointed a finger at their Gary. "Kings Cross queer."

Sonny's father lowered himself to a bench, grunting when his
rear end settled on wood.

"We'd drive yer truck into the river," one of the others said.
"Only we wouldn't want to get AIDS from touchin' it."

"Yearrrrrr!" The boy on the hood slid off and brushed at the
seat of his pants.

"We're leaving," the boy named Gary said. "No worries."

When he moved towards the driver's door, the bald youth
stepped behind him and put his forearm across his throat, pulling
him back. He drove his knee between his legs.

Sonny was already down the steps. "You fellows can go home, we're just passing through." Before it got worse, you had to pretend you thought this a harmless joke.

"A Yank poofter!" one of the others yelled. He ran at Sonny, half crouched, as though to drive his shoulder into Sonny's chest. But Sonny stepped aside, grabbed the boy's arm and twisted it behind his back. Then he shoved him away, and spun to deal with the bald youth, trying to pry the arm free of Gary's throat.

The bald youth spat in Sonny's face. The boy who had tried to shoulder him came back and shot out one foot, slamming it into his ribs. Then he kicked again, this time in the thigh. Sonny caught the foot and twisted it, but someone – it must have been the third boy – walloped the back of his head. He dropped to the pavement, his face against a scattering of loose crushed gravel. Someone put a foot on his head, to hold him there. "What're we gonna do with 'em?"

"Call yer dad."

"Tell 'im they tried to get us into their truck."

One of the boys giggled. "I'd rather piss on them."

Sonny stared into the gravel. To struggle was to invite more jabs and cuts. Hadn't he learned anything in half a century that could help him overpower a boy who weighed less than a medium-sized dog? Were there no adults in this town? If there were, they were glued, like the mechanic, to their television sets. The truck drivers had not come out to investigate. So here lay Sonny Aalto with a foot on his head, listening to the sounds of a struggle.

Fortunately, the foot's owner possessed a short attention span. He stepped aside to try something else – maybe to get some distance for a decent kick. The moment the foot was lifted Sonny grabbed the ankle and brought the boy to the ground. He stood up quickly, to face the others. Gary was still held from behind but now his shorts were down around his ankles.

Sonny dashed to the back of the LandCruiser and grabbed the tire jack. "Now, get out of here." He came back open-mouthed and roaring at them, swinging wide. He wouldn't think about what he was doing, threatening kids with a length of steel. The hand that held the jack was once again sticky with blood.

Their attackers fled. Sonny tossed the tire jack after them, clanging along the pavement. Then went out to retrieve it, his hair and face and chest as sweaty now as they'd been in the worst of the afternoon heat.

The boy leaned into the opened driver's door, breathing hard. "Let's get outta here."

But the truck drivers had come out to fuss over someone at the foot of the steps. Timo Aalto lay with his face on the gravel much as Sonny's had been, his walking stick over near the road train's huge front tire.

"I seen him topple," said one of the men when Sonny pushed through to crouch at his father's side.

My fault. He should not have taken the old man inside without his wheelchair. There was a pulse in his father's throat but his flesh was pale, his eyes dull and apparently unseeing. "This town got a doctor?"

"Doc Wallace might be sober," said one of the men, though not with much conviction.

"There's a man in trouble here!" Sonny said. "Get somebody! Paramedics. Whatever you've got!"

"Jeeeeez," his father said. He pulled in his hands to push his shoulders up off the ground. "Lost . . . footing's . . . all." His voice was barely strong enough to bear the weight of the words.

"There," said one of the truck drivers. "He'll be right."

The men stepped back. One said, "You 'n' your boyfriend can get him to his feet." Distaste was thick in his throat.

The old man was parchment-pale and shaky. His eyes swam unfocused like those of a week-old infant. Propped up between Sonny and the boy he seemed barely able to move his legs. When they'd got him to the Toyota, he resisted their efforts to lift him in. "No ambulance!"

"This isn't an ambulance," Sonny said. "This is the same damn stupid truck that got us into this mess!"

He thought, *stroke*, *heart attack*, words used everywhere you went that had never meant anything much to him. But his father would not hear of emergency rooms. He asked only for time to catch his breath. He was coming around, or putting on a pretty good show of it. "The lad okay?"

"We'll stay close by for the night – orright?" the boy said. "In case we need to get their doc out of bed. There's a caravan park up ahead, with some cabins."

His father smelled of booze. How could he be drunk from a couple of beers? He leaned closer. This wasn't beer he smelled. "Scotch?"

The old man slapped a hand over his trousers pocket, but didn't do it fast enough. Sonny glimpsed the cap of a silver flask that must have begun to fall out while they were getting him into the truck. His father had probably been sipping from it while he watched the fight. He may have been sneaking quick drinks while they were driving, too, though it was hard for Sonny to believe he hadn't noticed. Hadn't smelled!

"Are you crazy?" He turned to the boy. "You see where he got this?"

The boy shrugged. "Yesterday he came out on the street and shoved money at me. Said he's gonna drop dead anyway, he might as well die happy."

Their cabin was one in a row of several small buildings shaped like railway boxcars, each of them up on posts in a grove of eucalyptus trees. There was no overhang to the roof. Why would there be? You couldn't imagine rain in this place. One small window looked out from either side of the door. The interior was equally modest – a bed, a cot, a table with two chairs, and a tiny bathroom.

Inside, his father stood at the sink to swallow his pills, one from each of two bottles, then removed his dentures and placed them on a chair beside his bed. "If I forget where I put them I'll remember when they bite my arse in the morning." Stripped to his long johns, he pulled back the blankets and more or less rolled onto the bed.

The boy had remained outside. Perhaps he was being discreet. More likely he needed to be alone. To curse or cry or kick the hell out of whatever weeds got into his path – whatever it was you did when you'd been attacked and beaten by country "larrikins" for being who you were. If he didn't come in soon, Sonny supposed he would go out to him.

But first, there was his father. He put his hand to the old man's forehead. "You sure you're okay?" His flesh was cool and clammy. But then, so was his own.

His father swatted the hand away. "Ah hell, I'm just tired." He lay back on the pillow and closed his eyes. "Worn out from all the excitement!" He opened his eyes again and grinned. "You've got to feel sorry for the poor buggers that have to ride on boring air-conditioned buses!"

"You should toss that goddam mickey into the bush." Sonny opened cupboard doors in case breakfast things were provided for a bedtime snack. None were. Not even something you could dismiss as "chook food." There was nothing in the little fridge either. "But it's your business, not mine, if you want to arrive at your wife's place falling-down drunk."

"It's almost empty," his father said, looking away. A little embarrassed, Sonny thought. "It's just my throat gets awfully dry out here."

"Sure," Sonny said.

It was no wonder the old guy was drinking again, when you thought of what he was being dragged through. "We'll turn around and go back first thing in the morning. You can drink yourself to death in Sydney as easy as anywhere."

"No!" The old man's hand reached out to clasp Sonny's wrist, his eyes large with what looked like panic. "I want to see the look on her face." His mouth tried to find the words he wanted. "She'll probably think you're dumping me on her doorstep . . . so she'll have to nurse me through my final days."

For a moment Sonny wondered if this was what his father really hoped for, to see his wife obliged to look after him. He used his handkerchief to wipe away a spot of ketchup at the whiskery corner of the old man's mouth. "She may not even remember you after all this time."

"If you turn back now I'll take off on my own. I'll peg-leg it through this goddam heat, and crawl if I have to, all the way to her door."

Now that the ketchup had drawn attention to his father's beard, it was clear he'd done a piss-poor job of shaving this morning. Patches had been missed. A tuft of white hairs near one ear looked as if it had been neglected for a week. There were any number of small scabs healing where skin had been broken. His father looked like a homeless street-person who shaved with a rusty razor only when the spirit moved him. Since he could see well enough to read, the problem was either impatience or a shaky hand.

Sonny was anxious to shed his torn and dirty clothes. Unfortunately, he would have to put them on again in the morning. He had nothing else. Rinsed out in the sink, underwear and socks would dry overnight in the heat this cabin had stored from the day. If they went on, he would arrive in Mistake Creek half-naked and bleeding, he would meet his mother in rags.

Two new pairs of Lee Cooper jeans were in that suitcase. A copy of *Voltaire's Bastards. John Graham, Convict* with his boarding pass marking his page. There were three new shirts. A $58 bottle of Homme cologne, from the Wolfgang Joop Collection. A new pair of high-top runners, never worn. A hooded raincoat from Pacific Trekking. Fortunately, his passport and Visa card were in the money pouch attached to his belt, down inside his pants.

When his father had begun to snore, the boy came inside with a first-aid kit from the truck and hoarsely offered to apply Vaseline and Band-Aids to the lacerated face. But Sonny laboured over his own face with hot water and a washcloth, cleaning grit from chopped flesh, examining himself in the small square mirror above the sink.

The boy refused the cot. He also refused the cabin floor. He hauled his sleeping bag from the back of the LandCruiser and unrolled it at the foot of a white-barked gum not far from the door. It was impossible to know if they were being punished for something, or if he wanted to nurse his hurt in private. Dogs howled in the distance. Insects screamed in the trees. When Sonny went to the screened door, he could make out the boy's shape propped against the wide white bark, the glow of his joint flaring as he drew on it.

"How was I supposed to know you didn't want him to drink?"

"Doctor's orders," Sonny said. "I didn't think there was any need to tell you. I'm sorry, I guess there was."

"I didn't ask those ratbag sons of bitches to attack me neither. You see why I friggin' hate it out here? You learn how to watch out for yourself in town, you know who to stay clear of. But you get, like, used to yourself, you forget about these bloody bash-up merchants out here in the bush." He paused. The joint flared up for a moment, the boy's eyes briefly visible in the pale light. "Maybe you're wondering if I'm what they said."

This was not a conversation Aalto wished to encourage but he was going to get it anyway. He pushed the screened door open and went out to sit on the narrow step. "I guess I took it for granted. Just as I took it for granted that you're a thief when you have to be, and probably a beggar as well if you need to be a beggar. And God knows what else."

"It's what I do sometimes instead of starving. You got a problem with it?"

"Only if it means more thugs will want to push my face in the gravel."

"Here's my key." He raised an arm, but the key or whatever was in his hand could not be seen. "A room above a shop on Darlinghurst Road. A bed, a sink, and a stack of videos."

"That's okay," Sonny said, one hand raised to discourage more. "I didn't ask for a job description."

Still, there were questions he might have asked. The alleys of Kings Cross, the sleeping drunks, the syringes they warned you about – how did he ever feel safe? Did his parents know about his life? Sonny did not want to think how he'd lost those fingers. The meat cleaver was not so far-fetched after all.

"Look at the sky. Southern Cross is turning in front of me eyes."

It was true that there was something magnificent about the sky, though none of it meant anything to Sonny Aalto. Just random nameless stars, shining with an intensity that seemed hysterical. What had Holly Fitzgerald told him about the black intervals? Nobody knew what they were, they were just part of the landscape of space. Like all the other black spaces that kept you from seeing beyond the apparent borders of life.

He would buy a postcard for her son and tell him about the Southern Cross. Holly would have to read it aloud.

He wished she were here. She could be wishing the same, though of course she would have something to say about the accommodations. As shocked as Dora Mitchell or Judith Buckle, he imagined. Still, you could imagine Holly Fitzgerald making the best of a bad situation, and being one hell of a lot more cheerful about it than he was.

"I'm looking at the Magellanic Clouds," the boy said. "They aren't clouds, they're galaxies – our two closest neighbours. You won't see these at home." He got up from the ground and crossed the space between them, offering his hand-rolled joint.

"Naw," Sonny said. He hadn't smoked since his twenties, not even cigarettes. But the hand he'd raised to wave away the short damp twisted tube of paper-wrapped leaves took hold of it instead. It had been a rough day.

Now that he held it, he wasn't crazy about putting something in his mouth that the boy had put in his. He looked at it cupped in his hands. Embarrassed. It was something he'd never had to think about before.

The boy laughed. "Hey, that's cool, no worries. I'll give ya the shit so you can roll your own."

"That's okay," Sonny said. He breathed deeply of the sweet smoke that curled up from his hand, then handed the joint to the boy. Was his name really Mingary? Sonny hadn't yet said the boy's name aloud.

Whatever his name, he seemed oblivious to Sonny's offence. "You should sleep outside," he said, returning to his white tree. Now that Sonny's eyes had adjusted to the dark he could see the pale uncertain stripes of white gums all along the narrow river.

"Forget it," Sonny said, getting to his feet. "I'll sleep behind the screen, away from the bugs."

"Suit yourself. The two of youse are startin' to get on my tit anyway."

Inside, he lay awake, smelling the scent of marijuana through the window screen and listening to his father's snores. Wondering if they ought to turn back in the morning, whatever his old man said. Wondering how he would convince Timo Aalto to let him shave him. How did other people know when they no longer had any choice but to become their father's father?

Cars could be rented. Small planes could be chartered. Buses might be cramped but at least they'd be safe. Still, his father insisted on going on as they were. He claimed to be his old self again, though Sonny was uncertain what this meant. The boy promised an airfield later today in his mother's town, and a medical clinic if they needed it. He reminded them that the old woman of Kalevan Station expected him to deliver not only her LandCruiser but her overseas guests as well. Sonny began to feel like the parent of two belligerent teenagers. Before agreeing to continue, he'd insisted on new tires and a thorough checkup at one of the service stations in town. He also insisted on driving.

The heat was already more oppressive than yesterday's. The rolled-down windows continued to clatter. The door to the glove compartment rattled. Even though he was behind the wheel again, he knew what the swimmer felt who'd gone beyond the point of no return. He could only hope for a surprise landfall ahead or an intervention of some kind, divine or human.

Jerrod Hawkins would have intervened. When Aalto phoned him during breakfast he'd been horrified to hear what had happened. "My God, what a welcome! Stay where you are, I'll fly down and pick you up. No, wait." Papers rustled, voices muttered. "Shit. I'm sorry. I can't get away until tomorrow. We're in the midst of a trial. I should have made arrangements to fly down to Sydney and drive you myself."

His father had not only recovered, he behaved as though he'd taken command. He insisted on sitting up front in the passenger seat. Sonny and the boy were merely pilot and navigator, ferrying the rejuvenated captain to his destination. Sonny could imagine him having his wheelchair strapped to the roof so that he could scan the horizon and tap commands with his wooden leg. Ahab looking for his whale.

The world was flat and reddish-brown to the extent of human vision, decorated here and there with a gracefully lonely tree. The bodies of kangaroos and wallabies lay beside the road, presumably killed in the night. Some were so flat you could tell they'd been there awhile, their innards eaten out, their bones picked clean, their hides sucked dry by sun. If his father did go hobbling off into this landscape and found what he claimed to want – an invisible death – his body would not be found for years, mummified and flat.

On their right, dirt tracks ran off across country towards a cluster of buildings and trees. The highest thing was a windmill, a water tank standing beside it on narrow legs. Sun glared off metal roofs.

"It wouldn't hurt to take a gander down one of them roads," his father said. "I'm getting a little bored with this one."

Aalto could not imagine lasting very long in this baked hostility. The land looked back at you with a hateful glare. A human presence had barely troubled the surface. The rare house sat high on posts above an expanse of dirt as though ready for flight. The occasional vine clung weakly to a bit of verandah trellis, more by accident, you suspected, than by human design. "People can't have lived out here very long," he said. He meant they'd made little difference.

"Only a century or two," the boy said. Sarcastically, Sonny thought.

"I know somebody who didn't stick it out," Timo Aalto said. "My old man was born here but didn't stay."

"What?" Sonny said. "What do you mean by 'here'?"

"I mean in Queensland," his father said. "His folks left Finland with a bunch of immigrants to start a socialist colony. The *Kalevan Kansa.* Your mother's folks too. Where'd you think they got the name for her ranch?" He squinted into the wind, fumbling at the same time in his shirt pocket for his Copenhagen. "They were hired to build a railway. Lived in tents some place up behind Cairns. But my grandfather got fed up with being treated like a slave and followed Matti Kurikka to *Malcasaari.*"

Malcasaari was Malcolm Island, where Timo Aalto was born. "Not far from Cape Scott," he added unnecessarily. "You heard of that place? One more colony that didn't pan out. My old man moved us out when he come home from the Great War." He tapped Sonny on the arm with his wrist and offered the open Copenhagen, which Sonny rejected with a quick jerk of his head.

He was almost sorry for it, now that the lid was on and the little round container back in his father's shirt. He had no desire to taste what he remembered as bitter, but his father was in an expansive mood. And he was grateful – so long as his father had that stuff in his mouth he wouldn't be sneaking sips from his mickey.

In Queensland the pavement was just wide enough for one vehicle. Road trains forced him over, Sonny dropping his outside tires onto dirt to avoid a collision. Even so, one driver had little choice but to run his heavy tires and three-tiered trailers over a dead kangaroo to avoid forcing them off the road altogether. Bloody bits of flesh sprayed up. The boy cursed, and reached across Sonny's shoulder to turn on his wipers. But the wipers only beat the dust into arcs of pink greasy paste.

He was saying little today. At breakfast, he'd talked a bit about his family. An older sister had married a former pearl diver in Broome. A second sister had started training as a teacher in Adelaide but ran off with a greenie to live in the bush above Townsville. She threw herself in front of the large equipment pushing roads into the rainforest. She was even more of an embarrassment to the family, he said, than the sister who married a Jap. But once they'd got out onto the road, he'd withdrawn into a sullen sort of quiet. Maybe it was only that he hated being demoted to the back seat. In the rear-view mirror, when he didn't know he was being observed, the look on his face seemed to say, "I could tell you what you're looking at but I won't." That endless plain could be the scene of a famous massacre, that lonely house the place where a secessionist movement was formed; they would never know.

The roadside carnage had been increasing as they travelled north. At one point Sonny had to slow down to manoeuvre in and out amongst body parts spread along a hundred metres of pavement. It looked as though half the animal population of the state had tried to cross in the night – the scene of a slaughter. A swollen grey kangaroo lay in the dirt with limbs extended. A cow reclined on its side, its stomach eaten out. Some of the victims were unidentifiable, except as random legs and haunches, squashed midsections, spilled innards scattered and flattened by traffic. One head attached to a pair of shoulders was definitely pig.

"Wild?"

"You get a whiff?" the boy said.

Sonny hadn't smelled it, though the head and shoulders had flashed by below his window. Coarse black hair, a long narrow head, a dark snout, coils of pink and grey innards spilling out from an opened chest. A leg with its pale dainty hoof was several metres farther up the pavement.

Bitumen, the boy called it. Not pavement. Bitchm'n.

"They smell bad? Alive, I mean."

"Yair. I'd rather stick me head up a camel's arse. A smell that leaves a taste – you'd be, like, brushing your teeth for a week. Totally villainous. Eat the clothes off your back."

"'All vines and grasses burnt beneath his breath,'" said Timo Aalto in a singsong voice, obviously quoting, though not necessarily for their benefit.

"What's that supposed to mean?"

"Wild pig, with bristles like spears. According to Ovid. You don't know this tale? Young fellow shows up at a hunting party and falls for this naked beauty. He gets to kill the boar but jealous relatives start a fight and the poor bugger's killed while cutting up the carcass. So he don't get to take the lady home, or the trophy either." The surprise was not that the old man knew these things but that he was showing off. "That mess back there, you can see why a person wouldn't want his carcass lying around for people to stare at."

"They're dead," Sonny said. "They don't care."

"Who says they don't care?" his father said. "That's just our notion of them out there, what we can see. Their own notion of themselves could be different, we don't know what they're thinking."

"What's this? What are you talking about?"

"My old man died a couple of times before he finally kicked the bucket for good, didn't I tell you that? Once on the operating table. He said he got up and left his body behind and walked away. When he looked back from the door he could see the doctors tryin' to bring him back. 'They was hammerin' away at what looked like me to them,' was what he told us afterwards, 'but that wasn't me to *me*.' He said he could've left altogether but decided he mizewell go back, he wanted to finish clearing that field behind the barn.'"

"Bloody hell," the boy said, and dropped back to his seat.

"He did, too. Work was all he cared about. Cleared that field and then went in and laid down and started fading away so slow it killed my mother looking after him."

A sign cautioned: DO NOT OVERTAKE. Evidently the six or seven Aborigines crowded into the dusty black LandCruiser didn't believe the order was meant for them. They passed in the kicked-down roar of a lower gear, the stained blue shirt snapping about the aerial, their happy faces pressed to the windows like undergrads crammed inside a phone booth.

They stopped to fill up with fuel in a tiny hamlet where half a dozen buildings huddled together, their metal roofs blinding in the sun. When Sonny came back from paying in the iron shed, the boy who'd manned the pump was leaning into the driver's-side window chatting with their Kings Cross boy, who'd moved up behind the wheel. This was a lad of perhaps twenty, with long straggly hair, a hint of goatish beard on the tip of his narrow chin. He was naked except for a pair of dirty shorts, every rib as distinct and defined as the slats on a rail fence, one dirty bare foot rubbing up and down on the other instep.

"Sally," the driver said, by way of introduction. He ran a hand affectionately down that washboard chest. When Sally smiled, his upper lip snagged on the single tooth that stood clean and white between dark gaps. "He's going up the track to visit a mate. You can have the wheel back after we drop him off."

"Sally's a hitchhiker?" Sonny said, climbing in to sit beside this Sally in the back seat. "Or is he someone you know?"

"Yeh," the driver said.

Later, when they approached a road-end marked by mailboxes and a cattle grid, the old man started into his theme song again. "Let's see where that one goes."

"The beaut thing about this country is," their driver said, "you can just about see where that one goes without having to leave this one."

"Christ Almighty," his father said. "A person would think you two were union drivers of some scheduled bus. Would it kill you to poke around a bit to see something that isn't out smack against the highway staring back at you?"

"No skin off me arse," the boy said. "Orright, Sal?"

Apparently it was Sally who must be consulted rather than the old man's son. Sally leaned forward and shouted something that might have been "Cherruppin-ya!" Whatever it was, it must have meant, *Go ahead, who cares about the shithead who paid for the petrol.* Without slowing down, the boy swung off the narrow pavement at the first pair of tracks that might be thought of as a road.

Sonny's protests meant nothing. They bounced across a dusty plain in the direction of what could only be more dusty plain. At the first fork in the road his father said, "Turn here, keep right." Why *right*, when it offered nothing different from *left*?

"Haven't you been down enough back roads in your life?" Sonny said. "It feels like my whole childhood was spent down one or another of them."

"When you weren't being worked to death, you mean," his father said. He didn't turn to look at Sonny, he spoke to the road ahead. "Let me tell you something. I only had to mention going for a drive and you were out sitting on the front seat before I'd found my wallet. You held the map, for chrissake. You whined when I started home."

This was probably true. He'd had a private guide to the wonders of nature. There was no telling how much of his adult life had its roots in those journeys. Which was one good reason not to give them too much praise.

"Did you go alone?" he said. "Afterwards, I mean."

"Tommy Reimer came sometimes. There was a year or so I never went nowhere Sunday afternoons without Nora Macken beside me. Whaddaya think of that?"

"Not true! Nora Macken wouldn't cross a street with you."

"Not if someone was looking she wouldn't. But she used to bring her picnic basket down through the bush where nobody could see. She liked to eat potato salad with her feet in a lake. There was a while that tribe of Mackens was so busy raising more of their kind that they forgot they had an old-maid aunt."

"But she's older than you."

"We weren't planning to have a family! I'm talking about a picnic at places she never seen."

When the tracks petered out alongside a dry riverbed, his father instructed the driver to turn back. They found another set of tracks that led them farther west. They came across a calf nudging the swollen body of its dead mother, and nearly hit a pair of kangaroos vaulting blindly one behind the other across in front of the van, leaving the broken-line prints of their springboard tails in the dirt. In this fashion they eventually found themselves turning around in the playground of a tiny isolated school made of raw concrete and corrugated iron, then rattling alongside a gravel riverbed and coming to an abrupt stop at a cattle station gateway whose signs were pointedly hostile to visitors. GO BACK!

A primitive road led them around what the boy referred to as a turkey nest. This was a raised circular dam around a wàter reservoir for livestock, though there wasn't a cow or horse or even a sheep in sight of this singular landmark. In all this blankness it was an extraordinary feature, as the mouth of a volcano might have been, or an ancient circular fortress. They watched it as they approached, as though it might speak, or move.

The engine coughed, cut out for a moment, and caught again. Quailing, possibly, before this peculiar Presence. The boy leaned ahead as though to encourage forward movement.

The engine did not respond to begging. It cut out a second time, then started briefly again before dying altogether. They coasted to a stop, the boy cursing, then pleading with the engine, while grinding away at the starter. He continued this until it began to seem like a form of abuse. "You'll wear the battery down," Sonny said.

The boy turned to give Sonny a look that admitted to knowing less about engines than he did about changing tires. Sonny got out and looked at the engine long enough to determine that the fan belt hadn't broken, the water hose wasn't leaking, and the electrical wires were not hanging loose – the extent of his expertise. Then he returned to his seat and hoped a rest might renew the engine's willingness to co-operate.

"Whose idea was this?" his father said.

"No sense going for help," their driver said. "There's nothing within a three-hour walk."

They were probably the only vehicle on these roads without a radio-phone, it occurred to Sonny now. The few cars and trucks they'd seen had all been sailing under the curved masts of one or two or even three tall aerials. Some had winches mounted on the front bumper, to get themselves out of this sort of mess. Had their Gary pawned these accessories at Grace's Money Lent?

Throwing open the doors made no difference to the heat. Sweat trickled down from beneath Sonny's hair, ran freely down his neck. The boy's bare chest was slick with a gleaming film of sweat.

The boy reached across Timo Aalto and fetched a joint from the glove compartment. Then he got out to open the back door and offer his pal a toke. They muttered words at one another that caused at least one of them to snicker.

"Satisfied?" Sonny said, to his father. He got out of the truck and slammed the door behind him.

"Blame Viira," the old man said through the open window.

"Not this, goddammit! This is nobody's fault but yours. If this is the kind of stupid fix you got into when you were married it's no wonder she left. She probably left me behind because she was scared I'd turn out like you! Sometimes I think I *have* – your stupidity, anyway. Anyone else would have shoved you in a nursing home and left you there."

His father replied to this but Sonny had already walked out onto the dusty earth to put some distance between them.

The sky in the east had taken on the unfriendly purple hue of bruised flesh. Lightning flashed – thin staggering lines down to flat earth. Soon there was a roll of thunder. He imagined Dora Mitchell setting her mouth in a "told you so" manner.

If they died here, it needn't be of dehydration. They could drink the cattle's water from the turkey nest and slowly bake to death. If they sat up to their necks in the pool, this might discourage the dingos and the carrion birds long enough for a farmer to come across their remains. Not that this would please his father, who would probably rather just go down this road and disappear off the face of the earth. In a sense, he already had. They all had.

He took deep breaths to swallow his anger, then returned to stand beside the LandCruiser.

Their driver ducked to address the old man through a window. "You worried?"

"Not him," Sonny said. "He hasn't got the sense to be scared. This man has fought off wild animals with his bare hands. If he hadn't been so busy boozing, and trying to break his neck on those steps, those punks would've wished they'd stayed home. It's amazing what a weapon he has in that wooden leg. Nobody knows this better than I do."

"So all this," the old man said, "all this damn *sandbox* we're stuck in, you say they figure it's sacred – the natives?" His tone suggested he'd been brought here for a lecture and was impatient to hear it. "My son, here, he's thrown away a fortune chasing after such places. You think he's found what he's looking for – sky and dirt and blazing sun?"

"For Christ's sake," Sonny said.

The boy shrugged. "Mumbo-jumbo," he said. "They claim the Rainbow Serpent made it. Ancestors roamed it."

"Gods walked here," Timo Aalto said to Sonny. "Ancestors walked here." To the driver he said, "Heroes too?"

The boy sucked long on his cigarette, held the smoke in his lungs, and tilted up his head to release it. Even then, a shrug was all he gave. Evidently the subject didn't interest him much. His friend Sally giggled.

"Well, it must've told them something about themselves they didn't know," his father said. "Mallee over there." He spat brown juice out his window. His face gleamed with sweat. "A lot of stems instead of a trunk."

"Poisonous?" Sonny said. Sarcastically. This catalogue of meaningless names had become an irritation.

"Trees won't kill yiz," their driver said. "The brown snake will. Spiny-tailed geckos. Spiders. Yellow-faced whip snakes. Myall snakes." He turned to grin at Sonny's father. "You can't see none of them but they can see you."

"Let's hope whoever's coming sees us," Sonny said. "Or is it just a mirage?"

It wasn't a mirage. A dark truck travelled this way beneath a cloud of its own dust. As it drew closer it became a dusty black LandCruiser, and soon the dusty black LandCruiser they'd seen several times before. The shirt was no longer flapping from the aerial. Sonny helped his old man out of the truck. It seemed – he didn't know why – a good idea to abandon ship.

When the truck stopped, four, five, seven grinning black men tumbled out and stood clucking and tssking around the zebra-striped Toyota. Black curls peeked out from dusty toques pulled down almost to their eyes. They ignored the boy's "You reckon you could help us?" but when Sally stepped out from behind the truck they welcomed him with shouts and laughter, and drew him into their huddle. A low rumble of vowels followed.

Then, as though at a signal heard by no one else, they moved as one towards the zebra-striped LandCruiser and surrounded it, and bent to place their hands beneath the body. A collective grunt, a word, and the truck rose from the ground and floated in a wide arc until it was facing the opposite direction and was lowered again to sit on its own new tires. The men stepped back – all but one, who ducked his head beneath the hood and shouted. The engine started – possibly from shock. Sally laughed, slapping his hands together, and did a small loose dance on his skinny legs.

No one spoke while the black LandCruiser raced on down the track, taking Sally with it, and disappeared into its own dispersing cloud of dust. Sonny took the wheel again, and kept the van moving at a speed exceeding anything it had achieved so far on this journey, every nut and bolt enrolled in getting them back to the main road as fast as possible.

With tires once again on bitumen it seemed safe again to speak. "Those were Sal's people?"

The boy shrugged, "They are now," and reached from the back seat to turn on the radio. "Sal lives alone in an ol' shed out beyond everything. He gets adopted a lot."

Someone on the radio was telling the history of cricket in Australia. The first team to go to England in the nineteenth century was made up entirely of Aborigines, the voice asserted. A bit of a shock for those who'd invented the game. The visit had contained no real disasters, except for one unfortunate incident where a boomerang carved the head off a lady spectator.

The boy laughed. Sonny smiled, reluctantly. "That can't be true?"

No answer. The first truly good team of Aussie cricketers to go to England, said the announcer, quite literally caused heart attacks amongst the startled Brits who watched them play. "One titled lord gnawed the handle off his umbrella."

"But do we believe it?" Sonny said, when a male voice had started into a country-and-western song.

The boy grinned, and shrugged. "No worries. You're in Oz – orright? This int your place, you don't *need* to understand."

Beneath a few scraggly trees at the side of the road a half-dozen horses grazed on the dusty grass. Most were a chestnut colour, two were custard-pale. "Brumbies," Gary said. After this much time the boy might as well have a name, even if Sonny didn't believe it was his. "I wanted to be a jackeroo once, long ago. Break me own horse and ride with a kelpie on me lap. *The Man from Snowy River.*" He slapped the seat twice with the heel of his hand.

Timo Aalto had nodded off by the time an announcer's voice had interrupted the song. Someone named Ibrahim Ibrahim was on the announcer's mind again t'dye, as it had been yistadye. "Ibrahim Ibra-scum," he called him. Apparently this recent migrant from overseas had beaten his wife, then rubbed glue in her eyes and hair and pushed her into the shower yelling "Take that, you bitch!" But he'd been given only a short prison sentence, a chance to live in luxury at taxpayer expense. "But this is

Australia, yes, oh we wouldn't do anything bad to this poor scum, would we? No. Not just because he beat on his wife and rubbed glue in her eyes. Ibraham Ibra-scum will eat well off you and me, mate. Scum is what I call him and scum is what he is! And the taxpayers of this country will feed this Ibrahim Ibra-scum while decent blokes are lined up at the soup kitchens."

Apparently this was a phone-in show. A woman's high-pitched voice came on, protesting.

"Go ahead, sweetheart. What is it? I'm listening." *Oim leestnin'*.

"Well George, I was shocked yistadye when my little boy called me a scum? This was after we'd listened to your program? He learned that kind of talk from you, George."

"Well, there's a proper wye to use the word *scum* and an improper wye to use it," George explained. "The wye I use it is the proper wye. Tell your boy that. Tell him to mind his manners and to use his words in the proper wye."

"I will," the woman said. "Thank you, George."

The boy reached to turn the volume down. "Welcome to mulga country!" he said. "Me 'ome!"

The old man sat bolt upright out of sleep and looked from one side to the other as though all of this landscape was a surprise to him, though it looked no different to Sonny than what they'd left behind. "Something's wrapped around the axle," he said. "We're draggin' something behind."

Neither Sonny nor the boy could hear anything unusual but the old man brought it up again a few minutes later. "You better stop and get it loose or it'll pull the damn wheels out from under us."

When Sonny pulled the LandCruiser off to the side of the road, the boy got out and walked around the truck and got back in. "Nothing," he said.

The old man grunted. "Must've been dreaming," Sonny said.

The landscape hadn't changed much – more red dirt, a few scraggly trees at great distances from one another, a long broken line of horizon completely encircling them. Sonny believed he was beginning to see some beauty in it. In the simplicity, perhaps.

If you ignored what you knew about the dangers and thought only of the aesthetics, you noticed the clean lines, the simple colours, the repeated patterns. The world was reduced to a nearly naked monochromatic stage where the single eucalyptus with its scrawling limbs was more lovely than it could have been in a forest. A tree with a swollen trunk, sitting out in a fenced paddock, looked like a giant urn sprouting greenery.

"Bottle tree," his father said, and tossed his field guide out the window.

Sonny touched his foot to the brake. "What was that about?"

"Damn thing tells me names but they don't mean a damn thing."

They rode in silence for a few minutes. "You hear that?" his father said. "That cable again. You gotta get right down and look under or we'll be stranded here with no axle."

This time Sonny got out. Of course there was nothing. There was nothing dragging behind them either. Dammit, what was happening now? Would paratroopers soon be falling from the sky, dropping onto horses and stabbing them to death? He made a great deal of noise kicking the rear bumper and banging his fist against the door for his father's benefit. He would bang his fists against more than Toyota if he met the god who'd invented old age.

"Got it," he said, once he was behind the wheel again. "I threw it in the ditch with your book." The boy did not try to catch Sonny's eye in the mirror.

No hospital could be imagined out here, if you needed one. Were they so far out they would have to rely on the famous Flying Doctor service?

Eventually there were signs of a town ahead. They crossed a railway track and passed by a large brown hotel out of an earlier century. They passed a school, a motel, and a square building with "School of Arts" over the door. It seemed like a genuine town, with a main street of several blocks and glimpses of modest houses at intersections. One or two of the buildings had a flowering bush in the yard.

"We'll bunk in with Ma tonight," the boy said. "Mistake Creek tomorrow."

Sonny protested. He'd seen hotels. But the boy insisted that hotels were meant for shearers. "She wouldn't speak to me for a year if I let you pay for a bed." It seemed he meant it. Being back in his hometown must have improved his mood. Either that or there was some reason he suddenly needed their company. The look he gave Sonny in the rear-view mirror suggested he had given up his sulk. He directed Sonny to pull in at a service station and held out a hand for cash. "She'll need food for our tea. I'll get us some chops."

With a bag of groceries on the floor at the boy's feet, they turned beside the Railway Hotel onto a dirt road, then turned off that road too. Then they drove down an alley between fenced-in backyards and stopped by a tilted gate. Neither fence nor gate nor the small house had seen paint in decades. A stone pathway crossed a yard of packed-hard dirt, bare of plants or even weeds except for a few clusters of prickly pear.

The woman who came frowning to the door of the screened-in porch said "Lachlan," and tilted up her face for a kiss. She wore a loose faded blue housedress over a pair of khaki pants rolled at her ankles. Though she might have been younger than Sonny, she had the face of a much older woman, dry, cross-hatched with creases. Her grey-and-black hair was pulled tightly back, held in place at the sides with bobby pins. Her lips were thin, tight, dry with flakes of peeling skin.

"Lachlan?" Sonny said.

"Of course," the woman said, as she ushered them into her kitchen. "Lachlan Macquarie Hall!"

"Sounds like a friggin' opera house," the boy said. "Named after a bloody governor, a river, and an auditorium. We're starving, Ma. You reckon I could fry us up these chops?" He brought tomatoes out of the bag as well, and a squash, and a couple of spuds. "You sit and talk with our guests here, come all the way from America."

From a tiny kitchen radio on the windowsill came the shrill

sounds of a soprano doing something that ought to have been impossible for the human voice. This was definitely not the station they'd listened to on the road, but it might have been Stanley's station, pouring an Italian aria into this modest kitchen of scrubbed-raw countertop and duct-taped chairs.

"What's happened to your face?" the woman asked.

"He fell, Ma. Tripped over his own feet."

The woman's gaze went to Sonny's shoes. "How is it the three a youse are travelling together?"

"The old one's lookin' for his wife," the boy said. Lachlan now, not Gary. "She shot through and he's off to drag her home by the hair." He pulled a pan out from a cupboard and banged it onto the stove.

The woman led Sonny and his father into the tiny living room, but turned back to her son, who was laying out knives and bowls on the counter. "But how is it you're up this way, love?"

"Heading for Mistake Creek," the boy said.

The woman winced. "Flooding's started up that way." *That wye.*

Sonny parked his father's wheelchair in a corner beneath a shelf of knick-knacks and perched himself on the worn-through arm of the chesterfield. A blanket had been thrown over the middle section, probably to hide the wear and tear. He allowed his legs to sprawl across the polished lino, relieved to be out from behind the wheel.

From the kitchen doorway her son explained, "Me mate there is going to visit *his* mum tomorra, up at her station. You remember Mizz 'awkins?"

"Ahh!"

"You know her?" Sonny's father said.

She nodded solemnly. "Only by repu-tye-shun. Me sister-in-law in Brisbane sees her at the theatre. Oh!" Something suddenly made sense. "Merrilie it was that suggested my Locky drive youse. She knew he couldn't afford to visit on his own." She examined Sonny's father with something like awe. "A grand lady, Mizz 'awkins." She raised her voice for her son. "You brought her truck?"

But didn't wait for an answer. "Down to earth she is, like a regular bloke, they tell me. Always open-handed when there's a need."

The old man said nothing to that. Neither did Sonny. He recognized a jab of disappointment – that she might not be the monster Errol had warned him of.

"Placido Domingo," the boy's mother said, tilting her head towards the kitchen and the rich sounds now rolling out from its radio. Had they stumbled across the Great Australian Secret – a nation famous for its passion for sports was actually a country of opera buffs? "So whaddaya think of the world situation?" she added, dropping into the vacant chair. Her accent was more pronounced than those he'd heard in Sydney. *Sitch-oo-eye-shun*. Like the call-in woman on the radio.

"Aw, Ma," the boy said, chopping vegetables. Lamb chops were already hissing in the pan. "Give it a miss."

"Something is going on, love," the woman said, defiantly. "They're cooking up something, them presidents and all that mob. Plans for one world government. American Jew bankers are behind it." To Timo Aalto she said, "Whitlam signed a paper with them back in the '70s. Five families will soon be running the world."

"We'll show 'em," shouted Lachlan Macquarie Hall from the kitchen. "We'll carve off their heads with our boomerangs!"

"Of course it won't do them no good," the woman went on. "The end of the world is coming any-wye, like the nuns told us. What else can it mean? All these terrible things – volcanoes and people out of jobs and divorces. That rising water could be the start. Maybe He'll try another Flood."

When Lachlan called them to the wooden table in the kitchen, his mother turned her radio volume down a little. "River's rising bad?" he said, dropping into the chair at the head of the table.

"Not over the bridge yet," she said. So this town's river warranted a bridge. "Traffic's still moving but it's coming, the end of the world!" She smiled as though the notion pleased her.

"Well, let's hope not," Sonny said, taking up his utensils. He looked to the boy and found him grinning.

"Why?" she said. "It's supposed to be better in the next one, innit?" Her tone was as flat and dull as the expression in her eyes. "That's what they told us, any-wye." She tilted her head towards the radio, intent on listening. "Fritz Wunderlich," she said.

They waited through the aria without speaking. Afterwards a voice reminded them that it was Fritz Wunderlich's birthday this week. Unfortunately, the singer was not around to enjoy it, having suffered a tragic early death years ago. "At thirty-five, the height of his powers. Fell down the stairs at a friend's hunting lodge. An untied shoelace was the culprit."

"Shoelace?" Lachlan clearly doubted this.

His mother said, "A shoelace and a jar or two of plonk, I'd sye."

"Pissed," Sonny's father said. "After a day of shooting pigs." He aimed his grin at Sonny.

"You know this?" Sonny said.

"I may live at the farthest reaches of the known world but I can listen to the CBC like the rest of them. Poor bugger had a nice career ahead of him, too." Smirking, his father added, "A man who don't waste his life for wages has the time to learn a few things."

"These two blokes will need to keep their laces tied – orright?" Lachlan informed his mother. "They're on their way to a pig shoot."

"Oh!" she said. "I read about one of them." Timo Aalto was not the only reader here. "Murdered guests are left out on the paddocks for a boar to finish off? A feral pig will eat up everything, bones and all?"

"Fritz Whatsizname must have fallen to his death inside the lodge," Sonny said, "or he'd have disappeared without a trace. We'd still not know where he'd gone."

His father said, "One wild pig could save the cost of an undertaker." Looking about as innocent as anyone could.

After supper, the two visitors were given the main bedroom to sleep in. "I want the old gentleman to have our best," the woman said. She would sleep in the boy's old room. Lachlan would visit with his mother awhile, then sleep on the lounge-room couch.

There were twin beds in the room, each with a worn-thin satin spread and a doll at the centre of a wide circle made by its own skirt, pleats perfectly arranged. Photographs of flowers, cut from magazines, did not quite fill the frames mounted on the walls. A Bible and a half-filled glass of water sat on the table between the beds.

"You feeling okay?" Sonny said.

His father had trouble getting out of his clothes but swatted away Sonny's attempts to help. "Fine. Good. Never been better. We shoulda done this years ago."

"Glad to hear it," Sonny said. The axle business hadn't happened. "You want to show me those pictures?" When his father looked confused, he explained. "Warren? Charlotte? Are they in your bag?"

His father unzipped his tote bag and sorted through his jumble of clothing until he came up with a brown envelope. There were fewer than half a dozen coloured snaps inside. Outside their craft shop, Warren and his Lori were less distinct than the birches. Charlotte smiled down from an iron balcony. More beautiful even than her mother, more relaxed, it seemed, than Elaine had ever been.

He put the first two photos to the back. On the next, Charlotte was with her musician, the two of them at a kitchen table. This would be New Orleans again. There was also a smiling child. He turned the photo over. *Charlotte, Ryan, and Ciaran, 2 years.*

"The musician's kid?"

His father sat on his bed to kick off his long wool pants. "A sort of step-child for a while." He'd worn long johns again today, one leg loose around the wooden stump. They were grey with age, and stained at the crotch. "Step-grandchild to you, I suppose. But not any more."

"And she walked away from this little boy?"

"It wasn't hers." He seemed to be having no trouble getting these long johns off. "The guy was a brute. Turns out he was a drug dealer and a woman-beater."

"So she left the child with a brute?"

"Maybe it runs in the family." Timo Aalto shrugged. "It looks like I'm the only decent parent in the bunch!"

The laugh was involuntary. "The earth should open up and swallow you for that."

"You think I'm joking?"

Since you couldn't raise your voice in someone else's house, Sonny lowered his to a growl. "Have you lost your memory? Or do you think I've lost mine?"

"Well, tell me then, why isn't it your son that's driving us across the floor of this bloody furnace, instead of that hooker-boy out there?"

"It's *me* that's driving us, haven't you noticed? Driving my bull-headed vacant-memoried father who seems to have forgotten that this was his idea as much as mine."

"And why isn't your daughter with us? You, your mother, and Charlotte – the three of you make me look like the Model Parent of the Century." He stood up and turned away, chuckling, and began to stuff his rolled-up long johns inside the front of his pyjama bottoms. "I'm an old man. Let me get some sleep."

"What are you doing?"

His father rolled himself onto the bed, pulled up the sheet, and turned away. "I wouldn't sleep a bloody wink for wondering if I'd wake up when I need to. This way I can take my old-man-pee stink away with me."

On his back in the dark, hoping for sleep, Sonny found the road continuing to unroll beneath him, the sound of tires on pavement a steady growl. Snatches of conversations returned. The radio interviewer. The Finnish-Australian colony. And Nora Macken.

"Nora Macken?" he said aloud.

The old man snorted. "She didn't have to be famous Aunt Nora with me. She made it clear I had to be a gentleman."

"I don't suppose that was too hard," Sonny said.

"Don't be so sure. She was a good-lookin' woman once. An intelligent woman too. We argued about *Anna Karenina* all the way out behind Constitution Hill and halfway up Mount Washington and back. But then one day she run into one of Colin's boys while she was coming down through the bush and that was the end of it."

The snores began almost immediately – uneven, interrupted by bursts of coughing, brief choking fits, but anyway sawing on through time. Sonny Aalto was left with nothing to do in this small room but wonder what other humiliations he hadn't noticed his father trying to hide. Someone ought to be making sure he put on fresh underwear every day. Someone ought to be making sure his shirts were clean. Someone ought to be asking him if he should buy some of those diapers they made for adults now.

He had not yet fallen asleep when voices in the kitchen began to rise. At first it was only the woman, her monotonous tone becoming one of complaint, the words not distinct enough to be heard through the door. *Your father* might have been one of the phrases that rose above the others. Soon the boy's voice began to increase in volume too, and in anger. Sometimes both spoke at once. Threats were being exchanged. It was possible, now, to hear whole sentences thrown about. A girl had sworn she'd drink bleach before she'd speak to Locky again, "a young man's opportunity for happiness thrown away." This girl (whose name seemed to be either Mary-Anne or Marian), the boy was convinced, would be better off with dirty old Dabby Deacons if all she wanted was a wedding ring. "Oh, I didn't mean that, I didn't mean marriage, if only you'd come home and act normal." A father would be told the truth at last, if his son did not soon change. When word reached the old darlin' up fossicking for gold in the Gulf, it would either kill him or bring him home with murder on his mind. "What would I do?" the boy said. "What do you reckon I could do? I'd kill myself." A door slammed. Voices were muffled again. Passing by the bedroom, the woman could be heard weeping, her skirt swishing against the walls. A second door slammed – or the same one again. "I'll stay in bloody Sydney so you can forget I was ever born."

Some time during the night, Sonny awoke. Moonlight streamed in through the window curtains and fell on Lachlan Hall asleep on the floor between their beds. His breathing was shallow, steady, the deep sleep of a satisfied guide. Once he grunted and turned onto his back, kicking back the cover. He ground his teeth. Asleep, even a Kings Cross hooker was an innocent child, one hand down inside his underpants.

"The world may end any day now," said the manager of the Centretown hotel to his wife, over dinner, by way of justifying his infatuation with his receptionist. "It's important to make the most of life while it lasts." In his parliamentary office, the senior Cabinet minister shouted into his telephone, promising a colleague that he would get these goddam premiers talking to one another if he had to fly all over the country himself collecting them. Still unaware of the approaching end of the world, Colin Macken set out in his truck for a soccer game in town, while Holly Fitzgerald stood under a hot shower, having separated sword ferns into plastic pots for customers who might drive in to see what she had to offer. In his living room, Harry Sylvester watched a *séparatiste* politician enumerate, for the benefit of the television audience, a dozen hideous crimes the Anglos had committed against Quebec, for which they must never be forgiven.

The world hadn't ended yet when Lachlan drove them out of his mother's town, but by the time they'd finally reached Mistake Creek it seemed that *something* was up. Rains to the north and east had so swollen the river that it swept across the foot of the main street; people had come down to the wooden barriers to stare. In this baked-dry landscape it wasn't easy to believe in water. Even this late in the day, despite the clouds along the horizon, the sun

232

flung down its harsh light and stifling heat from a terrible sky. The bridge out of town, if there was one, had disappeared.

The town was just barely a town: two blocks of tin-roofed buildings, many of them up on posts. Latticework verandahs gave them the look of neglected birdcages. If a wind were to blow them away there would be little evidence that humanity had ever been here.

Lachlan pulled in before the yellow Australia Post building so that Sonny could make use of the public phones. He knew the family was gathering at a local hotel but didn't remember which – he'd counted two, as well as one motel. Once he'd found a V. Hawkins in the directory he dialled, and waited to hear a voice he hadn't heard in half a century. Flies as big as his thumbnails buzzed at his ear.

Store folds were still sharp in the shorts he'd bought this morning. Stiff and itchy, his reason for hating new clothes. Because his pale shoulders would fry if he wore only a singlet like so many men on the street, he'd bought a long-sleeved cotton shirt to wear open and hanging loose. Of course the singlet was wet, and sticking to his skin. To follow the lead of just about every man he'd seen outside of Sydney he'd got himself a pair of elastic-sided boots – a loop at the heel like the handle on Aladdin's lamp. "The country boot that went to town," the shop window posters boasted. He used his new Akubra to fan away the flies.

"Who?" The voice on the other end of the phone was so deep he could feel it rumble in his own belly. "No, I won't call her to the phone. You'll state your business to me."

The hotel where the family was to meet was The Kalevan. "Same as the station."

"Has a Charlotte Aalto arrived?"

"Are we expecting her?"

Across the street a huge billboard sat on the roof of an Ampol service station, pointing out the road to the left as the route to the dinosaur stampede. A cartoon *Tyrannosaurus rex* was two or three metres tall.

Since the voice on the phone had never heard of Charlotte, Sonny thought she might have checked in at one of the hotels to wait for him. It was just as likely, of course, that she was far from here, photographing Ayers Rock or the Bungle Bungles.

"Dinosaurs?" he said to Lachlan Hall, who leaned against a power pole, watching the river.

"Out past those jump-ups. Half a day's drive from here."

Beyond the houses on the short residential side street there was only the flat red dust, an expanse of pale grass, and then dead-level empty plain broken here and there by isolated trees so thin and leggy you could see right through to the tent-pegged edges of sky. What the boy called "jump-up" must be the long red sawed-off rise, a free-standing plateau. Dinosaurs were beyond the curve of the earth.

The familiar black BOUND FOR GLORY truck pulled up at the wooden ROAD CLOSED barriers. Doors flew open. Men leapt out and gathered at the water's edge. One of them put a foot in. Another took off his woollen toque, drove a fist into it, returned it to his head. They bent forward, talking. Their voices, from this distance, sounded to Sonny as if they were all speaking at once. Sally was amongst them, his pale face widely grinning.

Then, abruptly, they returned to the truck. One of them climbed onto the roof, and sat forward with his legs down the windshield and his feet on the hood. The engine roared to life even before all the doors had been slammed. The truck backed up as far as the public telephones. Dark round faces grinned through the glass. The man on the roof saluted – three fingers to his brow.

Gears clashed. The truck stopped and moved forward again, accelerating fast. Someone inside it yelled. The flimsy wooden barrier splintered, a piece of it flung aside. The truck roared down the slope and into the water, which quickly rose up its wheels and above the wheels and above the BOUND FOR GLORY bumper sticker and even halfway up the engine. A wake Ved out behind it, an animal swimming with its nose barely above the water. Then it began to rise up the opposite bank of the river, a muddy stream sluicing off it. It paused on dry land just long enough for the man on the roof to climb down, wave a long arm to the watchers, and get inside. Then it leapt forward and roared on down the road.

Three fat men crouched to examine the broken barrier. One of them picked up a splintered board and turned it over, then tossed it aside on the pavement. His face was decorated with shiny patches of pink where skin had been removed.

Inside the truck, Timo Aalto fanned himself with a paperback. His face shone with sweat. "Close 'er up and turn on the air-conditioning, willya? This thing's a bloody oven."

This morning the old man had sworn a cluster of bushes in the distance was a posse of furious Indians waiting to ambush them, and would not reconsider until they were passing close enough to see the individual trunks. He'd laughed at himself, but later got it into his head that one of the rear wheels was about to fall off, mentioning it so often that Lachlan agreed to get out and check. There'd been no further incidents, but two in one day were enough to justify a visit to a clinic when they arrived in town. His father, so far, had refused.

"I'll find us some shade," Lachlan said. He got in behind the wheel and – making a point of it so that Sonny would notice – turned on the air-conditioning with one hand while rolling up his window with the other.

The Hotel Kalevan was just a block up the street, one of those old hotels from the nineteenth century, a great two-storey structure on a corner, with a gallery down both visible sides of the second floor and glass doors off each of the rooms. Garishly coloured signs advertised "XXXX *our beer* XXXX," "*FOSTER'S LIGHT*," "VB: *For a hard-earned thirst.*"

It seemed important to walk the main street of his mother's town, to catalogue her world before he saw her in it. A newsagent. A chemist's shop. A drive-in bottle shop where a young woman in shorts came out to a truck to take an order, then went back and brought out a case of Fosters Light. Inside the TAB a handful of men watched horses racing across a television screen. In front of a menswear store, a big-bellied man in khaki shorts nodded to Sonny. Signs in the window advertised "Radios, Cassettes, Toys, Gifts, Stationery, Pools, Sporting Goods, and Firearms." Above the recessed entrance a sign promised a barber inside.

The stink of mutton fat escaped from the doorway of a small café. Inside, a woman studied a newspaper opened out on the counter. Checkered tablecloths were stained with patches of grease. A sign on the back wall said, *Toilets in back. Towels and soap for 50¢ – ask at counter.* A blackboard menu told what there was: T-bone and eggs for 9.50, Vegemite for 1.50, chicken leg and chips for 3.50. The wall behind the woman displayed alternatives: plastic bags of snack food.

His mother must have done her weekly shopping in this town. Would she look like that thick-legged woman gazing at the blouses in the clothing-store window, a loose yellow shirt over her shoulders, purse hanging from a strap? Or one of the women chatting in front of the newsagent's, all in cotton-print dresses and high-heeled shoes, made up for some kind of meeting. "Yayce, yayce," said one of them. "I would sye so, Mary, yayce. Forty dollars at least." These women's sons would be helping their fathers on the farm.

Across the street from the hotel, his own father and Lachlan waited in the LandCruiser, back end to the curb amidst a row of four-by-fours. Nissan Patrol, Daihatsu, Suzuki Sierra. All were equipped with what looked like iron bedsteads mounted in front of their radiators. "Roo bars," Lachlan had called them. Behind the cabs, angle-iron cages contained winches and extra tires and loose tools and cans. Some contained dogs as well, chained to the rails. All of these trucks were coated, like their own, with cinnamon-coloured dirt. Dust, he supposed, mixed with blood.

In the manner he was almost used to now, night had fallen in the few minutes it had taken him to walk that one long block. Night here did not *rise*, as it apparently did at home. From across the street he could see the figure of a man in a white T-shirt leaning over the railing of the second-floor gallery to smoke a cigarette, which flared up crimson when he sucked on it and glowed tightly red when he let it hang from his fingers below the railing. Behind him, light shone from a narrow window. Light shone from an open doorway as well, where a woman in silhouette leaned with her arms crossed at her breast. She was, he thought, in a slip.

Travellers stalled by that river, he supposed. Lovers travelling north to some large station, where he was employed as a drover. Returning from a honeymoon in Sydney, taking advantage of this unexpected hitch in their plans to spend time in a hotel-room bed. Sonny had found them cooling off.

It was a picture Charlotte would thank him for, he thought. He took up her camera from the seat of the truck and aimed it just as the man put the cigarette to his mouth. The automatic focus whirred but brought the woman, not the man, into clarity, just as she raised a hand to her hair and turned towards the light from the room. The shock of seeing a stranger for whom he had invented a life turn suddenly into someone familiar was enough to send all sorts of nonsense through his head while his confused brain tried to adjust. How could Charlotte be on a honeymoon? Why would she marry a cowboy? Of course, when he had shaken off his own ridiculous fictions, he recalled this same mistake happening once before.

Still, he felt compelled to go in and check. It was at this hotel they were supposed to meet up with the others. She might have got here early, she might be waiting for him.

The pub was so crowded that he had to push his way through a confusion of shouts and laughter and a low rumble of continuous palaver. Everyone was talking flood. You were scared to take your eye off that damn river for a minute, said one fellow in a black high-crowned hat, in case the bloody thing swelled up and took you away. "Y'd be down in Lake Eyre, swimmin' like a barrafuckin'-mundi for yer life."

"Shoulda gone straight to the Gold Coast and laid in the bleedin' sand fer the duration."

"I hear five t'ousand sheep is trapped down Boulia way."

He went up the stairway and down the hall. Dull lights. Threadbare carpet. An impression of dark peeling wallpaper. These rooms were probably never used except in times of disaster, when people with no intention of stopping were forced to spend the night.

Second room from the end. He didn't know how he knew this, some sort of instinct had taken over. He hammered on the door and stepped back. Footsteps crossed the room. The door was opened by Errol Hawkins, holding a can of Foster's. For a confused moment Sonny could not imagine why the host of the north shore dinner party was here. "You?" he said.

Errol shrugged. "Why not?"

"I thought I saw Charlotte," Sonny said. "Out on the verandah."

"The gallery? Better get your eyes checked, mate. She's not here." As though to prove it to himself, he went to the outside door. Sonny followed. There was no one down at this end of the gallery at all.

The sloped roof above them was of galvanized tin, stamped GUINEA beneath a circled drawing of a naked horseman with a flat-blade sword. Slatted chairs were set out along a hundred feet or so of worn floorboards, like the deck of an ocean liner. Doors to all the other rooms stood open. Below, at the traffic intersection, the triangular sign said GIVE WAY. "You were at the railing. She was in this doorway."

The half-brother only smiled, as though waiting for Sonny Aalto to realize what a fool he was making of himself.

The interior looked like a 1940s renovation of a Victorian hotel. The room was small, high-ceilinged, with a single light bulb hanging in the middle. The door was scraped, battered, even split open near the handle – someone had forced his way in. "Why would you stay here?" Sonny said.

"We do this every year, the family. We get together, have supper, stay overnight – for old time's sake. Our granddad owned this place. Our dad grew up in these rooms. It was considered a palace then."

A woman came down the gallery and joined them. She wore shorts, and a skimpy singlet that showed her nipples. She was dark – dark-haired, dark-skinned. There was something about her that made him think of Janis. A languorous walk, a slightly petu-lant set to her mouth. "Toni Papadoupolis," Errol said. "This is Sonny, from America."

The woman nodded without looking at Sonny and went inside, where she dropped onto the bed. A cosmetic case was open on the shelf in the corner.

"I hate this heat," she said. "Why don't they get air conditioning?"

"Find something better if you can," Errol said. He winked at Sonny. "This town's still waiting for its Waldorf Hilton Astoria."

Sonny passed through the room and stepped out into the hall.

"We'll be down to the carvery in an hour," Errol said, removing a shirt from a hook on the inside of the door. "Ms. Papadoupolis will freshen up a little before she makes her entrance."

"I might." The woman fanned her face with her hand, but did not otherwise stir.

"Get into the shower," said Errol, shutting the door in Sonny's face.

The staircase was broad, of shining red wood, and turned twice as it descended to a rather grand foyer that he'd barely noticed on his way in. There was a marble fireplace, a cluster of red-plush chairs, panels of stained glass in the windows.

The bar was a little less crowded now than when he'd entered the building. Some people must have gone home for supper, or back to stare at the river. Only a few sat here and there on the stools at the marble-topped counter, which made a full four-sided barrier around the bartender's pit. The pale green tiles on the floor and walls gave the room the bare, shiny look of a public washroom, as though it were meant to be hosed down after hours.

"There he is, the mad skater!" On the far side of the room a couple sat over schooners. The man got to his feet, "Sorry we couldn't arrange for a little snow," and came around the bar with his hand out. This had to be Jerrod – Gerard – though there was little to recognize him by: no woollen gloves, no fur collar, no heavy coat engulfing his large frame. "Joanie, come here, love, and meet your brother-in-law. This man has come halfway round the world to find us." His vowels, after all these Queensland voices, were a surprise: slightly British, with little trace of the accent he'd adopted for Ottawa. He clasped Sonny's upper arm, his face bright with boyish elation. Sonny Aalto had, it seemed, been claimed.

So they had arrived at the shooting party. Or the start of it, at least. Everyone would be staying here tonight and going on to the station in the morning by some alternative track that avoided this part of the river. But once they'd checked in to their room, his father dropped onto the narrow bed nearest the outside door and refused to go down to dinner. He and Lachlan would find some greasy spoon, he said, but only after he'd napped. He wasn't in no mood for a party.

Not in a mood to face his wife, Sonny assumed he meant. After coming all this way. And why would he be? Even with friendly Jerrod Hawkins showing up to make him welcome, he felt anxious enough himself. The old woman would make a grand entrance at the dinner. She'd be the centre of attention for a while but there was little doubt she would eventually turn the attention to him.

Lachlan would not share their room, and wouldn't let Sonny get him a room of his own. He would look up a few old mates, he said, or sleep under the stars again. "I'll fetch yiz in the morning, to drive to the station."

"But you'll stay with my father till I'm back? You'll make sure he eats, make sure he gets back to the room?" *You'll let me know if he has any more of his spells. Or starts drinking again.*

Lachlan examined the truncated fingers of his left hand. "Maybe I got a talent for looking after old blokes – orright?"

"That would be a nice surprise," Sonny said.

He thought of last night's overheard conversation – a dangerous father would be disgusted, a distraught mother was pressing for a more conventional lifestyle. The woman had gone past the bedroom weeping for her failure, but who could know what the boy had gone through before choosing to sleep on the bedroom floor? Sonny was surprised to discover that he wished he'd offered something. But what? And what made him think it would be welcome?

Strangers crowding into the dining room could be his relatives. Some might be celebrities. His mother could be amongst them somewhere. A blown-up grainy black-and-white photo of a bristly boar filled much of one dining-room wall. He assumed the shooting would not begin tonight.

The long smorgasbord counter and carvery stretched the length of the room, its glass and stainless steel the only signs of modern life. Everything else was early twentieth-century: dark wood panelling to shoulder height, oval portraits high on the pale yellow walls, potted ferns on leggy wooden stands. Along the wall of windows looking out on the street, two young families sat whispering at their tables. Across much of the rest of the room several tables had been pushed together and covered with lilac cloths. A crowd had begun to assemble, some already sitting with drinks.

"Used as a ballroom in my father's time," said Jerrod, his hand behind Sonny's shoulder. "Debutante balls. Bachelors-and-spinsters balls. Vice-regal dinners when the super-poms came through – which wasn't often, believe me. Celebrations after the picnic races."

Unlike Errol with his pale and freckled complexion, Jerrod was tanned and leathery, his teeth a startling white beneath a dark, straight-line moustache. He wore navy shorts and an open-necked white shirt, and a blue silk scarf hanging loose from his neck. Had he worn it in Sonny's honour, having seen so many

Canadians in scarves he thought it a national costume? "When you refused our invitation," he said, "I assumed you had no need, your soul already full and singing in its place."

"But as you see, I'm here," Sonny said.

Jerrod pulled out a chair halfway down the long table. "Now, this isn't Prussia. Don't expect hunting lodges with animal heads on the walls. What you can expect is tennis, swimming, a grand feast tomorrow, and a party lasting through most of the night. The chase very early next morning. Here now, meet some of these people, a few of your rellies amongst them."

Jerrod's wife sat across the table, beside a woman she introduced as Aunt Clara. "Gerard's father's sister." Aunt Clara wore a bead necklace and a wide green cotton dress with short sleeves that revealed arms thicker than Sonny's thighs. She leaned forward with her forearms resting on the table and told Sonny he'd better watch out, she liked the look of him. "Since Teddy passed on I been waiting for someone like you!" She laughed. She was seventy or maybe seventy-five years old.

"Viira's son," Jerrod said.

Aunt Clara's painted eyebrows rose. "A skeleton from Viira's closet?"

Other conversations stopped, while the skeleton from Viira's closet was introduced. Uncles. Aunts. A cousin and her husband. A niece – Errol's daughter. Three dentist mates of Errol's were just joining his end of the table, none of them familiar from the dinner party. A small round man with a giant moustache insisted that he was no blood relative to this mob but only a foolish widower who'd married into the family by mistake.

"Sweet Jesus, don't he know how to lie?" Aunt Clara cried. "That bugger hung around our Liz till she couldn't think of nothing else to do *but* marry him! Don't you give us that, you piss-tank, you're as related as anyone here." She swung on Sonny while she sucked in air for more. "You found yer room?"

He nodded.

"Number 21 I think we gave you," Aunt Clara said. "Top of the stairs, to the right."

"Clara owns the hotel," Joanie explained. "You see waiters cringing, that's the reason. Watch them put the biggest slab of beef on her plate."

"I should bloody hope so," Aunt Clara said, shifting her shoulders around. "If I don't enjoy me tucker somebody gets the axe."

"Sleep with one eye open," Jerrod said. "She has the extra keys in her purse."

"But doesn't need them," Joanie said. "Anybody closes their gallery doors we know something's goin' on."

"Errol's the only one closed his door last year," Jerrod said, lowering his voice.

"Last year was the first time whatsername came, that's why."

Jerrod's fingers slid repeatedly along the surface of the silk scarf, as if he were stroking a cat.

Other cousins arrived. Marg and Norm, with two sulking teenagers. Marg was a tall woman who carried a bust-and-stomach combination the size of a bachelor's fridge; Norm was shorter, with a fairly impressive gut of his own. Both wore T-shirts and khaki shorts, and rubber thongs on their feet. Flip-flops.

"All the way down from Karumba," Marg said, loud enough for everyone. She made a face, and dug with the nail of her little finger at something caught in her back teeth. "We got caught up there in the wet!"

"They're from Geelong!" Aunt Clara could outshout them. "Can't stand it away from the sea!"

Norm shook Sonny's hand and held a steady gaze while he explained that they had been travelling now for several months. Working their way around the continent. He pointed out his cherry-red Mitsubishi Pajero 4WD parked on the far side of the street, attached to a long boat with a Yamaha 90 motor on the back. "That's home for now," he said. "So far we've been up the east coast, Cape York, across to the Gulf of Carpenteria."

Marg was still pursuing something with that fingernail but this did not seriously hinder her speech. "My favourite place was Mount Surprise." She laughed. "The surprise is – there's no mountain! Not that we could see, anyway!"

Norm's dark eyes still held Aalto prisoner. "Sold our house," he said. "We'll build a new one when we get back."

"Don't get him started," Marg said, flapping a long wet hand at Sonny. "Where do we sit? Norm's a talker. Neighbours call him Avvachat. 'Let's 'ave a chat, shall we, mate?'" She laughed, and chose the nearest empty chair.

The daughter poked at one of her mother's boobs. "Avvachat Two."

An elderly couple arrived. "Pastoralists," Jerrod said. "Old friends of the family. Marcus and Lucy." The man was much shorter than his wife, his bare legs thin below his yellow plaid shorts. The small bony face was decorated with patches of shiny pink new skin. He gave Sonny a weak "G'day," but went directly to an empty chair to sit. He did not remove his stockman's hat.

"Bank took their property," Jerrod said. "Gave them forty-eight hours to get off, sold it at auction. It's happened to others around here too. Neighbours rescued everything that wasn't nailed down. They've had to move in with a daughter. Marcus is bitter – blames Canberra for everything." When he noticed Sonny watching his hand stroke the scarf he said, "Purchased in Montreal," and lowered his hand to his lap.

"Here's Lois," Aunt Clara cried. For Sonny's benefit she added, "Bush poet."

The "bush poet" was tall and thin, with wiry grey curls heaped on the top of her head. She entered laughing. She looked as though she was never not laughing. Her eyes appeared to be much higher up her forehead than they ought to be.

"You wouldn't have heard of our Lois Nugg," Jerrod said. "Wins prizes every year for her Banjo Paterson imitations." He raised his voice. "Come and meet your cousin, love. He's never heard of you. Or Banjo Paterson either!"

The woman laughed into Sonny's face and pumped his hand. "We'll set you right on both accounts soon enough!"

"You've penned a new poem for us?" Jerrod said.

"Have I ever failed you?" She rested an open hand on Jerrod's chest and let her gaze flicker around the room, perhaps to estimate the size of her audience.

"Wait until dessert," Jerrod suggested.

"Last year's party," she promised. "One verse about you scrambling up that red gum, yelling for someone to rescue you from your own dog." She trilled a happy laugh. "But I'll wait until you're begging for it," she said cheerfully, and swished off to brush cheeks with women down the table.

"She'll wait until she's got enough of us mustered to make it worth her while," Jerrod said. He turned his attention to Aunt Clara. "That river make you nervous?"

The big woman threw up her hands. Dimpled forearms quivered. "Hell, I'm scared to go to sleep at night. I'd move to Toowoomba if it wasn't for your mother's party."

"Oh lord!" someone near the window end of the table said. "Aunt Clara's remembering the flood."

"Tell them about Aunt Clara when you get home," one of the women suggested to Aalto. "If there's anything left for you to go home to."

"It was in today's paper," the young man beside her said. *T'dye's pye-pah.* "Your PM begging the French to stay."

"It was all predicted in the Bible, wasn't it?" said the sad pastoralist who had been kicked off his property. "In the last days – the breaking-up of nations."

A small silence followed this. Avvachat One and Two directed impatient glances at one another.

"The Hells Angels say they'll vote against separation," said the woman who'd brought the topic up. "That must be comforting news." She snickered for a neighbour's sake.

Avvachat rested his elbows on the table and leaned forward. "You Bananalanders tried that once yourselves," he said, shaking an accusing finger at the locals. "Central Queensland its own colony!"

Aunt Clara waved history's failure aside. "But we went our own way anyway, in everything that matters."

"When the flood hit," Joanie said to Sonny, "Aunt Clara was getting ready for a funeral, her house was filled with visitors sleeping on the floors."

Aunt Clara was all of a sudden shy. "Teddy, me 'usband, died. Of course he was always useless in an emergency anyway?"

"Clara!" Joanie was shocked.

"Well, he was! The bugger would sit and wait to be told what to do if the roof was falling on his head. May he rest in peace." She quickly crossed herself, her fingers catching for a moment in her beads.

"We didn't get Uncle Teddy buried for two weeks," Jerrod explained.

"Woke us up in the night," Aunt Clara said. "Water was lapping at the steps. We had to get up and put me linen in the attic? Then we waded across the street to Cheryl's house, which was on higher ground? By this time, the water was up to my, up to here!" She cut a line with her hand across her bosom.

"Tell him!" one of the cousins shouted.

Aunt Clara boldly smiled at Sonny Aalto. "Took me clothes off to cross the street. All but me bra and knickers? Put everything on me head and around me neck."

Several people applauded. "One day they'll erect a statue," said Jerrod Hawkins. "*Aunt Clara Crossing the Flood*."

Silence followed, perhaps as people contemplated a marble version of Aunt Clara in her underwear, out on the main street of town. Absurdly, Sonny imagined a marble version of Darryl Maclean, standing on the bank of the St. Lawrence River, near the location of his drowned childhood home.

You could hear the water roar, she said. Over where the river was supposed to be. And smell a frightful smell. From across the street she could see it running through her house, where she'd purposely left the doors and windows open. Dead dogs and cushions floated past, and furniture. Shoes. A few hours later they were coming by in boats to evacuate people. "To take us across to where the helicopter would land on the hardware's roof." Aunt Clara put her hands over her mouth. "I never been in a boat before! This was a tiny little thing."

"Like moving a house on a wheelbarrow," Jerrod said.

"Oh, I was frightened," she said. "'Sit in the middle!' they told me. They was scared I would tip us over. Then they motored us across to the building, to the foot of a ladder, and told me I had to go up!"

"I'd rather drown!" Joanie said.

"They put the legs of the ladder right in the boat, which was bobbing up and down," Aunt Clara said. "The men stood up in the boat and prodded me bottom to keep me moving! I prayed me way up the wall. Once I got up I was right, but we had to wait for the helicopter to take us out to what they called Tent City."

"I've rendered this in verse," cried Lois Nugg, the bush poet. "Twenty-seven stanzas."

"Later," someone pleaded.

But the bush poet might not have heard. "There was worry in the township, for the word was spreading fast, / That the rains up in the north would bring a flood. / The funeral guests had gathered at Aunt Clara's place at last, / Though most of them had had to wade through mud."

"About time!" one of the women shouted. A commotion had erupted at the door.

"Haw!" said a large bald man in the doorway. Heads turned, including heads at other tables. "A mob of starving bushies lined up at the trough! Lois droning on in rhyme."

"Trev!"

He was alone. If this was the brother who lived at the station he'd apparently come by himself.

Women stood up and threw out their arms in case he would hug. Men stood, to see whose hands might be taken. Trevor

Hawkins shook no hands and gave no hugs; he went down the length of the table squeezing the occasional shoulder. Saying names. "Joanie. Gerard. Auntie Clara. George. Errol – where's what's 'er name?"

"Down in a minute," Errol said, though he did not look as though he hoped for it.

Sonny watched the doorway for a second entrance. Someone asked the question for him. "Viira didn't come?"

Trevor made the sort of face that meant *You know what she's like*.

"Wandering the paddocks again?" someone said. "Sleeping under the stars?"

Aunt Clara rolled her eyes for Sonny's benefit. "Indisposed." Then she shouted for the others. "She'll perk up when she sees who's here! I've lost me heart to the bloke, I may embarrass m'self."

Jerrod stood behind Sonny's chair. "Now, look here, Trev, would you recognize this gentleman if you met him behind the woolshed? Resemble anyone you know?"

Sonny had seen no one yet who resembled the person who looked back at him from mirrors. This was a meaty lot. Even Errol and Jerrod, who weren't fat, had jowls. Not a single Karelian cheekbone, no Scandinavian noses, no Siberian eyes.

Getting to his feet, Sonny held out his hand. "Dennis Aalto," he said.

Trevor Hawkins did not take the offered hand. "I heard the ol' lady named you Sonny."

"She named me Risto," Sonny said. "But she didn't hang around long enough to hear my father ignore it."

"Risto," Trevor said. And repeated it, exaggerating a little – "Rees-toe" – so that the others wouldn't miss it.

"Now Rees-toe," said Trevor Hawkins, passing down behind them to the end farthest from Errol and the carvery, where the man who'd accidentally married into the family gave up his chair. "Have you come in the mood for a party? Have you come in a mood to kill?"

"If it's pigs we're talking about," Sonny said. "If that's the only way I'll get to play with the grown-ups. I haven't shot a thing since I was a kid."

"He shot a bear once," Errol said.

Aunt Clara reached across the table to give Sonny a poke. "I love a dangerous man." She hugged herself and shuddered.

Trevor was not impressed. "A bear? Well, I reckon you haven't met a beast that's a match for the Terror of Kalevan Station. I speak, of course, of our mother."

Wearing a grim smile, he led the way to the food. Others stood up to follow. "Trevor's the oldest," Jerrod said. "That's why he swans around as if he owns the hotel and the town and the people too. Thinks he's squattocracy. He's ignorant as dirt, but at least he loves the farm. Last year when prices fell he went out and shot thirty thousand of his own sheep. He's the only man in this crowd that could have done it."

"Don't hog the Canuck," Aunt Clara said, taking Sonny's arm. "I'll make sure he gets his share, we need him strong tomorrow."

"You'll take part in the hunt?" he asked.

"Depends what shape I'm in?" Aunt Clara said. "Last year we went skinny-dipping in the bore. I nodded off to sleep and they left me behind. I damn near drowned but Viira threw a squawking leghorn in my face and woke me up. Feathers everywhere!"

"I'm told she has a bit of a mean streak," Sonny ventured.

Aunt Clara hummed while she thought about this. "She was the first one there to help me after the flood. Brought food? She took charge of Teddy's funeral too. Trevor mocks her for it, bullies her about money, treats her like she's senile."

"And she isn't? Senile?"

Aunt Clara pressed her brightly painted lips together and shook her head. "Some reckon she's a bit of a nutter but she's just a little forgetful at times, it's only natural. But if she don't watch out, Trevor will have her convinced she's got kangaroos in her top paddock, as me old mother used to say. She muddies things by being sane. Also by being alive." With plates in hand, they looked down through glass at bleeding roasts and steaming pans

of roasted potatoes and chopped vegetables. "Take plenty of everything, the food's good. None of that New Australian Cuisine
they'll give you in Sydney – which I'd rather hang on the wall
than put in me mouth."

"Now, Rees-toe," Trevor said, when everyone had returned to
the table with heaping plates of roast beef and lamb and gravy
and roasted potatoes. He'd raised his voice so that it would carry.
Also so that others between them would stop their talking to
listen. "Did you telephone us earlier out at the house? Benno
radioed while I was on my way in."

It seemed that Sonny Aalto had become either the guest of
honour or the goat, it wasn't yet clear which.

"I did," he said. "Asking about my daughter."

"Well, Benno reckoned it could wait till I told you myself." He
paused while he used his knife to push meat and potatoes and vegetables into a heap on his fork. "We've got her under what you
might call house arrest." He lifted the load to his mouth.

"What!" Errol Hawkins protested before Sonny could be sure
of what he'd heard.

Trevor seemed to be taking pleasure in this. "One of the boys
came on her out behind the old homestead yesterday. Taking
photos where she had no business being. Never had the decency
to ask."

"Would you have given permission?" Errol said.

"Naow!" Trevor said. "We would have showed her the gate."
He sat large and red-faced and happy at the head of the table,
shovelling up another forkful of food. He seemed to be the only
one eating. "We'd've showed her the gate when we caught her
too, like we did to that driver of yours that brought her, only she
said she had connections to somebody coming tomorrow. Don't
worry, nobody hurt her." He said this to Sonny. "But Ol' Benno
give her a bit of a scare." He chuckled. Others chuckled as well.
Whoever Ol' Benno was, the effect he had on trespassers was
apparently known.

Charlotte was in trouble again, he could understand that much.

His stomach understood that much. The crowd had broken into dozens of conversations now, while Errol moved up the table to confront Trevor. Shouting seemed to be all that would happen.

"They'll end up in court, them two," Aunt Clara said, "If they don't kill each other first. Your daughter must've took sides." She shifted about in her seat and propped her elbows on the table. "Errol's got himself mixed up with them World Heritage people, they want to turn the whole catchment area into park – a third of the state!"

"Not a park," calm Jerrod said. "Just make sure it's protected."

"To save an endangered frog and a stupid fish," Joanie said.

"That's how Trevor sees it," Jerrod said. "He's ropeable. Somebody telling him how many sheep he's allowed to graze."

"Telling him how much he can sell the property for when Viira's gone," Aunt Clara said, louder than necessary. "Errol must have hired your girl and didn't tell her why."

All of this was being said too quickly for Sonny to make any sense of what he was hearing. No one seemed to be concerned about Charlotte, or think that *he* must be. Of course it was hard to believe she hadn't known what she was risking, after all she'd brought down on her head at home. But still. What wasn't clear was just how serious this was.

Apparently they weren't about to tell him. "I'm a moderate greenie myself," Jerrod said. "These pastoralists have done a piss-poor job of caring for the land – Trevor included. It's time to let the land take care of itself for a while. But I'm always surprised when the people you think are on the side of the angels behave like perfect bastards."

"I blame that Holmes woman," Aunt Clara said. For Sonny, she explained: "Sold her property to the state government? Just to protect the critters – black falcon and a little rabbity sort of bandicoot called a bilby! She's put ideas into the politicians' heads."

He felt a sudden and acute sense of being the foreigner here. Excluded while they talked falcons and bandicoots. Arguing politics while his daughter was held against her will. Did they think he could sit here and listen to this? He pushed back his chair to stand, though he didn't really know why. He'd been anxious since she'd left Sydney on her own, but didn't know if this was because he was worried about her safety or because there was something he wanted from her. If there was something he wanted from her, he didn't know what it was, having learned how little she would give.

Jerrod put a restraining hand on his arm. "She'll be safe enough with Benedict in charge, believe me. We'll be up at dawn to get an early start."

While Sonny hovered, undecided, behind his chair, Lachlan Hall appeared in the doorway to the foyer, waving his arms about. Alarmed, but afraid to cross the dining-room floor.

"I reckon the heat's got him," he said, when Sonny joined him. He'd pulled a shirt on, but not shoes. Dirty feet were splayed on marble tiles. "I took him to the clinic around the corner." He led Sonny onto the street. "We started out for our tea, but when he got out of the wheelchair he, like, toppled to the footpath before I could catch him. An old bloke like that, I reckoned I better not fiddlearse around, I took him where people can check him out. Lucky there was a nurse on duty, innit?"

"Good for you," Sonny said.

It was almost embarrassing to see how pleased the boy was to hear this.

The neighbours had been right. Judith Buckle as well. He'd had no business bringing the old man down here. However determined his father had been, it was Sonny Aalto who would be left to live with his mistake. He should get them out of here tomorrow, if it weren't too late already. Book a plane to Sydney. A plane to Brisbane would do. Back to ocean breezes and a plane for home.

As it happened, it might not be too late after all. A doctor had been called in. "A little heat prostration," he explained. "Dehydration. We've given him liquids but I'd like to give him a thorough checkup in the morning."

When the doctor led Sonny into a second room, his father was sitting back against the raised pillows of a cot, talking with a nurse. His head went up, he looked relieved, perhaps even surprised. He grinned. It must have been thirty-five years since Sonny had seen that reaction to his entering a room. There was a time Sonny could stand in the Men's entrance to the Riverside beer parlour and know that eventually his father would look up, sensing he was somewhere close, and grin with pleasure upon seeing him.

On that immaculate white cot he was dressed in the same long-sleeved shirt and wool pants he'd been wearing since they'd left home, refusing to let Sonny buy him anything lighter. He looked small, as though the heat had dried him out.

"He's travelling with medication, I understand," the doctor said. He was a slight man, with reddish hair on the backs of his hands. "You've made sure he's been taking it?"

"He doesn't like me seeing," Sonny said. "But he swears he doesn't miss."

His father's smile was sheepish. It was impossible to know whether he was apologizing for something he couldn't help or enjoying something that had turned out much as he'd planned. A man of his age and state of health, the doctor said, should not be travelling in this heat. "I would find him a comfortable room and stop a few days here. Someone could be called at any time." With the confidence of one accustomed to the authority granted him by almost everyone, he decreed that Mr. Aalto would stay overnight. "For observation." His cool eyes recognized in Sonny Aalto a man who could not be trusted.

When the doctor had left the room, Timo Aalto looked at Sonny and shrugged. This could mean either "What are you going to do about this mess?" or "Don't tell me you didn't know this was coming."

Lachlan Hall studied his own dirty toes.

"Maybe it's time to give this up and fly home," Sonny said.

His father's bristly jaw thrust out. "You scared I'm gonna kick the bucket here? Just wait and see how fast I bounce back. I done it before. I mean to get to that pig shoot. That's what we come here for."

"You're sure that's why we came? It wasn't just an excuse to get us out on the road awhile – any road?"

An impatient hand waved this interpretation aside. "You're not leavin' me behind. I'm going even if I have to be carried on a damn stretcher!"

Sonny laughed. "My god! What do you think is going to happen when you get there – a Hollywood reunion? You got hopes the marriage can still be saved?"

His father glanced at Lachlan. Had they talked about this already?

Sonny turned to the nurse. "Is there a phone in another room?"

His hand was on the doorknob when his father spoke. "She can shrivel up and blow away in this dusty hell of hers for all I care. What I want is to see her trying to explain herself to you. Maybe ease that burr you got in your pants, that keeps you dissatisfied with everything." He looked at the embarrassed nurse. "I don't hold out too much hope, but I want to see if she tries."

The telephone was answered by Holly's son, who sounded as though he would have to think hard to remember who Sonny Aalto was. Maybe it was only that he'd been asleep. Sonny hadn't thought – it must be, what? Six in the morning? Even earlier?

Then the boy's voice said, "You seen the dinosaur tracks?"

"Hold on a minute, son. I need to talk to your mother."

"I'd rather believe this was harassment," Holly said, "but I'm afraid to hear it isn't. Is he okay?"

"Heat stroke mostly, I think. But he's weak. I think he only wants to make sure you're alerted. I think this might be his way of alerting *me*."

"Are you okay?" The sound of her voice set off jangling pleasure in his chest.

"A bit shaky. I'm getting used to the bugger again. I'm not ready to let him go." Through a window he could see a horse cropping grass on someone's front lawn. People were still gathered at the barriers above the river's flooded bank. "You don't suppose he was planning to die in my mother's house? Some sort of revenge?"

"I'm not sure it would be a good idea for me to be there, I'd want to be the one who holds his hand."

"If you were here I'd make sure you were doing more than that. I was a fool not to talk you into coming with us from the start."

"Well, just think how glad you'll be to see me when you get back. If I'd gone you could be tired of me by now."

"How so? I'd get to shake out your shoes every morning before you put them on, to make sure you don't drop dead after one or two steps. I'd get to smear the sunscreen on parts of your body you can't reach. Swat the flies that get into your hair. Wash out your sweaty underwear three or four times every day."

"Good lord, such a romantic place might spoil me for ordinary life. What would I get to do for you?"

"You have to ask? Put Rohan back on for a minute, will you? I was rude."

There were muttered voices as the telephone was exchanged.

"Yeah?" the boy said. Suspicious.

"I haven't seen the dinosaur tracks but I'm getting close. If there's any sign it was a meteor wiped them out I'll let you know."

"Okay."

"I mailed you a card," he said. "Told you something about the southern sky. Get your mum to help you sound out the words."

Even a grunt could sound pleased.

When Holly came back on, he said, "His father?" The boy's father had shown up that other summer, spoiling things.

"His father is living on the reserve again, married to someone else." Then she seemed to have guessed a question he hadn't even thought of yet. "Yes, his father can read. But he hated the residential school so much he refuses. Rohan thinks –"

"I can imagine."

"But he hasn't seen Joseph in three years or more. Nor have I."

"Will you come if he doesn't improve? He refuses to go home."

"If he wants me to. I won't go far from a phone the next couple of days. Uncle Harry can take a message if he has to. I miss you too, you know."

This was a natural place to hang up. Nothing he could think of seemed important enough to keep her on the line, yet he didn't want her to go. He was grateful this woman was thinking of his father while she tended her mock orange bushes and her western wahoos. And thinking of him, too, down here in this unfamiliar baking fly-blown valley of death.

"Is he complaining much?" she said.

"No more than usual. He seems to be having a better time than the rest of us."

Before returning to the other room, Sonny sat for a moment on a narrow chair he'd noticed only now beside the phone. His hands were shaking. It had been all right while he was talking with Holly, he was doing something about it then. But now he was back with the facts. So long as they'd been on the move it seemed that the facts might be outrun, but they had caught up to him now. It seemed that suddenly he was aware of the accumulated weight he was carrying: his father's deteriorating health, his daughter's welfare in this unfamiliar world, and his own surprising concern for a boy he would gladly, just two days ago, have left behind on the road. All of them had got too far from home.

When he rejoined the others, his father's eyes were greedy for his news.

"She doesn't trust you, she's waiting to hear you're too weak to threaten her virtue."

"Be serious," his father growled.

Lachlan sat awkwardly on the edge of the bed, his eyes on the floor. Uncertain whether he ought to be here, Sonny thought. Yet his hand rested on the old man's shoulder. His father, usually uncomfortable with physical contact, didn't seem to mind.

"She wants me to phone her every day. Bulletins, like an ailing pope. She'll get here fast if I ask her."

The nurse came back into the room carrying a pillow. "Your

father tells me you're going to Kalevan Station," she said. "A friend of mine is a live-in there." She lifted the old man's head and placed this second pillow behind it, pounded it a bit before lowering Timo Aalto's head. "The lady keeps a nursing sister in the house. So he will be cared-for there as well as anywhere."

"Well, there you are," Sonny said to his father. "You may get what you want after all."

He wasn't sure if he cared one way or the other, now. They had already succeeded at something. They'd got as far as his mother's doorstep without spending too much time at each other's throat. And he hadn't lost the old man to this landscape. Not yet, anyway.

Lachlan looked up at Sonny with a puzzled squint, still waiting for something.

Maybe it wasn't true that he didn't care one way or the other. He needed, amongst other things, to get at least a glimpse of the woman who'd chosen not to be his mother, and to meet the boar who'd set out statues and mutilated corpses along the way in order to lead him here. And he needed to give his father the chance to finish something that had begun in his sauna. What he hadn't thought until now was that he also needed to deliver this young man and the stolen LandCruiser, he couldn't let the poor bugger face the music on his own. If the old woman didn't tear a strip off his skinny hide, Trevor certainly would. Or their famous Benno. After three long days together in that battered zebra-striped Toyota, he could not abandon the boy now.

By the time they arrived, Kalevan Station was in a state of excitement. Viira Hawkins had disappeared. She was out there somewhere on the land, she hadn't been seen for three days. It wasn't unusual for her to go walkabout, apparently, but according to radio and television reports the flood was heading this way much faster than anyone had expected. This meant the old woman was in more danger than she might have realized.

"You think I scared her off?" Sonny said. "Bringing my father with me?"

"She doesn't want to see any of us, really," said Lois Nugg. She and Aunt Clara had brought their coffee outside the sprawling house onto a verandah that overlooked a broad grassy space shaded by acacias. "God knows why she puts on these parties." Like Aunt Clara she was wearing shorts this morning, her narrow freckled legs a contrast to Aunt Clara's dimpled white calves. "Once, she sent out cancellation notes the day after she posted the invitations and some were delivered in the wrong order." This was followed by a rise and fall of laughter. Light glinted off her frameless glasses.

This flood also meant they did not have the luxury of waiting until the next morning for the pig shoot, Aunt Clara said. "Night's best, while the pigs are feeding. Early morning's second-best, when they're heading back to camp. But I reckon the flood has given some urgency to things."

As though to demonstrate the urgency, a white truck roared in to the compound and came to a stop beneath a shaggy-barked gum tree, dogs turning and passing over and under one another inside angle-iron cages behind the cab. Shovels, chains, and other tools lay heaped on the boards. When three men spilled out from the cab, all laughing, Aunt Clara raised her voice: "You wrote me name on a fat one, I hope. Tied it to a tree?"

"One for each of us, Clara," said the little man who'd married into the family by mistake. He put a hand on Sonny's shoulder as he passed by to go inside. "Big ol' granddaddy asked us not to forget the foreigner." And laughed again. "If that flood don't drive us off first." He nodded in the direction of a television visible through the opened wall of the kitchen. Muddy water swept past buildings and the crowns of isolated trees.

"My daughter?" Sonny said.

"Eating with them others down the far end," Aunt Clara said. She slapped dust from her voluminous shorts. "They've treated her better than she has any right to, but that hasn't made her what you'd call a happy little Vegemite."

He could imagine. He had been imagining Charlotte's displeasure since waking up this morning, and all the long way out here to the station. The others had set off from the hotel at sunrise, but he had first to collect his father from the clinic, where the doctor had left word he wanted to talk. There was a possibility, the doctor said when he'd been called in from his home, that the old man had suffered a series of minor strokes. "Has he had periods of confusion?"

"He nods off," Sonny said. "He falls. His legs can't be trusted. Sometimes he's a little confused afterwards. Yesterday he was seeing things that weren't there."

The doctor looked almost pleased to hear this. "He may be using the falls to mask what's really happening. Bring him back if

it happens again, we'll have him flown out for tests. The receptionist will give you my number."

"You don't think we should be flying straight home?"

The doctor stared down at his own hairy legs, thinking about
this. "Consider where your father would like to be. Just try to
avoid excessive heat."

Once they'd got out of town, by a route that took them downriver to a bridge that hadn't yet been swamped, the journey to the
station was through some of the loneliest landscape yet. With the
nearly bald world slipping over the horizon in all directions it was
easy to imagine the planet turning beneath them. They travelled
along the curved rolling ridge at its top, silent most of the way,
the old man speaking only once during the two-hour drive.
"Christ, this is desolate."

The *Kalevan Station* sign hung from a twisted crossbar spanning
a pair of gateposts. A battered and rusted mailbox sat on a tilted
stump. Once they'd crossed over the cattle grid the road became
a pair of tire tracks, winding like a lazy stream across the nearly
featureless landscape. After ten or fifteen minutes a cluster of
roofs and trees appeared against the sky. A dark oasis in a desert
of light. When the tracks had led them in through a gap in the
shrubbery, they could see buildings set around an oval of grass,
some up on posts like seaside cottages capped with metal roofs.
Cars and utes and four-by-four trucks were parked to one end of
the compound.

So many palms and flowering shrubs grew against the largest
building that it appeared to be only a great expanse of roof sus-
pended above a jungle. The nearest wing was obscured by
draperies of fragrant vines and a netted aviary, where brilliant
birds roosted on the limbs of leafless trees. From some far part of
the house a confusion of excited voices rose to a burst of laughter
before subsiding.

Once he'd got past bushes and under the wide overhang, he
could follow a wall of louvred doors past patio furniture and a
jungle of potted plants. Around a second corner a giant stood up

from a chair. A black Lab leapt to its feet and came barking down the floorboards prepared to tear out Sonny Aalto's throat, but a shout from the tall man yanked the dog into a cringing retreat.

"Got lost, did yiz?" The voice was so deep that Sonny felt it in his lower diaphragm. This was the person who'd answered the phone. The low brim of his hat kept much of his face in shadow but did not hide a broad snub nose and patches of fresh pink skin. His arms and legs were long and skinny but a hefty gut strained the buttons of his khaki shirt. He looked off into the dust still rolling in from beyond the bushes, perhaps for more stragglers. Then, seeing none, he decided a small token of hospitality wouldn't kill him. "Benedict Morrow," he said. "General foreman here. Boss cocky when Trevor's away." He put a hand on the dog's head. "This is Thor. We're having a short smoko now between chores." He found himself amusing.

A Benno had been mentioned at the banquet. His employer had found him amusing too. "My father is with us," Sonny said.

"Sister Grimes has been watching for him." Sister Grimes was presumably the young woman in a loose red tank top who'd come out to stand behind the giant and size up the intruder.

Once they'd wheeled the old man inside, the nurse led them down a hallway to a bedroom where the covers of a single bed had been turned back. Timo Aalto protested. He hadn't come all this way just to be dumped into bed. He did not consent until Sonny had explained that this rest would give him time to prepare himself for curious strangers asking too many questions. "And I have to make sure Charlotte's okay."

Sister Grimes helped the old man out of the wheelchair, and turned him to sit on the bed. "Now we'll take off these shoes."

"Surprise," he said, placing the end of his wooden stump in her hands. "When our brakes failed they made me drag my foot, wore shoe and foot right off and started up my leg."

"I can point yiz to your room," Benno said. Even while speaking to Sonny he seemed more interested in Lachlan, who had stayed in the doorway, apparently uncertain of his status here. "I

can take the lad while you find something to eat. Shearers' quarters are just minutes up the track."

He'd followed Lachlan and the giant outside as far as this open
verandah where Aunt Clara and the bush poet sipped coffee and
watched brightly coloured birds squabble in the upper branches
of a gum tree. Once the zebra-striped Toyota had driven off, and
the scouts had gone inside to make their report, he set off down
the length of the house in search of Charlotte.

The food was laid out on a row of tables that stretched from the
kitchen through the opened louvres and onto yet another wide
verandah. Stacks of pancakes, dishes of boiled and fried eggs, pans
of bacon and sausage, jugs of various coloured juices, bowls of
tropical fruit. People took their loaded plates outside and down to
the tables and benches in a tiled courtyard. For some, brunch was
a sweating can of Powers from the ice chest.

Excited conversations overlapped, exploded into shouts, a
burst of laughter. A small child ran in from outside, bounced off
Sonny's legs, ducked under the table, and came up on the other
side running again. He was followed by one, two, three others, all
squealing. Beside a post in the opened-up wall a young man with
a beard strummed absently on a guitar.

Outside, Charlotte was sitting on a bench in the midst of a
crowd, listening to what must have been highlights of the
Avvachat family trip so far. "You can keep your Cairns," the big
woman said. "When we woke we thought they'd sold the ocean to
the Japs – tide was out so far you couldn't see nothing but mud!
The Mareeba Rodeo was worth seeing, though. A blackfellow was
gored by a bull. We don't know if he died, the ambulance took him
away." Eggs and bacon were washed down with beer. "Suzy here's
been worrying about him ever since. Wants to call up and ask."

"Do not!" her daughter snarled. The mother laughed.

As soon as one of the younger people left, he moved out to take
the vacated space beside Charlotte. "Aha!" she said, apparently
pleased to see him. She gave him her movie-star smile and kissed

the air beside his ear as though she'd been looking forward to his arrival. "Everyone's on edge," she said. "The old woman's out there somewhere. 'Talking to the rocks' was how it was put." She smiled the smile of one who was thinking more than she'd said. "Well, a madwoman in the family could be fun."

"But why are you here?"

Surprised innocence. "This is what we planned. This is why we came."

"I meant why *were* you here, where Errol has put you in danger."

It was clear she'd hoped he wouldn't ask. Her smile was withdrawn, her beautiful face turned away. "He offered me a job that night at his house. He wanted photographs taken, discreetly, of certain parts of his mother's property. I turned him down at first but changed my mind. He'd offered me a guide, and I was in such a hurry to get out into this fabulous continent with my camera. No mountains, no old-growth forests, no clear-cuts. Not a hint of green! Not real green, anyway."

"But you weren't as careful as Errol must have intended."

She smiled. "I seem to have stumbled into another war zone. Errol wanted photos of places that Trevor doesn't want the world to know about."

"Isn't that dangerous, putting yourself between them?" Not to mention, he thought, that it was out here that white supremacists practised with their guns. He'd picked this up from a television program. The farther you ventured into this continent the more likely you were to encounter extremists. Trevor could be Grand Dragon of some local version of the Klan.

"Native paintings in a cave is what Errol wanted proof of. He has hopes they'll be on some tribe's dreaming journey."

"Meaning?"

"Survival knowledge. Laws passed on by their ancestors. Like the Ten Commandments. Apparently any site they consider sacred is protected by law. Errol says the area would have to be cleared of sheep."

Errol says.

The dispossessed pastoralist had overheard. "Another plot of the federal government." He leaned closer with his elbows on his naked knees, his face bland and patient. "Look at Fraser Island – no more sand mining allowed. The Great Barrier Reef – no more oil searches. Tasmania – logging halted. Lives here will be ruined. It will put a halt to shearing, cattle transporting, the pastoral and rail industries, all in one blow."

"But will save the freckled duck from extinction," said Lois Nugg passing by with her mug. "Also the grey falcon and the golden perch." She laid a hand on the back of Sonny's neck and then moved on.

"And the bloody skink!" The pastoralist sneered towards Lois Nugg's departing back. Then, for Charlotte, he adopted his reasonable tone again. "Our land values will drop – unsaleable, except to the government, which is exactly what they want. We'll have to take what they offer. Can you blame Trevor for putting up a fight?"

Charlotte observed him as she might a servant who had delivered an unwelcome lecture on the management of an estate. Sonny knew how this felt. But the pastoralist was not so easily scared off. "It's a way for the federal government to override the state. Canberra's a front for the coming world government. I'm sure they've found a way of taking over your country as well."

This time Charlotte's silent icy stare unnerved him and he turned away. Remembering, maybe, that he'd already lost one battle and would probably lose this one as well. When she turned to Sonny again, it was to draw attention to his unoccupied hands. "You didn't get yourself any of their *tucker*?"

"No I didn't, not yet. But I should take something to my dad. He'll think I've gone home and left him here."

Inside, he forked a few pancakes onto a plate, poured syrup over them, and explored hallways until he found his father's room. The old man was asleep, or pretending to sleep. "It's just me. Sonny." He put the plate on the bedside table.

Without opening his eyes his father said, "Sonny?" As if the name meant nothing.

"A relative. I believe we've met."

A grunt. The sunken mouth chewed on itself. The eyes opened, but quickly closed again, as though the light were too bright. "Where the hell am I now?"

"What do you mean?"

The eyes opened again, and looked hard at Sonny with something like fear. "Just what I said. Where've they put me? I can't tell nothing from this bloody box of a room."

"You're in her house. You don't remember us getting here?"

"Oh." The embarrassed half-laugh was unconvincing. "What's the matter with me?" Again the fearful eyes looked to Sonny for help. "Whaddya mean, her house?"

"Viira Hawkins's house. You must've dozed off for a while, it's made you confused."

"I guess so." He looked at the plate of pancakes on the bedside table as though these, too, were part of a puzzle he was expected to solve.

"You okay?"

"Yeah. Sure." The old man shook his head as though to dislodge a cobweb. "She bit your head off yet?"

"Not yet. She isn't here. Nobody knows where she is."

His father seemed pleased to hear this. "Well there you are, she hasn't changed." It brightened his mood to say so. "Don't forget to ask her if it was me that drove her away." He watched Sonny's face for a reaction.

"You think I'd ask her that?"

"What else is worth coming all this way to ask?" He pulled himself into a sitting-up position. "Isn't that why I brought you here – so you can hear that it wasn't me?" A good deal of his colour had returned to Timo Aalto's cheeks. "Hand me that plate." He struggled to work his shoulders up against the pillow. When Sonny had put the plate in his hands, he frowned at the pancakes. "No eggs? No bacon? What kind of cheap outfit does she run here anyway?"

On his way back to the kitchen, he passed by Joanie Hawkins talking on a telephone. She smiled and wriggled fingers. A radio phone. Before going to sleep last night in the hotel, he'd dialled the long complicated series of digits that led to an operator, and then another series that ended, finally, with a distant ringing in Warren's craft shop up the Ottawa Valley. "I'll be meeting your grandmother tomorrow," he'd intended to say. "What do you think of that?"

"Warren isn't here," his partner Lori said. Without waiting for his next question she added, "He doesn't tell me where he's going." She was not impressed that he was calling from Queensland. She asked no questions of her own. She did not say she would tell his son he'd called. "It's thirty-nine degrees here," he said. He should have known better than to try.

In one of the rooms he had to pass through, this morning's *Australian* lay on the top of a stack of newspapers. It seemed that interest in tomorrow's referendum was genuine. According to headlines, his country was being pushed to the brink of balkanization. Bureaucrats were reporting a record number of passport applications from Quebeckers. To help Australians visualize this vote as a geographical war, they were given a map labelled "Language Divide."

Ceiling fans paddled air to keep it moving. In this sprawling one-storey house you were under a sheltering roof but, with so many outside walls thrown open, only the surrounding bushes, alive with birds, were between you and the baking landscape. Living here would be like making your home in a vast open tent. What must Jerrod have thought of the houses in Ottawa? Sturdy brick walls, narrow storeys stacked upon one another, double sets of doors between inside and out, glassed-in sun porches, outer walls behind a palisade of icicles hanging off the roof. Inside and outside as distinct as you'd find in any fortress under siege.

His mother's walls were decorated with framed black-and-white photos. A long-skirted grim-faced woman stood on the front gallery of a shack, one hand against a post. Was this his mother's mother, wondering what she'd got herself into? In another photo, a truck from the earliest years of the century was piled high with what he imagined were bales of wool. The driver's raised hand might have been waving away the flies. There were portraits of women – all strong-jawed and squinting with impatience – but hair and clothing suggested an earlier age. Viira Hawkins must be camera-shy. Either that, or she had removed her image from the accessible parts of her house.

"Careful you don't knock Herman off his pedestal." Laughing Lois Nugg came into the room with a mug in her hand. "Herman" was a sculpture built of spark plugs, the shape of some vicious bird vaguely reminiscent of a turkey vulture. "Something she purchased at the Eumundi market. Whenever Viira has the money, she can't resist anything resembling art. Gets up Trevor's nose, makes him wild."

Other strange figures, constructed of wire or metal fragments or marked-up Plexiglass, stood about on dark gleaming tables. Some stood on the floor. A brightly decorated didgeridoo leaned against a wrought-iron gum tree at the centre of it all. If you thought of this as a trophy room, or a museum of looted artifacts, a battered old lunch bucket would not be out of place. It was not, however, currently on display.

"You never know when you may find an ancient black man in the yard with his pots of paint. She spent time on the board of directors at the state gallery."

"And didn't make enemies of everyone?"

"Viira has the knack for charming lifelong foes into getting along." The pause seemed calculated. "If she wants to."

"Obviously she hasn't much interest in charming me."

"You'll notice that Errol is missing." She seemed determined not to leave him. "He and Trevor got into a boil-up last night.

After you deserted us." Her short salt-and-pepper hair was so tightly curled he thought of scouring pads. Her blouse may have been unbuttoned a little lower than it had been a few minutes before, perhaps to enjoy the breeze from the ceiling fans.

"Afterwards, Errol went up to his room and knocked two teeth out of his floozy's head. Apparently he didn't want her here this year. There's someone else he's set his sights on, I don't have to tell you who. He hasn't shown his face this morning, so far as I know."

"And his, uh, young woman?"

"Gone." Lois Nugg raised her eyes to the ceiling, perhaps for his careful choice of words. "Each year we expect one of them to do some damage to the other. Maybe that's what keeps us coming. Maybe that's why Viira sometimes doesn't show. You can see for yourself why she can't bear to see them at one another's throats." She reached up to tap at a rectangle of framed words amongst the photos.

> *The only road to a better life lies in co-operation, love,*
> *and generosity . . . virtually impossible in a society*
> *based on competition and internal strife.*
> *Matti Kurikka: "The Harmony Idea"*

"Not exactly original," she said. "But it was the basis of the *Kalevan Kansa* colonies – up in your part of the world as well as here. My grandfather and your mother's father were part of it for a while, in the Atherton Tableland. Brothers. So we are cousins, you and I." She studied Sonny with the sort of concentration she must apply to thinking up a line for a poem. "If you came looking for an apology, you won't get it. She may believe in co-operation and the rest of it, but she isn't big on apologies." She laughed at some inner thought. "I hope you didn't come with some notion that you could be born, like Wainamoinen, in middle age! I don't suppose you know the poem?"

She didn't wait for an answer, but stood up straight like a reciting schoolgirl:

"There's no getting the Sampo
and no bringing the bright-lid
    out of dark Northland
from dreary Sariola!
There the Sampo's been taken
    the bright-lid carried
into Northland's rocky hill
inside the slope of copper
    locked behind nine locks;
in there roots have been rooted
to a depth of nine fathoms
with one root in mother earth
and one in a riverbank
and a third in the home-hill."

She paused only long enough to refill her lungs. "I know great
chunks of it by heart! Years ago I visited the family's village in
Suomi. Mid-summer. The entire population out in the square,
reciting the epic in turn." She rested a hand on his wrist. "My own
verses are poor imitations, but I like to think the voices that told
those tales to Elias Lönnrot speak faintly also to me on occasion.
All this distance away."

The hand slid a short way up his arm. "We must talk more
about the *Kalevala*." There was a fruity smell about her. Perhaps
she'd been drinking cheap wine with her brunch. "Have they put
you in the shearers' quarters as well?"

"They have," he said, "but I haven't been out to see."

"Then I can take you there." She seemed to mean she was
ready to do that now.

"Maybe later," he said. "I promised my daughter I would get
myself something to eat."

Once Lois Nugg had passed on to another room he recalled her
veiled reference to Charlotte. Bloody Errol! Though she would
deny him the right to do so, she could not prevent him from speaking to the man. He hoped the dentist was too hungover this

morning to pursue anyone. Maybe Brother Errol was smart enough
to see her motives were purely selfish, or at best only professional.

As soon as he'd rejoined Charlotte, the dog Thor came trotting
down the verandah and flopped by his feet. His tongue slurped
experimentally at Sonny's hand, I'm right here if you need me.
Sonny pulled his hand away and wiped it against the leg of his
shorts. "You haven't asked me how he is – the man you came to
help me care for."

"What about the other one? What have you done with the
back-alley boy from Kings Cross?" Although she was seated beside
him she was turned slightly away, and so spoke as though over her
shoulder. "The only thing I regret is not being there to see how
long it took you to start hating each other's guts. Did you drive the
whole way here in silence, or did you dump him and fly?"

"Right now he's taking our luggage back to the shearers' quarters, wherever that is. It took him a while to warm up to us but
eventually he was the helper I couldn't do without. I'm thinking
of adopting him."

She turned, wide-eyed, to be sure he was joking.

"I meant only that he filled the gap you left," he said. "Left
me free to spend more time worrying about what had happened
to you."

Her shoulders stiffened. "You've no reason to worry about me.
You've no reason even to *think* about me."

If she weren't his daughter would he even try to care about this
woman? When she seemed to get pleasure out of thwarting him?
"Do you want me to believe you never think of that child you left
in Louisiana? It seems you have more reason to overlook my shortcomings than I'd imagined." He lowered an overcooked sausage to
the dog at his feet, who gulped it down and yawned his gratitude.

Though she shifted her gaze to something in the middle distance, he could see her facial muscles fighting an impulse to
scowl. "Don't you dare pass judgement on me! Don't you dare
pretend it's the same!"

Sonny stood up to return his plate to the kitchen. This sudden surge of anger was dangerous. So was the sense that he'd handled everything wrong. Again. He would see if he could find the shearing quarters without the help of Lois Nugg. For all their talk of moving up the hunt, he'd seen no sign they intended to leave very soon. Some of them were keeping an eye on the television, where a gleaming muddy sea extended to the distant horizon, animals and furniture bobbed and turned and floated past, and tiny human figures waited on rooftops for rescue. "Charleville's gone under," someone announced, with what sounded like satisfaction.

He should telephone Judith Buckle, to tell her they'd arrived. There was no point in writing postcards now. His Sydney card to Colin Macken would not have got there yet, and probably wouldn't get there until after that anniversary party Harry'd mentioned. Thirty-seven, thirty-eight years married? Colin was probably sitting down to dinner about now, talking over Theresa's suggestion that they go to Europe for a change, to celebrate, though he'd rather stay at home and fell trees. Down in Harry Sylvester's house, Holly's son picked sulkily at his supper, punishing his mother for refusing to read him the locations of upcoming sky parties. Even farther east, some of the M'sieur Patates chip wagons were preparing to close for the night, business just beginning to fall off after a busy day. Inside a canal-side tavern, while he delayed finishing his last drink of the evening, the senior Cabinet minister held his cellular phone to his ear. "That is bullshit," he said. "This country is going down the drain while he sits on his fat ass doing nothing!" At the far end of the room, Warren Aalto shared a plate of stuffed mushrooms with an attractive maker of beeswax candles, before adjourning to her Sandy Hill apartment. "I've been feeling trapped," he said. "Thank God you came along when you did."

Sonny Aalto, this far away, could not remember whether the water level of the Rideau Canal would have been lowered yet, in preparation for the first big freeze.

A few hundred metres up the dirt track was a cluster of tin-roofed buildings, the largest the size of a barn, with corrugated walls reflecting the blinding sunlight. All faced in to a central dirt yard stitched over with a network of vines and small green melons. Benedict stood with fists to his hips, contemplating the zebra-striped Toyota. He pushed back the brim of his hat and squinted at Sonny. "The lad's from the city?"

"Raised in the country." The mother's defeated face had been as dry and scored with lines as Benno's own. "Lives in Sydney now. But before he goes back he'll probably want to work off whatever he owes your Mrs. Hawkins."

A tree off the far end of the shearers' quarters looked like a bouquet of tail feathers from some giant bird. Another drooped with heavy snatches of what might have been long green horse's hair. Casuarina, his father's book had named it. Small black birds noisily settled in a gum tree whose trunk was as pale and smooth as human flesh.

The foreman held an open palm above the hood. "I've got him filling sandbags with some of my men. You reckon he's worked on a station before?"

"He says he likes horses," Sonny said. "I figure what he needs is someone willing to teach him reasons to be pleased with himself – like doing a good day's work. If expenses are more than he can reasonably work off I'll –"

"Nuh!" Benno waved the offer away before it could be made. "You'll find some old hats hanging outside my door. Here's the boy now."

Lachlan appeared in an open doorway of the barn. "Wool shed," he said, once Benno had disappeared around the side of it. It wasn't a barn. His grin could not have been wider if he'd built the wool shed himself. The wide-brimmed hat he'd crammed on his head came right down to his bleached eyebrows, and made him look like a twelve-year-old boy. Someone had persuaded him to wear a long-sleeved khaki shirt and a pair of beat-up and proba-bly dog-chewed elastic-sided boots. "We're over here." He started across the powdery dust towards the longest of the other buildings, a sort of primitive motel with a row of doors and tiny windows under a wide metal overhang. "Benno's got me fillin' sandbags with some other blokes."

Thor followed close on Sonny's heels, as he had done all the way from the house. "He say anything about the happy reappearance of the vanished truck?"

"Grinned around 'er a bit, that's all. Shook his head. I reckon the old lady'll have enough to say for both of them."

"You worried?"

"Naow!" The very idea was dismissed with a shrug.

"I don't imagine those stripes were on it when she saw it last. She probably remembers a radio phone as well."

The boy pushed a hand up under his hat. "Maybe I am a bit worried – orright?" His eyes met Sonny's then quickly shifted away. More than worried, he was scared. "If I had a friggin' brain I'd shoot through before she shows up." This was said with a sigh, giving the future an air of inevitability. He led the way along beneath the wide front overhang, loose boards clattering beneath their feet. "I reckon you'll have to put up me bail." He stopped at the second door from the end and pushed it open.

The room was no larger than it had to be, for two single cots. Walls were whitewashed. The floorboards were painted the colour of dried blood. A piece of checkered cotton hung over the little window. Sonny's new tote bag had been tossed onto one of the narrow beds, Lachlan's backpack on the other.

"The big man's quarters are there." Lachlan tilted his head in the direction of a separate building up on posts. "If there's anything we need in the night, is what he said." The boy's grin could not be misunderstood.

"You'll get yourself killed," Sonny said. "He could have meant a flashlight. Or extra blankets. I'd watch my step if I were you."

Thor settled on the floorboards by the door, his eyes following Sonny's hand. Hoping for more sausages, perhaps.

"You reckon you could take on Benno if you had to?"

"I *reckon* I don't want to find out. Just stick to the job and he might defend you when the old woman throws a fit." Sonny ducked to look into a small, cracked off-kilter mirror on the wall, and prodded gently at scabs. He was beginning to look like a stranger. "What makes you think I'd want to put up your bail?"

"I dunno," Lachlan said, starting away. "I've gotta go. We're movin' sandbags down to the house." Thor went panting after him.

Maybe it wasn't the point – whether some friendly gesture would have been welcome that night in his mother's house. Maybe you weren't supposed to wait until you were welcome. If you were a father. Which of course he wasn't, not to the boy – though for a while that night what he'd felt for Lachlan Hall was probably more fatherly than what he felt for the two blood children who claimed they didn't need him. Whatever it was, he felt something like it now, watching the boy's skinny frame stride down beneath the overhang and out across the dirt towards the wool shed. Of course this scrawny young man didn't need him, or would never admit it if he did. That, too, was probably beside the point.

Sonny was left at the centre of a great lonely silence. Sun glared off the unmoving metal blades of a distant windmill. Beside the building that housed showers and toilets, sun glared off a corrugated metal water tank on spindly legs, a giant soup can stripped of its paper label. Sun glared off the side of the Toyota LandCruiser, as well, out on the square of dust. Sonny's singlet was soaked down the front. Sweat ran in rivulets down out of his hair. Heat rash had started in the sweaty creases inside his elbows and knees. Even dressed, he felt naked here. Too much had been left behind.

Unused to keeping track of hats, Sonny had left his new one somewhere. From the row hanging by Benno's door, a beat-up ancient sweat-stained Akubra with a tear in the brim appealed to him most. He pulled the front down over his forehead and looked out through the ragged hole. These things, he'd heard, were made from rabbit skins.

He smeared Ombrelle on his wet face and arms and the bare parts of his legs. Then he hung Charlotte's camera from his shoulder and started down the tire tracks towards the bushes that hid the big house from the rest of the world. The song of some kind of bird etched brief scribbles of sound against the silence.

The land spread out on all sides to the wide curve of the earth. Tracks to the left led across reddish-brown dust to the horizon. Tracks to the right led to horizon as well. Here and there, dusty sheep snatched mouthfuls from tufts of dun-coloured grass. Sun's heat pressed from above and below at the same time. The dirt, dust, whatever it was, might not have lost yesterday's heat before having to absorb today's. A kangaroo – it took some effort to distinguish the figure – lounged sidelong in the thin shade of a scraggly bush.

How close would it allow him? He walked out to see, and discovered that it wasn't just dust that he walked on. Hammers might have reduced a sprawling city of red clay bricks to rubble. When he pressed his toe to a tuft of grass, it crackled like brittle sticks. Whatever the sheep were getting from it wasn't moisture. Colours were weak, as if the sunlight had sucked all pigments from earthly things. The few skeletal trees were jagged strokes of blinding white.

Behind the peculiar songs of the magpies, he could hear the distant roar of a machine working hard in low gear. Pulling his hat down lower, he squinted along the line of horizon for sign of movement. Nothing moved. Then, where a fence line vanished, some kind of vehicle appeared. It was coming, slowly, in this direction. Eventually he could see that it was the heavy bottom half of a truck. The kangaroo leapt from its lazy rest and hopped off – at first in jerky leaps, then in gradually lengthening tail-propelled bounds. A second was up and leaping too, a little behind, a little to the right of the other.

The front of the engine carried not only a roo bar but a pair of large truck tires wired to the top of the iron framework like two monstrous black-ringed eyes. Maybe animals were taller here than elsewhere. Maybe these people would rather bounce them aside than kill them.

The truck, tractor, whatever it was, swung off the fence-line track and growled across the dry paddock towards him. The word *Toyota* peered out from the grille but there was little left of the original truck. The top had been removed and replaced with a framework of pipe. Spotlights had been mounted at the top front corners. The tires were oversize. The half-doors were cut down from another vehicle of another colour, some kind of blue.

The machine roared slowly closer and didn't stop until the right-hand buffer tire was inches from Sonny's chest. He stepped to one side. The engine dropped into a noisy idle. Two hands gripped the oversized steering wheel in the ten-to-two position advised by drivers' manuals. This driver wore grease-smudged cotton pants, a long-sleeved khaki shirt, and a high-crowned hat with a brim wide enough to hide the face in shadow.

Sonny removed Benno's damaged hat and fanned himself. His hair was soaking wet. So was his singlet.

"Put it back on," the driver said, pushing back his own hat. It was Jerrod Hawkins. He propped a boot, scuffed and rubbed raw at the toes, on the top of the low half-door. "There's that hole in the sky they keep talking about, and everywhere people with pieces of face cut away."

Obediently, he returned the hat to his head. "You?"

"You expected a holy apparition? Our Lady of the Paddocks, perhaps?" He kicked open the half-door. "Come on up."

Relieved and disappointed both, Sonny climbed onto the trembling seat, placing his feet amongst rusted cans and pieces of machinery. The vehicle jerked into life, and started its slow roaring crawl. But instead of carrying on towards the house, Jerrod hauled on the steering wheel and turned them through a wide arc in the tussocky dirt. Then they started off towards the horizon. "No worries," he shouted. "They'll think you're lost. Chasing you will be more fun than chasing a pig."

"I don't know why she invited me if she can't be bothered showing up."

"Hold on, mate – we may be the ones to find her."

If she couldn't be bothered showing up, why should he go chasing after her? "You sure this is a good idea? They seemed in a hurry to start."

Jerrod laughed. "Trevor's probably just waking up about now," he said. "What have they told you about her? A lot of cock, I'm sure. Painting her face and dancing with the Abos – that sort of thing."

"I think they're worried – a woman her age out there."

"She's at home out there. She's paying her place a *visit*."

"Not offering blood sacrifices to the rocks?"

Instead of smiling this time, Jerrod adopted a businesslike tone. "You're a landscapist, right?" He waited a moment, perhaps in case Sonny wished to object. "You already know a landscape's manufactured by the human mind, like everything else." They were moving along the fence line, following the tracks he had just made in the dirt upon all the tracks before them. "I mean, it means something different to everyone. When Trevor looks at this, he sees food and space for stock. Possible profit, if only the damn wool prices would rise or the government come through with another grant." One hand swept out to take in everything on this great brown disk of earth. "Errol huddles against the coastline, scared of this. But he wants to save it anyway. What he sees is delicate plants and endangered animals. Now tell me, what do you see?"

They'd come to an iron gate. Beyond it was another paddock identical to the one they'd just crossed. Dirt, tufts of grey grass, grey-brown lumps of sheep. A few scraggly trees. On and on and on. Far off, a horizontal bar of earth the colour of dried blood. This might be beautiful but it was naked, hostile earth. "The floor of a red-brick crematorium," he said. "Everything burned away except bones and ash."

Jerrod dipped his head. "Then that's what you came here for. To walk on the ashes. Somewhere inside that head you must know what it means."

He didn't know. Or didn't want to know. "Is it only the rocks and dirt she loves? She shoots the pigs."

"She has a license to cull the kangaroos. She doesn't like it, but she's got to protect the stock." Jerrod leaned forward, resting both arms on the wheel and his chin on his arms. "The water brings them here. The kangaroos come to eat the grass, the pigs to eat the lambs. She loses as many as 30 per cent to the feral pigs." He pushed back his hat and studied the horizon for a moment before going on. His nose, in profile, was not unlike Sonny's own. "They root up the earth around water holes, destroying vegetation. They eat crops meant for farm animals. They prey on nesting birds. They sire more pigs to do still more damage on a continent where they don't belong. They wouldn't be here at all if some damn fool hadn't brought them." He sat abruptly upright again. "And there wouldn't be so many if we weren't here with our water supply. It's a matter of keeping a balance. Now get down and open the gate."

Once Jerrod had driven through, Sonny closed the gate behind them and climbed aboard again. He brushed away the flies that buzzed at his ears. Flies interested in the sweat at his inner elbows were more persistent. "I don't know one direction from another here," he said, as they started to move again. "We could be heading for those dinosaur tracks you promised."

"You won't get to Lark Quarry this time. Not unless you stay till the flood subsides. It looks as if the whole channel country's going under."

Within minutes they'd come to a pool – a dam, Jerrod called it. This was a great muddy reservoir scooped out of the ground, the dirt pushed up to create a surrounding dike surmounted by a wire fence. Sheep were meant to drink at the outside trough, fed by a pipe that ran along the ground, but a few had got in where strands of barbed wire had been broken. Two, three, four of the sheep were mired at the water's edge. They looked at nothing and waited. On the far side a cluster of sheep looked out from the shade of acacias upon their mired sisters and the purring truck with equal indifference.

"Shall we save Benedict the bother?" Jerrod said, swinging down out of the machine. Grabbing up a coil of rope, he walked ahead of Sonny down the slope and through the gap in the fence. Posts were short and twisted, barbed wire mended here and there with rusted haywire twists.

The nearest sheep was belly-deep in the slick grey muddy edge of the water. Jerrod slipped a noose over its neck and stepped back up the slope, letting the rope uncoil. When he set in his heels and leaned back, pulling the rope tight, it seemed to Sonny that the sheep's neck was stretching. The head might soon come off.

"Up here," Jerrod said.

Sonny took hold of the rope and dug his heels into the soil. This time the sheep panicked, and its front legs emerged, flinging mud and water. "Again!" They heaved again. The sheep slipped, and fell, and came up sidelong out of the mud, slithering along the surface, kicking all four legs. When it lay above the water's edge, Jerrod went down and slipped the rope from its neck and nudged it with his boot. When it didn't move, he used both hands to raise its rump. It stabbed with its front hooves until they found purchase. Standing, it seemed about to collapse. Jerrod pushed, so that it was forced to take steps. But it fell, and had to be raised once more. By the third push, the sheep was steady enough to keep going, and hobbled up the slope towards the shade.

They helped two more sheep to their feet, and watched them stagger up the slope to join the others. But the fourth was too weak to struggle, and had to be dragged out as dead weight at the end of the rope. When Jerrod removed the noose, he raised the ewe to her feet and nudged her ahead, as he had the others. Like the others, this one staggered and fell. Raised a second time and nudged again, she hadn't the strength to walk. Again she fell.

"Maybe once she's rested," Sonny said. But when they were back in the truck, though the three rescued sheep were indistinguishable now amongst a crowd looking out from the acacias, this last one still hadn't moved. It lay with its neck stretched out on the mud.

Jerrod reached under the seat and brought up a small pistol. He swung one foot down to get out, then paused and pulled his foot in and handed the gun to Sonny.

Sonny Aalto looked at the cold metal in his hand. He could smell the oil.

"This is the childhood you missed, remember? This is what the old woman cheated you out of. Go down and find out what it means to be a Queensland grazier."

Sonny walked through the fence gap and down the slope towards the muddy water and bent over the sheep. Its knobby eye looked up, then rolled away. "You sure you can't walk?" Just in case, he raised its rump and set it on its feet again. This time it did not even stagger ahead, but dropped where it was.

The old woman was watching him from somewhere, as skilled as his father at manoeuvring him into corners he couldn't get easily out of. Had he become another of her employees? His boots were sinking. Dirty water spilled across his toes. He walked back up the slope to the truck and handed the pistol to Jerrod. "It's your family that raises them. It's your mother who's responsible for their welfare." He did not ask if it was her habit, even here, to expect others to care for what she ought to be caring for herself.

Apparently satisfied that Sonny meant what he said, Jerrod took the gun and went back down the slope to the mud. He braced one hand on a knee and with the other held the pistol behind the sheep's ear and pulled the trigger.

"Well," he said when he'd returned. "I thought this might get your blood lust up for the chase!" He laughed. "If any grunters witnessed this they'll breathe a sigh of relief."

"So this is the childhood I missed?"

"Maybe she convinced herself you were better off where you were. This is rough country out here. I was trampled by cattle more than once." For a moment he was quiet, as though remembering this. He hauled out a handkerchief and wiped the sweat from the moustache on his upper lip. "When Errol was small he disappeared. Two days later this bloke rode in on his horse, he'd found Errol down at your dinosaur site, alone. Nobody could tell us how he got there. He couldn't tell us himself, though he swears he saw cave paintings somewhere. Her three dingoes, she called us. She doesn't like us much. Never has. Maybe she thought she was giving you a chance you wouldn't have here."

Jerrod forced the gearshift into reverse and backed around to face the direction they'd come from. When they'd passed through the one long paddock and the gate and then the next paddock, he pulled to a halt where Sonny had climbed aboard and rested his arms on the steering wheel to study the scene. "So there they are, behind those trees, baying and milling and sniffing the air for blood. Don't make the mistake of thinking this family is typical. Some neighbours think Trevor and the whole lot of us are mad."

These brown paddocks, that wool shed and shearers' quarters off to their left, and the treed oasis ahead with the floating roof had been Jerrod Hawkins's childhood home. And beneath that roof there'd been a mother – the mother who'd been absent from the Aaltos' back-road farm. That Sonny Aalto was here and looking at it with an irrational envy was enough to make him wonder if this was what all his racing over the globe had been about – looking for home. He hoped it was not so simple.

"So she invited me to show me what she chose instead?" Because the engine was still running, it was still necessary to shout.

"Maybe it was as much my doing as hers," Jerrod said. He was silent a moment. Then he said, "Well, why not admit it?" He raised his hands and dropped them again on the steering wheel. "It was all my doing. I didn't even tell her till I knew you'd decided to come." He'd ducked his head, to speak to some point between his feet. "Even then, she wouldn't have anything to do with it. I booked your hotel in the name of the station. I engineered your trip in the LandCruiser. I had no idea what shape it was in. And I assumed the boy was just another country lad going to school in town. I thought it was a way of getting her truck back and giving you a chance to see the country. I was horrified when you called about the tire."

"But you forged the invitation before you'd even met me."

"I'm the youngest, remember. I spent a good part of my life trying to please the others but it never worked. When I discovered there was one more I hadn't known about, I reckoned I had to try again. I did some research. I hoped to have more in common with the foreign brother than with the others. You've seen how little friendship there is amongst us. Maybe the brother who didn't share our childhood could be the brother I'd always wished I had."

"I'm not good at family," Sonny reluctantly admitted. "As you can see. I'm out here when I should be in with my father."

Jerrod shifted into first. "Your old mum hasn't gone native, if that's what you think. Her dreaming doesn't include totems and rock spirits requiring blood. But she believes there is only the one soul, and everything her thought touches is included in it." He cocked his head and grinned. "Be glad she didn't bring you up, she might have driven you as bonkers as she is herself." He eased the accelerator down and the machine moved slowly ahead.

"You think I've been lucky?" Sonny hardened his voice for this.

"You've had a life, haven't you? To make of it what you could." Jerrod laughed. "You didn't come all this way to thank her for it?"

When Trevor stepped out of the truck he was all but naked – fat and furry, pale and freckled where he wasn't smeared with paint. A skimpy breechclout hung below his belly; his face was painted over with orange circles and brown-and-white stripes. Of course he wore socks and elastic-sided boots on his feet. Apparently, neither threat of flood nor the fact that he was fairly drunk caused anyone to question his decision to set off in the early afternoon sun.

Sonny remembered the Greeks. "Does he expect us all to strip?" He felt naked enough already in this glaring light.

"I wouldn't recommend it," Jerrod said. "This sun would take the skin right off your North American carcass. Trevor's been half-naked most of his life." He stepped back and spread his arms, to draw attention to his own long-sleeved khaki shirt and full-length cotton pants.

The dogs on the trays of the two white trucks yelped and howled at one another from inside their squat iron cages.

Sonny yanked the front of Benno's hat down far enough to look through the tear in the brim. Though a dark cloud was slowly moving this way like a sliding lid from the north-northeast, the light from the still-uncovered sky was so harsh it lay like a heavy weight on his head. He felt not only naked but misplaced as well. Going into battle. All of a sudden he wondered what he was doing here.

Holding both arms high, Trevor turned in a slow circle, the hair in his armpits matted with sweat. "Listen here! Listen here!"

"No speeches!" Avvachat shouted, from amongst the gathered crowd.

"Only this," Trevor said, his voice raised to speech-making pitch. "To remind you of the . . ." He teetered a little, but braced himself with a hand against the truck. ". . . to remind you of the Rural Lands Protection Act of . . . of . . . just wait a minute." He reached into the truck for a piece of paper, which he then had some trouble unfolding, his fingers too thick for the job. "Here it is. The Rural Lands Protection Act of 1987 . . . which states, and I'll read the important part to yiz now. Here we are. Here we are. 'It is the responsibility . . . of every landholder to . . .' uh. . . ." The paper slipped from his grasp and fluttered to the ground. Grunting, he bent to pick it up, then fumbled with it until he'd found his place. "'It's the responsibility of every landholder to control feral pigs.'" He stared at the document as though uncertain whether to read on, his eyes racing ahead. Then he folded it up with such satisfaction he might have written it himself. "So what you're about to do is help us with our civic duty. Come up and get yer weapons before that mob of mugs in Canberra make them illegal."

He reached into the cab again and this time started pulling out rifles and handguns, which he distributed to those who came forward. "If one of those grunters decides to charge, you want more than bare hands to hold him off with." When Sonny did not step forward with the others, he made a point of offering him a .22. "I reckon our blow-in brother can protect himself with this." The sarcastic eyebrow looked ridiculous in that painted face.

Sonny stepped back, surprised to discover he was prepared to refuse the gun. "I'm the outsider here. I think I'd better just watch."

Was this really why he'd come? To be a tourist? Trevor didn't think so. "You pushed yourselves on us, you can take the fuckin' gun!" He thrust the .22 into Sonny's hands. "They told me yer some kind of mighty warrior. Bear, was it? Our little pigs will be like shootin' wooden ducks."

Sonny felt the weight of the gun in both hands. One of the dogs, he saw, was staring at him, its muzzle pressed to the bars while the others continued to turn and twist, flowing over and under one another, impatient to get on with their job. "Bull-mastiff crosses, most of them," Aunt Clara said. "The one that's fallen for you's a ridgeback." All the dogs wore leather collars wide enough to cover throat and chest and even shoulders.

"Thor doesn't take part?"

"Thor! That fool would want to *play*. Pigs would eat his simple heart."

With this gun in his hand he felt as out-of-place as Thor, but before he could say as much to Aunt Clara, she'd opened the pas-senger door of Trevor's truck and started handing out sheathed knives. "Just them that's taking part," she shouted. To Sonny, she said, "Strap that to your belt." When he slid the knife out of the sheath he saw it was long and thin, a gleaming steel blade sharp-ened on both sides.

"For sticking," Jerrod explained, accepting a knife for himself. "Heart or throat is quickest." A turn of his wrist illustrated how quick you had to be.

"I won't need it," Sonny said. He saw that most of the others were refusing knives – just going along for the ride. Some said they weren't coming after all, they were heading home, the flood was making them nervous. A few insisted on staying close to the house in case they were needed here.

"G'on," said Aunt Clara. She grabbed the sheath from Sonny's hand and strapped it herself to his belt. "Play along with the boys. Something to tell yer grandkids."

"No spears?" Sonny said.

Aunt Clara turned a sidelong critical eye on grinning Jerrod. "That's because the last time we used spears we'd forgot we had a bloody javelin champion with us."

"Lois's poem made me famous," Jerrod said, "but not popular."

Those who were joining the hunt did not refuse hats, which were handed out by Avvachat Two to those not already wearing something on their heads. Her daughter distributed dark glasses. Sunscreen was smeared on exposed flesh until everyone was greased and shining in the sun. The dispossessed grazier wound his sad way through the crowd distributing cans of cold beer – xxxx, Powers, Victoria Bitter – the pop and hiss of cracked-open tabs forming a sound-trail behind him.

Seeing all of these people gathered here, Sonny was struck by how many of them had taken on the sunburnt colouring of the soil. Many had hair the reddish hue of the distant jump-ups as well. Was this the landscape's doing? Some of them – Avvachat One, for instance – even had the long lashes, the strong high nose, and long upper lip of the kangaroo. There was something of the emu in Lois Nugg – her long neck and high starey eyes. He saw no faces that made him think of *Il Porcellino*. How long would the wild pigs have to live here before Australians began to resemble them as well?

Benno drove a third truck into the compound, with still more dogs yelping in the cages. "This one's for us," Jerrod said. Benno stepped out, leaving the driver's door open, and started away on foot. He wore the expression of a man who was merely following orders. A young man slid an ice chest of beer cans behind the cab.

Half a dozen motorbikes sputtered into the yard – youths with faces shaded by their hats. Two followed on horseback, one of them Lachlan Hall on a shining black gelding. He made a quasi-military salute in Sonny's direction, his narrow face and pointed features somehow softened by his obvious delight.

"The Man from Snowy River?" Sonny said. "You know how to ride!"

"Rode me own old nag to school for a year." He leaned forward and rubbed the horse's neck, making an effort to look solemn, or at least unimpressed. The horse snorted, and danced a few steps to the side. "Benno hired me."

"Then why aren't you staying behind to keep the station from harm?"

The boy's gaze passed across the sprawling house. "He told me to come – to watch. He's got a mob back there shovelling sand." The impatient horse snorted and pounded a front hoof. "Here comes that woman gave you grief in Sydney."

Charlotte was dressed conspicuously, her shorts too white, her blouse too expensive. Even her hair, which was no different than usual, seemed now to be too perfectly and expensively cut. He saw her as he thought these others must – a North American come to gawk at the locals. Of course her camera bag hung from her shoulder.

"Trevor let you keep your camera?" Sonny said.

"He took the film I'd used. He knew better than to try taking this." She patted the leather bag at her hip.

"This means we won't be going near sensitive areas," Jerrod said. "All the same, I'd keep both cameras out of his sight."

Sonny wasn't ready to give up the Minolta yet. He'd forgotten to buy a pair of binoculars in Mistake Creek. Because so much of what you saw in this landscape was too far away for the naked eye, he needed the zoom.

"I'm here to photograph the big mother-son reunion," she explained to Jerrod. "I figure it'll happen while he's playing chase-the-pig with his rustic Down Under kin." She ran an appraising eye up the length of Lachlan, who looked down on her from the saddle. "I understand you got along so well he's thinking of taking you home, to make a permanent nursemaid of you."

"No bloody way," the boy said, laughing even as he looked to Sonny for an explanation.

"I made the mistake of praising you for your help with the old man," Sonny said. "This was Charlotte's way of saying she's sorry she couldn't have done it herself."

"You're a long way from the Cross," she said. She was the beautiful movie star now, tilted a little to one side and smiling up. "I hope he's compensating you for all the business you're losing."

"Yairs, he's buying me this horse," Lachlan said, looking straight-faced directly at her. "Also, I caught him smoodging with me mum the other night so he promised to put me in his will."

"Don't count on getting anything," she said. "He'll spend it all on trips to places no sane person cares to see. Cliff dwellings and standing stones and painted caves."

"And shooting parties," Sonny added.

"I'd better go join the others," Lachlan said. The other horseman and the motorbikes were waiting beside a gate.

Sonny placed a hand against the horse's shoulder and felt a quiver run through the flesh. "You'll let me know when they induct you into the Stockman's Hall of Fame."

He knew, even before the boy had cantered off across the yard, that of course he had no business going along on this savage entertainment. "I can't take the chance," he said to Jerrod, who was standing now inside the opened door of the third truck, one elbow resting on the roof of the cab. "My father . . ." He didn't know how to finish the sentence except with action. He went up the nearest steps, alarmed to think that he hadn't gone in to check sooner.

But the old man was heading out to meet him. They almost collided just inside the house. "Where do you think you're going?" But his father went right on past him and outside, using his homemade walking stick for support.

"I didn't come all this way to lie in bed and listen to lectures from a damn nurse!"

"Jesus Murphy. You recover just whenever you feel like it! That ride will be rough."

The old man's shirt was misbuttoned. Sonny moved closer to straighten it out, but his father swatted him away. "I've been over more rough roads than you've even seen. What more can it do than kill me?" There was an almost feverish gleam in his eyes.

"That doctor will charge me with criminal negligence."

"So hire yourself a lawyer."

"Anyway, you and I have got to get out of here," Sonny said. "We can't risk being trapped by a flood."

His father stepped back in order to glower from a safer distance. "I never said I was going on the damn hunt, for chrissake. I just want to stay out here and watch for you to get back." He squinted up his eyes and cast an amused look at Sonny. "Covered with pig shit and bleeding gore from a thousand gashes."

Suddenly the nurse was beside them with the wheelchair, her lips pinched. "There you are!"

"I'm okay, I'm okay," Timo Aalto said.

"I'll take him back to bed," the nurse said.

"No you won't!" the old man said, though he backed himself up and dropped into the wheelchair with a grunt. "I'll sit right here till they're back."

"Not in this heat, you won't." Sonny said.

"I'll sit in the shade. I'll read a book, if there are any books in this joint."

"There's a radio-phone in Trevor's truck," Jerrod said. "Miss Grimes will call us back if there's a need."

"There is the telly," the nurse said. They could see it from here: helicopters lifting people off their roofs. "And we have a library. Perhaps I can get you something?"

"You have any Plutarch?" Sonny said.

"Just bring me a picture magazine," the old man growled. "Jesus Christ! Anything, so long as it's interesting enough to keep my brain from collapsing altogether."

"They will be back within the hour," the nurse said. "Most of them. The excitement usually wears off fast, for everyone except the bloodthirsty few."

"Just go," his father said. "I promise not to kick the bucket before you get back."

Before he'd joined Jerrod at the truck, Sonny was intercepted by Lois Nugg with her notebook in hand, her glasses hanging on a chain from her neck. There was a spring in her step, like

someone anxious to get a tennis match started. She placed an
open palm against his chest to stop him in his tracks, her finger-
tips tapping the flesh above his singlet. "I'll ride with you, so I can
see it all from your point of view. For my poem."

But Aunt Clara put one hand on her arm and turned her away.
"Benno's expecting me and you in the next one."

Errol came out of the house then, the dark bruised flesh
swollen above one eye. Trevor flung out an arm that gestured for
him to get into his lead truck. "C'mon – pull your finger out!" Errol
hesitated, then shook his head. Muttered words were exchanged.
Then he snatched the rifle out of the hands of Avvachat One and
directed his Adelaide cousin to get into Trevor's truck in his stead.
Taking Charlotte by one arm, he guided her down towards the
fourth truck.

"Let's go," Sonny said. "I might be in the mood for killing
something after all."

"Righto," Jerrod said. He walked over to consult with Trevor, who
shrugged as though Jerrod's words meant nothing to him. Instead,
he yelled something at his noisy dogs, who went silent. Two of the
station hands abandoned their motorbikes and leapt onto the
tray of the lead truck, where they crouched beside the dogs.

"They'll pick us up at the homestead," Jerrod said, and got in
behind the wheel.

They moved out of the compound and up the dirt road past the
shearers' quarters and the great blinding corrugated walls of the
wool shed. Then they swung left through an open gateway into a
dusty paddock of pale dry grass where they followed tire tracks
along the fence line. A dead sheep had all but melted into the
earth – there was little left but bones and tufts of wool. A single
leaning tree raised pale and sharply pointed branches towards the
sky, like the rack of antlers off some giant elk. When he looked
behind, buildings were slipping beyond the horizon. There was
nothing different from what there was in front – endless surface
of earth.

They crossed a flat expanse of reddish dirt populated by the skeletons of more dead trees. These bleached and twisted figures looked as though they had been struck dead in the midst of a conniption fit, trying to pull themselves free of the ground. The truck abruptly dipped into a dry creek bed and bounced up the slope to an area of level ground, populated by still more twisted white skeletons.

Eventually he saw, far ahead, a long low bar of raised land-scape gradually growing nearer. This anvil-flat plateau looked as though someone had sheared the top three-quarters off a small mountain. As they drew near along a row of fence posts, he could see rubble at its base. Pale spiky plants grew here and there amongst the stones.

They began to pass by a row of twisted fence posts leaning this way and that, unconnected by wire to one another. "Original homestead," Jerrod explained. He pointed out a group of knee-high stumps. "House stood on those. A two-room battler's hut."

He stopped so they could get down and walk amongst the ruins. A collapsed bedstead. A tilted iron cookstove. A few scattered mud bricks. Everything was coated with a fine dust. Sonny sat on his heels and freed a crockery pot from beneath the bedstead. It crumbled into shards in his hands. Some kind of small dark image had been worn nearly away, a flower symbol perhaps, or a word. The short stumps that once held the house above the ground were from twisted irregular trees, each of them a different thickness, a different shape. Weather had sharpened the lines of the grain, stark as bones, distinct now as the threads on a screw. When he put a hand to one of these, it tilted and came free of the ground.

Jerrod pointed out a grave not far away. "Her sister." A tiny wooden headstone tilted beneath a tree. "Died of whooping cough in her first year," Jerrod said. The headstone was surrounded by a fence made of the type of wire used for chicken pens. To keep the wild dogs out, Sonny imagined. And the pigs. "She likes to visit sometimes when she's feeling maggoty."

The gravesite was outside the house yard, which was enclosed by a fence made of upright stakes wired together at the top, slabs of twisted wood worn by weather to knots and hardest grain. The old wool shed was a corrugated roof collapsed across a confusion of leaning posts. It wasn't hard to imagine the work her parents had put into this. It wasn't hard to imagine, either, how they would feel if they could see what had become of it now.

"You thought we'd find her here?"

"It was worth trying. But of course she isn't that predictable." Jerrod stepped up into the truck. "She'll probably be back at the house waiting for us!"

They moved out onto the plain again, increasing their speed as they left the homestead and faced open fields. "They didn't know how to live here, she says. They were afraid of it. They fought it. They tried to impose another world upon it. They still do, all of these graziers out here. She thinks they ought to have learned something from the people who've lived on it for sixty thousand years."

"The blacks?"

"They survived because instead of trying to make the landscape into something different, they allowed the landscape to make them into people who could live on it. They are who they are because of this." *This* was everything around them, his hands implied. All this lonely landscape Sonny had considered hostile. "Their voices, their eyesight, their ways of thinking have all been formed by where they are. She didn't know until she moved to your part of the world that some of this had started to happen to her, from living here. She must have been open to it. But she didn't know this until she was over there and saw everyone making the same mistakes they were making here." He seemed to be thinking about his own words for a minute. "Like you, now. Making artificial landscapes for people who've turned their backs on the real one."

"That's how she would see it?"

"Well. The rest of us cause her some grief when it comes to fitting us into her hopes for the world. I reckon the old-time blacks had their version of the lawyer to keep people in line, but I don't know if they had people getting rich from straightening teeth."

A cloud of dust announced the arrival of the others. They were a parade of trucks and motorbikes and horses with Trevor's truck in the lead. Jerrod started their truck moving out alongside, gaining speed, so that eventually they were able to fall into place behind Trevor, close enough beside Benno for one of the station hands to leap from the tray of that truck to this. Benno raised his can of Foster's in a salute.

"Look back," Jerrod said. "A vanguard."

They'd formed a large **V** to cross this sparsely treed space. Lachlan and the second horseman brought up the rear of either arm. Sonny thought of a military operation, but Jerrod said it made him think of geese. "That kind you have in America. Honking across the sky."

For a while they followed the edge of what looked like a muddy lagoon. "Flood water," Jerrod said. "That's Mistake Creek. Over her banks." Water leaked across the landscape here because some river was swollen by rainstorms hundreds of kilometres upstream in a flattened landscape. The green leafy crowns of scrub trees stood mired along what must have been the creek bed. Leaves and twigs lay on the surface of the khaki-coloured water, where flocks of dark birds cut **V**-shaped wakes. A few sheep had gathered on a tiny island at the base of a crooked tree. If the water rose another foot they would be swept from their perch.

"It's moving," Sonny said. "Where does it go?"

"Draining all the way to Lake Eyre," Jerrod said. "A gigantic garden will spring into bloom where there's been nothing for years but salt pan."

Sonny wondered if the dark shape on the far side of the nearest water was human. Again he imagined Viira Hawkins watching from a distance. He raised the camera to his eye and twisted the zoom. A bleached eucalyptus filled the viewfinder. Green lights flashed down the right-hand side. The figure beneath the tree might have been human, might have been another kangaroo, but before he had time to get a clear enough focus it moved too quickly out of his viewfinder to be identified.

He twisted the thick tube of the lens. What he saw this time was a pig, a tusked boar, trotting along the shoreline. The size of a house, it seemed, in the viewfinder. With quick tiny steps it trotted along the far side of the flood on top of its own reflected self, its long snout lowered, probably snuffling or grunting. Hairy-backed but dainty! A monstrous fat man hurrying along in a pair of high-heeled shoes.

Then it darted outside his frame and couldn't be found.

They passed by a cluster of small trees tilting around a yellowish mud hole. "Pig wallow," Jerrod said. The mud around the edges had been churned up with footprints. "I read somewhere about those geese of yours. All their honking's really troops encouraging the leader. Keep on! Keep on! You think our Trev would appreciate that?"

"He'd shoot you for it," Sonny guessed.

"They take turns replacing the lead goose when he tires – right? I heard if one is shot another escorts it to the ground but I don't know that I believe it. Ah, Trevor's sighted something."

Ahead of them, Trevor waved a decorated arm out his window, hand jabbing in the direction of a row of trees not fifty metres away. Dogs on both trucks set up a hullabaloo.

"Camp ahead," Jerrod said. "Look – there's a mob scattering."

Dark pigs shot out from under the scrub and dashed in all directions across the dirt.

"Small," Jerrod said.

Two dogs passed their truck, set free from one of the trucks behind, streaking at an astonishing speed across the dirt. The dispossessed grazier was down on the ground and running on his short legs, two of the station hands passing him.

Jerrod did not slow down, but stayed close to Trevor's tail.

"Will you eat them?" Sonny said.

"Naow!" Jerrod said. "We leave them for the eagles. If you had a peek inside their gut you'd know why."

There were shots somewhere behind them.

Trevor's truck continued down a dirt track that once again skirted the thick moving edge of the flooded creek. Then it turned away and followed tracks in through a stand of sturdy trees, some of them broken as though by a terrific windstorm, their leafy crowns gone dry and withered on the ground. He might have been following a map through a maze. There was no hesitation in the way he manoeuvred in and out amongst these trees. Their perfect military chevron was put to the test here, though Sonny noticed Benno's truck moving at the identical speed on the far side of the trees to their left.

Another explosion of black pigs shot out from somewhere behind a knot of scrub, most of them disappointingly small. Some went left, some right. Some went straight ahead of Trevor's truck. Again Trevor's arm made its extravagant gestures.

"He wants us to take these runts," Jerrod said. Then, abruptly, he sped up. "There's a big one up ahead he's marked for himself. I want you to see this."

They swung out and roared past Trevor. Soon they broke free of the trees and once more onto open plain. Three dark pigs raced ahead of them, zigzagging around bits of debris, skidding at a sudden change of mind. One, perhaps the largest, split off from the others and headed for a clump of scrub. Dogs set free from the back of their truck streaked after it. When Jerrod slowed, the station hand leapt down and followed.

Then, after a brief spurt of speed, Jerrod braked. "Come on, get out!" He leapt out himself. Sonny slid out his door with the .22 and started to run.

Ahead, the dogs had come up on either side of the boar, nipping at his shoulders, dancing around him, darting to this side and that, barking, and finally herding him to a standstill just as he was about to run into a patch of scrub.

By the time they caught up, the boar had turned to face them, its rear backed into a bush. Its long snout and sharp tusks slashed at the dogs every time they made a move for him. They leapt in to nip at his throat, and quickly jumped back out of reach. Then, as though they had been communicating with one another, both dogs leapt at the same moment and seized an ear. The boar squealed and tried to fling them off. They held tight. Hunched down on the grass, they used both weight and strength to pull the boar's head low.

He hadn't expected the beast to be so dark, or so hairy. This fellow was out of a sinister European tale. Not a Disney pig or even a farmyard pig gone wild but a black monster snuffling around the edges of a child's nightmare. He wasn't the shiny handsome figure of Il Porcellino, either. He had more in common with the shadowy figure that trotted across the back of Sonny Aalto's mind in times of bone-weariness, confusion, and self-loathing, snuffling and grunting and running free but unable to stop, the figure of a son no mother could possibly want to keep. His smell caught in the throat, prompting a gag reflex – the high sharp stench of pigpen muck, with a hint of putrefying corpse.

"He's bowing to you," Jerrod said, stepping back.

"Take out your knife." Aunt Clara's voice.

The boar's small eyes regarded Sonny Aalto with loathing. The smaller pigs had not been killed with knives.

"You're the honoured guest," Jerrod said. "You came the far-thest. You'll have the tusks for a trophy."

The yellow tusks curved up from the bottom jaw – not daggers to stab you as he'd imagined, but scythes to rip you open. Six or seven inches long. A sudden twist of the boar's head shook one dog loose from the ear, the tusk opening a gash in the leather armour at its throat. But the dog scrambled back to set his teeth again into the ear, his rear legs finding solid purchase in the dirt, his whole body straining to drag that long dangerous head down again to the earth.

Errol's truck had pulled up and Charlotte stepped down for her pictures. Errol got out and stood inside his open door, and said what Sonny was thinking: "Too dangerous for a first-timer. If those dogs let go, the man is dead."

"Go for the throat," said Aunt Clara's voice somewhere behind him. She spoke as though she'd done this countless times herself.

Sonny lowered the .22 to the ground and unsheathed the knife at his belt. He hadn't really wanted this, he'd only wanted the idea of it. It was the idea of things, and not the things themselves, that had kept him moving across the face of the world. Visiting, observing, admiring, and then moving on. In all his journeys he'd been just an observer passing by, even when he'd reached his destination. Not once had he left behind a story about himself. Why, now, did he think this time would be different?

The wire-brush hairs that rose along its back were more frightening even than the tusks. The hairs on the back of his own neck rose. He had failed her at the water hole. She would show herself only after he had done this thing. Some kind of stupid bloody Australian test she'd learned from her Aboriginal friends. A male initiation, along with pulling teeth, drilling holes in the penis, and sending sons out to fast to the brink of starvation.

The pig was going to die today anyway. Jerrod had told him the reasons, the most important of which was that he would sire more pigs to do still more damage on a continent where they did not belong. His crime was that he lived in the wrong place. He was no more native to this landscape than was Sonny Aalto. Although the pig had had no say in his exile, he would pay for it with his life.

His father could imagine how it felt to be inside that doomed pig's head, facing the moment that divided before from after. "He knows what he's looking at," the old man would say. "Don't make him wait." Of course Sonny had his own idea of what the boar was thinking. If their situations were reversed there'd be none of this hesitation. *No ears left for trophies. In fact there'd be no trace left at all, once I'd made a meal of you.*

"Use the gun." Lachlan Hall had come up to stand beside him. "Don't listen to these bastards, they just want to see the blood."

The small explosion of blood happened before the sound. A rifle from somewhere off to the side. It was impossible to know if the scream came from the pig or from humans who watched. Someone shouted: "Whacko!" Both dogs yelped, and scrambled back, their tails between their legs. Whimpering, they crawled away on their bellies toward the trucks. The boar sagged, one front hoof weakly jabbing at dirt, and then collapsed. The head tilted, laying the long crooked snout along the ground. Blood leaked from the mouth. Blood leaked from a small hole behind the shoulder.

Evidently Trevor was an expert shot even while drunk. If he was drunk. Though his drunkenness may have been exaggerated, his anger probably wasn't. He came into the glade as though he would shoot them all. Jerrod first. He pushed at Jerrod's shoulder, knocking him back a step. "You stupid arsehole, whaddaya think you're doin'?"

"He's our guest," Jerrod said, standing his ground.

"He's no guest of mine." Trevor pushed Jerrod aside. "He's another bloody trespasser, like Errol's whore."

Somewhere, in one of the trucks, a voice squawked and buzzed on a radio-phone.

Sonny wasn't fast enough to prevent Trevor's arm from striking out like a thick club and thumping him, back-handed, across the side of the head. His brain recoiled against the back of his skull. He tasted blood on his bottom lip. Pain shot up along his jaw. Instinctively he threw himself at the painted fat man, and discovered that his long knife had gone to Trevor's throat. Gasps on all sides, and a few blocked screams. The point rested against the bristly flesh but hadn't pierced it yet.

Trevor's eyes, this close, were as furious as the boar's had been, and more contemptuous. If he hadn't gone stiff, and if his hand hadn't taken firm hold of your wrist, you might believe he was daring you to draw blood. For a moment no one moved. Then Trevor's powerful grip began to crush flesh on the way to breaking bone. Sonny had barely the time to realize what Trevor intended before they were both grabbed from behind and pulled free. A steadying hand from Lachlan kept Sonny from falling.

The radio-phone crackled again. Benno's voice shouted, "Yeh?" Then, "Trev! Y' better come and take this!"

Cursing, Trevor shoved his way through the crowd to snatch the instrument out of Benno's hand.

The boar exhaled a long shuddering disappointed sigh, its dim eyes still on Sonny Aalto. You and I had expected something of one another, it said, but you see what these damn fools have made of that.

Trevor slammed the squawking radio-phone back into place and climbed inside his pig rig. "Back to the house, all of yiz!" he shouted. "She's brought her bloody lawyer home, some fuckin' announcement she wants to make."

The station hand who'd stayed to watch the television broke the news – they were running out of time. The swell that had started with the heavy rains up Carnarvon way had swallowed much of Charleville. The swollen Thompson was spreading out through Longreach. Mistake Creek was backing up.

By the time Jerrod's truck had pulled into the yard this news had already sparked alarm and disorder amongst those who wished they'd left earlier. As soon as Trevor abandoned his truck to rush inside, someone grabbed his radio-phone. Others stood by for a turn. "Naow! Naow!" A woman shouted into the transmitter. "You take Tim and get out of there. We'll meet you in Rockhampton if we get through. O-kye? You understand me? Take Tim and start for Rockie now!" You'd think this flood had not been mentioned before.

Avvachat began to manoeuvre his Mitsubishi Pajero and boat trailer out from amongst the confusion of other vehicles. He stopped for his frightened wife to herd their pouting children aboard. Maybe floods were rare in Geelong. "Going west!" she shouted, to whoever might care to know. "It'll be hot but at least it's still dry."

Lois Nugg showed no interest in following their example. She leaned against one of the trucks to scribble notes, catching people by the arm and asking for observations she might quote.

Verses would be recited at bush-poet meets. *Kalevan Goes Under.*
As Sonny set out to find his father, she grabbed his nearer hand
and turned up his palm. "No blood," she said. He would be punished, he supposed. Mocked in her poem. A disappointing
Lemminkainen, unworthy.

Lachlan was suddenly between Sonny and the house. "There's
an airfield in town," he said, already starting away. "You get the
old man – orright? I'll get yer bags."

His father was not where they'd left him. Sonny briefly imagined him wheeling his chair down the dirt road or peg-legging his
way through the dust. Of course he had probably gone back to
his bedroom, keeping out of the way. But before Sonny could go
in to find him, Sister Grimes placed herself in his path. "No one
but the immediate family."

It seemed she was prepared to use her body as a roadblock if
she had to, but Jerrod Hawkins appeared in a doorway and
called him over. "In here. Follow me, you've as much right as
anyone."

Once he'd seen where Jerrod had led him he was certain he had
no business here at all. The walls of this room had been painted
in murals of stylized lizards, naked stick-figure humans, and
uprooted trees caught up in a tail of white light spiralling out from
a brilliant yellow sun into diffusion. Dwarfed by these brown and
orange images, family members sat on chairs and couches, most of
them with their backs to the door. Errol was alone to one side,
leaning against a wet bar with a xxxx in his hand, scowling out
from under his swollen discoloured eyelid. Trevor's children and
older grandchildren were crowded onto a rigid Victorian divan.
Trevor went along the far wall closing the louvred doors between
them and a passageway beyond. When he saw that Jerrod was
showing Sonny to a vacant chair, he demanded the visitor leave.
"Immediate family only, ya wanker!"

"I'll go," Sonny said, and turned to do so.

But Jerrod gripped his arm to stop him. "He's staying, Trevor.
We invited him."

"*You* invited him. If she wants him she can see him later, outside."

"Oh for chrissake, Trev," Errol said. "What difference does it make?" He brought two cans of Powers across and handed one to Jerrod, the other to Sonny. "If she doesn't want him here she'll tell him to leave. Sit down and shut your hole."

Trevor slammed the last pair of shutters closed and joined his family. You could see that Sonny Aalto was not the only one he would have liked to exclude.

Fronds of potted ferns floated in the breeze from the overhead fans. At the far end of the room, Thor lay beneath an empty captain's chair, his muzzle resting on his paws, his eyes on the humans gathered before him. Behind a small table a white-haired man in a short-sleeved dress shirt and yellow tie appeared to be reviewing the papers in his hand. He put the papers down and fished a white handkerchief out of his pocket to mop his face. Then he set the handkerchief on the table. They were waiting, it seemed, for the empty chair to be occupied. An eccentric monarch, Sonny thought. Those papers might list the names of those who would lose their heads.

He didn't want to be here, but he couldn't leave now. Flood or no flood.

Possibly the white-haired man did not intend to wait. "These documents," he said, "have been signed." He spoke with his eyes on the papers, one hand clutching his handkerchief. His brow was already shiny again with moisture. "There is only the matter of informing you of their contents."

The muttering was short-lived. Curiosity was stronger than indignation.

"For much of the time you believed your mother was wandering under the stars," the man began. He paused to clear a phlegmy throat and began again. "For most of the past few days she has been down in Brisbane taking care of the final touches to these arrangements, which have been in confidential negotiation for some time. She has brought you here to inform you –"

"Where is she?" Trevor said. "Let her *inform* us herself!"

"Well, in fact," the man said. Presumably he was the woman's lawyer. "There is some business she wishes us to deal with first. A matter of courtesy before we get on to today's real business." He put his elbows on the table and laced his fingers together across his chest. "Wool prices are down again. No surprise to anyone. Leasing paddocks to the Harpers for their beef cattle brings you a little cash, but not much. The last time you met, your mother invited suggestions, and we have two she wants me to address."

Errol protested. "She brought us in to *address ideas*? Where the hell *is* she, Fraser?"

"Save your indignation, Errol, you'll need it later. Let's deal with these suggestions first. Trevor thinks you ought to consider raising emus."

"Dear God!" said Joanie. Someone laughed.

"The Japs are buying all the emu meat the Swansons can raise," Trevor said. His tone suggested that anyone who doubted his wisdom was a fool.

"Swansons have been earning a few yen, that is true," the lawyer said. He seemed to be more than lawyer. The company chair, perhaps. Conducting a board meeting. "But Ed Swanson reports they're being driven mad by the noise. Like a grumbling mob plotting revolution, he says. Nobody sleeps."

"Swansons are idiots," Trevor said. "All we have to do is pen them out by the western dam."

"Eating emu is a fad," the lawyer said. "By the time you'd raised your chicks the Japanese will have thought of something even more outlandish to eat and you will be feeding a thousand hungry birds for the pleasure of it. I am only speaking for your mother, understand."

This man was not a company chair addressing the board. There was no board. These others weren't part of the business at all. He may be sounding like a CEO but he was merely the mouthpiece of a mother dismissing her family's advice.

"This is ridiculous," Errol said. "We have guests who are being ignored while we talk about bloody emus."

"Patience, Errol. Now, Gerard has suggested taking in guests as a solution. Get into the holiday-farm business, like everyone else out here with the banks breathing down their necks. Let rich Americans pay for the thrill of fixing your fences and crutching daggy sheep, so they can go home and boast that they've experienced the bush."

"While we listen to them complain," Trevor said. "About the food, the accommodations, the heat, the flies, the distance from civilization – everything including the *other* Yanks."

"Apparently Gerard was so enamoured of this idea that he invited a North American guinea pig for a preview. He would be given the chance to invest a little foreign money in the business."

"Jesus," Sonny said, under his breath.

Jerrod shot to his feet, his face colouring. "That isn't what I had in mind at all." He didn't look in the guinea pig's direction.

"I'm only speaking for your mother, understand. Kalevan Station is not about to become Disneyland Down Under. If we have to destroy the place in order to keep it there's not much point in keeping it, is there? Which brings us to why you're together in this room when you'd rather be out there killing things."

The lawyer mopped his brow again and put his handkerchief down on the table in order to pick up the documents. "Mrs. Hawkins will not be joining us this afternoon. In her absence, she has asked me to inform you of this transaction she has been negotiating for more than a year. With the assistance of my firm, of course."

"And without the family's knowledge," Errol added.

"Kalevan Station is to become something of a nature sanctuary," he said. "A park." To go on, he had to raise his voice above the protests. "Publicly owned. Protected property. She has sold the thirty thousand hectares to the state government."

Naturally the growls of dissent exploded now with Trevor's shouted "By God, she can't do that!" He leapt to his feet, his face shining scarlet through his silly makeup, his belly going in and out with his heavy breathing. "She's mad!"

The lawyer rapped his knuckles on the table. "Sit down. Sit down."

Trevor did not sit down. "I'll challenge it in court. Psychiatrists will queue up for a chance to testify." He was a child in a tantrum, ridiculous in his breechclout and furry belly and elastic-sided boots. "It will be easy to prove she wasn't in her right mind when she signed the papers – she hasn't been in her right mind for years!"

The lawyer sat with one hand curled against his forehead, listening to this rant, or at least waiting it out. Then he went on as though Trevor hadn't spoken. "She will be permitted to live out the rest of her life on the property. She may engage in a little subsistence farming. She may even allow members of the family and a few necessary employees to live on it with her. If she wishes."

This did not hold frenzied Trevor off for long. "She'll have dingoes whelping in the kitchen, blackfellas tearing down my buildings for firewood. I'll see her committed first!"

"She should have consulted me," Errol said. He did not rise from his chair, though it was obvious that he was as angry as Trevor. "I know people who could have helped." He was not only angry; it was clear he was hurt. By taking the initiative, his mother had deprived him of the chance to be a philanthropist, admired by those who cared about such things in Sydney. He'd wanted to be the grazier's son who'd forced a World Heritage listing on his reluctant family. The old gal had robbed him of his chance to be a hero.

The lawyer looked at Errol with an air of sorrowful resignation. "She didn't need your help, Errol. The only thing she needs is for you to understand that you have no say in the matter. We'll give the land a chance to heal itself. That is the least that is owed it. Then perhaps one day it will teach those of us who are patient how we might live on it again."

"She won't get away with this," Trevor said. "She's just started the fight of her life."

"Your mother is a thorough woman," the lawyer patiently explained. "I'm afraid there isn't anything you can think of that she hasn't anticipated. If you are quiet for a minute you'll see where we have worked a little compensation into the deal, for your years of service. Gerard?"

Jerrod had stood up again. "If Trevor's determined to take this to court, he should be aware that the son she seems to have forgotten may demand some rights to the property as well."

"Like bloody hell," Trevor said.

"And may want me to represent him when he lays claim to his share." There was a pleased edge of sarcasm to Jerrod's voice. "Compensation for the trauma inflicted by the mother who abandoned him. He may claim an equal interest in making sure the station isn't bequeathed to the goannas and marauding tuskers of Trevor's imagination."

"You keep him out of this!" Trevor yelled, pointing. "This has nothing to do with anyone else. It don't even have anything to do with you. Or bloody Errol either. You gave up any rights you had when you left me to work my stupid arse off for *her*."

Without waiting for the meeting to end, Sonny set off for the nearest doorway, hoping his instincts would lead him to the bedroom wing. But Jerrod was quick to catch up. "Wait." A hand on the shoulder.

Sonny shook off the hand and ducked out into the corridor. "I want out of here before we're trapped by the flood."

"Keep going that way and you'll never be seen again. Follow me." Jerrod led the way down the hall and turned to the left. "She may not have been here to welcome you but she has been entertaining you, I suppose you could say. By remote control. Viira says there's no fun being old unless you can run everyone else's lives. She's always had to be the say-so. You're determined?"

"We just want to get home before we're trapped on the wrong side of the flood."

"Well, that will depend upon forces greater than hers, I'm

afraid. She may be a tyrant but she doesn't pretend to have power over floods."

"You said she and the landscape have a special understanding."

"She'll be glad to hear I drove you out to the homestead," Jerrod said. "I was right about her feeling for the land. You could hear that for yourself inside. But that doesn't make her Queen Canute. The flood will probably reach the house but it likely won't be any deeper than the stumps beneath us. If it is, we'll put a few things out of harm's way before it gets here."

His father was not in his bedroom. Lachlan must already have taken him outside.

Lachlan had parked the LandCruiser just about where they had stopped when they arrived earlier in the day. He'd also brought Timo Aalto and his wheelchair out and down the steps and helped the old man into the truck. When Jerrod and Sonny came outside he was folding up the wheelchair to store at the back with their luggage.

"You'll get home and start to wonder about those dinosaur tracks you didn't see." Jerrod said. "When your country falls apart – it's today, isn't it, whenever 'today' arrives at your part of the world? – or when it's devoured by the neighbours – you'll have a place down here amongst the brethren!" He laughed and stepped back. "We can keep our distance from Trevor. He'll be foaming at the mouth along the borders of the property, looking for some way to reverse history."

When Charlotte appeared from around the side of the house, Sonny was alarmed to discover he'd been about to leave without giving her a thought. She was in the company of a young man in jeans and T-shirt, and obviously hadn't expected to encounter her father. They were on their way to the parked vehicles.

"If you want to come with us," he said. "We're heading for Brisbane. To see about getting home."

She laughed. "Are you crazy? And miss this?"

Maybe the young man was taking her where there'd be good photo possibilities. If he was taking her to meet his mother, her father would be the last to know. At least it wasn't Errol she was going with.

The muscles in her face carefully rearranged themselves into deliberate expressions of polite shining-eyed charm. She left the young man and came over to remove her Minolta by its strap from Sonny's shoulder. "You won't need this any more." She started away but paused and came back to kiss his cheek. "And I *am* grateful that you brought me to this fabulous new world. It could be months before I leave." This time when she started away she spoke over her shoulder. "Or maybe I never will."

As she hurried past the LandCruiser she bent at the knees just long enough to wiggle her fingers at the old man inside. Sonny couldn't see whether his father responded with a friendly wave, a puzzled scowl, or a look of surprise that this was all he was getting from the granddaughter who'd left him behind in Sydney four days ago.

"We have a daughter living in Perth," Jerrod said, watching Charlotte and the young man get into a two-door Honda. Perhaps he was recommending distance. Perhaps not. Once the Honda had driven off he added, "There's still the Devil's Marbles if you'll wait for the flood to subside." He put a hand on the roof of the LandCruiser and quickly removed it. "I'd hoped, well. . . ." He opened and closed his fingers, to see how badly they'd been burned.

"That I might be persuaded to invest in Disneyland Down Under?"

With a hand to his forehead, Jerrod looked to the ground as though to express his shame. "I knew as soon as I met you there wasn't a hope of that." Then he straightened up, breathed in. "But after you'd already crossed the Pacific, Errol mentioned a comment your daughter made. About looking for something to invest in." Both hands rose to surrender. "I'm sorry. It seems an ugly sort of scheme when you think of it."

"And really, you just wanted me to kill a wild boar." Laughing, to make this a little easier. "That smelly bastard's already grown to twice its size in my head. By the time I get home he'll be famous for gobbling up half the graziers and boss cockies and pastoralists of central Queensland. A vicious servant of Canberra. Of course I'll be the one who killed him."

Jerrod's face had taken on an extra degree of seriousness. "We'll mail you the ears and tusks." He laughed, but only tentatively, perhaps in case the offer was more welcome that he'd expected. "It was your pig. There must be some lady at home you can give them to."

"Please don't," Sonny said. "The lady I have in mind would ram them down my throat." He imagined Holly Fitzgerald turning back folds of tissue paper to find she was holding items sliced from a slaughtered boar. "You'd better get back. The others are making decisions without you."

Jerrod threw up his hands in a sort of comic pantomime. "Oh, the horror, the horror!" Then, more seriously, "We were brought here to listen, not to make decisions. If she were here, she'd be chasing us off by now. She gave us life, now she takes it away." He waved his arms like someone shooing chickens. His voice took on that high harsh-edged quality you sometimes heard amongst Finnish women. "You do not exist, any of you. Poof!" He was his mother waving away whatever remained in the air before her. "She gave us this land to live on, now she's taken it away. We don't deserve it. How we survive, she would say, will depend upon our relationship with our own piece of landscape." He cocked an eye at Sonny, as though there were more she might have said to this particular son if she'd been here. "Now go. If she were here she'd tell us all – including you – to save our selfish hides before we're washed with the rest of the carrion down to Lake Eyre."

Jerrod ducked to speak to Lachlan through the Toyota window. "The road you came on has the only bridge that's likely to be still above water. Otherwise you'll have no choice but to take the Capricorn Highway all the way down to Rockhampton on the coast."

For most of the way to town they saw little evidence of flooding. The dark cloud had spread over much of the sky by this time, but hadn't reached the sun still shining on the endless dry brown fields. It wasn't easy to believe this was all about to go under because of rain a thousand kilometres away.

"You'll go back to Sydney?" Sonny said. "Or to your mother's?"

"Benno hired me," the boy said. "I'm employed on the station." He said "employed" like someone who might never have had reason to use the word before.

"But you should know that everything's about to change."

The boy reached across to open the glove compartment and remove his package of hand-rolled smokes. He seemed uncertain how to act now, what expression to wear on his face. Sullen would no longer do, and it seemed he didn't want his satisfaction with recent developments to show. He'd gone all businesslike. "So long as she don't fire Benedict I'll be there for a while."

"Working with horses."

The boy laughed and removed one twisted cigarette before tossing the package back and closing the door. "When that woman writes her poem? I'll tell her to squeeze in a line about you – orright?"

"Saying what?" the old man said from behind. "He never accomplished nothing he come here for. I haven't heard that he killed a pig. Didn't have it out with his daughter. He didn't meet his old lady to give her hell. He didn't even find my damn lunch kit."

Sonny admitted all of this. "Neither did I get to see those dinosaur tracks. But I did get to see her property. Some of it. Saw why your ex-wife cares more about her land than about you or me or anyone."

"Flood water over there," Lachlan said, indicating a row of distant trees. Light shimmered weakly off the wet surface of earth beneath them.

"Well, it don't matter," his father added after some thought. "I never understood why you cared about such things – somebody else's idea of what's important. What's important to someone else don't have to mean nothing to you."

Certainly no one could say that something important had happened in that little grove where the boar had made his stand. Two confused and stubborn creatures had looked at one another for a while, though only one of them was held in place by hounds. Lois Nugg had expected something that would bloody his hands. What his father had expected he didn't know, but it had little to do with the killing.

"I always figured it was a waste of time," his father said, "all your chasing after them so-called sacred places. You won't find 'sacred' in rocks or trees or places where something happened, you'll find it in what was *done*."

"We have an expert with us," Sonny said to Lachlan. "I should have read those big fat Russian novels of his."

"Bah!" His father opened his window and spat. "All you shoulda done is just kept your eyes open. Most people chasing after something, they find out they had it all along. If you just poke around back roads like me, you don't have none of that, you just get to see where they go. More water over there."

Beyond the wide brown tussocky paddock to their right, water had spread out around a row of distant trees. This would be another of their dry riverbeds filled up and overflowing. Each tree was isolated from the others by a shimmering milky brown surface of moving water, making islands of them all. Less exciting than those aerial shots on TV, maybe, with houses and vehicles stranded in a muddy sea, sheep standing in clusters on the roofs of cars. Yet this was real. Here they could not have been a foot above the water level, with only a wide flat field between them.

Sonny recognized nothing. Nothing looked as it had this morning. Like the old man with his inadequate guidebook, he didn't know what anything meant. He didn't know much at all. If there were any truth to what Jerrod said, raw native landscape was something he'd spent his lifetime escaping, much as he'd tried to escape his father.

His father must have been keeping an eye on that water. "I hope to hell this truck don't leak."

"I think you're enjoying this," Sonny said.

"So long as that water stays where it is," his father said.

"You admit you're glad you came here, then," Sonny said. "Instead of Cape Scott."

There was a moment of silence before his father said, "I've just been lucky so far." When Sonny half-turned to look at him, his eyes had narrowed. Meanly, Sonny thought. "The bad stuff could happen any time. Don't think bringing me here has changed my mind."

"You think that's what I wanted?"

"I wouldn't put it past you. You probably think you're what's-his-name in the play. You know."

"No I don't. Who?"

"Gloucester's son – I forget his name."

"I don't know any Gloucester's son. What did he do?"

"He pretended to push his old man off a cliff. The poor old miserable bugger wasn't kidding about wanting to die, but being blind he was easy to fool. He pushed him, all right, but not over any cliff."

"And?"

"The old guy was surprised as hell to find out he was still alive. Even more surprised to find out he was relieved. So he decided to live out his life to the end. There would've been a different tale to tell if it was me. Shakespeare would know better than to think dragging me across Australia would change my mind about anything. He'd have paid a little more attention to start with. He'd have a better idea of why."

"It doesn't matter why, for God's sake! I know your why! What you ask is too much. You don't ask that of someone. You especially don't ask that of someone close. Did the old man think about what he was asking of his son?"

"He didn't know it was his son. He was blind, for chrissake! He thought it was just some fool he come across in the bush."

"Well there you are. He wouldn't have asked it of his son if he'd known. You don't ask that of people who love you."

A few more fence posts flew by. "Well," his father said. "Maybe that's why I asked you." He let more posts go by before he added, "Instead of Rosie, say, or Dora, or Tom Reimer."

Silenced, Sonny wasn't sure if he had the right to be offended.

Soon there were indications they were approaching town. Mailboxes had begun to show up. Two houses sat high on posts. A horse grazed behind a barbed-wire fence. But here and there brown water had begun to appear close to the road, leaving each bush on its own small island of spiky grass.

"Christ!" his father said. "We're at sea!"

There was water on both sides of the road now. They were driving on what appeared to be a shallow land bridge barely a hand's breadth above the muddy surface.

"Maybe we'd better turn back," Sonny said.

"The friggin' airfield's on the other side of town," Lachlan said. He slowed but didn't stop. He turned his radio on but got nothing but static. "Our only other choice is to go back – orright? Take the Capricorn Highway, then down across the Dividing Range to Brisbane."

Sonny turned to his father. "You willing to take the long way 'round?"

His father had moved forward to rest his arms on the back of Sonny's seat. "Them blackfellows yesterday didn't take the long way."

"That was yesterday," Sonny said. "Things have changed. I've still got a chance of getting you home in one piece. You're the one who thinks you're Moses with your rod. Just carve us out a channel and we'll cross, Egyptians screaming for help on every side."

His father's contemptuous snort was a familiar sound.

They had almost passed it by before Sonny realized that he was looking at a ROAD CLOSED sign attached to a wooden barrier tilted against a tree. No doubt swept from where it had been placed. His "Stop!" was an attempt to shout without causing too much alarm. One hand braced itself against the dashboard for the expected jolt.

It was too late now to stop. The jolt was from their tires dropping into potholes or channels where pavement had been washed away. The road had disappeared beneath mud. Where there should have been only fields and a shallow creek there was now this wide expanse of brown river. There was no sign of the creek. Even the white stakes were too far away to be read from this distance.

Though Lachlan pumped the brake pedal, the LandCruiser continued moving ahead. Brown foamy spray flew up on either side. It seemed the waters were indeed parting for them, the truck an amphibian plough. But a floating tree limb slammed against the driver's door before sliding off and passing by. The LandCruiser turned as though to go after it. Lachlan yanked on the wheel, but he had begun to lose control. They could feel the truck lift beneath them, shift a little, touch bottom again. Then it began to slide away with the current, turning in a slow arc to face downstream.

Lachlan pounded his horn.

The water might have been liquid manure, a brownish-yellow rising up the outsides of their doors. Leafy tree branches knocked against them and floated off. A cow with a bloated belly rolled over and disappeared beneath the surface and then appeared again metres on. A small tilted shed ploughed past and disappeared. The truck was being slowly dragged downstream with the debris.

A small black dog came swimming down the current, gulping and whimpering. It thumped against a tree trunk, and was thrust out into the stronger current. Its head sank out of sight, reappeared for a moment, then sank again. Above, a helicopter thrashed into sight above the town but did not come this way. It turned, tail up, and passed back over the town a second time.

They slid past a small island of trees, low limbs dragging across their hood, and came up with a thump against a second. The truck rocked from the current's efforts to dislodge it. A resident sheep stupidly observed their arrival. Water had begun to leak in around their feet.

Sonny pushed open his door and stepped cautiously onto the hump of grassy soil. The nervous sheep moved two steps to the side, but had come to the limit of his world. Lachlan got out as well. "Don't leave the old one inside," he said. "It won't take much for the truck to go off without us."

His father waited in the doorway, his walking stick in his hand. Sonny tucked the stick in behind his own belt, then lifted the old man free of the truck. They stood, the three of them, with their backs to the tree, water less than a metre from their feet. There wasn't much room for the sheep.

Directly across, perhaps a hundred metres away, a row of houses stood half-buried in water. Beyond these was the recognizable shape of the Kalevan Hotel. No doubt it had been evacuated, though several figures were gathered on the roof of a neighbouring building.

Tree shadows rippled across the gleaming surface of water, all of it moving past without regard for designated rivers or creeks. Slower on this side of their little island, it seemed, than what they'd just been through. Unimaginable quantities of muddy water moved across earth that appeared to be perfectly level. Gravity seemed to have little to do with it.

A stuffed chair sailed past. A plastic shopping bag. For all he knew there could be crocodiles. He could be looking at one now – a dark floating log. Of course, if they stayed where they were they could be swept away by that promised "swell," which he imagined to be something like a tsunami, a house-high wall of water sweeping up everything in its way.

"Is all this really heading for some empty lake?"

"If it don't evaporate before it gets there," Lachlan said. He sat on his heels and laced his hands together. "A big dry basin of salt, not a thing alive. Then every so often there comes a friggin' flood like this and – I seen this on TV – flowers start blooming, the whole place is screaming with birds."

"An instant garden," Sonny said.

"An instant graveyard," said his father. "I just seen a dead sheep go past to rot amongst your flowers."

Voices from across the water were strangely distorted – loud, though it was impossible to hear the words. A two-cylinder motor puttered somewhere. Something knocked hollowly, the soft thud of wood against submerged wood.

"How long do we wait?" the old man said.

"Until somebody notices," Sonny said.

"Or the friggin' water rises," Lachlan said.

"Or some big brown snake decides to come ashore," Timo Aalto said. "He might not be willing to share like our timid ewe."

The timid ewe stood patient and unmoving on her narrow side of the island.

"Or," Lachlan said, getting to his feet, "I can swim for help."

That narrow sharp-featured face may have looked like a small adult's even when he was eight or ten years old, those fox eyes always a little wiser than you and suspicious. He looked the small boy now, however, in that ridiculous too-large hat – he was the one in charge, the one who knew he could save them.

"Don't try," Sonny said. "You'll find yourself riding a dead cow into the next state."

"You haven't been looking. Most of the stuff's going by behind us, i'n'it? We must've crossed the creek. This side is paddock. Flat and shallow. Current's weaker."

"The Mysterious Manly Swimmer," Sonny said.

"I wanted to be a surf lifeguard once." He stepped into the water. "The two a yiz stay."

He waded into the brown water, the surface rising up his legs to his thighs. As he walked, the surface dropped for a while to his knees and rose again. Twenty metres out it hadn't got any deeper than mid-thigh. "I can walk it," he said. "So could you if you're careful. We can carry your dad." He started back towards them.

Sonny turned to his father. "How do you feel about that?"

"What about the sheep?"

"We can rescue only one of you. Take your pick." He stood up and crouched for his father to climb on his back. Then, with Timo Aalto's arms around his neck, his bony thighs in his hands, he waded in towards Lachlan Macquarie Hall.

It seemed the boy had been right. They could be crossing someone's level field. The earth seemed fairly solid and reliable, the current not too strong. But even the flattest of farmer's fields could have sudden rabbit holes or piles of rocks. When one foot dropped into a hollow he stumbled forward into deeper water, bent from his father's weight, and stopped himself from a fall by grabbing at a sturdy uprooted tree.

"Easy," his father said, his breath hot at Sonny's ear. "Take it slow."

As he worked his way along the trunk towards its naked roots the water rose again up his thighs. He found purchase on a rise of earth and for a while he was able to walk again, though the water rose to his waist. Ahead, Lachlan was getting close to the far side – some sort of low bank of trees and muddy soil that formed a long island or peninsula between them and the town. He walked backwards, keeping an eye on them while checking occasionally over his shoulder.

"Careful," he said. "There's a drop to your right."

Sonny heard his words even as he felt both feet slide out from under him and down a sudden incline of mud, the water rising up past his neck and into his mouth. By the time he'd got himself up again, spitting and thrashing about, trying to swim, trying to get his footing, he was aware of his father's weight gently lifting from his back.

His shoulders were suddenly free, the pressure of his father's thighs against his waist had gone. He turned, slapping his arms in the muddy current. At first he couldn't see the old man at all. Then, when he did see him, he was already out of reach, three or four metres away, a floating face-down figure slowly turning, moving past a dead dog hung up in weeds, past the tilted shed turning in an eddy, and right on past another of those small islands of twisted trees.

five

He'd come out onto the back porch of Colin Macken's house to escape the crowd. It was a clear day, unusual for November, but chilly enough. A brown squirrel darted across the backyard and ran up the trunk of a Douglas fir, then from the safety of a high bare limb worked itself up into a fury of scolding chatter. When Holly joined him on the bench, she was carrying a large crystal platter heaped with sandwiches she was supposed to be serving the people inside. "I still can't believe you're wearing a suit and tie." She put the platter to one side and made a small adjustment to the knot at his throat. "New clothes!"

"Admire it while you can, you may never see it again. Not on *this* body."

Taking his hand in hers, she placed it over her knee where it made a sharp angle in her skirt. She was wearing a moss-green sweater-jacket, long and loose and open over a darker green skirt and blouse. "Okay. The rest! Tell me before they come looking. So maybe he just wanted to give you a scare?"

"Or maybe he saw his chance and decided to sail on down that river and disappear." With all that had happened since getting home, this was his first opportunity to tell her about the flood in any detail. "Lachlan had already started to run. I splashed my way to shore as fast as I could and ran like hell to catch up."

Paavo Nurmi might not have run any faster. He caught up to Lachlan and passed him, aware that they were running along a sort of dike with water on both sides of it, a strip of land that was gradually getting narrower, the earth becoming mud and starting to crumble. Eventually the dike narrowed almost to a point and collapsed altogether into disintegrating clots of muck. Ahead, the world opened up to a lake, spreading through the streets of town and spilling out over fields and paddocks and fenceless plain as far as the eye could see. Trees that must have looked lonely enough at any time seemed entirely banished now.

He bent forward with hands on his knees, panting. It was impossible not to think, *Maybe this is best. Maybe this is what he wanted.* But he also thought, *This will save me from Cape Scott, from having to make a decision* – and so he knew, too, that things weren't going to be that easy. When he spotted what looked like someone caught up in a floating tree, he knew he had no choice. "I plunged down into the mud, and thrashed my way out the best I could. It didn't take long, but it was long enough to curse myself for taking the old man to that country in the first place." By the time he'd splashed his way back, Lachlan had run in to help carry his father out.

When the little State Emergency Service boat came along, Timo Aalto had regained consciousness, thanks to Lachlan's amateur lifeguard efforts. But he didn't understand what had happened. He fought Lachlan off, or tried to; he seemed to think the boy was trying to do him damage.

"There were two people in the boat. A short, stout muscular black man in an orange jumpsuit sat at the stern, steering the outboard motor. Down on the flat-bottomed hull by his feet was a small boy whose face was filthy with mud and tears and who looked as though he didn't welcome new refugees. 'A bloke's been electrocuted,' the man said, once he'd got us aboard. When we'd laid the old man into the vee of the prow, he opened up a blanket over him."

"Electrocuted?" Holly said.

"Climbed onto a floating bit of fence to keep from drowning and was swept right into the power lines."

The boatman clamped a half-smoked cigar between his teeth, gunned the little outboard motor, and turned in the direction of town.

"The medical clinic?" Sonny said.

"Town's evacuated," the man said. "They've got a clinic set up at the airfield."

They travelled right up the main street in that boat, past people on roofs still waiting for someone to rescue them. The false fronts of the stores were the banks of a canal. Some windows were broken, walls torn away, the water flowing through the interior of buildings. On the roof of the bottle shop, four people huddled together, a family with children, watching the approach of another orange boat with "State Emergency Service" printed on its side. A Ford sedan and a Holden ute bobbed like bathtub toys. A delivery van, nose up, nudged at a wall. Above the Ampol petrol station, two boys and a dog sat along the base of the billboard advertising the dinosaurs of Lark Quarry.

The helicopter thrashed into sight again, and paused for a moment above a solitary man on a rusty corrugated roof, its rope ladder dangling near his head. On the peak of the roof, a small terrier barked twice, and then sat silently watching, its ears alert, while the man waved the helicopter away. It throbbed, tail up, across the street to hover above a group on the opposite roof, who were happy enough to climb in and go swinging across town towards safety.

Their little boat navigated around a shed roof, which moved ponderously by with three chickens roosting on its peak. "There's hundreds out at the airfield already," the man said. "They've got tents. And medical supplies. And food."

The pallor of the old man's face was emphasized by the streaks of drying mud that Sonny's handkerchief had missed. The puzzled gaze in those eyes never left Sonny's face. Sonny didn't know what to think. He didn't even know how he felt. Relieved to see him alive, at least with a fighting chance, but angry, too. The old man looked at Sonny as if there were still something more for him to do. Something for Sonny to say.

"There's a whole family gone missing," their rescuer said. "Five of them. Left their property in a rowboat and haven't been seen. Swept downriver, I reckon. How d'ye like it so far – the Big Wet?"

"Well, it looks as if some of us may survive it," Sonny said. "Thanks to you." He swatted at the flies around his ears. Benno's old hat had been lost in the swim. "This sort of thing happen often?"

"Flood? Yeh? Often enough for most people's taste. Whenever we aren't having drought." He chuckled, and raised his hat to relocate it on his head, and squinted off into the distance. "It don't always happen this bad."

Sonny leaned forward on Colin Macken's bench to rest his chin on his hands and look down at the planks between his shoes and his nearly empty glass of rye-and-ginger. The squirrel had been quiet for a while, but now it took up its scolding again. Holly placed her open palm on his back and moved it around in a wide circle. "The little boy?" she said. "What was he doing in the boat?"

"He hadn't been able to find his folks, the man told us. Nobody knew who he was. Poor little bugger didn't even know his own last name. The boatman had taken him along in case they passed something that reminded him. I asked him what would happen if they didn't find the family. Lachlan was sure someone would recognize him, that people in small towns know one another. But the boatman said he'd lived in that town all his life and had never seen the little tyke before.

"'So, what if they don't find his family?' I asked him again. My father has come this close to death and I'm worried about a kid I've never seen before. But Lachlan gave me this warning look and said, 'He'll have grandparents.'"

"There must have been reporters and TV cameras," Holly

said. "Someone would know." Her hand had not stopped moving around on his back.

"There wasn't anything we could do for him," Sonny said.

When the boy noticed the others looking at him, he wiped the back of his hand across his eyes and made his face into a defiant scowl. Then he crawled up the length of the boat and slipped under the blankets beside the old man. The look he gave Sonny might have been saying *This is what you should have done yourself, to keep him warm.* Or maybe Sonny was the one who thought that, shocked to think he hadn't thought of it earlier. Or maybe what the boy was saying was only *If you save him, you have to save me too.*

"This is as far as I can go," the man said, cutting the motor. "You'll have to wade up to the Railway Hotel and a truck'll take you to the camp. Make sure you get in the queue for your tea. Don't want you complaining Mistake Creek didn't feed you."

"And did they find out who the boy was?" Holly said.

"Not while we were there. I don't know what happened afterwards. How could I? I might still be wondering about him twenty years from now. Or I might not think about him again."

"I'll think about him," Holly said. "You should write the mayor or someone." They watched the squirrel come down the tree and skitter across the grass and up another. "I've got to get back inside and help. Theresa will think I've run off with her platter."

Hundreds of mourners had crammed into the funeral home, filling up the chapel and its overflow room, with some standing outside to hear what they could through the open doors. All of the Finns had turned out for the funeral, of course – the Korhonens, the Koskelas, the Aaltonens. They had made Colin one of them after his marriage to Theresa, just as they had tried long ago to make Sonny one of them because of his ancestral blood and their own sympathy for a mother-deserted boy. So did

all the various families of Mackens attend, those who still lived in
the settlement as well as those who'd moved down-island or
across the strait. Theresa brought Aunt Nora out of Extended
Care for the service, but the old woman seemed to think she was
attending her own father's funeral and expressed aloud her aston-
ishment that so few of her brothers had shown up.

Not everyone had come to Theresa's afterwards, though there
were enough family and neighbours and close friends to fill up
every room and spill out onto the porches and even into the yard.
Fortunately the cool weather was pleasant enough for at least half
the men to take their beers outside where they stood in clusters
amongst the parked vehicles in the nearest field.

Sonny had little interest in joining them yet. Abandoned by
Holly and alone on the porch for the moment, he chose to think
about the man who'd built this house and started this family but
wasn't here today "in person," as they liked to put it. He hadn't
known about Colin until yesterday. Just a few hours off the plane,
with his father settled in hospital for observation, he'd stopped in
at the store to replenish the empty fridge and found neighbours
brooding in a booth against the window wall. They asked about
his father, of course, but as soon as they'd heard that his condition was stable, they'd fallen over themselves to explain why the
anniversary party would have to be a funeral instead.

According to Harry Sylvester, the protesters, who usually
waited until summer when they could stir up their trouble without too much discomfort to themselves, decided that they
couldn't afford to wait for next year's warmer weather. Word had
gone out that because the snow line had come down pretty low
the company was about to move into a new watershed valley and
start logging in the same clear-cutting manner they'd been using
since the local company sold out. "Right back here behind
Carter's Canyon. There isn't any old growth left in this area,
hasn't been for years, but they've started to talk about this as
'virgin second growth,' for cryin' out loud, if you can believe it.
They came in from all over the damn place in school buses,

wearing their beards and long skirts and hippie beads, you'd think it was the sixties all over again."

"That's only what they showed on TV," Dora said. "We know plenty of regular people who joined them, some of them as normal as me and you."

Rob Mitchell put a hand on her arm. "Imagine how you'd feel now . . . if you'd went . . . with them."

Dora bridled. Her tiny legs jerked as though he'd tapped a rubber hammer to her knees. "Well I wouldn't, would I!"

Harry stood beside them, a hand on the high back of Dora's seat as though he ought to be going out the door but couldn't pull himself away. He insisted that Sonny take his place, and the waitress brought him a cup and filled it with coffee. Plates were empty except for a few crumbs and a red smear of jam. It was one of those rainy November afternoons when the sky seemed to have moved down to sit on your head. Inside lights only emphasized the gloom. The traffic hissed by in an almost steady stream.

Dora thought that history would eventually show the protesters' ideals to be admirable and good, "but good ideals mixed with hate and blame aren't good any more, I don't care what anyone says."

Apparently the whole settlement was more or less united in their opinion of the press. "Reporters who'd come up from Victoria and across from Vancouver were like sharks smelling blood." Rob Mitchell's hand rested on folded proof of this, news stories from recent papers, lying on the sheet of glass that itself lay over more pleasant stories out of history. Only Charlie Mackinaw, who'd been a reporter and editor himself in his day, had defended them. "He said they'd had no choice," Harry said. "To make sure they did their jobs, they sought out the biggest blowhards on either side, so people watching or reading about it at home could work up their own good hate."

Rob Mitchell slurped his coffee and said "Ahhhh," then placed his mug precisely on the dark ring it had left on the table. "Colin . . . should've . . . known better."

"He wouldn't have gone," Harry said, "if he hadn't turned on the TV to get the results of that goddam referendum. A skin-of-our-teeth win and ugly accusations from the losers. You probably didn't hear anything about it – that nasty little premier blaming it on everyone that isn't 'pure French,' whatever he means by that!"

Then the TV news switched to something closer to home. The *séparatistes'* attempt to break up the nation had been little more than a spectator sport. A local squabble over timber, on the other hand, had the urgency of a family fight. "Colin spotted a few of his friends in the crowd. This is what Theresa tells us. He just thought he'd go up to have a look, maybe talk to some of them. You know him, big happy guy, took it for granted everybody liked him as soon as they saw his smile. He figured it wouldn't hurt anybody if he just drove up there and talked with this one and that one about what he's been doing down here for years, making a half-decent living out of selective logging his own property. He didn't expect to stop anything. He just thought – he talked this over with Theresa first – he just thought he'd plant a few little seeds for people to chew on once the protest was broken up."

Then one of these reporters spotted Colin chatting with people around the edges of the angry loggers, showing his big white teeth and putting a friendly hand on people's shoulders. And then moving up closer to the bridge and chatting with one of the protesters chained to the railing – a friend of his son's, as it happened. "This reporter notices he's just as friendly with this young protester as he was with the loggers, so he goes over and sticks his microphone in his face."

"You forgot to say there's people up in the trees since the night before," Dora put in. She used her paper serviette to scrub at stains on the table glass. "Threw their own, um, excrement down on the loggers. There's people chained to the bridge, too, sitting on cans of gas."

"There's the cops," Harry said, "trying to convince the protesters to let the workers go through and rely on the courts to decide their case, saving them all the trouble of arrests and a night in jail."

"And there's this TV . . . camera . . . on Colin," said Rob Mitchell.

"Big naive lunk," Harry Sylvester said, "he thinks the TV camera wants to hear him talk about his own logging operation but everybody wants him just to tell which *side* he's on. He didn't get a chance to tell much of anything because just then someone throws a stink bomb and the police decide to move in and clear the way for the logging crew to go to work. Nobody even wondered what happened to the big white-bearded fellow. Maybe they thought he'd gone home. Theresa waited two or three hours before she started phoning around, he'd promised to be back for lunch."

It was the next morning before someone spotted him. "Carried a mile or so downstream," Dora said. "Caught up on some rocks." She rubbed her serviette hard at a resistant stain, while the others looked at traffic hissing by in the rain.

"Rusty . . . will be up for the funeral," Rob Mitchell said.

"He was a long way from the bridge at the time," Harry said, "down in his Victoria office with a bunch of others trying to revise the forest practices code to satisfy half a dozen competing ministries. When he heard about Colin he packed 'er in. Put in for early retirement. He said it's somebody else's turn to find a way through this mess."

"Colin was murdered," Rob Mitchell said.

"But not by any one person," Dora said. "Hatred can do its own sort of damage. So can blame."

"Oh, for heaven's sake, Dora!" Harry said. "Somebody pushed him off the bridge."

"You can put me down as saying nobody done it. It was the ugly feelings of all them people in one place." She folded her tiny arms and blew air down her nose, and jerked her head in one quick nod that meant she'd said her final word. Her feet, crossed at the ankles, swung back and forth beneath the bench.

"The problem was that somebody had to be right," Harry said.

"You hiding here or what?"

Rusty Macken had come around the corner of the house carry-ing an empty glass. He wore a black tie and a lightweight dark-grey suit that made him look even longer and skinnier than he'd looked in his loose cottons up at the Blueback. His dress shirt was precisely the same colour as his faded once-red hair.

"I don't know what I'm doing here," Sonny said. "Yes I do. I'm waiting for Colin to come walking up out of that bush back there to tell me how this thing could have happened."

Rusty glanced in the direction of the woods as though he too expected to see Colin. Then he came up the steps to the porch, straightening the little round glasses on the bridge of his nose, and sat where Holly had been sitting. "It's going to take some getting used to." He bent forward and looked into his glass, which he held between his hands like something that needed restraint while he studied it. "Maybe we never will. Maybe nobody *does*."

"Rob Mitchell says it was murder."

"All we know is that he died in the river. We'll have to let the police look for answers – not that knowing answers will change anything."

Sonny picked up his own glass, which had been sitting on the planks between his feet. The ice had melted long ago, but he drank the diluted inch or so and put the glass back on the planks. Then he pushed it back with one foot until it was safely beneath the bench. "Well, one thing's changed. I hear you quit your cushy job with the government. I didn't think anyone ever did that."

"I was ready." Rusty leaned back and stretched out both long legs and crossed them at the ankles. "I could see the future – forest companies will lobby for changes to any code we come up with, and eventually get their way." Tiny drops of moisture from the grass still clung to his shiny black shoes. "Colin will be sorry to miss out on all that movie-making business over at your –" He interrupted himself with a short surprised laugh. "I actually thought *When he gets back*! I mean, he *would* have been sorry. It

wasn't the movie stars that interested him, it was the idea of
seeing all their big machines. He hoped they'd want to borrow
something, or ask him to get a few trees out of their way."

"Well, they might yet," Sonny said. "I wasn't home twenty
minutes when they descended – two fast-talking baby-faced types
awfully pleased with themselves. They wanted to see how I felt
about a little 'pruning.'"

"Well, it's Colin's son they'll have to see about it now. Unless
you've decided to take up logging yourself."

"Only what I can do with my hands. They drove me down to
the old sawmill and offered to rent that too, and tried to hire me
to clear away a couple of spots where they'll want to set up their
cameras."

"You going to do it?"

"I'm thinking about it. I feel like taking an axe to something."

"I could give you a hand, if you wait till I'm out of this suit." One
long-fingered hand lifted a lapel away from his shirt, as though he
wished somehow to distance himself from his own costume. "If I'm
going to be retired I ought to see what skills I've got left."

"Handling tools isn't one of them," Sonny said. "I'm the one
that knows how many nails you bent and lost and probably even
swallowed while we were building that tree fort. Even when we
decided to blow it up you nearly killed us both, misreading the
directions in the stump-blasting book."

Rusty looked surprised, pleased, and amused all at once. "Well.
We should've asked Colin to help. The thing would not only get
finished but it'd be standing even now, occupied by half a dozen
of his grandchildren."

"You forget, he was too busy growing up faster than anyone else
to waste his time on play. While we were fooling around with that
tree fort Colin was only a couple years away from building a real
house – for his teenaged bride and first-born son to live in."

"He got a faster start than we did," Rusty said. "Maybe he had a
hunch he might not get to be an adult for as long as the rest of us."

"Well," Sonny said, getting to his feet. "We've already outlived the poor bugger by most of a week. He'll want to know what we've done with it."

His father had been only vaguely aware of the world as the emergency boat took them up the main street of town. They could have been speeding up the Grand Canal in Venice. But he began to show a little frowning curiosity once a truck had brought them to the airfield, an expanse of dry reddish dirt behind the town. Here the old man had been shifted onto a stretcher and carried through a milling crowd and past a row of tents towards a large building with "ROYAL FLYING DOCTOR SERVICE" painted high up the gable end.

Inside, there was a row of cots along the nearer wall, with several occupied stretchers amongst them. Men with stethoscopes bent over beds, some with hands at wrists. Women with clipboards met newcomers, asking for names and relevant statistics.

The first doctor free to examine Timo Aalto was the one who had checked him over in the clinic last night. He showed no sign of recognizing the old man, and paid no attention at all to Sonny. In the circumstances, maybe even his neighbours and regular patients were faceless refugees. A quick examination was the most he had the time for. The old man was breathing; he was conscious; there was no blood, no visible sign of bruising. The stethoscope delivered no alarming news. A woman in a nurse's uniform was called from another bed to take over. Sonny supposed this was good.

"How old?" the doctor said, turning suddenly to Sonny.

"Eighty-five."

The doctor turned again to the nurse, who was already wrapping her blood-pressure apparatus around his father's upper arm. "We'll send him out."

"To Brisbane?" Sonny said.

"We're sending some to Brisbane, some to Toowoomba." He looked at Sonny now, perhaps because of his accent. "We'll get your father on the next one out. Possibly you too, if there's room." He might have recognized them after all. "Make sure we have all the correct information," he said to the nurse.

"How soon?" Sonny asked.

The doctor turned away to tend to someone else.

"There should be another leaving within the half-hour," the nurse said. "The minute the supplies are unloaded we'll have you on it – along with these others." While she was jotting information on her clipboard, the nurse's gaze took in Sonny's soaked and muddied clothing, his mud-thick hair. No doubt his face was streaked with mud as well. "There are showers outside. The sun will dry you off."

He looked down at himself. His new clothes were no longer stiff and itchy, they were heavy and loose, thick with drying mud. To stand under a shower fully dressed might be enough improvement for the time being. There would be clothing stores in Brisbane. For the second time since arriving in this country he was being forced to clothe himself from the skin out. The only things he still owned that he would go home with were his watch and the waterproof pouch, attached to his belt, containing his passport, his credit cards, and a little cash.

"A shower won't do me no good," his father said, a weak but worried mumble.

The nurse put a hand on the old man's shoulder. "I didn't mean you, Granddad. You'll have to stay dirty. If I could spare the time we could take a shower together, but I've got all these other gentlemen screaming for attention."

"Christ," Timo Aalto said. His mouth opened to say more, but closed again. It seemed he didn't have the energy.

Sonny put a hand on his shoulder. "I won't be far away. Okay?"

His father made a brief noise in his throat, but didn't open his eyes.

Against the far wall of the hangar a soup kitchen had been set up. Behind a long table, three or four women and a couple of young men in military uniforms ladled food onto plates, which were taken back outside by those who had waited in a line that extended down the length of the building and well into the midst of the crowd outside. A youth in a soldier's uniform passed along the queue, pausing to crouch beside each child he came to. He appeared to be making jokes even as he examined hands. Most were sent up to the far end of the building to wash.

Lachlan was not in the queue. At least he was not in the part of the queue that had got in under the roof. Sonny moved back to the open hangar doorway in search of him. He could not fly off without some final words.

Those who weren't in the lineup for food were walking around in a kind of daze, it seemed, uncertain where they were or what they ought to be doing with themselves. Some sat on their heels to eat. Others had found stumps or bales of hay to perch on. Two red-faced men in white shirts and ties were engaged in animated discussion with a soldier. "Who's making sure we aren't looted, then?" It seemed they were prevented from returning to their businesses. "I hope they're armed. I've left a million dollars' worth of stock unguarded."

"Wastin' 'is breath." A short round Aboriginal man wearing the orange jumpsuit of the emergency volunteers said this to Sonny Aalto as he passed by. "His precious stock'll be spread from here to Birdsville." A rueful joke, delivered with a wink.

Off to one side, a family seemed to be living out of a panel van. Wet clothing was draped all over the top of the van to dry. Mattresses lay on the ground. A row of small children in wide-brimmed hats sat on a bench, eating food from the plates on their laps. Behind them, a wide grey-haired woman leaned against the van and wept into a handkerchief.

Nearby, a cluster of women had gathered around the nameless boy who'd shared their boat. He shook his head vigorously, his face wet with fresh tears, and pushed away an offered cup.

"Doesn't know his own name," one of the women explained. "Poor little soul has lost his folks."

The elderly woman who'd offered the cup was short and round – a Mrs. Korhonen with slightly goitrous eyes and weathered skin. Apparently offended by the rejection, she handed the cup to one of the others and turned away. "I've got to get back and put my ladle to work." She strode off through the crowd towards the hangar brandishing a long-handled soup ladle.

Noticing that his was not a familiar face, the woman who had inherited the cup said, "Maybe he's yours?" This was asked with enough hope to turn the attention of the others Sonny's way.

He was forced to disappoint. "We shared a rescue boat, that's all."

He didn't attempt to get the boy's attention, certain that his eyes would only accuse him of something. He would ask Lachlan to watch out for developments. Surely a miraculous reunion would be reported in the newspapers read at Kalevan Station. This would mean leaving an address, something he hadn't thought to do earlier. But in order for him to do this, Lachlan would have to be found.

In case this didn't happen, Sonny turned to the woman with the cup who might have been one of the dressed-up ladies he'd seen in the street yesterday. "Could I give you my address?" he said. "So you could let me know if the boy is reunited with his family."

Even to his own ears, it seemed a peculiar request. Why would a stranger with a foreign accent want to know such a thing?

"Oh, I'm no letter writer," the woman said, stepping back, perhaps suspecting that Sonny was not someone a decent person should get involved with. "Best leave your address with the Salvos, I would think – wouldn't you, Dorothy? They'll take care of it."

"There are showers down the north side of the building," the woman named Dorothy suggested. Perhaps he was beginning to smell.

Sonny assumed that by "the Salvos" the woman had meant the Salvation Army, since she'd tilted her head in the direction of a man in the familiar uniform. At the moment he was dealing blankets off an armload to members of a family that sat silent and stunned and probably disbelieving in a row along a makeshift bench of planks. When this gentleman had placed the remaining blankets on a child's lap and pulled a crumpled envelope from his trouser pocket, Sonny scribbled his father's address, and then, before handing the envelope back, added his Ottawa address as well. How could he know how long he would be at the one, and whether he would return for any length of time to the other?

Lachlan did not reappear until Sonny and his father were being loaded into the Hercules. There was time for little more than a quick handshake, and for Lachlan to draw their attention to his mate Sal. They'd come across one another somewhere in the crowd. Sal grinned. "Me boyhood chum from school – orright?" Lachlan said. "We reached puberty together – same day, same minute." Whatever this was supposed to mean, both of them found it hilarious.

"What's Sally doing here?" Sonny said.

"He's with them." Lachlan jabbed a finger here, and then there, and somewhere else into the crowds. The volunteers? The Aborigines. Those faces could be the faces that had grinned out at them from that dirty black LandCruiser. Which was probably parked off to the side of all this somewhere, BOUND FOR GLORY printed across its bumper. While they performed more of their wonders.

When he saw that Sonny and his father were being escorted to the plane, Lachlan said that he would stick with the station as long as he could. "Maybe till I've earned enough to buy me own horse. I'll let yiz ride it when yer back." He may have meant Timo Aalto – he gently punched the old man's arm.

Sonny made one request, that Lachlan keep track of the little boy. That was about all there was time for. They were being escorted by men in uniform, after all, who were impatient to get this next load of the sick, the elderly, and the troublesome out of their hair. They were whisked aboard, and Lachlan became a figure on the packed red dirt of the airfield, almost indistinguishable from the others in the crowd.

He supposed, as the Hercules engines began their roar, that his request might have shown questionable judgement. But it was too late to retract it now, and anyway a small abandoned boy would be open to far worse risks than any Lachlan might represent. And of course, he could count on the sober members of the Australian "Salvos" to keep a watchful eye.

How quickly Lachlan and his chum became the inhabitants of a miniature universe that rapidly lost any resemblance to reality. Within moments, all had fallen away to become a vast spectacle of pinkish water decorated with the occasional crowns of tiny isolated trees, a cluster of little roofs and water towers representing a station far from any others, a small stone ridge that he supposed from ground level would be a "jump-up." What reality was there now in the tracks of long-extinct dinosaurs, or the unhatched eggs of serpentine gods? The one inescapable part of his world was going with him, beneath a rough grey blanket, rising with him above the earth to fly southeast towards Brisbane and whatever else lay ahead.

Apparently the location scouts had found inspiration in the overgrown and dilapidated farm, which, to the young man who arrived in the first truck, was, "like, totally excellent." Within days of Colin's funeral, a crew began converting the property into a hillbilly farm devastated by a war where cousins killed one another over the right to separate. A truckload of potted magnolia trees arrived, all of them in bloom. There were chinaberry trees as well. This was to be Mississippi and not Kentucky, as Colin had believed. Young firs were cut so that men could plant the imported trees. Blackberry bushes were rearranged to look even more invasive and menacing than they already were. An overturned coal-oil lantern was placed on the front step, torn flour-sack curtains were hung at the windows, a long-eared mule was tethered to a stake in the yard.

More trucks moved in and parked in the second field. "The circus," they called it. The actors' dressing rooms would be parked in that field too, when they arrived from some other location where shooting was still going on. His father's trailer was dragged out of sight behind the barn. "We'll put it back where we found it," the foreman assured him. "You won't even be able to tell it's been touched."

Sonny was expected to move to a motel in town but he chose to stay on in the trailer. This meant carrying water from the well.

It also meant that his electricity depended upon a single exten-
sion cord from a pole beside the old house – easily disconnected,
coiled up, and tossed out of sight if it got in anyone's way. But the
important thing was that he could keep an eye on things, and
report to his father, who was confined to bed in a "respite house"
and straining hard to come home and witness it all for himself.

No one knew when this would happen. When they'd returned
from Australia, Doctor Chandler had slapped Timo Aalto in hospital for observation. Then he found him a bed in a private rest
home in town. The old man was a little anemic, a little confused,
and weaker than he ought to be. He needed to regain his strength.
Of course the old man was convinced that he would be hauled
down to the Extended Care wing and wake up with Nora Macken
glaring at him from the foot of his bed. There he would be forced
to stay till they wheeled him through the connecting tunnel to
the death-row prison of Acute Care. "Plugged into machines,
hooked up to tubes, and trapped in a goddam crib." He wished the
flood had carried him safely out of reach. Failing that, he said, he
wished he were still in Brisbane, where he'd felt one hell of a lot
safer than he did here.

The few days in Brisbane had been an opportunity, between
visits to the hospital, for Sonny to spend some time with Jerrod
Hawkins. They drove northeast to observe the Giant Pineapple,
and to laugh at themselves climbing the stairway inside. And to
walk the long sandy beach at Maroochydore, before driving south
to observe the Japanese occupation of Surfers Paradise. They
snaked their way to the top of Mount Marvellous, and walked
through the whip-bird eeriness of a rainforest. And because the
dinosaur tracks were out of the question, they visited the state
museum where Jerrod pointed out the large wall-mounted cast of
footprints crossing a slab of Lark Quarry, "Just to put a picture in
your head of something to come back to."

The picture it put into Aalto's head was of a flock of oversize
turkeys running across a slab of pink cement before it had set. It
was only because you'd been told you were looking at footprints

several million years old that you felt this sense of awe. If you felt
you were looking at a message from another world, it was because
you trusted the experts who wrote the museum guide. This wide
expanse of tracks made you feel you'd risk alarm bells just to touch.

He tried not to tie his brain up in knots contemplating
whether observing the original footprints might have been
more or less rewarding than standing before these impressions
removed from their landscape. It was the kind of thing that
could bring on a headache, the question of whether looking at
the original *mattered*.

It wasn't all that hard to believe a landscape could be in two
places at once if you remembered that a town's main street could
be captured on 35 mm film, its street signs and vehicle licence
plates changed to those of a foreign country. If you were looking
at a movie filmed in Vancouver but set in Seattle, were you
looking at Vancouver or Seattle while you ate your popcorn? It
depended, it seemed, upon what you'd been told. Readers of the
Vancouver papers would know they were seeing Vancouver, while
three hundred million Americans would discover parts of Seattle
they hadn't known existed.

You had only to remember that a landscape could be stolen,
drowned, or buried. It could be borrowed, blasted, burnt, and
covered over. Worse, it could simply disappear. You understood
that people could vanish, though you might not like it much.
And so could bad ideas, unpopular makes of cars, and movies you
weren't quick enough to catch. What was harder to get into your
head was that places, too, could disappear, sometimes without
moving an inch. A childhood home could vanish beneath the
waters of a seaway project, an old-growth forest could be wiped
out for distant housing. Whole countries had been gobbled up by
neighbours, their names erased from the map.

If the Devil's Marbles were moved by barge and truck to
Saskatchewan, say, would the sacred site be the abandoned patch
of ground, or the transported collection of Marbles? If a site was
important because of its association with some event, did the

location of the site have any significance at all? It was something he might have asked his mother.

He went back to stare at the wall-hung dinosaur tracks a second time, and a third, but the headache only got worse. There was relief only when physicians finally declared his father fit for travel. His indifference to his own survival, they said, had been undermined by his natural interest in the world – including his curiosity about what had gone on at home.

What had gone on at home was recorded in the newspapers stacked on the chair by his father's bed. The old man intended to take them with him. Otherwise, he said, no one would believe that foreign papers had noticed. The front page of *The Australian* remained at the top of the stack, its blaring headline "CANADA AVERTS SPLIT – JUST" followed by a subheading, "*Violence follows knife-edge poll.*" He'd counted seven stories in that one issue: the lead news item, a front-page analysis, two facing pages of photographs, a back-page editorial, a letter to the editor, and two opinion columns. He insisted that Sonny read them. "If Canada, which is noted for its global decency (such as peacekeeping) and domestic civility (such as its innovative multicultural policy) can't work out a constitutional and political settlement to head off separatism, then who can?"

The writer of a letter to the editor, on the other hand, saw "the looming collapse of Canada" as a warning for his own country. "Multiculturalism is exposed as an ideological threat to a stable society. If Australia is to develop as one nation, we must have one language, and one mainstream culture."

"Makes you think we're going home to a war zone," his father said.

"If you're ready to give up this charade," Sonny said. "You convinced me your days were numbered but you've already used up more lives than a cat. You'll probably outlive me. You'll outlive your grandchildren too."

"No thanks to you." It was not possible to know whether his father was pleased to be going home or happy to be giving his son a hard time. "What you dragged me through . . . would finish . . . most old guys my age. Drowning in mud ain't a hell of a lot of fun."

Sonny swallowed a laugh. This wasn't the time to bring up the chilly waters off Cape Scott.

While he was helping his father into the new shirt and pants he'd purchased on the Queen Street Mall, the old man brought up the cougar incident again, something he'd been thinking about in his bed. "I heard you mention it to young Lachlan."

"So which part of it was a lie? Was it my mother who scared it off? You didn't want me knowing even one good thing about her?"

The old man kept his eyes towards the window, though there wasn't much he could see but Australian sky. "There wasn't any cougar."

For a moment Sonny could think of nothing to say to this. A kind of indignant outrage had paralyzed his brain. Yet one hand had risen of its own accord to finger the dents in his skull. "Let's get you dressed and out of here. Tell me the rest on the plane."

But the old man was determined not to leave without confessing. "It was one of them times . . . when Rosie turned me down. I went on a terrible tear. Probably lasted a week. I may have left you alone the whole time too. I don't remember."

It left him gasping, but he rested a moment. He might have been drunk, he said, or maybe the hangover was so bad it was the same as being drunk, but at any rate he knew he was trying to get through the next day with the help of a little fresh air. He was sitting out on the doorstep of the sauna, trying to get up the energy to tidy the vegetable garden. "Maybe I forgot to feed you. I don't know. Anyway your whining was like a buzz-saw . . . in my head. I swung the garden rake . . . to bat you out of earshot. But the teeth of the rake come down on your little head."

Sonny didn't know if this swell of indignation was for the blow itself or for the loss of the cougar. "I liked the original version better."

His father allowed him to raise the arm and slip it into the sleeve of the new checkered shirt. "But that's not the end of it," he protested. "Dammit. Let me finish."

"You can finish in the taxi. The other arm!"

His father ignored this. "I just about decided to give you up after that."

"What?"

"I pretty well decided . . . that if Rose wouldn't have me . . . I'd find some strangers I could turn you over to."

Sonny took his hands from the shirt and stood back a step. "Jesus, Dad. You wanted to get rid of me."

"For your own good. I'd been thinking how you got nobody . . . but me . . . to keep an eye on you. Then this rake business, it scared me so much . . . I decided to sell you off for sure."

"Sell me?"

"Give you away. Whatever. I never found out how it works. For your own safety, was what I was thinking." He lay back for a moment on his pillow, breathing hard. Then he said to the ceiling, "But without you I was sure I'd drink myself to death. Probably fall off a bridge or under a truck. This scared me even more than the rake business so I changed my mind. Decided to bring you up myself . . . so I'd have a reason to try harder."

"My childhood was an example of you trying harder?"

"I was doing the best I knew how. It was a way of keeping myself alive. And keeping you . . . out of the hands of strangers."

Suddenly his father was interested in getting dressed. He started to do up his own buttons. "Let's not miss the damn plane over it," he said. "If I'm going home alive, I want to get there in time . . . to keep an eye on them movie people. I figure we mizewell wait till they've done their job before we head up to Cape Scott."

His father was not the only one looking forward to the "Hollywood invasion" that would transform the old farm into a corner of

Mississippi. This was clear from the information exchanged
amongst people coming and going at the store. Theresa Macken's
daughter-in-law was disappointed to learn the film company had
its own caterers to feed the crew of more than one hundred
people, but she'd managed to secure a contract for providing the
caterers with fresh sandwiches daily, and hired three other
women to help. Al Price had rented them some of the ancient
and mostly useless farm machinery from behind his barn, including the gas caterpillar his grandfather had used for pulling stumps,
and lent them the team of sway-backed Percherons he kept only
for the pleasure of seeing them in his field. Sandy Morris ordered
an extra supply of cigarettes, snack food, and cold drinks for the
store. Several people drove into town for auditions, and registered
for crowd scenes in case they didn't get speaking parts. Linda
Maguire was prepared to use her skill at the sewing machine on
costumes for those lucky enough to be hired.

Holly Fitzgerald was already talking about a big party for the
movie's premiere. She knew the actual premiere wouldn't happen
here, since most of the movie was being shot somewhere else.
But there would have to be a screening in town eventually, and
so there would have to be an opening night. Those outfits run up
on Linda Maguire's machine could be put to good use a second
time. The community hall would be the scene of a costume
party. She would wear the torn and partially burnt flour-sack dress
of some backwoods hermit-woman, an expert on the healing
properties of local plants, perhaps, a character who'd been abused
by the marauding Northern soldiers but didn't actually appear in
the film. Her apron would be embroidered with words advertising her nursery.

She needed the attention. Sales of native plants were already
proving to be as disappointing as Sonny had predicted. Nobody
wanted their gardens to look like the wilds, and those few who
liked the idea didn't want to pay for what they could steal for
themselves from the bush. She still believed, however, that if she
could only take over Sonny's overgrown nursery garden, people

would be tempted to drive by out of curiosity. At least it had a history. She would sell fruit trees as well as native plants. "If you're going to landscape with ornamental trees you might as well use apples or pears. Instead of just looking at your garden, you can have a relationship with it."

"You're planning a relationship with an apple tree?" Sonny said.

This was after her shift at the Blueback one moonless night. They had gone down the beach and sat on a driftwood log, the white spindrift sloshing in the dark, gleaming gravel not far from their feet. "Just come in there with me, will you? Let me show you what I've found."

"You've told me what you found. It's just a little wilder and more crowded than it was."

He told her then about a recent dream. "You were naked except for a sort of drapery of vines, and beckoned me into that overgrown jungle, just as you're doing now with your clothes on. Eventually we knew we were lost. You suggested we set up house-keeping in one of the little glass houses, if I'd clear away the brush and build us a bed."

She laughed, but was not distracted. "You can hire someone to go in and start cleaning it up. Some of the local unemployed would be grateful. Or you could bring over that young fellow you left behind in Queensland, pay him to do the job."

It made you wonder what went on in that head of hers. "Bring Lachlan over here?"

"You know he'll be back on the city streets eventually. This would be a nice distraction for him. For you, too – you could teach him a few new skills."

He put an end to this conversation by tilting up her chin and pulling her in for a kiss.

Before long there were so many movie people swarming over the place that he didn't know one from another. One of these strangers met him at the gate as he returned from grocery shop-ping and suggested he read the screenplay. It seemed important that Sonny understand this was not a two-bit outfit, this was a serious movie with a budget of several million dollars.

"No thanks," he said, pushing the script aside.

But Holly suggested that his father might be interested in reading the script. "So he won't feel left out."

Not only did the old man let Sonny read the screenplay to him in the respite house, he made suggestions. "Tell them the poor bugger who lives in my house should put up more of a fight when his wife and children are kicked around by the soldiers." Sonny reported this to the man who had given him the script, but had no idea if this was someone with the power to change things. "He also thinks the man's son should show more gumption. Shoot one of the soldier's horses, or hightail it through the bush to get some help." A family poor enough to live on this broken-down farm, the old man suggested, would have some of their old folks living with them, a grandfather chewing tobacco on the front porch.

He was proud to think that his place was so dilapidated it could be used for a Southern farm devastated by war. "They mizewell use my chickens too," he said. "They can turn them out to run in the yard. But tell them they'll have to replace any that go missing."

The movie was one good reason to stay alive a bit longer. Telling neighbours about the Queensland flood was another. Of course he wasn't always coherent enough to make the best of it, but on his good days he could get himself worked up. They didn't care to hear it from Sonny. Even with Sonny in the room they encouraged the old man to tell again how they'd tried to get to the far side of the flood, how he'd stared into the eyes of venomous snakes and bumped his nose against the floating carcasses of sheep and wallabies, how he'd been caught up in a bush until someone hauled him up by the armpits and dumped him in a boat and took him off to a refugee city of tents.

The story was still unfolding behind them. Sonny passed on any news he received from Jerrod Hawkins. The flood had subsided. Lake Eyre was in bloom. But several human lives had been lost, and several thousand sheep and cattle drowned. Before coming home, their mother – who, it turned out, had been working as a volunteer at the airfield camp, "ladling out bowls of soup for the refugees," according to Jerrod – continued to devote her time to helping the people of Mistake Creek put their damaged houses back in order. Two of her sons were doing all they could to stop her plans for her property, so far without success. Trevor had got himself so worked up that he'd flown down to Errol's Sydney dental clinic and knocked out three of his brother's teeth. "Them Australians aren't like the rest of us," his father said. He left it to you to guess how.

Sonny passed on word of Charlotte to his father but not to the others, who hadn't cared enough to ask. She was still in Australia, still taking photographs, and still not sure she would ever return. She said she just might stay in that country of spectacular scenery and relaxed, friendly people. If she ever left, it would be to move back to that country, south of the border, where, she said, she could join that big chorus facing north and singing "Why can't you people be just like us?"

The old man was always pleased to see visitors but wasn't always lucid enough to entertain them. Sometimes he drifted off to sleep in the middle of an anecdote. Sometimes he told them things he'd told them before. Occasionally he didn't recognize his friends at all for a few minutes. Once he believed that Sonny was a realtor come to cheat him out of his farm. This sort of thing didn't happen often, but when it did they tried to laugh about it. Still, Sonny saw the puzzled fear in his father's eyes, and felt a chill in the movement of his own blood.

Occasionally his father veered away from his broken narratives and talked as if he'd just come back from an adventure with Tommy Reimer down one of the Island's back roads – a deer-hunting expedition, or a hike into Strathcona Park to look at the copper mines. He didn't seem to notice that while Reimer was sometimes the subject of his tales he was never amongst the listeners. According to Harry Sylvester, Tom Reimer had not forgiven either of them for going to Australia. "The fact that you came back alive may have unhinged him a little. He invested a good deal of energy in the conviction that at least one of you would not survive. He was hoping it would be you."

Rose Ferguson was another who didn't visit. She had been accepted into a home while they were away, Dora reported, but was in constant danger of being kicked out. "They take away her cigarettes but she has a way of finding more. They're terrified she'll cremate them all while they sleep."

Anticipating the movie shoot hadn't caused the old man to give up his plans for Cape Scott. They hadn't been back even long enough to get used to the rain, or the dark, low, autumn sky, before his father had asked for his map, which he opened up across his lap in order to trace the Cape Scott trail with his crooked index finger. They would go as soon as the filming was completed.

Occasionally he wondered aloud if it might already be too late. So much effort to commit suicide might kill him. Yet, so long as he was still within reach of that hospital he could wake up one morning in Extended Care. Sonny tried to convince him that if he was alert enough to worry about it, he wasn't far enough gone to have much reason to worry.

While Sonny had the trailer to himself, he made the necessary telephone calls to Ottawa and the Valley. Darryl Maclean was surprised to learn that M'sieur Patates hadn't opened a chain of chip wagons Down Under. Judith Buckle said, "Don't ever do anything like that again. My heart was in my throat the whole time you were away!"

"Your son dropped by last evening," she reported. "I hadn't seen hide nor hair of him for months. He has a new lady friend in Montreal and wonders if you're interested in buying out his share of the shop."

Sonny's laugh was mostly a whoop. "He still owes me for most of his half. This was his way of saying he intends to skip."

"I'm afraid you'll have to deal with that yourself," she said. "I have quite enough to handle. An acquaintance of mine from the gallery has been charged, I can hardly believe this, with attempting to kill her husband. The manager of one of those newer Centretown hotels? Of course she isn't capable of such a thing, but she's in the papers so there must be something to it. That referendum has had everyone acting strange. Those people have a lot to answer for."

Eventually his father was well enough to come home – or had nagged his doctor into submission. Sonny moved out of his father's bed and into the trailer's second bedroom at the end of the hall. This meant tidying up enough paperbacks for a small-town library. The floor was piled high with books, some of the stacks collapsing, some still standing as high as his waist. Strewn across the tops of these piles were items of clothing his father had not put away. Sonny hung some in the closet, stuffed some into dresser drawers, threw most of them into the laundry basket. Then he forced a passage through, removed fifty or sixty Penguins from the bed, and made it his own.

He listened to his father's noises, waiting for his father to fall asleep before falling asleep himself. Heavy breathing deepened into snoring, which got louder until it erupted into a choking cough. Then the procedure started again, with a few shouted words thrown in. Sonny was wakened some time during the night by the crash of a body slamming against furniture on its way to the floor. "Sonofabitch!"

He was already out of bed himself before he was aware of the smell.

"I was trying to get to the damn toilet," his father said, while Sonny helped him up off the floor. The words were garbled by swallowed sobs, snuffed-back snot, an animal sound in his throat. "Get away, I don't want you to see."

"See what?" Sonny said, as they hobbled to the bathroom. "You got something new I haven't seen before?" While he waited for the shower water to heat up, he stripped off his father's pyjamas. He was wearing an adult diaper beneath.

"You see?" his father said.

Sonny tried to suggest that he wasn't impressed. "I guess I'm supposed to buy you some of these things. What has Plutarch got to say about them?"

"I hope the poor bugger didn't live long enough to need them."

His father wasn't able to stand on his own in the shower stall so Sonny stepped in with him. Stepped in, that is, as far as he could. He had cleaned up his old man before, after some of his drunks, but the mess had never been of this nature, and a shower could always be put off till morning. "Goddammit," his father said. "You shoulda let me be."

"I guess you cleaned me up a few times," Sonny said.

When his father had been thoroughly soaped and scrubbed down and rinsed, Sonny towelled him off and helped him back to his bed. Then he went back to the bathroom and dried himself off, and exchanged his wet boxer shorts for a new pair.

No extra diapers had been sent with his father's things. For the present emergency, he would have to tear a bedsheet in half. This was easy enough with a worn-thin sheet. What wasn't so easy was figuring out a way of folding it. After the first step – folding corner to corner in order to make a triangle – neither of them knew what to do next. While his old man sat on the side of his bed with a blanket over his shoulders, Sonny knelt at the foot, experimenting with every geometrical shape that might yield something he could wrap around his father's skinny loins. "I don't suppose there are safety pins in this place?"

"Old age is gonna finish me off," his father said. "You'll be feeding me Pablum next. If you'd left me in that flood this useless body would be down in their lake and rotting with the sheep by now. I'd've forgotten already that I ever owned it. I want to go to Cape Scott."

Silence, except for the hum of the electric wall clock out in the kitchen.

"Let's just think about this for a day or two," Sonny said. "I haven't figured out how I can pull it off without landing one of us in jail."

The old man had come home too late to see any of the actual filming, which had lasted only three days and hadn't been all that interesting after all. The actors had already left. The trailer had been dragged back to its former spot just behind the old house. While Sonny and his father watched, a remaining crew dismantled what was left of the sets. They stripped away the lanterns and hammocks and butter churns that had turned the house into a nineteenth-century hillbilly's shack. They removed the mules and old-fashioned farm equipment and magnolia trees that had converted his father's property into a backwoods farm, peeling back the facade they'd laid over the place. It occurred to Sonny that, even unmasked, his father's derelict farm was still a facade – laid over, or grown up through, the farm he'd worked on as a boy.

One day, when the director returned to engage the cleanup crew in an animated conversation across the top of his Honda, Sonny asked for a few minutes of his time. The director was already a little cranky, the shoot had not gone as well as he'd hoped, and they were behind schedule and over-budget. Sonny's request was not only unconventional but a bloody nuisance as well. Also, there were union rules to consider. Even so, money was briefly discussed. In return for this small favour, the payment for the use of the farm would be passed on to the director and a cameraman of his choice.

A night passed while the proposal was considered. In the morning the director, crankier than ever and perhaps embarrassed by his own capitulation, reluctantly conceded that, "What the hell, it can be done in a couple hours if we're lucky." He had talked it over with the others and some had volunteered. A little more footage could come in handy, so long as they confined themselves to shots that required nothing in the way of dressing.

It started out as one of his father's bad days. Sonny had to talk him past a horrifying dream of flood waters filling his lungs before he began to understand a little of what was happening. People setting up lights. Tripods being opened, and cameras attached. Sheets and blankets were removed, and replaced with one pale sheet. This would be a single close-up – so close that only the man and his sheets would be seen.

The cameraman tossed a dirty battered hat onto the cover near the old man's hand, looking as if it had been tromped on and chewed by a dozen mules. "You're sharing the room with the hero of our story," the director instructed. "You understand?" He spoke louder than he needed to, in case the old man was deaf. "You're a backwoods farmer who was caught in the crossfire, and you don't go anywhere, not even to the hospital, without your hat." His father exaggerated his hollow grin, giving himself the appearance of someone who'd lived far from a dentist for eighty-five years, his teeth having rotted from his head because of inadequate diet.

"Don't I get to say nothing?"

The director released an exasperated sigh and left the room for a few minutes. They could hear him muttering to himself in the kitchen. When he came back, apparently making an effort to keep his composure, he taught the old man to say, "Ah reckon I'll lie here till they've done finished their war without me." The cameraman winked at Sonny.

Timo Aalto's grin lasted long after the Hollywood crew had departed for parts unknown.

"Okay," he said. "They're gone."

Sonny concentrated on heating a can of mushroom soup for their lunch.

"I been thinking," the old man said. "One of Harry's sons owns a helicopter company. He could pick us up at the trailhead, fly us in to the Cape. Then you wouldn't have to carry me."

"You planning to do this right away?" Sonny said. "Without telling anybody about being a movie star?"

"Well," his father said. "I guess they'll be pissed if they don't hear it from the horse's mouth. I can wait a couple more days before we go."

"**N**ow listen," he tells the boy. "Up there to the north there's a cliff on the mainland that rises out of the sea. My father told me this. It's too far to see from here, he never saw it himself but he read about it somewhere, he saw pictures of it. At the top of the cliff there's the shape of a man's body pressed into the stone – arms out, legs apart, the head a round bowl filled with water on a night like this. The Indians call him the Man Who Fell From the Sky."

"What is it really?" Rohan says. "Did somebody carve it?"

"What makes you think it wasn't a man who fell from the sky?"

"And dented solid rock?" Only a seven-year-old would dare to express such disgust.

Because of the wind and the washing waves, they have to shout to be heard, though they are shoulder-by-shoulder inside the tent. It is late afternoon and already getting dark. This time of year there is not much of the day you could call true "daylight," especially when the clouds have lowered so far the world has to live inside them. The leaping waves can be seen only because of the whitecaps. In this pale light, the spray that shoots up where waves meet rocks is like a white fountain of fireworks. Here in this rain, slashing down from one direction and then another, the entire world appears to be underwater.

"What do you think?" Sonny shouts. "There's ocean ahead of us, all the way to Alaska. There's ocean to our left, all the way to Japan. And there's the sound to the right, between here and the mainland. There's just us on this lonely spot. The world's not very big."

Inside his tent the world is even smaller. The nylon sides rattle and snap in the wind. They sit just inside the opening, the two of them, to watch the day fade to its end. They are dressed against the cold in everything they've brought – sweaters, jackets, even a sleeping bag opened up around them. It is a stupid place to set up a tent.

Holly has set up a tent for herself and the boy a hundred metres down the beach, closer to sheltering trees. She would take her chances with the wolves and cougars rather than perish in this wind. She has chosen to be close to the toilets at Guise Bay, and the official bear cache meant for storing food.

"I put more wood on the fire," she says, appearing from around the side of Sonny's tent. She hugs herself as she crouches low to find whatever protection there might be inside. She is wearing her camouflage pants again but her top half is a shapeless bulk in a shiny yellow slicker. "It's nearly time to rustle us up some grub. I've got things started." To Sonny she said, "He wanted to watch me turn those little packages of dust into something we can eat."

"He was about to tell me a story. He doesn't think much of my version."

She kisses him abruptly on the forehead. "You can tell me your version later." Then, grabbing her son by the hand, "Hold on, so your old lady doesn't get blown out to sea."

Sonny stays where he is for the time being, and wraps the sleeping bag around his shoulders. They have set up camp beyond the remains of the vanished Danish settlement. They are down at the hard-packed beach at Guise Bay, just before the narrow neck of sand dunes, as close as he dare get to the cape itself, and the lighthouse. For all he knows he may be breaking the rules out here. A park warden, if there is one, could appear at any moment from somewhere to tell him so. But this is where his father would have insisted on pitching the tent. A big-enough tsunami could wash them off this peninsula like a hand scraping crumbs from a table, tossing them into the swirling deep with the whales.

There were no other vehicles parked at the trailhead. Walking in, they soon discovered why. The rain did not let up or even pause to gather strength, it fell as though wild with fury, switching direction as if whipped by a giant egg whisk. You thought that if you kept your head down and your eyes on your toes you might keep your face fairly dry, but this rain was capable, it seemed, not only of falling from every direction at once but of defying gravity, too, and falling upward. Their faces streamed. Most of the trail was a stationary river of mud, sometimes thigh-deep, as they discovered whenever they slipped. The occasional section of wet boardwalk was as treacherous as ice.

Last night, slathered with mud, they set up their tents in a designated campsite, near a privy and under the dripping evergreens. This morning, he was the first to step out of the dark of the forest into the site of the disappeared colony. *Watch where you step*, the map warned. *There are still undiscovered wells.*

They watched their step but didn't stop long to explore. Tomorrow they will take the time to poke around, find whatever is left of the houses, examine the remains of the dike built by the Danes to hold back the tide from their hay meadows. A collapsed tool shed. Pieces of farm machinery, too – a wooden cart, a caterpillar tractor lodged in the trees. They can take all the time they want on the way out.

Holly will return to the tall gravestone she came across in the underbrush, past weathered fence posts and a rusted stove. "A twelve-year-old boy," she said. She has read about this somewhere. "Died of blood poison from stubbing his toe because there was no way to get him out." A father had inscribed his heartbreak deep in granite: *The sun went down while it was yet day.*

He recalls thinking, as they passed through the colony site, that there was something disturbing about the beauty of this place. Was this, like the beauty he sees in clear-cuts, his aesthetic sense mocking his better judgement? How beautiful would this seem to those Danish farmers if they could see it now? Back-breaking work had accomplished nothing. A child buried who might have been saved. There was sadness in this type of beauty, not as much like the stark abandoned homestead on Kalevan Station, or the chaos that had overtaken Sonny's childhood farm, as like the luxurious growth that had overwhelmed his nursery.

The boy is suddenly beside him, squinting against the wind. "Food's ready!" Sonny follows him, head down, leaning into the wind, across the hard sand towards the small fire the three of them built in a sheltered sandy hollow near Holly's tent. Mother and son sit on a log beneath a blue tarp they'd tied with yellow plastic ropes to driftwood and the lower branches of twisted scrubby trees.

"It's hot," Holly says, sipping at her cup of thin chicken-broth soup. "That's about all I can say for it. It'll warm our bones."

They are shouting still. The roar of the waves is constant.

"I hate the rain," the boy says. "I hate the dark!"

"He expected to lie under the sky and read the constellations," Holly said. "Our own private sky party!"

"No reading material up there tonight," Sonny says.

"I can see them in my head," Rohan says. "The story starts in the Whirlpool Galaxy."

"The man who fell from the sky," Sonny explains to puzzled Holly. To Rohan he says, "Tell us where this Whirlpool Galaxy is. I don't know about your mother but I've never seen it. I've never even seen Venus."

"Rohan found the wiener sticks," Holly says. She holds out one of the long, dead-fir branches to Sonny. "Crooked as pretzels but they'll do, I wouldn't let him wander far."

While they hold the wieners above the coals at the nearer fringes of the fire, the boy closes his eyes for the first part of his telling. The Whirlpool Galaxy, which is also known as M51, is so far away that it is one of the deep-sky treasures. The people who live on the third planet of the eighth sun in that galaxy, he says, have body temperatures of ninety thousand degrees. "It wasn't a man that fell from the sky, it was a boy. The people of that galaxy are giants. His father went off to fight in a war against an evil band from Andromeda and never came back. Everyone thought he was killed, but Sorhan was sure he was captured, so he went off to look for him."

Sonny removes his blackened wiener and uses his stick to push one log in closer to the others. Sparks fly up. Rain sizzles on the wood at the outer edges of the fire. You didn't bring wieners on a hike like this unless you were bringing a boy.

"First he steals Orion's sword, which he took to the lip of the Big Dipper, where the evil band was gathered. But they chased him all the way across to the Charioteer, the brightest star in Auriga." In the firelight, his black eyes shine, his round face seems to have grown even more moonlike with the wonder of his own telling. "When they cornered him he sliced off some hands, but the leader pushed Sorhan over the side and he fell straight into the Milky Way and landed on the top of that cliff. His body temperature was high enough to melt his shape in the stone."

"Well," Holly says. "That sounds pretty convincing to me."

The boy's eyes slide to the side as he consults his imagination. He hasn't finished yet. "This was where the evil band send their captives. The next day his father found him there and they started plotting how to get home to Sorhan's mother."

For a few moments all three of them watch their wieners blistering above the fire.

"Do you think they ever got home?" Holly says.

"I don't know," the boy says.

"I'll tell you what," Sonny says. "When we get home ourselves I'll scribble it down so your friends can read it. I'll read it back to you, to make sure I got it right."

The boy says nothing to this. His wiener has fallen into the fire. Rather than get another, he tears open a bag of marshmallows.

"You know, there's more than one way to read the stars," Sonny says. "Your pals with the telescopes use certain names but the

Tlingit people north of here see something different. To them, the Milky Way is the tracks left by one of their heroes while chasing a monster across the sky."

"Uh-oh," Holly says, seeing trouble ahead. With her hand wrapped in a corner of her sweater, she lifts the coffee pot from the flames and fills Sonny's mug and then her own.

"How would you know that?" the boy says.

"I read it. The Snohomish people south of here tell a story about how they got fed up with the sky being so low they were always bumping their heads on it – like today – so they decided to raise it. They made giant poles from fir trees and pushed as hard as they could until they'd got it up to where it is on a nice clear day. But the trouble was they accidentally trapped some people and animals up there, including three hunters chasing an elk. The elk became the stars in the bowl of the Big Dipper. The hunters became the handle. And their little dog became the tiny star next to the middle hunter."

Rohan studies Sonny's face. "My father's Coast Salish."

"Well then," Holly says. "The Salish probably have their own way of reading the stars. Maybe that's something you can find out about and tell Sonny. Risto, I mean." Since his father's death, she sometimes calls him "Risto," sometimes "Dennis." She hasn't yet decided on one or the other. "Sonny" is not in the running. A man who's lost his father needs an adult's name.

When the boy has crawled into his mother's tent, they sit for a while longer by the fire. "Just don't let him see that you're doing what his teacher would do if he'd let her," she says. "He may read it to his classmates, but only if he doesn't realize it's what everyone's been trying to get him to do. He usually doesn't make things easy."

"I don't imagine any of them do," he says. "It just seemed like a good idea."

She moves closer down the log to sit with an arm through his and her head against his shoulder, while they look into the fire without speaking. There could be a dozen wolves out there.

There could be seals and sea lions up out of the water for all they know. But the fire has reduced the world to this small flickering circle. Her tent is barely in it.

"You can't expect me to come out to you," she says. "I won't leave him alone."

"I need to be alone tonight," he says. They speak in lowered voices, as though there are more ears than the boy's to hear them. "City girl thinks she's fallen off the world?"

"I'm not exactly an alien, you know." The beautiful eyes of this offended "city girl" narrowed to object or threaten, he wasn't sure which. "My mother's father grew up in Portuguese Creek, before he ran off to the city."

"I know. I heard about him every time I threatened to run away myself. He and the old man were friends when they were boys."

"He never told me that!"

"Afraid you'd take it as encouragement."

She pulled back, indignant. "For what? To be friends? We *were* friends, at least I thought we were!"

"I used to think that too, when I was a kid. It took me nearly twenty years to see that we were something else." He stands to kick the cramps from his legs, ready to return to his tent. "I could never have guessed that, in the end, in some ways I'd become his father, too."

She pulls his hand to make him sit again, then puts her arms around his neck and speaks with her mouth close to his. "You won't admit it, but even after all your staying away, he knew you well enough to know what you needed most."

One of his tent pegs has been pulled from the ground, leaving the front corner rope to slap freely about in the wind. With that corner collapsed, his father's old tent appears to be going the way of his house. Inside, there is a dampness where the wall has rubbed against itself. Part of his sleeping bag is wet. For a moment, he thinks the walking stick has disappeared. He imagines the wind has entered the tent and somehow carried the converted umbrella out through the doorway and tossed it up in a tree, or wedged it somewhere in the rocks where he'll never find it. There is a moment of panic before his hand discovers it beneath the collapsed wall. He holds onto it now, and has the idea he will sit in the entrance to his tent through the rest of the night.

"I don't suppose I told you how I came by that cane," his father told him. This was soon after Sonny had arrived from Ottawa, over an early dinner at the Blueback. Holly had joined them, to share Sonny's strawberry-rhubarb pie, but the old man didn't tell this story until she'd gone back to showing customers to their tables. "Me'n Tommy Reimer took the old Dodge for a run, one drizzly afternoon. We dropped in on Davy Chalmers for as long as we could stand him, then decided to poke around the Camp Three Road we hadn't been up for years. We heard some foreign outfit turned the Stokes place into a dude ranch – horseback riding, mini-golf, that sort of thing. There wasn't nothing left we recognized. Everything cleared so far back you can see the bottom of Constitution Hill."

He was a little short of breath but he seemed determined to tell it all. "Then we seen this new dirt road pushed through the only bush left standing on Stokes's old place. And there's this trailer sitting in there. Surrounded mostly by mud." They'd meant to turn around and take off, he said. But this old woman came out on her step as if she'd been waiting for them. "A tiny old thing, bent over, with hair knotted on top of her head." She put up her long-handled umbrella to come out across the mud. "You remember Stokes."

Sonny did. An old man when Sonny was a boy. Everyone knew he'd lost his temper and thrown a rock that killed his own son. His war bride had taken off for England and never returned. "Well, this was Mrs. Stokes, come back. I don't know if she hoped to find old Stokes alive but he'd been gone for years."

She had made tea. Cups waited on the table for someone. She

chattered on about how well the folks at the dude ranch treated her. She never mentioned her husband. Neither did her visitors, but they thought about him. "The rain was pissing down. When I started to turn the Dodge around to leave, she sunk to the axle in mud. We threw rocks and planks and gunny sacks under the tires but they didn't do nothing but spin. There wasn't no telephone in the trailer, so the old lady gave me her umbrella and told me to walk to the ranch and ask for help."

He'd forgotten all about this until one day he spotted the umbrella under the seat of the Dodge. A long-handled English umbrella. "When I went up to return it, the trailer was gone. The woman had disappeared. I brought the damn thing home and kept it with the other junk that might come in handy one day."

"Which it did," Sonny said. "For fighting off walkers and wheelchairs as long as you could."

"It saved me from some bad falls."

"Not enough of them. You thought that thing made you some kind of Old Testament prophet, but poking at those caves – remember? – got you nothing but a couple of sneering rednecks!"

His father laughed. "Well, even Moses' rod was a venomous snake for a while. At least he figured it was. Until he picked it up and saw it was something he could lean on."

While his father was still in the respite house, Sonny called in Al Price to see if the old house could be salvaged. He imagined putting it up for rent, though he would not be surprised to hear that it ought to be burned to the ground. But the contractor announced that most of the weakened structure at one end could be repaired, and portions of rain-rotted wall replaced. "But she'll need a new roof if you want to keep the weather where it belongs. And you'll want to clean 'er out and give 'er a new coat of paint."

The thought of cleaning out the house kept him from making a start. The inside was a confused clutter of damp, abandoned furniture, broken light fixtures, and mouldy clothes. He kicked through a pile of odds and ends spilled from an overturned box and uncovered a rolled-up braided rag-rug that might have been made by Mrs. Korhonen or sent by someone in Finland. Every room had its share of junk. Metal hangers in the shape of men's work socks. Stacks of yellowing newspapers from Finland, dating back to his grandparents' day. An old wooden hand plane. Propped against a wall of the spare bedroom was the pair of cross-country skis his father had made him from an alder plank, planing the wood with his sharpest axe and subjecting it to steam in order to get the perfect curve. Sonny hadn't had many chances to use them here, and hadn't wanted the old man to see him care enough to take them to Ottawa.

He preferred to start with the outside, chopping back the blackberry bushes in the front yard, pruning the orchard trees. Once his father had come home and the movie people had gone, he took advantage of the old man's naps and visits from the old man's friends to brace up the sagging chicken shed and replace some of the fallen shakes on the barn roof. There was a kind of numbing pleasure in stretching unused muscles till they ached. Getting calluses again on his dirty hands.

Occasionally he drove down to the site of his overgrown nursery garden and chopped at underbrush, pushing Colin's trail on past the old sawmill and through the fallen debris and jungle towards the hidden blooms and exploded glass houses that Holly claimed to have found. He left untouched a trellis and bench of willow twigs that had sent down roots and sprouted new limbs to become its own peculiar grove. He cleared away the ivy that had climbed up and engulfed one Douglas fir before crossing to another, draping a thick green leafy blanket-wall between the two. Everywhere there was evidence that colonies of oddball plants had taken advantage of the sunless, undisturbed nature of the place – plants that couldn't manufacture nutrition for themselves: saprophytics sprouting from decaying vegetation, parasitics connected underground to the roots of shrubs and trees, insectivorous plants that dined on flying things – a pale, short, weird population of freakish life.

Working outside seemed to give him more freedom to think things through. Late in the dim light of an overcast afternoon they packed the rented car – a BMW this time, they would go in style. They turned at the general store and followed the Island Highway north through the quiet little stump ranches and then past the dairy farms and strawberry farms of Black Creek. *Firewood. Sewing. Puppies 4 Sale.* There was surprisingly little traffic. As they passed the old Macken property where the Blueback Restaurant sat at the high-tide line, he thought of Colin levering nacho chips up to his mouth, and felt a pang of sorrow at his loss, and a wash of admiration, or perhaps of envy, for his life.

"You feeling okay?"

"Good enough," his father said. "Keep going." He spoke carefully, his weakened voice strained. He swiped his sleeve across beneath his nose. It was dripping again.

"We'll take it in easy stages," Sonny said. "Stop in Campbell River, maybe, for tonight."

His father grunted and fished his Copenhagen out of his shirt pocket. Once he'd removed the lid and scooped a wad behind his bottom lip he held the little round box out to Sonny. A decent son would take up chewing snoose, however vile the taste.

"You really want me to?" Sonny said, thumb and index finger ready.

"Christ no." His father snatched the cylinder back, slapped the lid on, and returned it to his pocket. "It's a filthy habit. Don't go starting now." He left it to Sonny to wonder why he'd persisted with his frequent offers through the years.

The world outside looked fairly typical for a January day. A low sky was building towards another downpour. Rocks gleamed. Soggy grass lay flattened and pale. Stalks of late-flowering plants were bent or broken. Evergreen boughs sagged with the weight of moisture. Roof eaves dripped. You would think a flood had only just receded.

"I've spent a little time on the phone," Sonny explained. "Found us a cabin not too far from the trailhead. Small, but warm and comfortable. There are dozens of logging roads nearby that you've never seen. Hundreds of lakes and inlets – fjords. A doctor nearby in Port Hardy if we need one. We can do some exploring until you've had your fill. When you give me the high sign I'll phone Harry's son and get us one of those helicopters."

His father didn't seem to find any of this surprising.

"And nobody knows?"

"Even Dora's radar will never find us."

On along the coastline they went, past the homes and scattered shops and motels of Willow Point. A row of condominiums looked out across the traffic to an almost colourless world. A near-white flannel sky had pulled down like a window blind, obscuring the mainland mountains and dissolving along some indistinct line into the choppy grey waves. The shoreline trees might have been bludgeoned into shape from shafts of lead.

The town's first vacancy sign was in front of a motel that had probably seen no improvements since the fifties, aside from a paint job to the stucco. It was high above the water, looking across to the lighthouse off Cape Mudge. Sonny drove on past to watch for something better, but his father insisted they go back. "Reminds me of that hunting trip," he said. "Could be the same motel."

They'd had to spend a night in this motel or another like it because his father's car had broken down not thirty miles from home, with a three-spike deer on the fender. It was too late in the evening to find a mechanic or telephone a friend. A night in a motel had been so unusual that they'd hardly slept, each of them thinking of something that needed to be told just as the other was about to drop off. Sonny was fourteen. This was his first time in a public bed. To prevent theft, the old man had stored the deer in the bathroom, its window open to the cool night air.

Since then, the smells of forty more years had accumulated inside. Sonny opened the sliding glass door so that the salty tang of sea air could wash them away, or at least compete with the chemical cleaning fluids.

It was plain but it would do. Walls were cement blocks painted pale yellow. The furniture was made of chrome and fake-wood Arborite. The orange-and-yellow drapes had soaked up decades of cigarette smoke. Above one of the beds hung a coloured photo of a rower in a narrow boat, his back to the camera, approaching out of an impenetrable mist. The word PERSEVERANCE was printed across the lower part of the water, and, below that, a quotation attributed to Thomas Edison: *There is no substitute for hard work.*

"Obviously this was put here for you," Sonny said.

His father turned from the window to read the words for himself, then twisted his face in an exaggerated grimace. "For shy honeymooners, maybe."

Sonny suspected its purpose was to suggest how hard the owners of this motel were required to work on your behalf, never getting a holiday themselves. Who did they imagine would find this a welcome sight? He took the picture down and stored it in the closet, leaving behind an rectangle of unfaded yellow paint. A dusty cobweb trailed from the spike imbedded between the bricks.

In bed, the old man wanted to hear again about the place they were going. "I can't remember nothing no more. Things slide off my brain like it was slicked with Vaseline."

"I only know what I was told. A small but comfortable cabin not far from the trailhead. I've got a number for Harry's son in my bag."

His father said, "Hmmmf," which seemed to suggest content-ment, at least for the time being. "Look, I meant to tell you the rest of that cougar business."

"You told me, Dad. In Brisbane. Remember?"

"You sure of that?" His father sighed. "I thought I might've dreamed it."

He was soon asleep, though not for long. This time he was able to get to the bathroom on time. From behind the door he said, "We should have flown."

"To Cape Scott?"

"No," his father said, impatient with such stupidity. "Here. To your mother's. Instead of that long drive."

"We're not at her place now. We're in Campbell River."

When his father reappeared in the doorway, his brow was lowered in a doubter's frown. "You sure?"

"I'm sure."

"Where are we, then?"

"Still asleep, I think. Sleepwalking in Campbell River. You ready to go back to bed?"

Not long after his father had gone to sleep a second time and Sonny had just crawled into his own bed, the door rattled from a tattoo of impatient knocking. Wrong unit, Sonny thought, and waited for whoever it was to go away. But when the hammering started again he got out of bed and pushed one of the curtains aside. Backlit by street lights, Tom Reimer's enormous bulk could not be mistaken for anyone else.

"Go away, Reimer," he said through the door. "My father's asleep."

Reimer rattled the doorknob. "Did you think there wasn't nobody watching out for him?"

Sonny opened the door a crack without releasing the chain. Reimer stood less than a foot away. Behind him, a taxi sat idling, the driver's head tilted down in order to watch what was going on.

"He's asleep. This isn't any of your business."

"The cops might think it's *somebody's* business, if I tell them."

"What's the matter with you, anyway? You think I'd do something to hurt him?"

"Is that Tommy?" his father said. "Jesus Christ! You mizewell let him in or he'll have the whole damn place down around our ears."

Reluctantly, Sonny held the door open for Reimer, who moved his heavy body forward one slow step and then a second and third, putting much of his weight on his walking stick, until he was just far enough inside for Sonny to close the door behind him.

"Turn the light on," his father said. When the weak hanging lamp came on, he raised his head from the pillow. "For chrissakes, Tommy, what's the matter with you?"

"I just don't like the smell of it," Reimer said. He levered his slow way across the floor towards the bed, where he put two fingers out to steady himself against the wall. He carried his head as though it would roll off his shoulders and drop to the floor if he strayed from the perfectly vertical. "You okay?"

"You should know me good enough by now." His father's eyes were wide with too much innocence. "All I want is just to poke my nose down a few more roads before he takes me home."

Reimer lowered himself carefully into the chair by the bed, and grunted loudly when it didn't collapse beneath him. "Shoot." He wasn't going anywhere in a hurry, taxi or no taxi. Sonny checked at the window to make sure that he hadn't dismissed it. "I don't know what the hell you two are doin' here."

"We don't know why you're here either," Sonny said. "We're the ones paying for the room. Since we got back you never came across to see him even once. Now you chase him up the highway and interrupt his sleep."

"You scared he's gonna dump me in the saltchuck?" his father said. His voice suggested this was the most outlandish thing he could think of.

"Goddammit!" Reimer said. His voice was loud now. Those tarnished-penny eyes were steady as a dead man's, aimed at Sonny Aalto's face. "I want to know what's going *on*!" Sonny thought of a child too frightened to move, shouting above the noises in his head.

"Life is going on," Sonny said. "His and mine. Yours too, if you insist on it."

"Why aren't you in your own bed?" his father said. "You'll be cranky as hell tomorrow."

"I'm cranky now!"

It wasn't every day you got to see someone explode without using any muscles except those needed for his voice. Someone

knocked on the far side of the wall. Something metal – probably
a chair, a fist could not have been heard through cement blocks.
Reimer answered by swinging his cane off his wide-apart knees
and thwacking his side of the wall. One arm moved to do it, but
immediately returned to the knee, a flying buttress holding his
head and torso steady in their place.

Then they were witness to a terrible sight: Reimer started to
cry. At first there were only the tears sliding down the wide
impassive face. A man of good instincts, it seemed, Reimer sensed
that something was going on that he wouldn't like. The world, in
other words, was probably falling apart. Muscles erupted into
movement that had not for years been seen in public to move.
Chins convulsed. An entire network of invisible facial muscles
stretched in all directions at once, as if trying to pull the face
apart. The shouting voice, to make things worse, became a wail.
"I'm. Not. Leaving. Here. Until you tell me!"

A rat-a-tat-at on the wall's far side protested. So did Timo
Aalto, who looked at Sonny and swore. Sonny opened the door
and gestured for the taxi driver to come in.

"He has trouble walking," he explained to the driver, who
stood in the doorway scratching in his shaggy hair. "He'll need
your help."

"Stay where you are!" Reimer shouted. Facial muscles had
snapped back into place. "I mean, get back in your taxi and wait!
I have something more to say."

Apparently the something more he had to say was not on the
tip of his tongue. He looked at Timo Aalto in his bed as he might
once have looked at his own father when he could not understand
the reason for some punishment. Eventually, after two or three
false starts, he said, "I thought we might've gone down some of
them back roads together like we used to. I always wanted to go
back to them caves – remember?"

"You don't drive any more," Sonny said, as kindly as he could.
"My father doesn't drive any more. And neither of you would be
safe inside those caves."

Reimer ignored this. "When I seen you go past today I got it into my head that that was where you were going. But they told me at the store you turned left instead of right, so I figured I better find out what's going on."

Turning left instead of right was the giveaway? Reimer looked more pleased with his detective work than he ought to, though Sonny didn't intend to point this out. Neither did he intend to let this man upset his father, who looked a little besieged. It was his world and not Reimer's that was falling apart.

Sonny crossed the room and put a hand on Reimer's arm. "If we ever go to look at those caves we'll take you along. Now please, his doctor would be furious if he knew you were keeping my father awake."

He didn't get to say all that he heard himself saying. Somewhere after "doctor" Big Tom Reimer's stick slashed out and slammed against him, part of it catching his arm and the end of it slapping into organs he didn't usually think about. The blow was hard enough to cause the muscles in Reimer's face to flinch. Something in his legs shot him upright in a single rapid movement so that he could bring that stick back in a quick hard slash from somewhere higher, and catch Sonny on the side of his head. His left ear felt as if it had been sliced from his skull. It hadn't – his hand checked – but it felt as if it had.

"Goddam you," Reimer said. "Get out of my way."

Bent over his own pain, Sonny was happy to open the door for Reimer's exit, which, despite his sudden uprearing from the chair, was no faster than his entrance had been. That walking stick might have been levering an awkward giant boulder across the floor in small difficult moves.

"Jesus," his father said, as soon as Sonny had closed the door. "You all right?"

"I'm okay," Sonny said. With the hand that wasn't holding his ear he pulled back the curtain to watch the taxi cut a wide arc in the parking lot and head south. "It hurts like hell but at least the sonofabitch has gone."

"The poor bugger's goin' senile faster than me."

"That isn't senility, Dad. Reimer is jealous."

The old man dropped his head back onto his pillow and blew something that was more raspberry than exhausted sigh.

"He's your lifelong friend. I suppose he loves you."

His father flinched at such language. "Arrrrgh!" Which meant, Sonny supposed, that either Sonny or Reimer was a fool.

"Maybe he suspects you're planning to cheat him out of something."

"What's that supposed to mean?"

What that was supposed to mean was something Sonny suspected he knew but not something he could tell his father. They'd both learned long ago to skirt language that might embarrass them. If Reimer was filled with resentment – and Dora Mitchell and Harry Sylvester and any number of others who felt much the same – it was because anyone who cared about the old man and even vaguely suspected his plan to desert them was bound to feel robbed. What they were about to be robbed of could be, if you were in the habit of confronting such thoughts, an opportunity to practise love. By stepping off the planet, however strong his need to do so, Timo Aalto would be robbing his friends of the chance to fill their own old age with acts of kindness. Not to mention an opportunity to fill their heads with something other than their own decline.

Maybe there wasn't anything more important you could do – a thought so startling that he felt his face heat up to think it – than make yourself available to the love of others. A person could look at those old folks in Extended Care and think, as Colin Macken had suggested, *If I get like that I hope they take me out and shoot me.* Or you could see them being cared for by relatives and staff and decide to marvel at how many lives were being enriched by this opportunity to love people when they needed love the most.

Was his father being selfish, to deny his friends the opportunity to see him out? Sooner or later Sonny would have to wonder whether his own role in this – so far as he was willing to go, that is – ought to be reconsidered in the light of Reimer's loss.

But not yet.

"He's upset," Sonny said – all he dared in the circumstances – "because he knows that with you gone he'll have to take up visiting Nora Macken until it's someone else's turn to visit *him*. Come on, I think we'd better get out of here."

"Now?"

"Do you trust him to leave us alone? We can move to another motel, somewhere off the main road."

"You're not taking me back!" His father's entire body was stiff with resistance.

"We've got that cabin waiting for us. We aren't doing anything permanent yet."

"You brought the camping stuff, I hope."

It caught him by surprise every time – his father's forgetting, this having to remind himself to be patient. "It's in the trunk. You watched me put it in – remember?"

"You phoned the helicopter?"

"We're still in Campbell River, Dad. We've got a long drive ahead of us. There's all those roads to explore."

"But we're going to the cape," the old man said, while Sonny helped him out of his pyjama top.

"Not until you want to give up the cabin. Then we'll set up a tent as close as we can get to the Cape, and send the helicopter away."

"And?"

On with the undershirt, on with the shirt, both from the back of a chair.

"That's it."

"How can that be 'it'?"

"I mean – as far as I'm concerned, that's it. We'll be tourists come for the view. We'll stay until you've had enough. I'm only the tour guide here. And the pack horse. Anything else is up to you. I'm calling your bluff, if it is a bluff. I'll take you there to see what's there to see, but the rest is up to you. I've got my cellphone activated in case I need to call the helicopter back for us both. Or I'll start back on foot and let you decide if you're coming with me. As I said, it's up to you."

They reached the isolated cabin late the following day. While Sonny started a fire in the stove, his father inspected everything – beds, the contents of the cupboards, the view into the woods through each of the little windows. He looked so pleased you'd think he'd found the place himself. "Why didn't you think of this last August?" he said. "Save a lot of time and money, not to mention bickering."

"Well, maybe I was a bit stupid then. Maybe we needed to spend some time where we couldn't get away from each other. Or maybe we needed to nearly drown in a flood."

His father waited until Sonny had come in with the cooler, two sleeping bags resting on top. "Look," he said. "If you ever go back?"

"Back?" At this point, "back" could mean the old man's farm, Ottawa, Queensland, or any number of other places he might return to one day.

His father closed his eyes. "If you go *there* again –" His eyes opened, but narrowly. "Will you see if you can get my lunch kit off of her?" When Sonny didn't respond immediately he went on. "It don't matter what you do with it – bring it home and throw it in the dump, I don't give a damn. Just get it away from her."

"You should've looked for it yourself."

"What do you think I was doing while you were chasing your pig? Sneaking around her house like a thief, driving that nurse up the wall."

Sonny started putting cans of soup, boxes of crackers, packages of Kraft Dinner in a cupboard above the stove. A canister of oatmeal. "Then you should have come clean and asked the nurse to help you when you had the chance."

"Don't be a fool. I didn't want them to know I give a damn."

The next morning while Sonny was still asleep he heard his father's voice, "Getting a bit of fresh air," but he might have dreamt it. Only later did he discover his father had gone outside. To explore the limits of the small clearing, he supposed. To congratulate himself on having got this far. The trouble was – and this brought him leaping from his bed – the old man had apparently forgotten he couldn't walk far without help. His stick leaned against a chair. His wheelchair was parked against the wall.

No one answered his calls from the doorway. The damn fool must have gone into the woods. He wasn't likely to have started down the road, where there was the chance a driver might stop and ask questions. Sonny didn't notice until he'd skirted the clearing that there were several overgrown trails into the woods, most of them laced with surface roots. He spotted the sharp holes made by his father's wooden stump in the dirt, and followed them up a trail to where an ancient privy tilted sharply amongst the thick, waist-high salal. There was no one inside. Yet he could find no more wooden-leg holes leading on from there. Narrow paths wandered in four or five directions into the dense underbrush. Deer trails.

He started down one of these trails but found no sign that anyone had passed this way. A second trail was equally undisturbed. He came back to the privy and started down a third. Shouting, of course. Expecting to find his father crouched behind a bush, waiting to surprise him, delighted to think he had his son in a panic. Expecting, at the same time, to come upon his father laid out on the ground, his head beside a sharp stone. Having got so close to the cape, had the man decided on some other way to disappear?

A hundred metres down a fourth trail, imprints from the wooden stump were suddenly visible again, each of the holes driven deep into mud as if with increased hurry or determination. He followed them down a long damp stretch tunnelling through a stand of hemlock until the pathway suddenly ran up onto a long curve of stone exposed to sky, some of the stone furred over with moss, much of it bare. No impressions had been left upon the moss. He found no more imprints where the stone dipped and disappeared again beneath soil and underbrush.

At noon he went back to the cabin and dialled 911. Police arrived. A small posse of volunteer firemen began to comb the woods. RCMP experts studied the maps. A Search and Rescue helicopter thrashed its way from one side of the island to the other, back and forth above the trees, looking for signs of his father. Sonny was allowed to ride with them for most of a day. He was glad his father didn't know about these professional attempts to bring him back to the land of the living. Of course he could not be sure of this. That is, he could not be sure his father didn't know. If he were like his own father before him, he might have been witnessing the whole procedure at some distance from his own body, before deciding whether to return and allow them to save his life or to turn away and leave.

Searchers went into the woods every day for most of the following week. Rainstorms made the work miserable. For two of those days a thick fog rendered the helicopter useless. When the search teams eventually admitted defeat, he supposed he ought to feel relief on his father's behalf, but what he felt was the loss of something too large to be named. Something he had in common with Tommy Reimer, he supposed. He felt as thoroughly cheated – of the final journey itself. Or rather, the final leg of the journey. Absurdly, he thought of the thousand back roads he would never see. At least he would never see them with his father. They had recommenced their travels far too late.

Of course, when he got back to his father's farm he was surprised in the midst of his first solitary breakfast by a sudden upheaval of anger. Fury, really – he could have taken a sledgehammer to these trailer walls. Helplessness, too. He threw his plate into the sink, and relished the sound of its shattering. The cup went in after it, with even more force, coffee splashing up onto the tiny window. To save the rest of his father's chipped and mismatched china he slammed his way outside (kicking a crease into the flimsy metal door) and laid into some orchard brush with an axe, hardly able to believe he had begun to cry. He supposed this was grief, if grief was a kind of intense frustration, a sense of irreversible deprivation. It could as easily have been fear. Despite all the warning, it was as if he'd believed there would be decades yet for them to explore the world together. Maybe he'd believed his father would be permitted the occasional visit afterwards.

He was interviewed by the local paper. If his story was suspect, he saw no sign of this in the report, heard nothing of this from those who spoke to him. Rather, his father's neighbours were quoted admitting that the old man had told them this was what he wanted, though they hadn't taken him seriously. "Like an old watchdog who knows his time has come." Dora even suggested that Timo Aalto may have tricked his son into this. "Dennis knew his father loved nothing better than exploring back roads. I believe Timo took advantage of that to get himself a driver." Tom Reimer was not quoted in the write-ups. He said nothing about the business to Sonny. He said nothing to Sonny at all.

Since then, Sonny has often experienced fleeting images of his father crashing through the early-dawn woods, grabbing at the lowest limbs to keep from falling, trying to put distance behind him. He sees the old man losing his footing on a steep incline, and sliding, tumbling, falling down the face of a rock cliff, the world revolving around him. He sees his father freeze as the trail passes beneath a series of overhanging limbs, sensing a cougar about to drop on the back of his neck. He even imagines his father about to come upon a large wild boar, tusked and bristly, foul-smelling and mean, waiting around a bend in the trail, planning not to leave a single bone uneaten. Since there are no wild pigs on the island, so far as anyone knows, this was unlikely, but that didn't mean his father mightn't expect one.

It is also unlikely that his father, faced with the possible realities of perishing in the bush, wished he'd followed old Kharlov's example and stood up on a roof to toss down shakes and rafters until the building collapsed beneath him. It is unlikely he got confused, forgot what he was up to, or changed his mind and hoped for rescue. Not when you considered how long he'd held to his plan. He may even have reached the Cape, still determined and fully aware of what he was doing, and found his way to the sea. It would have taken him exhausting days to do so, but the old man's will was strong. It would not surprise Sonny, even now that he has come here to the Cape himself, to find prints left by that homemade wooden leg, evidence that his father had passed through here on his way to the end of the world.

Theophrastus, who classified all plants in the known world, granted his slaves their freedom at his death, but only on the condition that they continue to work in his gardens for an additional year. Apparently he'd known something about the nature of attachments. In the two months since his father's footsteps disappeared, Sonny Aalto has begun to suspect that those slaves, by the time they'd earned their freedom, must have wondered why they'd ever believed true freedom possible.

He has got into the habit of following his own trail in through the underbrush to visit the neglected nursery garden, carrying his axe and machete and shovel in case he feels like exploring farther. Often he is content merely to sit on a log, or on a rotting bench beside the muddy bog that had once been a pond of lilies, taking pleasure in the silence, the solitude. It seems no animals had made this their home – he has disturbed no raccoons, no deer, no foxes. Sometimes he discovers plants he hadn't noticed before: round-leafed sundew, pinedrops, candystick – plants he would likely be killing off if he continued with his clearing. Sitting in the midst of all this rich chaotic growth, he wonders why his father had shown no interest in this place, had never – so far as he knew – ventured onto it, either while it was a working nursery or in all the years of neglect. Unlike Holly and the others, he never even rebuked Sonny for leaving his parcel of land untended.

Some of the neighbours have begun to recover from their disappointment. They were cheated not only out of Timo Aalto himself but out of a proper funeral as well. But they have only to look at one another to see there are plenty of funerals still ahead. They may even have decided there's something to be said for disappearing. Some of the Finns would have their ashes taken back to Suomi, but they would not expect this of Timo Aalto. At any rate, if it is ritual that they want, they know that his walking stick will complete the journey he didn't complete himself.

Yesterday, it seemed for a while that the walking stick might also fail. In Port McNeill they stopped for lunch in a seaside café where Malcolm Island and the village of Sointula could be seen from the window. "Where my father was born," he explained to Holly and her son. A whole community of houses had been built in the same style as his father's, though these, unlike his father's, had obviously been cared for. There were families over there with names like Salo, Rihtamo, Hantula, and Jarvinen. His father had mentioned them, though in all their years of exploring he'd never taken Sonny across.

"We should go over some time," Holly said.

"Maybe," Sonny said. "Not today. The old man didn't say anything about wanting to go back there."

Still, when they saw the little ferry come in, they walked down near the slip to watch the cars drive off. Sonny expected to see familiar characteristics: high cheekbones, slightly Asiatic eyes, ski-jump noses, blond hair. Some could be his relatives. But the drivers and passengers in the sedans and trucks might have been any mixture in any town in the country. It took imagination to see traces of Finnish blood. The costume, too – what could be seen – was anonymous: baseball caps turned backwards, denim jackets and fleece-lined vests over T-shirts with logos. *Blue Jays. Roots.*

The only foot passenger was a youth with a red backpack towering above his shoulders. A few minutes later they saw him
again, out on the highway with his thumb up, his backpack lying
on the gravel beside him. "Bradley Price," Holly said. Sonny had
already driven past before he realized this was the boy he and
Charlotte had come across in Butchart Gardens, the youth with
the bullet wound in his cheek. "Alan Price's son," Holly said.
"Sometimes helps me out at the nursery after school."

"You sightseeing?" she said, when the boy had climbed in to
the back seat, his backpack propped between him and Rohan.
"You look like you're running away from home."

"No kidding," the boy said. "I took all their shit I'm going to."

"Me too," Rohan said.

"Rohan," Holly said.

"I'll crash with my grandparents in Port Hardy."

"We saw you come off the Sointula ferry," Sonny said.

"So?" Apparently Aalto's words were taken as an accusation.
"Girl I know lives there, okay? I stopped to say hello."

"Your grandparents know you're coming?" Holly said.

"I phoned."

They let the boy out at the end of a residential street, but
Rohan waited until they'd driven three or four kilometres farther
up the road before he stood up behind his mother's seat and said,
"He took the walking stick."

"What?" Holly said. "And you didn't say anything?"

"You want me killed?"

They drove back to Port Hardy and spent half an hour knocking
on doors. When the old man had called him out to the front porch,
the boy was indignant. "What's the problem? I didn't see nobody in
the car that needed it, I figured my grandpa could use it."

Sonny looked into the old man's cataract-blurry eyes. Was this
one of those times when God pushed you up against an opportunity to do the one right thing and then sat back to see if you took
it? "You might have asked," he said. How could Sonny be sure this
wasn't exactly why he was making this journey?

Fortunately, it wasn't necessary to know. The old man didn't want the walking stick. "It was nice of the boy to bring it but Olive drove me down to Nanaimo last week, made me spend my pension cheque on a new one with a fancy handle."

"Makes you wonder, would he have stolen an urn of ashes?" Sonny said, once they were back on the highway. "To give his grandma a vase for her flowers."

Thinking now of that boy scowling out from behind his grandfather, he is reminded of that sullen youth on the far side of the globe: Lachlan Hall in his new life, riding out to check on the water holes, pulling sheep from the mud, shooting the hopeless ones behind the ear. What would he think of this place? Slashing rain, exploding waves, a daylong semi-dark with the sky down low enough to sit on your head. Green, green, green, and yet entirely grey. Wind thrashing the tent flap, tugging at the pegs, threatening to brush you off the world. A far cry from the pigeons and tourists at the fountain square, the harsh light and dusty paddocks of Kalevan Station.

He will phone Lachlan as soon as he gets home from Cape Scott. He telephoned before leaving Brisbane, and again when his father disappeared, but this time it will be to discuss plans for this coming summer. It isn't hard to imagine his laugh when he is told of Holly's idea, an offer to let him try out a different sort of landscape for a while.

For Lachlan it is already tomorrow afternoon. At this time of day he is probably keeping out of the mid-summer sun, possibly brushing down the coat of his horse while he calculates how long it will take to save enough wages for a week in Sydney, looking up old mates at the Cross. In his Brisbane office Jerrod Hawkins is looking over his brothers' latest proposal for challenging their mother in court, a desperate attempt that can't possibly work, as he will advise Trevor once he's summoned the will to pick up the phone. Beneath these papers on his desk is an array of colourful brochures advertising Lark Quarry, the Bungle Bungles, Kakadu National Park, an endless supply of places that promise to get him away from his office. None of those brochures advertises the attractions of Ottawa, where, at this time of night, only a few skaters remain on the canal. They wipe the frost from their nostrils, drink hot chocolate from M'sieur Patates. Or they keep themselves warm with endless movement, in rhythmic patterns down the scratched and glistening ice past Judith Buckle's canalside mansion and the tall apartment buildings and beneath the towers of *centre-ville*. Here, the manager of the new hotel has just returned to work after a slow recovery from a near-death experience at the hand of his wife. On the Quebec side of the river, the Museum of Civilization is safe for another few years from the threat of secessionist claims. The office of the archivist is locked for the night, tomorrow's tasks laid out on her desk while she sips a late-night drink in a small Irish bar in the Glebe, brought here by a new manager who claims to recognize her potential. Neither of them notices the young man escorting the Montreal fashion designer out into the snowy night, though both recognize the middle-aged man drinking with friends in the corner, a senior Cabinet minister already discussing what can be done to fend off the next attempt to break the country apart.

Every journey in pursuit of something new, his father said (on one of those Australian roads), ends with discovering what you didn't know you already had. And then, he should have added, having to fight your way back home in order to hold and make use of it. When they get home from Cape Scott, Sonny will take them on another journey, the boy and his mother, into the mysterious centre of his overgrown nursery garden. At least he imagines he will. Past the old sawmill, past the large dogwood. Getting scratched and wet, with old man's beard in their hair. Risking injury just to see what is there. "Foxglove here," he will say. "Poisonous." He'll hear his father's voice saying these things, but it will not be his father's voice. "Cow parsnip," he'll say. "Fatal." Eventually they will reach the destroyed glass houses and the stagnant ponds and the hill with the underground pool where there was once a pair of blind fish. "Here is where I used my new axe for the first time," he will tell the boy. He doesn't know if the boy will be Rohan, or Lachlan Hall on a working holiday. "There is where I turned over the first shovelful of my very own dirt. This is where the garden started, this is where our journey to Cape Scott began."

"It's a mess," the boy will say.

"That's why I've brought you here. To see if we can decide what ought to be done about it, if anything. The way it is now, the movie people have stolen it and moved it to Mississippi. Someone was shot right about where you're standing. So what we have to do is decide if we want it to belong to us again, or to leave it as it is. What do you think?"

He doesn't know what he thinks himself. Here in his tent, buffeted by the wind and deafened by the crashing waves, he doesn't even know whether he will take this other journey. He doesn't know what he will do with the rest of his life. He's travelled so long and at such a distance from the person he had started out to be that he isn't sure now which of them is going forward from this day. He hasn't achieved anything he intended, has accomplished none of his goals. It seems he has achieved something else instead, though he doesn't know what that is. There is a difference, he thinks, in how he feels about things. If this is a sort of visceral wisdom, he assumes the day will eventually come when he'll discover what he's learned. He can't imagine the rest of his life without Holly, but the surprise is that he cannot imagine the rest of his life without his father, either. The old man has made a permanent travelling companion of himself, their conversation bound to continue in Sonny's head. He suspects that Holly and Rohan and Lachlan, and even Jerrod, will, amongst them, make sure he never becomes the grouch of Darryl Maclean's prediction. But if the future is to reveal anything of itself to him, it will not be until after this long-handled former umbrella has been taken out to the end of the island, tossed into the waves, and, like that Hollywood crew and the old man himself, has departed for regions unknown.

ACKNOWLEDGEMENTS

There are several creeks named Mistake Creek in Australia, but I know of no town with that name. I have tried to make no other changes to the landscape of Queensland but I have taken some liberties with time.

For introducing me to their worlds, I am grateful to the Robinson family, formerly of Lorraine Station, to Roger McDonald and members of his family, to Annu Jylhä-Pyykönen and members of her family, and to Roy MacGregor. For impressions of the flood of 1990, I am grateful to a number of citizens of Charleville, and especially to Dawn Claire.

Quotations from Australian coverage of the Quebec referendum of 1995 have been taken from the pages of *The Australian*. Quotations from *The Kalevala* by Elias Lönnrot are from the translation by Keith Bosley, published by Oxford University Press. Information about the Tlingit and Snohomish interpretation of the stars is from *Stars of the First People* by Dorcas S. Miller. The concept of the landscape shaping people to suit it has no doubt been explored by many, but my introduction to an Australian interpretation was a brief passage in Steve Biddulph's *Manhood*.

For assistance, advice, and support, I am again grateful to members of my family, and for practical assistance, to Tyler Zurowski, Grant Sheppard, Rob Wooldridge, Dr. Arthur MacGregor, Bill New, Jeanette Taylor, Harry Erickson, and Kevin Roberts. Special thanks to Doug Gibson for his patience and persistence.

During his later years, my father often wished aloud that he could give his failing legs away. I've borrowed them (or rather, one and two-thirds of them) for a fictional character who has almost nothing else in common with the man who got around on them just fine for almost all of his eighty-seven years.

PUBLISHED BY McCLELLAND & STEWART LTD.

BROKEN GROUND: A novel *by* Jack Hodgins
It's 1922 and the shadow of the First World War hangs over a struggling
Soldier's Settlement on Vancouver Island. This powerful novel with its
flashbacks to the trenches is "a richly, deeply human book – a joy to read."
W.J. Keith   *Fiction, 5⅜ × 8⅜, 368 pages, trade paperback*

THE MACKEN CHARM: A novel *by* Jack Hodgins
When the rowdy Mackens gather for a family funeral on Vancouver Island
in the 1950s, the result is "fine, funny, sad and readable, a great yarn, the
kind only an expert storyteller can produce." *Ottawa Citizen*
                              Fiction, 5⅜ × 8⅜, 320 pages, trade paperback

INNOCENT CITIES: A novel *by* Jack Hodgins
Victorian in time and place, this delightful new novel by the author of *The
Invention of the World* proves once again that "as a writer, Hodgins is unique
among his Canadian contemporaries." *Globe and Mail*
                              Fiction, 5⅜ × 8⅜, 416 pages, trade paperback

A PASSION FOR NARRATIVE: A Guide for Writing Fiction *by* Jack
Hodgins
"One excellent path from original to marketable manuscript. . . . It would take
a beginning writer years to work her way through all the goodies Hodgins
offers." *Globe and Mail* The Canadian classic guide to writing fiction.
                    Non-fiction/Writing guide, 5¼ × 8½, 216 pages,
                    updated with a new Afterword, trade paperback

THE SELECTED STORIES OF MAVIS GALLANT *by* Mavis Gallant
"A volume to hold and to treasure" said the *Globe and Mail* of the 52 marvellous stories selected from Mavis Gallant's life's work. "It should be in
every reader's library."   *Fiction, 6⅛ × 9¼ , 900 pages, trade paperback*

LIVES OF MOTHERS AND DAUGHTERS: Growing Up With Alice Munro
by Sheila Munro
"The book will thrill anybody with a serious interest in Alice Munro."
Edmonton Journal "What Sheila Munro says about her mother's writing
could be just as aptly applied to her own book; you trust her every word."
Montreal Gazette
              Biography/Memoir, 6 × 9, 60 snapshots, 240 pages, trade paperback

A PETER GZOWSKI READER *by* Peter Gzowski
The man who affected the reading habits of millions of Canadians gives us the work of a lifetime in this selection of his best writing, much of it never before published in book form.

Anthology/Essays, 6 × 9, 228 pages, trade paperback

REMEMBERING PETER GZOWSKI
This lively and varied volume of tributes includes pieces from well-known friends like Robert Fulford, Alice Munro, and Shelagh Rogers, and from ordinary people touched by Peter Gzowski's life and work.

Anthology, 5½ × 8½, 248 pages, including photographs, hardcover

RAVEN'S END: A novel of the Canadian Rockies *by* Ben Gadd
This astonishing book, snapped up by publishers around the world, is like a *Watership Down* set among a flock of ravens managing to survive in the Rockies. "A real classic." Andy Russell

Fiction, 6 × 9, map, 5 drawings, 336 pages, trade paperback

THE GRIM PIG *by* Charles Gordon
The world of news is laid bare in this "very wicked, subversive book . . . it reveals more than most readers should know about how newspapers – or at least some newspapers – are still created. This is exceedingly clever satire, with a real bite." *Ottawa Citizen*

Fiction, 6 × 9, 256 pages, trade paperback

AT THE COTTAGE: A Fearless Look at Canada's Summer Obsession *by* Charles Gordon *illustrated by* Graham Pilsworth
This perennial best-selling book of gentle humour is "a delightful reminder of why none of us addicted to cottage life will ever give it up." *Hamilton Spectator* *Humour, 6 × 9, 224 pages, illustrations, trade paperback*

THE CANADA TRIP *by* Charles Gordon
Charles Gordon and his wife drove from Ottawa to St. John's to Victoria and back. The result is "a very human, warm, funny book" (*Victoria Times Colonist*) that will set you planning your own trip.

Travel/Humour, 6 × 9, 364 pages, 22 maps, trade paperback

CONFESSIONS OF AN IGLOO DWELLER *by* James Houston
The famous novelist and superb storyteller who brought Inuit art to the outside world recounts his Arctic adventures between 1948 and 1962. "Sheer entertainment, as fascinating as it is charming." *Kirkus Reviews*

Autobiography, 6 × 9, 320 pages, maps, drawings, trade paperback

HIDEAWAY: Life on the Queen Charlotte Islands *by* James Houston
This gentle book is a song of praise to the rainforest magic of Haida Gwaii, its history, its people, and the little green cottage the author loves. "James Houston finally writes about his own backyard." *National Post*
Memoir/Travel, 6 × 9, 272 pages, 40 b&w illustrations, map, trade paperback

WHO HAS SEEN THE WIND *by* W.O. Mitchell
First published in 1947, this wise and funny novel of a boy growing up on the prairie has sold over 750,000 copies in Canada, and established itself as a timeless popular favourite. Complete text edition.
Fiction, 5½ × 8½, 384 pages, trade paperback

HOW I SPENT MY SUMMER HOLIDAYS *by* W.O.Mitchell
A novel that rivals *Who Has Seen the Wind*. "Astonishing . . . Mitchell turns the pastoral myth of prairie boyhood inside out." *Toronto Star*
Fiction, 5½ × 8½, 276 pages, trade paperback

THREE CHEERS FOR ME: The Journals of Bartholomew Bandy, Volume One *by* Donald Jack
The classic comic novel about the First World War where our bumbling hero graduates from the trenches and somehow becomes an air ace. "Funny? Very." *New York Times*
Fiction/Humour, 5½ × 8½, 330 pages, trade paperback

THAT'S ME IN THE MIDDLE: The Journals of Bartholomew Bandy, Volume Two *by* Donald Jack
Canadian air ace Bandy fights at the front and behind the lines in the U.K., gallantly enduring the horrors of English plumbing. "A comical tour-de-force." *Montreal Gazette*
Fiction/Humour, 5½ × 8½, 348 pages, trade paperback

IT'S ME AGAIN: The Journals of Bartholomew Bandy, Volume Three *by* Donald Jack
Bart Bandy's back, landing behind enemy lines in France, causing havoc in Halifax, and trying to roll back the red Russian Revolution in Archangel. "Outrageously funny!" *Hamilton Spectator*
Fiction/Humour, 5½ × 8½, 420 pages, trade paperback

ME BANDY, YOU CISSIE: The Journals of Bartholomew Bandy, Volume Four *by* Donald Jack
It's 1920, and fresh from fighting Bolsheviks in Russia, Bartholomew Bandy is in New York trying to establish an airline, a movie career, and a romance with a tycoon's daughter. "The Bandy Papers deserve to be read in private, where insane giggling can go unnoticed." Jack Granatstein
Fiction/Humour, 5½ × 8½, 304 pages, trade paperback